Peter Lovesey was born in Middlesex and studied at Hampton Grammar School and Reading University, where he met his wife Jax. He won a competition with his first crime fiction novel, *Wobble to Death*, and has never looked back, with his numerous books winning and being short-listed for nearly all the prizes in the international crime writing world. He was Chairman of the Crime Writers' Association and has been presented with Lifetime Achievement awards both in the UK and the US.

www.peterlovesey.com

Also by Peter Lovesey

Sergeant Cribb series
Wobble to Death
The Detective Wore Silk Drawers
Abracadaver
Mad Hatter's Holiday
Invitation to a Dynamite Party
A Case of Spirits
Swing, Swing Together
Waxwork

Albert Edward, Prince of Wales series
Bertie and the Tinman
Bertie and the Seven Bodies
Bertie and the Crime of Passion

Peter Diamond series
The Last Detective
Diamond Solitaire
The Summons
Bloodhounds
The Vault
Diamond Dust
The House Sitter
The Secret Hangman
Skeleton Hill
Stagestruck
Cop to Corpse
The Tooth Tattoo
The Stone Wife
Down Among the Dead Men
Another One Goes Tonight
Beau Death
Killing with Confetti

Hen Mallin series
The Circle
The Headhunters

Other fiction
Goldengirl (as Peter Lear)
Spider Girl (as Peter Lear)
The False Inspector Dew
Keystone
Rough Cider
On the Edge
The Secret of Spandau (as Peter Lear)
The Reaper

Short stories
Butchers and other stories of crime
The Crime of Miss Oyster Brown and other stories
Do Not Exceed the Stated Dose
The Sedgemoor Strangler and other stories of crime
Murder on the Short List

'No one has done this kind of thing better since Dorothy L. Sayers. A must for crime buffs' *Mail on Sunday*

'A consummate story-teller' Colin Dexter, *The Oldie*

'A comedy of bad manners, full of oddball characters and wacky events develops into a perfectly realised murder mystery' *The Wall Street Journal*

'A bravura performance from a veteran showman: slyly paced, marbled with surprise and, in the end, strangely affecting' *New York Times Book Review*

'A marvellous achievement – masterfully plotted and totally absorbing' *Deadly Pleasures*

'Peter Diamond may be my favourite fictional police detective – perky, dogged and very clever' *Scotsman*

'Diamond is forever' *The Sunday Times*

SPHERE

First published in Great Britain in 1997 by Little, Brown
Published in paperback in 1998 by Warner Books
This edition published in 2014 by Sphere

3 5 7 9 10 8 6 4

A CIP catalogue record for this book
is available from the British Library.

ISBN 978-0-7515-5364-2

Typeset by Palimpsest Book Production Limited, Falkirk, Stirlingshire
Printed and bound by Greta Britain by Clays Ltd, Elcograf S.p.A.

Papers used by Sphere are from well-managed forests
and other responsible sources.

Sphere
An imprint of
Little, Brown Book Group
Carmelite House
50 Victoria Embankment
London EC4Y 0DZ

An Hachette UK Company
www.hachette.co.uk

www.littlebrown.co.uk

UPON A DARK NIGHT

PETER LOVESEY

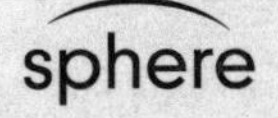

SPHERE

First published in Great Britain in 1997 by Little, Brown
Published in paperback in 1998 by Warner Books
This edition published in 2014 by Sphere

3 5 7 9 10 8 6 4 2

A CIP catalogue record for this book is available from the British Library.

ISBN 978-0-7515-5364-2

Typeset by Palimpsest Book Production Limited,
Falkirk, Stirlingshire
Printed and bound in Great Britain by
Clays Ltd, St Ives plc

Papers used by Sphere are from well-managed forests and other responsible sources.

MIX
Paper from
responsible sources
FSC® C104740

Sphere
An imprint of
Little, Brown Book Group
100 Victoria Embankment
London EC4Y 0DY

An Hachette UK Company
www.hachette.co.uk

www.littlebrown.co.uk

'It has been said . . . that there are few situations in life that cannot be honourably settled, and without loss of time, either by suicide, a bag of gold, or by thrusting a despised antagonist over the edge of a precipice upon a dark night.'

From *Kai Lung's Golden Hours,* by Ernest Bramah (Grant Richards, 1922)

Part One

Over the Edge

One

A young woman opened her eyes.

The view was blank, a white-out, a snowfall that covered everything. She shivered, more from fright than cold. Strangely she didn't feel cold.

Troubled, she strained to see better, wondering if she could be mistaken about the snow. Was she looking out on an altogether different scene, like a mass of vapour, the effect you get from inside an aircraft climbing through dense cloud? She had no way of judging; there was just this blank, white mass. No point of reference and no perspective.

She didn't know what to think.

The only movement was within her eyes, the floaters that drift fuzzily across the field of vision.

While she was struggling over the problem she became aware of something even more disturbing. The blank in her view was matched by a blank inside her brain. Whatever had once been there had gone. She didn't know who she was, or where this was happening, or why.

Her loss of identity was total. She could recall nothing. To be deprived of a lifetime of experiences, left with no sense of self, is devastating. She didn't even know which sex she belonged to.

It called for self-discovery of the most basic sort. Tentatively she explored her body with her hand, traced the swell of her breast and then moved down.

So, she told herself, at least I know I'm in that half of the human race.

A voice, close up, startled her. 'Hey up.'

'What's that?' said another. Both voices were female.

'Sleeping Beauty just opened her eyes. She's coming round, I think.'

'You reckon?'

'Have a look. What do you think?'

'She looks well out to me.'

'Her eyes were definitely open. We'd better call someone.'

'I wouldn't bother yet.'

'They're closed now, I grant you.'

'What did I tell you?'

She had closed them because she was dazzled by the whiteness. Not, after all, the whiteness of snow. Nor of cloud. The snatch of conversation made that clear. Impressions were coming in fast. The sound quality of the voices suggested this was not happening in the open. She was warm, so she had to be indoors. She had been staring up at a ceiling. Lying on her back, on something soft, like a mattress. In a bed, then? With people watching her? She made an effort to open her eyes again, but her lids felt too heavy. She drifted back into limbo, her brain too muzzy to grapple any more with what had just been said.

Some time later there was pressure against her right eye, lifting the lid.

With it came a man's voice, loud and close: 'She's well out. I'll come back.' He released the eye.

She dozed. For how long, it was impossible to estimate, because in no time at all, it seemed, the man's thumb forced her eye open again. And now the white expanse in front of her had turned black.

'What's your name?'

She didn't answer. Couldn't use her voice.

'Can you hear me? What's your name?'

She was conscious of an invasive smell close to her face, making the eyes water.

She opened her other eye. They were holding a bottle to her nose and it smelt like ammonia. She tried to ask, 'Where am I?' but the words wouldn't come.

He removed the thumb from her eye. The face peering into hers was black. Definitely black. It wasn't only the contrast of the white background. He was so close she could feel his breath on her eyelashes, yet she couldn't see him in any detail. 'Try again,' he urged her. 'What's your name?'

When she didn't answer she heard him remark, 'If this was a man, we would have found something in his pockets, a wallet, or credit cards, keys. You women will insist on carrying everything in a bag and when the wretched bag goes missing there's nothing to identify you except the clothes you're wearing.'

Sexist, she thought. I'll handbag you if I get the chance.

'How are you doing, young lady? Ready to talk yet?'

She moved her lips uselessly. But even if she had found her voice, there was nothing she could tell the man. She wanted to ask questions, not answer them. Who was she? She had no clue. She could barely move. Couldn't even turn on her side. Pain, sharp, sudden pain, stopped her from changing position.

'Relax,' said the man. 'It's easier if you relax.'

Easy for you to say so, she thought.

He lifted the sheet and held her hand. Bloody liberty, she thought, but she was powerless. 'You were brought in last night,' he told her. 'You're being looked after, but your people must be wondering where you are. What's your name?'

She succeeded in mouthing the words, 'Don't know.'

'Don't know your own name?'

'Can't think.'

'Amnesia,' he told the women attendants. 'It shouldn't last long.' He turned back to her. 'Don't fret. No need to worry. We'll find out who you are soon enough. Are you in much pain? We can give you something if it's really bad, but your head will clear quicker if we don't.'

She moved her head to indicate that the pain was bearable.

He replaced her hand under the bedding and moved away.

She closed her eyes. Staying conscious so long had exhausted her.

Some time later, they tried again. They cranked up the top end of the bed and she was able to see more. She was lucid now, up to a point. Her memory was still a void.

She was in a small, clinically clean private ward, with partly closed venetian blinds, two easy chairs, a TV attached to the wall, a bedside table with some kind of control panel. A glass jug of water. Facing her on the wall was a framed print of figures moving through a field of poppies, one of them holding a sunshade.

I can remember that this painting is by Monet, she thought. Claude Monet. I can remember a nineteenth-century artist's name, so why can't I remember my own?

The black man had a stethoscope hanging from his neck. He wore a short white jacket over a blue shirt and a loosely knotted striped tie. He was very much the junior doctor wanting to give reassurance, in his twenties, with a thin moustache. His voice had a Caribbean lilt.

'Feeling any better yet?'

She said, 'Yes.' It came out as a whisper.

He seemed not to have heard. 'I asked if you are feeling any better.'

'I think so.' She heard her own words. *Think so.* She wanted to sound more positive. Of course if her voice was functioning she had to be feeling better than before.

'I'm Dr Whitfield,' he told her, and waited.

She said nothing.

'Well?' he added.

'What?'

'We'd like to know your name.'

'Oh.'

'You're a mystery. No identity. We need to know your name and address.'

'I don't know.'

'Can't remember?'

'Can't remember.'

'Anything about yourself?'

'Nothing.'

'How you got here?'

'No. How *did* I get here?'

'You have no recall at all?'

'Doctor, would you please tell me what's the matter with me?'

'It seems that you've been in an accident. Among other things, you're experiencing amnesia. It's temporary, I can promise you.'

'What sort of accident?'

'Not so serious as it might have been. A couple of cracked ribs. Abrasions to the legs and hips, some superficial cuts.'

'How did this happen?'

'You tell us.'

'I can't.'

He smiled. 'We're no wiser than you are. It could have been a traffic accident, but I wouldn't swear to it. You may have fallen off a horse. Do you ride?'

'No . . . I mean, I don't know.'

'It's all a blank, is it?'

'Someone must be able to help. Who brought me here?'

'I wish we knew. You were found yesterday evening lying unconscious in the car park. By one of the visitors. We brought you inside and put you to bed. It was the obvious thing. This is a private hospital.'

'Someone knocked me down in a hospital car park?'

He said quite sharply, 'That doesn't follow at all.'

She asked, 'Who was this person who is supposed to have found me?'

'There's no "supposed" about it. A visitor. The wife of one of our long-term patients. We know her well. She wouldn't have knocked you down. She was very concerned, and she was telling the truth, I'm certain.'

'So someone else knocked me down. Some other visitor.'

'Hold on. Don't go jumping to conclusions.'

'What else could have happened?'

'Like I said, a fall from a horse. Or a ladder.'

'In a hospital car park?' she said in disbelief, her voice growing stronger as the strange facts of the story unfolded.

'We think someone may have left you there in the expectation that you would be found and given medical attention.'

'Brought me here, like some unwanted baby – what's the word? – a foundling?'

'That's the general idea.'

'And gone off without speaking to anyone? What kind of skunk does a thing like that?'

He shrugged. 'It's better than a hit-and-run. They just leave you in the road.'

'You said this is a private hospital. Where?'

'You're in the Hinton Clinic, between Bath and Bristol, quite close to the M4. Do you know it? We've had car accident victims brought in before. Does any of this trigger a memory?'

She shook her head. It hurt.

'You'll get it all back soon enough,' he promised her. 'Parts of your brain are functioning efficiently, or you wouldn't follow what I'm saying. You can remember words, you see, and quite difficult words, like "foundling". Did you go to school round here?'

'I've no idea.'

'Your accent isn't West Country. I'd place you closer to London from the way you speak. But of course plenty of Londoners have migrated here. I'm not local either.' He smiled. 'In case you hadn't noticed.'

She asked, 'What will happen to me?'

'Don't worry. We informed the police. They took a look at you last night. Made some kind of report. Put you on their computer, I expect. You can be sure that someone is asking where you are by now. They'll get a report on a missing woman and we'll find out soon enough. Exciting, isn't it? Not knowing who you are, I mean. You could be anyone. A celebrity. Concert pianist. Rock star. Television weather girl.'

The excitement eluded her. She was too downcast to see any charm in this experience.

Later they encouraged her to get out of bed and walk outside with one of the nurses in support. Her ribs felt sore, but she found no difficulty staying upright. She was functioning normally except for her memory.

She made an effort to be positive, actually summoning a smile for another patient who was wheeled by on an invalid chair, some poor man with the sallow skin of an incurable. No doubt the doctor was right. Memory loss was only a temporary thing, unlike the loss of a limb. No one in her condition had any right to feel self-pity in a place where people were dying.

Before returning to her room, she asked to visit a bathroom. A simple request for a simple need. The nurse escorting her opened a door. What followed was an experience common enough: the unplanned sighting in a mirror of a face that turned out to be her own, the frisson of seeing herself as others saw her. But what made this so unsettling was the absence of any recognition. Usually there is a momentary delay while the mind catches up. This must be a mirror and it must be me. In her case the delay lasted until she walked over to the mirror and stared into it and put out her hand to touch the reflection of her fingertip. The image was still of a stranger, a dark-haired, wide-eyed, horror-stricken woman in a white gown. She turned away in tears.

In her room, Dr Whitfield spoke to her again. He explained that her condition was unusual. Patients with concussion generally had no memory of the events leading up to the injury, but they could recall who they were, where they lived, and so on. He said they would keep her under observation for another night.

The loss of identity was still with her next morning. One of the nurses brought her a set of clothes in a plastic container. She picked up a blue shirt and looked at the dirtmarks on the back and sleeves. It was obvious that whoever had worn this had been in some kind of skirmish, but she felt no recognition. Jeans, torn at the knee. Leather belt. Reeboks, newish, but badly scuffed. White socks. Black cotton knickers and bra. Clothes that could have belonged to a million women her age.

'Do you want me to wear these?'

'We can't send you out in a dressing gown,' said one of the nurses.

'*Send me out?*' she said in alarm. 'Where am I going?'

'The doctors say you don't need to be kept in bed any longer. We've kept you under observation in case of complications, but you've been declared fit to move now.'

'Move where?'

'This is a private hospital. We took you in as an emergency and now we need the bed for another patient.'

They wanted the bed for somebody who would pay for it. She'd been so preoccupied with her problem that she'd forgotten she was literally penniless.

'We're going to have to pass you on to Avon Social Services. They'll take care of you until your memory comes back. Probably find you some spare clothes, or give you money to get some.'

On charity. She hated this. She'd hoped another night would restore her memory. 'Can't I stay here?'

She was collected later the same morning by a social worker called Imogen who drove a little green Citroen Special with a striped roof. Imogen was pale and tall with frizzy blonde hair and six bead necklaces. Her accent was as county as a shire hall. 'I say, you were jolly fortunate landing up there,' she said, as they drove out of the hospital gates. 'The Hinton is *the* clinic to get yourself into, if you're in need of treatment, that is. I don't like to think what it would have cost if you hadn't been an emergency. What's your name, by the way?'

'I don't know.'

'Still muzzy?'

'Very.'

'I'll have to call you something. Let's invent a name. What do you fancy? Do you object to Rose?'

The choice of name was instructive. Obviously from the quick impression Imogen had got, she had decided that this nameless woman wasn't a Candida or a Jocelyn. Something more humble was wanted.

'Call me anything you like. Where are you taking me?'

'To the office, first. You'll need money and clothes. Then to a hostel, till you get yourself straight in the head. They told me you cracked a couple of ribs. Is that painful? Should I be taking the corners extra carefully?'

'It's all right.'

The doctor hadn't strapped up the damaged rib-cage. Apparently if your breathing isn't uncomfortable, the condition cures itself. The adjacent ribs act as splints. Her sides were sore, but she had worse to worry over.

'I'm an absurdly cautious driver, actually,' Imogen claimed. 'Do you live in Bath, Rose?'

Rose. She would have to get used to it now. She didn't feel like a flower.

'I couldn't say.'

She thought it unlikely that she lived in Bath, considering it made no connection in her mind. Probably she was just a visitor. But then she could think of no other place she knew.

They drove past a signpost to Cold Ashton, and she told herself it was the sort of name you couldn't possibly forget.

'Ring any bells?' asked Imogen. 'I saw you looking at the sign.'

'No.'

'The way we're going, down the A46, you'll get a super view of the city as we come down the hill. With any luck, some little valve will click in your head and you'll get your memory back.'

The panorama of Bath from above Swainswick, the stone terraces picked out sharply by the mid-morning sun, failed to make any impression. No little valve clicked in her head.

Imogen continued to offer encouragement. 'There's always a chance some old chum will recognise you. If this goes on for much longer, we can put your picture in the local paper and see if anyone comes forward.'

She said quickly, 'I don't think I'd like that.'

'Shy, are we?'

'Anyone could say they knew me. How would I know if they were speaking the truth?'

'What are you worried about? Some chap trying his luck? You'd know your own boyfriend, wouldn't you?'

'I've no idea.'

'Stone the crows!' said Imogen. 'You do have problems.'

They drove down the rest of the road and into the city in silence.

At the office in Manvers Street, Rose – she really was making an effort to respond to the name – was handed twenty-five pounds and asked to sign a receipt. She was also given a second-hand shirt and jeans. She changed right away. Imogen put the old clothes into a plastic bin-liner and dumped them in a cupboard.

She thought about asking to keep her tatty old things regardless of the state they were in. Seeing them dumped in the sack was like being deprived of even more of herself.

In the end she told herself they were too damaged to wear and what were clothes for if you didn't use them? She didn't make an issue of it.

Then Imogen drove her to a women's hostel in Bathwick Street called Harmer House, a seedy place painted inside in institutional green and white. She was to share a room with another woman who was out.

'How long do I stay here?'

'Until you get your memory back – or someone claims you.'

Like lost property.

Imogen consoled her. 'It shouldn't be long, they said. Chin up, Rose. It could happen to anyone. At least you've got some sleeping quarters tonight. Somewhere to count sheep. You're luckier than some.'

Two

The bed across the room was unmade and strewn with orange peel and chocolate-wrappings. Not promising, the new inmate thought, but it did underline one thing: you were expected to feed yourself in this place. Imogen the social worker had shown her the poky communal kitchen in the basement. If she could remember what she liked to eat and how to cook it, that would be some progress. Surely if anything could jump-start a girl's memory, it was shopping.

So she went out in search of a shop. It would be pot-luck, because Bath was unknown to her. Or was it? She may have lived here some time. She had to get into her head the possibility that her amnesia was blocking out her ability to recognise any of it.

A strange place can be intimidating. Mercifully this was not. Viewing it through a stranger's eyes, Rose liked what she saw, disarmed by the appeal of a city that had altered little in two hundred years, not merely the occasional building, but street after street of handsome Georgian terraces in the mellow local stone. She strolled through cobbled passages and down flights of steps into quiet residential areas just as elegant as the main streets; formal, yet weathered and welcoming. At intervals she looked through gaps between the buildings and saw the backdrop of hills lushly covered in trees.

An unfamiliar city. Unfamiliar people, too. She didn't let that trouble her. She preferred the people unfamiliar. What if she *did* live here and suddenly met someone who knew her? That was what she ought to be hoping for – some chance meeting that would tell her who she was. But if she had a choice, she wanted to find out in a less confrontational way. She dreaded coming face to face with some stranger who knew more about her than she did herself, someone who expected to be recognised, who wouldn't understand why she acted dumb. Her situation was making her behave like a fugitive. Stupid.

So she was wary of asking the way to the nearest food shop. By chance she came across Marks and Spencer when she was moving through side streets, trying to avoid the crowds. She discovered a side entrance to the store. A homeless man was sleeping outside under a filthy blanket, watched by his sad-eyed dog. Her pity was mixed with some apprehension about her own prospects.

Hesitating just inside the door of the shop, feeling exposed in the artificial light, she found she was in the food section, where she wanted to be. To run out now would be ridiculous. She picked up a basket and collected a pack of sandwiches, some freshly squeezed orange juice, a mushroom quiche, salad things and teabags and paid for them at the checkout. The woman gave her a tired smile that reassured, for it was the first look she'd had in days that wasn't trying to assess her physical and mental state. Carrying her bag of food, she followed the signs upstairs to the women's wear floor to look for underwear and tights. She blew fifteen pounds in one quick spree. Well, no one had told her to make the money last. Outside in the street she dropped some coins into the homeless man's cap.

She saw someone selling the local daily, the *Bath Chronicle*. She bought one and looked for a place to read it, eventually choosing a spare bench on the shady side of the paved square beside the Abbey. She took out a sandwich and opened the paper.

This wasn't only about orientating herself in a strange place. If – as her injuries suggested – she had been in some sort of accident, it might have been reported in the local press.

She leafed through the pages. The story hadn't made today's edition, anyway.

Trying not to be disappointed, she put aside the paper and started another sandwich. People steadily crossed the yard carrying things that gave them a reason for being there – shopping, briefcases, musical instruments, library books, city maps or rucksacks, going about their lives in a way that made her envious. Seated here, watching them come and go, secure in their lives, Rose knew she was about to be overwhelmed by a tidal wave of self-pity. She had nowhere to go except that hostel.

Shape up, she told herself. It was stupid to let negative thoughts take over. Hadn't everyone said her memory would soon be restored? They'd come across amnesia before. It wasn't all that uncommon.

Even so, she couldn't suppress these panicky feelings of what might be revealed about her hidden life. Who could say what responsibilities she had, what personal problems, difficult relationships, unwanted secrets? In some ways it might be better to remain ignorant. No, she reminded herself firmly, nothing is worse than ignorance. It cut her off from the life she had made her own, from family, friends, job, possessions.

Lady, be positive, she lectured herself. Work at this. Get your brain into gear. You are not without clues.

All right. What do I know? I've looked in the mirror. Age, probably twenty-seven, twenty-eight. Is that honest? Say around thirty, then. Clothes, casual, but not cheap. The shoes are quality trainers and reasonably new. The belt is real leather. The discarded jeans were by Levi-Strauss. My hair – dark brown and natural, fashionably short, trimmed close at the sides and back – has obviously been cut by someone who knows what to do with a pair of scissors. As for my face, well, they said at the hospital that I wasn't wearing make-up when I was brought in, but it doesn't look neglected to me. You don't get eyebrows as finely shaped as these without some work with the tweezers. My skin looks and feels well treated, smooth to the touch, as if used to a moisturiser. The hands? Well, several of my fingernails were damaged in the accident – though I did my best to repair them with scissors and nail-file borrowed from one of the nurses – but the others are in good shape. They haven't been chewed down, or neglected. I'm interested to find that I don't paint my fingernails or toenails, and that in itself must say something about me.

No jewellery, apparently – unless someone took it off me. There isn't the faintest mark of a wedding ring. Is there?

Rose felt the finger again. This was the horror of amnesia, not being certain of something as fundamental as knowing if she was married.

The injuries told some kind of story, too. Her legs were bruised and cut in a couple of places, apparently from contact with the vehicle that had hit her. The broken ribs and the concussion and the state of her clothes seemed to confirm that she'd been knocked down, but it must have been a glancing contact, or the injuries would have been more serious. The likeliest conclusion was that she'd been crossing a road and the driver had spotted her just too late to swerve. It was improbable that she'd been riding in another vehicle, or there would surely have been whiplash injuries or some damage to her face.

She walked the canal towpath for an hour before returning to the hostel, where she found a policewoman waiting. A no-frills policewoman with eyes about as warm as the silver buttons on her uniform.

'I won't keep you long. Just following up on the report we had. You *are* the woman who was brought into the Hinton Clinic?'

'So I'm told.'

'Then you haven't got your memory back?'

'No.'

'So you still don't know your name?'

'The social worker called me Rose. That will have to do for the time being.'

The policewoman didn't sound as if she would be calling her Rose or anything else. Not that sympathy was required, but there was a sceptical note in the questions. Jobs like this were probably given to the women; they weren't at the cutting edge dealing with crime. 'You remember that much, then?'

'I can remember everything from the time I woke up in the hospital bed.'

'The funny thing is, we haven't had any reports of an accident yesterday.'

'I didn't say I had one. Other people said I did.'

'Has anyone taken photos yet?'

'Of me?'

'Of your injuries.'

'Only X-rays.'

'You should get photographed in case there's legal action. If you were hit by some driver and there's litigation, it will take ages to come to court, and you'll have nothing to show them.'

Good advice. Maybe this policewoman wasn't such a downer as she first appeared. 'Is that up to me to arrange?'

'We can get a police photographer out to you. We'll need a head and shoulders for our records anyway.'

'Could it be a woman photographer?'

'Why?'

'My legs look hideous.'

The policewoman softened just a touch. 'I could ask.'

'You see, I'm not used to being photographed.'

'How do you know that?'

It was a fair point.

'If this goes on for any time at all,' said the policewoman, 'you won't be able to stay out of the spotlight. We'll need to circulate your picture. It's the only way forward in cases of this kind.'

'Can't you leave it for a few days? They told me people always get their memory back.'

'That's not up to me. My superiors take the decisions. If an offence has been committed, a serious motoring offence, we'll need to find the driver responsible.'

'Suppose I don't want to press charges?'

'It's not up to you. If some berk knocked you down and didn't report it, we're not going to let him get away with it. We have a duty to other road users.'

Rose agreed to meet the police photographer the same evening. She also promised to call at the central police station as soon as her memory was restored.

She was left alone.

'Rose.' She spoke the name aloud, trying it on in the bedroom like a dress, and deciding it was wrong for her. She didn't wish to personify romance, or beauty. She went through a string of more austere possibilities, like Freda, Shirley and Thelma. Curiously, she could recall women's names with ease, yet couldn't say which was her own.

'I'm Ada.'

Startled, Rose turned towards the doorway and saw that

it was two-thirds filled. The one-third was the space above head height.

'Ada Shaftsbury. Have they put you in with me?' said Ada Shaftsbury from the doorway. 'I had this to myself all last week.' With a shimmy of the upper body she got properly into the room, strutted across and sat on the bed among the orange peel. 'What's your name?'

'They call me Rose. It's not my real name. I was in an accident. I lost my memory.'

'You don't look like a Rose to me. Care for a snack? I do like a Danish for my tea.' She dipped her hand into a carrier bag she'd brought in.

'That's kind, but no thanks.'

'I mean it. I picked up five. I can spare one or two.'

'Really, no.'

Ada Shaftsbury was not convinced. 'You'd be helping me. I'm on this diet. No snacks. Five Danish pastries isn't a snack. It's a meal, so I have to eat them at a sitting. Teatime. Three would only be a snack. If I was left with three, I'd have to blow the whistle, and that might be good for me. I'm very strict with myself.'

'Honestly, I couldn't manage one.'

'You don't mind if I have my tea while we talk?' said Ada, through a mouthful of Danish pastry.

'Please go ahead.'

'I've tried diets before and none of them work. This one suits me so far. Since my mother died, I've gone all to pieces. I've been done three times.'

'Done?' Rose was uncertain what she meant.

'Sent down. For the five-finger discount.'

Rose murmured some sort of response.

'You're not with me, petal, are you?' said Ada. 'I'm on about shoplifting. Food, mostly. They shouldn't put it on display like they do. It's a temptation. Can you cook?'

'I don't know. I'll find out, I suppose.'

'It's a poky little kitchen. If I get in there, which has to be sideways, I don't have room to open the cupboards.'

'That must be a problem.'

Ada took this as the green light. 'I can get the stuff if you'd be willing to cook for both of us. And you don't have to worry about breakfast.' Ada gave a wide, disarming smile. 'You're thinking I don't eat a cooked breakfast, aren't you?'

'I wasn't thinking anything.'

'There's a foreign girl called Hildegarde in the room under ours and she likes to cook. I'm teaching her English. She knows some really useful words now: eggs, bacon, tomatoes, fried bread. If you want a good breakfast, just say the word to Hildegarde.'

'I don't know if I'll be staying long.'

'You don't know, full stop,' said Ada. 'Could be only a couple of hours. Could be months.'

'I hope not.'

'Do you like bacon? I've got a whole side of bacon in the freezer.'

'Where did that come from?'

Ada wobbled with amusement. 'The back of a lorry in Green Street. The driver was delivering to a butcher's. He was round the front arguing with a traffic warden, so I did some unloading for him, slung it over my shoulder and walked through the streets. I got looks, but I get looks anyway. They shouldn't leave the stuff on view if they don't want it to walk. I've got eggs, tomatoes, peppers, mushrooms, spuds. We can have a slap-up supper tonight. Hildegarde will cook. We can invite her up to eat with us.'

'Actually, I bought my own,' Rose said.

'Good,' said Ada Shaftsbury, failing or refusing to understand. 'We'll pool it. What did you get?'

'Salad things mostly.'

'In all honesty I can't say I care much for salad, but we can use it as a garnish for the fry-up,' Ada said indistinctly through her second Danish.

Rose's long-term memory may have ceased to function, but the short-term one delivered. 'It's a nice idea, but I'd rather not eat until the police have been.'

'The *police*?' said Ada, going pale.

'They're going to take some photos.'

'In here, you mean?'

'Well, I've got some scars on my legs. If you don't mind, it would be easiest in here.'

'I'll go down the chippie for supper,' Ada decided.

'I don't want to drive you out. It's your room as much as mine.'

'You carry on, petal. If there's a cop with a camera, I'm not at home. We'll have our fry-up another day.'

She gulped the rest of her tea and was gone in two minutes.

The photography didn't start for a couple of hours, and Ada had still not returned.

Having the pictures taken was more of a major production than Rose expected, but she was relieved that the photographer *was* a woman. Jenny, in dungarees and black boots with red laces, took her work seriously enough to have come equipped with extra lighting and a tripod. Fortunately she had a chirpy style that made the business less of an ordeal. 'I can't tell you what a nice change it is to be snapping someone who can breathe. Most jobs I'm looking at corpses through this thing. Shall we try the full length first? In pants and bra studying the wallpaper, if you don't mind slipping out of your things. It won't take long.'

Jenny thoughtfully put a chair against the door.

'Okay, the back view first. Arms at your side. Fine . . . Now the front shot. Relax your arms, dear . . . My, you're getting some prize-winning bruises there. Sure you're not a rugby player? . . . Now I think we'd better do a couple without the undies, don't you? I mean the blue bits don't stop at your pantie-line.'

Rose swallowed hard, stripped to her skin and was photographed unclothed in a couple of standing poses.

'You can dress again now,' Jenny said. 'I'll tell you one thing. Whoever you are, you're not used to flaunting it in front of a camera.'

Three

Rarely in his police career had Detective Superintendent Peter Diamond spent so many evenings at home. He was starting to follow the plot-lines in the television soaps, a sure sign of under-employment. Even the cat, Raffles, had fitted Diamond seamlessly into its evening routine, springing onto his lap at nine-fifteen (after a last foray in the garden) and remaining there until forced to move – which did not usually take long.

One evening when it was obvious that Raffles' tolerance was stretched to breaking point, Stephanie Diamond remarked, 'If you relaxed, so would he.'

'But I'm not here for his benefit.'

'For yours, my love. Why don't you stroke him? He'll purr beautifully if you encourage him. It's been proved to reduce blood pressure.'

He gave her a sharp look. 'Mine?'

'Well, I don't mean the cat's.'

'Who says my blood pressure is too high?'

She knew better than to answer that. Her overweight husband hadn't had a check-up in years. 'I'm just saying you should unwind more. You sit there each evening as if you expect the phone to ring any moment.'

He said offhandedly, 'Who's going to ring me?'

She returned to the crossword she was doing. 'Well, if you don't know . . .'

He placed his hand on the cat's back, but it refused to purr. 'I take it as a positive sign. If there's a quiet phase at work, as there is now, we must be winning the battle. Crime prevention.'

Stephanie said without looking up, 'I expect they're all too busy watering the geraniums.'

His eyes widened.

'This is Bath,' she went on, 'the Floral City. Nobody can spare the time to commit murders.'

He smiled. Steph's quirky humour had its own way of keeping a sense of proportion in their lives.

'Speaking of murder,' he said, 'he's killed that camellia we put in last spring.'

'Who has?'

'Raffles.'

The cat's ears twitched.

'He goes to it every time,' Diamond insensitively said. 'Treats it as his personal privy.'

Stephanie was quick to defend the cat. 'It isn't his fault. We made a mistake buying a camellia. They don't like a lime soil. They grow best in acid ground.'

'It is now.'

He liked to have the last word. And she knew it was no use telling him to relax. He'd never been one for putting his feet up and watching television. Or doing the crossword.

'How about a walk, then?' she suggested.

'But it's dark.'

'So what? Afraid we'll get mugged or something?'

He laughed. 'In the Floral City?'

'But this isn't exactly the centre of Bath.' She took the opposite line, straight-faced. 'This is Weston. Who knows what dangers lurk out there? It's gone awfully quiet. The bell-ringers must have finished. They could be on the streets.'

'You're on,' he said, shoving Raffles off his lap. 'Live dangerously.'

They met no one. They stopped to watch some bats swooping in and out of the light of a lamp-post and Diamond commented that it could easily be Transylvania.

At least conversation came more readily at walking pace than from armchairs. He admitted that he was uneasy about his job.

'In what way?' Stephanie asked.

'Like you were saying, we're not exactly the crime capital of Europe. I'm supposed to be the murder man here. I make a big deal out of leading the Bath murder squad, and our record is damned good, but we're being squeezed all the time.'

'Under threat?'

'Nobody has said anything . . .'

'But you can feel the vibes.' Stephanie squeezed his arm. 'Oh, come on, Pete. If nobody has said anything, forget it.'

'But you wanted to know what was on my mind.'

'There's more?'

'The crime figures don't look so good. No, that's wrong. They're too good, really. Our clear-up rate is brilliant compared to Bristol, but it isn't based on many cases. They've got a lot of drug-related crime, a bunch of unsolved killings. See it on a computer and it's obvious. They need support. That's the way they see it at Headquarters.'

'You've helped Bristol out before. There was that bank manager at Keynsham.'

'I don't mind helping out. I don't want to move over there, lock, stock and barrel.'

'Nor do I, just when we've got the house straight. What about your boss – the Assistant Chief Constable? Will he fight your corner for you?'

'He's new.'

'Same old story.' Stephanie sighed. 'We need some action, then, and fast. A shoot-out over the teacups in the Pump-Room.'

'Fix it, will you?' said Diamond.

'Do my best,' she said.

They completed a slow circuit around Locksbrook Cemetery and returned to the semi-detached house they occupied in Weston.

Diamond stopped unexpectedly at the front gate.

'What's up?' Stephanie asked.

He put a finger to his lips, opened the gate and crept low across the small lawn like an Apache. Stephanie watched in silence, grateful for the darkness. He was heading straight for the camellia, the barely surviving camellia.

With a triumphant 'Got you!' he sank to his knees and thrust his hand towards the plant.

There was a screech, followed by a yell of pain from Diamond. A dark feline shape bolted from under the camellia, raced across the lawn, leapt at the fence and scrambled over it. 'He bit me! He bloody well bit me.'

Gripping the fleshy edge of his right hand, high-stepping across the lawn, the Head of the Murder Squad looked as if he was performing a war dance now.

Stephanie was calm. 'Come inside, love. We'd better get some TCP on that.'

Indoors, they examined the bite. The cat's top teeth had punctured the flesh quite deeply. Stephanie found the antiseptic and dabbed some on. 'I expect he felt vulnerable,' she pointed out in the cat's defence, 'doing his business, with you creeping up and making a grab for him.'

'My own bloody cat,' said Diamond. 'He's had his last saucer of cream from me.'

'What do you mean – "your own cat"? That wasn't Raffles.'

'Of course it was Raffles. Don't take his side. He was caught in the bloody act.'

'Red-handed?' murmured Stephanie, adding quickly, 'A fine detective you are, if you can't tell the difference between your own cat and the moggy next door. That was Samson. I saw the white bit under his chin.'

'That was never Samson.'

'Why did he bolt straight over the fence into their garden?'

'It was the shortest escape route, that's why.'

She chose not to pursue the matter. 'How does it feel?'

'I'll survive, I suppose. Thanks for the nursing.'

She made some tea. When they walked into the sitting room, Raffles was curled on Diamond's armchair, asleep. It was obvious he had not stirred in the past hour.

'Incidentally . . .' Stephanie said.

'Mm?'

'When did you last have a jab for tetanus?'

Four

Ada Shaftsbury's breathing was impaired by her bloated physique, particularly when she moved. With each step she emitted a breath or a sigh. Climbing the stairs sounded like competitive weight-lifting because the breaths became grunts and the sighs groans. The entire hostel must have heard her come in some time after eleven.

She stood for a short while by the bedroom door, recovering. Finally she managed to say, 'You're not asleep, are you, petal?'

'No.' But 'petal' had hoped to be. She was exhausted.

'I brought back a few nibbles from the pub, a pork pie, if you want, and some crisps.'

'No thanks.'

'Aren't you going to keep me company?'

'I thought you didn't eat snacks.'

'This is supper,' said Ada.

'Wasn't supper what you went to the chippie for?'

'That was dinner.'

'Actually, Ada, I don't like to eat as late as this.'

'How do you know?'

'What?'

'If you lost your memory, how do you know when you like to eat and when you don't?'

Rose couldn't answer that. 'What I mean is that I'm ready for sleep.'

'You don't mind if I have yours, then?'

'Don't mind at all. Goodnight.'

There was an encouraging interval of near silence, disturbed only by the smack of lips.

Then:

'I say . . . ?'

'Mm?'

'Did the photographer come – the photographer from the police?'

'Yes.'

Another interval.

'You want to be careful, getting in their records. You don't know what they do with the photos they take.'

'Ada, I'm really pooped, if you don't mind.'

'I could tell you things about the police.'

'Tomorrow.'

Ada wanted her say, regardless. 'We all have rights, you know, under the Trade Descriptions Act.'

'Data Protection.'

'What?'

'I think you mean the Data Protection Act.'

'Your memory can't be all that bad if you can think of something like Data whatsit at this time of night. Are you getting it back?'

'No.' Some hope, she thought, when I can't even get my sleep in.

Ada would not be silenced. 'I think it's diabolical, the way they pissed you about. That hospital was only too pleased to see the back of you and the social so-called services shove you in here and all the police do is take some photos. It's a bloody disgrace.'

Rose sighed and turned on her back, drawing the hair from across her eyes. She was fully awake now. 'What else could they have done?'

'Never mind them. I know what I'd do. I'd go back to that hospital where you were dumped and ask some questions. That's what I'd do. I'd insist on it.'

'What is there to find out?'

'I haven't the faintest, my petal, but it's all you've got to work on. Did they show you the place where you were found?'

'The car park? No.'

'Who was it who found you, then?'

'A woman. The wife of a patient. They didn't tell me her name.'

'You've got a right to know who she is. You're entitled to speak to her.'

'What can she tell me? She didn't cause my injuries. She just happened to find me.'

'How do you know that? I might as well say it: you're too trusting,' said Ada. 'They pat you on the head and tell you to go away and that's what you do. The well behaved little woman, God help us, up shit creek without a paddle. Do they care? All they're concerned about is the reputation of their sodding hospital. They don't want it known that someone was knocked down in their car park. You could sue.'

'It wasn't like that.'

'So they say.' Ada was practically beating a drum by now. 'Listen, petal, this may get up your nose, but you've got some rights here. If you want to exercise them, I'm willing to throw my weight in on your side, and that's a pretty large offer. I'll come with you to the hospital and sort those people out.'

'That's very kind, but I really don't think—'

'We'll talk about this in the morning, right?' said Ada, following it with a large yawn. 'I can't stay awake all night listening to you rabbiting on. I should have been in bed twenty minutes ago.'

Stephanie had fixed this. She had promised it would be done quickly and without fuss by one of her vast network of friends, a nurse who worked in Accident and Emergency at the Royal United Hospital. It was no use Peter Diamond protesting that he was neither an accident nor an emergency.

When he met the friend, he had grave doubts whether he wanted her hand on the syringe. She was mountainous.

'How is my old chum Steph?' she asked.

'Blooming,' he said. 'Shouldn't you be asking about me?'

'You look well enough.' She examined the cat-bite. 'Was it your own little kitty who did this to you?'

He said in an offended tone, as if the possibility had never crossed his mind, 'Raffles wouldn't hurt me. Steph reckons it was next door's, but I have my doubts. This was a big brute. You can see that from the size of the bite.'

'Probably on the run from a safari park,' said the nurse

with a look she probably gave men who made a fuss. 'Slip off your jacket and roll up your sleeve.'

'You think an injection is necessary?'

'Isn't that the point?' She gave a rich, unsympathetic laugh. 'Your tetanus jab is long overdue, according to your file. I phoned your GP.'

'Is that what he said?'

'First, I must take your blood pressure. That must have altered since – when was it? – 1986. You seem to be rather good at bucking the system, Mr Diamond.'

'Or saving the system from bankruptcy,' he was perky enough to respond. 'You need healthy people like me.'

'We'll see how healthy,' she said, tying the cuff around his arm and inflating it vigorously. 'Who took it last time?'

'My doctor, I think.'

'A man?'

'Yes. Is that important?'

'We can expect it to go up a few points. It's always that bit higher when someone of the opposite sex takes the reading.'

He stopped himself from saying anything. He was in no position to disillusion her.

Presently she told him, 'Too high, even allowing for the attraction factor. You'd best have a chat with one of the doctors. I'll slot you in. No problem.'

He was going to have to assert himself. 'I didn't come about my blood pressure. I came for a jab.'

She picked up the syringe. 'Which I'm about to give you.'

'I'm beginning to wonder if there's been some collusion between you and Steph.'

'I don't see how,' said the nurse. 'You don't think she arranged for the cat to bite you?'

She dabbed on some antiseptic and then plunged the needle in.

'Jesus.'

A woman in a white coat appeared in the room while he still had his finger pressed to the piece of cotton wool the nurse had placed over the injection mark.

'Superintendent Diamond?'

He didn't respond. Who wanted to socialise at a time like this?

'I'm Christine Snell. I don't think we've met.'

The nurse put a Band-Aid over the injection and said, 'I'll leave you with the patient, Doctor.'

He said to Christine Snell, 'You're a doctor?'

'That's why I'm here. How's Steph, by the way?'

Another friend. His thoughts took a lurch towards paranoia. Steph's friends, between them, had him over a barrel.

She said, 'Your blood pressure is slightly on the high side. We shouldn't neglect it. Do you smoke?'

'No. And the answer to the next question is yes, the occasional one.'

'So how do you cope with stress?'

'What stress?'

'Overwork.'

'Underwork, in my case.'

'Potentially even more stressful. It kills a lot of people. Have you got any hobbies?'

'Like collecting beermats?' said Diamond. 'You're trying to catch me out, Doctor. No, I don't do anything you would call a hobby.'

'Maybe you should.'

'I'll think it over,' he conceded. 'It wouldn't surprise me if the nurse just now got an exaggerated reading.'

Her eyes widened and the start of a smile appeared.

'Not that,' said Diamond. 'I was annoyed. Doesn't that increase it? I can't help feeling I was fitted up for this. I came here because of the cat-bite, but last night, before I was bitten, Steph was on about my blood pressure.'

The smile surfaced fully. 'Do you know what Kai Lung said?'

'I've never heard of Kai Lung.'

'I think I have it right,' said Dr Snell. '"It is proverbial that from a hungry tiger and an affectionate woman there is no escape." Seems rather apt, in your case.'

While Rose and Ada were waiting to speak to Dr Whitfield, a refreshment trolley came by and Ada's hand, quick as a lizard, whipped two doughnuts off it and into her bag, unseen by the woman in charge. 'Elevenses,' she said in justification.

'Does that count as a meal?'
'It's over two hours since breakfast.'
The breakfast the foreign girl Hildegarde had cooked to Ada's order had been enough to fortify Rose for hours yet. She could still taste the delicious bacon.
Bizarrely, the appointments secretary was announcing something about eggs.
'That's you,' said Ada.
'Me?'
'Rose X.'
'Dr Whitfield will see you now,' said the secretary. 'Room Nine, at the top of the stairs.'
'Stairs. I knew it,' Ada complained.
'You don't have to come with me.'
'I do. Someone's got to fight your corner.'
The door of Room 9 stood open. Dr Whitfield got up from behind his desk to greet them. He was shorter than he looked from the level of a hospital bed. 'Have you got it back yet?'
Rose shook her head.
'Not even a glimmer?'
'Nothing at all. This is my friend Ada Shaftsbury.'
Ada's hand must have been sticky from the doughnut, because after shaking it Dr Whitfield took a tissue from the packet on his desk. 'So how can I help you?' he asked after they were seated.
'We'd like to speak to the lady who found me.'
Dr Whitfield was slow in responding. He made a performance of wiping his hand and letting the tissue drop into a bin. 'I doubt if that would help.'
'I want to know exactly where I was found.'
'I told you. In the car park.'
'Yes, but I'd like the lady to show me where.'
'Not possible, I'm afraid. She doesn't work here. As I think I explained, she's the wife of a patient.'
Buoyed up by Ada's substantial presence, Rose said, 'It's a free country. I can ask her, can't I?'
'I really can't see the point in troubling her,' Dr Whitfield said.
This was too much for Ada. She waded in. 'Troubling her? What about my friend here? What about the trouble

she's in? Hey, doc, let's get our priorities straight before we go any further. This is your patient asking for help. She wants a face to face with this woman, whoever she is. She's entitled to know exactly where she was found and what was going on at the time.'

'I don't think there's any mystery about that,' Dr Whitfield started to say.

'Fine,' said Ada, 'so what's the woman's name and address?'

'Look, the lady in question acted very responsibly. She came straight in and got help. It was as simple as that.'

'So what are you telling us?'

'I'm saying I don't want her put through the third degree. She's an elderly lady.'

'Tough tittie, doc.' Ada rested her hands on his desk, leaned over it and said, 'You think my friend would duff up the old lady who came to her rescue?'

He gave an embarrassed smile. 'Not at all.'

'Well, then?'

Dr Whitfield must have sensed he wasn't going to win this one. 'If it's this important, I suppose it can be arranged. But I think it might be wise to speak to Mrs Thornton alone.' Pointedly excluding Ada, he said to Rose, 'I suggest if you want to meet her that you come back this afternoon. She visits her husband every day between two and four. See me first and I'll introduce you.'

Progress at last.

'There's something else, Doctor.' Rose spoke up for herself. 'I'm puzzled about this head injury. I've examined my head. I can't find any cuts or bruising.'

'Neither did I,' said Dr Whitfield.

She frowned, unable to understand.

'It doesn't follow that you had a crack on the skull at all,' he went on. 'You get concussion from a shaking of the brain. A jolt to the neck would do it just as easily.'

'You mean if I was struck by a car and my head rocked back?'

'That's exactly what I had in mind.'

Rose prepared to leave.

'There's something else I should mention,' the doctor said. 'When you get your memory back it's quite on the cards that you still won't remember anything about the accident. It may be a mystery for ever.'

'I hope not.'

'It's a common effect known as retrograde amnesia. The patient has no recall of the events immediately before the concussion happened.'

'I could accept that, if I could only get back the rest of my memory. This has gone on for three days already. Are you sure there isn't permanent damage to my brain?'

He put his hand supportively over hers. 'Nobody fully understands how the memory works, but it has a wonderful capacity for recovery. Something will make a connection soon, and you'll know it's coming back.'

She and Ada went downstairs and walked in the grounds. Through the trees they could hear the steady drone of traffic on the motorway.

Rose felt deeply disheartened. 'What am I going to do, Ada?'

'Talk to this old biddy who found you.'

'I'm not pinning my hopes on her.'

'She's your best bet, ducky. Like he said, something will make a connection. Who knows what talking to her might do?'

'Of course I'll talk to her now it's been arranged. All I'm saying is that I don't expect a breakthrough. What do I do if I draw a blank with Mrs Thornton?'

'Talk to the press and get your picture in the paper along the lines of CAN YOU HELP THIS WOMAN? With looks like yours, you'll get some offers, but I won't say what kind.'

'I don't want that.' They strolled past some patients in wheelchairs. She told Ada, 'I'm sorry to be a misery-guts. It's become very clear to me how much we all rely on our memories. You'd think what's past is finished, but it isn't. It makes us what we are. Without a memory, you don't have any experience to support you. You can't trust yourself to make decisions, to reason, to stand up for your rights. My past started on Tuesday morning. That's the whole of my experience, Ada. I don't have anything else to work with.'

'There's lunch,' suggested Ada.

Five

Meals-on-Wheels is a system as near foolproof as any arrangement can be that relies on volunteers. A couple of days before someone's turn to deliver the meals, she (the volunteers are usually women) will be handed (by the previous person on the rota) a white box about the size of a ballot box. It is made of expanded polystyrene, for insulation, and fitted with a shoulder strap. Being so large and conspicuous when left in a private house, the box is a useful reminder of the duty to be done.

On either a Tuesday or a Thursday, at a few minutes before noon, the volunteer reports to a local school canteen where lunch is ready for serving. Piping hot foil containers are loaded into the box by the dinner ladies. The box is carried to the car. With the meals aboard, the wheels take over.

'Now begins the tricky part,' Susan Dowsett explained to Joan Hanks, who was about to join the Acton Turville and District team and had come along to learn how it was done. Mrs Dowsett was the mainstay of the service, one of those admirable, well-to-do Englishwomen who plunge into voluntary work with the same sure touch they apply to their jam-making. 'They do look forward to seeing you, and most of them like a chat. Some poor ducks hardly ever see anyone else, so one does one's best to jolly them up. The snag is that you have to ration your time, or the ones at the end of the round get cold lunches.'

'I expect you can pop them in the oven if that happens. The meals, I mean.'

'That's the idea, and sometimes I've done it, but old people are so forgetful. More than once I've opened the oven on Thursday and found Tuesday's lunch still in there, untouched and dry as a biscuit.' Her chesty laugh jogged the steering. She drove an Isuzu Trooper that suited her personality.

Acton Turville alone would have been a simple task: meals on foot. The 'and District' was the part requiring transport. Many of the recipients lived in remote houses outside the village.

'I always start at the farthest outpost,' Mrs Dowsett explained as they cruised confidently along a minor road. 'Old Mr Gladstone is our first call. He's not the most pleasant to deal with and most of them leave him till last. Get the worst over first, I always say.'

'What's wrong with Mr Gladstone?'

'Hygiene. The atmosphere, shall we say, is not exactly apple-blossom. He's none too sociable, either. I've known him to be downright offensive about the meals. There's no need for that. It's plain food, but at least it's warm.'

'If he doesn't want us . . .'

'Social Services insist. He won't cook for himself, apart from eggs from the few wretched hens he keeps in his yard. Used to be a farmer. Lived there all his life, as far as I can gather, but he doesn't seem to have any friends. Sad, isn't it?'

'Perhaps he prefers a quiet life.'

'Perhaps,' said Mrs Dowsett, unconvinced.

The 'farthest outpost' turned out to be only a mile from the village, just off the Tormarton Road, up a track that Joan Hanks privately vowed to take cautiously in her own little car for fear of ruining the suspension.

'You'll need tougher shoes than those when the weather gets worse,' Mrs Dowsett advised when they were both standing in the yard. 'Every time it rains, this is like a mud-hole after the elephants have been by. Good, you've brought the box. Always bring the box into the house. It keeps the food warm. Let's see what reception we get today.'

As they crossed the yard to the door of the stone cottage there was an extraordinary commotion from the henhouse at the side, hens crowding the wire fence.

'Hungry, I expect,' said Mrs Dowsett. 'All they get is scraps, and not much of them.'

'Poor things,' said Joan.

Mrs Dowsett tapped on the door and got no answer. 'This is often the case,' she explained. 'They don't hear you. As often as not, the door is open, so you just go in. Try it.'

'He doesn't know me.'

'Don't let that put you off. He treats us all like strangers. Is it open?'

Joan knocked again, turned the handle and pushed. The door creaked and opened inwards just an inch or so. An overpowering stench reached her nostrils and she hesitated.

'You see?' said Mrs Dowsett. She called out in a hearty tone, 'Meals on wheels, Mr Gladstone.'

Joan held her breath and pushed at the door. The interior was shadowy and the full horror of the scene took several seconds to make out. Old Mr Gladstone was inside, slumped in a wooden armchair. The top of his head was blown away. A shotgun lay on the floor.

'Are you all right, dear?' said Mrs Dowsett, suddenly turned motherly.

In this bizarre situation, Joan was uncertain whether the remark was addressed to the corpse, or herself. She gave a nod. She was reeling with the shock, and she needed fresh air if she was not to faint. She turned away.

'I'd better get on the car-phone,' said Mrs Dowsett, a model of composure. 'Why don't you feed that meal to the chickens? I don't like to waste things.'

The old farmer's death was routinely dealt with by the police. A patrol was detailed to investigate. Peter Diamond heard of it first over the radio while driving down Wellsway. Nothing to make his pulse beat faster, some sad individual topping himself with a shotgun.

He drove on, his thoughts on his own mortality. High blood pressure, it seemed, was a mysterious condition. His sort had no recognised cause, according to Dr Snell. The symptoms were vague. He might suffer some headaches, tiredness and dizzy spells. He had not. If it affected the heart, or the arteries, he might experience breathlessness, particularly at night, pain in the chest, coughing or misty vision. He had told the doctor honestly that none of it seemed to apply to him. In that case, she said, he need not alter his life-style, except, she suggested, to reduce some weight, if possible, and avoid worrying too much.

Great, he thought. Now I'm worrying about worrying.

As he had time to spare, he called at the Central Library and looked up high blood pressure in a medical textbook. They called it hypertension, a term he didn't care for. But the author was good enough to state that if the condition caused no symptoms at all, it could not be described as a disorder. He liked that and closed the book. The rest of the article could wait until he noticed a symptom, if ever.

His hypertension level had an immediate test. Having returned the book to the shelf, he turned the corner of the stack and found himself face to face with the new Assistant Chief Constable, all decked out in black barathea, shiny silver buttons and new braided hat. Diamond managed a flustered, 'Morning, em, afternoon, sir.'

'Afternoon, Mr Diamond. Checking some facts?'

He didn't want the high-ups to know about his hypertension. Not for the first time in a crisis, he said the first thing that popped into his head, and it was so unexpected that it had to be believed. 'That's right, sir. I'm looking for the philosophy section.'

'Philosophy?'

'I wanted to find out about Kai Lung, if possible. I think he must be a philosopher.'

'Chinese?'

'I believe so.'

'Sorry. Can't help. Is this an Open University course?'

A low punch. Diamond's rival John Wigfull had got to the head of Bath CID on the strength of his OU degree. Further education was not on Diamond's agenda. 'No, something that was quoted to me earlier. I wanted to trace the source. It's my lunch-hour.'

'Good luck, then. I'm looking for *Who's Who.*'

Save your time, matey, Diamond thought. You won't make *Who's Who* for at least another year.

To support his story, he strolled over to the inquiry desk and asked if they had anything on Kai Lung. A tall young man looked over his glasses and told him to try under Bramah.

Thinking Bramah sounded Indian, Diamond emphasised, 'I said Kai Lung. I reckon it's Chinese.'

'Ernest Bramah. He was a fictional character invented by Ernest Bramah. *The Wallet of Kai Lung* was the first title of several, as far as I remember. Try the fiction shelves.'

'Ernest Bramah?'

'Yes, but don't pick up one of his Max Carrados books expecting to find Kai Lung. Carrados is the blind detective.'

Diamond didn't want to know about infirmities in his profession. 'I'll avoid those, then.'

He wandered over to the fiction shelves.

The hypertension definitely edged up a few points when he got back to his place of work, Manvers Street Police Station. Two of the youngest detectives were getting into a car when he drove in. The use of CID manpower was a constant source of friction. His old adversary Chief Inspector John Wigfull was in charge of CID matters, but Diamond headed the murder squad. In bleak spells like this when everyone in Bath respected everyone else's right to exist, the squad virtually disbanded. Most of the lads were employed on break-ins and car thefts. Like anyone keen to defend his small empire, Diamond insisted that certain officers were detailed to pick the bones of the three unsolved homicides he still had on his books. He felt sure one of this pair was last given orders to work for him.

'You're not skiving, I trust,' he called across.

'No chance, Guv,' said the less dozy of the two. 'Incident at Tormarton. Some farmer blew his brains out.'

'Didn't I hear a patrol being sent to that one an hour ago? How has it become a CID matter?'

'Mr Wigfull's orders, Guv.'

'Two of you? CID must be under-employed these days.'

He went up to his office and opened *Kai Lung Unrolls His Mat.* Concentration was difficult. John Wigfull had the nose of a tracker dog and the resemblance didn't end there. It justified a call to his office. A sergeant answered. Chief Inspector Wigfull, it emerged, was not in. He had driven out to look at a suicide at Tormarton.

* * *

When Wigfull got back towards the end of the afternoon, Diamond – remarkable to relate – met him coming in from the car park. 'Been down on the farm, John?'

Wigfull gave a guarded, 'Were you looking for me?'

'Nothing vital.'

'But you went to the trouble of finding out where I was?'

'Just out of interest. I'm not going to shop you if you need a break.'

'It was police business.'

'I know that.'

They eyed each other for a short, silent stalemate. Diamond had never been able to take that overgrown moustache seriously. He explained, 'I spoke to Sergeant Burns. How was your farmer?'

'In a word, high,' said Wigfull.

'Been dead some time?'

'Too long for my liking.'

'Straightforward suicide?'

'He blew a hole through his head with a twelve-bore.'

'Sounds straightforward to me.'

There was another interval.

'Not so straightforward?'

'I didn't say that.' Without understanding how it had been done, Wigfull found himself having to fill Diamond in on the incident. 'He was a loner. The farm, such as it is – more of a smallholding, in fact – is in a pitiful state. He was old, living frugally. It all got too much, and no wonder. You should have seen the inside of the house.' Wigfull paused, remembering. 'The saddest thing is that he wasn't found before this. Nobody visited. Anything up to a week, the pathologist reckons.'

'Who found him?'

'Two unlucky women who take the meals-on-wheels round.'

'He gets meals-on-wheels? Why wasn't he found before this, then?'

'It's only Tuesdays and Thursdays. He may have had a visit from them last week. We're checking. They work to a rota. The thing is, whoever was due to call may have gone away when they didn't get an answer.'

'Neighbours?'

'It's way out in the sticks. And he discouraged visitors.'

'Where exactly is it? North of the motorway?'

Wigfull's eyes widened. 'I don't recommend a visit, Peter. The two lads I have at the scene are still wearing face-masks, helping the pathologist find all the bits.'

'Quite a baptism for them.'

'Yes.'

'The shotgun?'

'At his feet. He was in a chair.'

It was apparent that Wigfull was playing this down for all he was worth. He answered the questions honestly because his sense of duty wouldn't allow him to lie. But he hadn't revealed what induced him to go out to Tormarton in person. There was something else about the case, and Diamond was too proud to ask precisely what it was.

Before leaving work that night, he asked Julie Hargreaves, his second-in-command, and the one person he could depend upon, to keep an ear open in the canteen. Wigfull wouldn't give anything away, but his officers might. Something about this business offended the nostrils and it wasn't only the dead farmer.

Six

Mrs Thornton was a sweetie. She was well over seventy, tall, upright and so thin that she must have been suffering from chronic osteoporosis. Yet her thoughts were all of her husband David, an Alzheimer's patient. 'I don't know what's in his mind, if anything, poor darling,' she told Rose in an accent redolent of a privileged upbringing more than half a century ago. 'It's very distressing. He rambles dreadfully. It's hard to believe that he once commanded an aircraft carrier.'

Rose explained that her own brain was impaired, but temporarily, she hoped. 'I'm trying desperately to find something that will get the memory working. Would you mind terribly if we walked over to the car park where you found me?'

They had to move slowly. Once or twice Mrs Thornton had to be steadied. This walk to the car park was an imposition, and it was clear why Dr Whitfield had been reluctant to encourage it. 'In case you're wondering,' the old lady remarked, 'I don't drive. I come in twice a day – afternoon and evening – on one of the minibuses. It stops outside my house in Lansdown Crescent. The drivers are so thoughtful. They always help me on and off. I get off at the gate and walk to David's ward. It takes me through the car park, which is where I found you the other evening.'

'Lying on the ground?'

'Yes, over there, by the lamp-post. If I hadn't spotted you, I'm sure someone else would have done. The car park was completely full. It always is in the evening.'

'Was anyone about?'

'I expect so. That's what I was saying.'

'But did you notice anyone in particular?'

'Hereabouts? No. I'm afraid not, or I would certainly have told them. Someone better on his pins than I am could have got help quicker. This is the spot.'

They had reached a point between two parked cars under an old-fashioned wrought-iron lamp-post with a tub of flowers under it. The small area in front was painted with yellow lines to discourage parking. In fact, there wasn't space for a car, but you could have left a motorcycle there.

'When I saw you lying there, I thought you might be asleep. With all the homeless young people there are, you can come across them sleeping almost anywhere in broad daylight sometimes. Only when I got closer, it was obvious to me that you weren't in a proper sleeping position. I can't say why exactly, but it looked extremely uncomfortable. I thought you might be dead. I was profoundly relieved to discover that you were breathing.'

'I suppose I was dumped there.'

'That's the way it looked.'

'Thank God they left me here and not in the path of the cars where I could have been run over.'

'Yes, it shows some concern for your safety,' said Mrs Thornton.

'And after you found me you came up to the ward and told someone?'

'That's right. The first person I saw was one of the nurses I know and she soon got organised. They're very efficient here.'

'What time was it?'

'When I got help? Some time after seven for sure. At least ten minutes past. My bus gets in at five past the hour, which suits me perfectly. Visiting is open here, but they tell you they prefer you to come after the evening meal, which is from six to seven. I think most visitors co-operate.'

Rose stood and stared at the place where she'd lain unconscious. 'It's fairly conspicuous.'

'It is.'

'I mean, you'd think somebody else must have noticed, if people were driving in for the seven o'clock visit.'

'Well, you would,' Mrs Thornton agreed.

'I can only suppose I wasn't there very long.'

Mrs Thornton said, 'Can we go back to the ward now? I

don't suppose David knows if I'm there or not, but I like to be with him and I don't think there's anything else I can tell you, my dear.'

Rose couldn't think of anything else to ask. She felt guilty she'd brought the old lady out here for so little result. 'Of course. Let's go back.'

Mrs Thornton offered to let Rose walk ahead, allowing her to follow at her own slow pace, but Rose insisted on taking her arm. In the last few minutes the light had faded. 'You want to be careful,' Rose advised. She'd become fond of the old lady. 'You won't be all that easy to see in your dark clothes. They don't all drive under the speed limit, especially if they're late.'

'Don't I know it!' said Mrs Thornton. 'The other evening I was almost knocked down by some people in a white car just as I came through the main gate. I'd only just left the bus. I had to dodge out of the way like a bullfighter. Perhaps I was partly to blame for not being alert, but you don't expect anyone to be driving so quickly in hospital grounds, unless it's an ambulance.'

'When was this?' Rose asked eagerly.

'Two or three nights ago.'

'Could it have been the night you found me?'

'Don't ask. I come every evening,' Mrs Thornton said with exasperating uncertainty.

'Would you try and remember?'

'One day is very like another to me.'

'Please.'

'Well, it certainly wasn't last night, and I don't think it was the night before, because I met someone on the bus who came in with me, the wife of one of the patients. It must have been Monday, mustn't it?'

'This white car. Was it coming into the hospital?'

'Oh, no,' said Mrs Thornton. 'That was why I was caught off guard. The car was on the way out. You don't expect a car to be leaving when everyone is arriving.'

'You know why I'm asking?' said Rose. 'It may have been the car that brought me here. I can't have been lying here very long, or someone else would have noticed me before you did. If this car was being driven away in a hurry, you may have seen the people who dumped me here. You did say there were some people in the car. More than just the driver.'

'Well, I think so, my dear. I got the impression of a man and a woman.'

'Anything you remember about them? Young? Middle-aged?'

'My dear, everyone looks young to me. I think I'm right in saying that the man was thin on top – well, bald – so he was probably middle-aged. I didn't see much of the woman, except to register that she was female. Dark-haired, I think. They simply raced through the gate and away. You could hear the car's noise long after it vanished up the street. Do you know, it didn't occur to me until this minute that they might have had something to do with you.'

'Do you remember anything else about them? Or about the car? You said it was white. White all over?'

'I think so. I'm sorry. A car is a car to me. I can't tell you the make or anything and I certainly didn't notice the number.'

'Was it large? You mentioned the engine-note.'

'I suppose it must have been.'

'A sports car? Like, em . . .' Rose cast around the rows of parked cars, '. . . like the green one over there, in shape, I mean?'

'No, nothing like that. It was higher off the ground than that. More substantial, somehow.' Now Mrs Thornton took stock. 'Not particularly modern, but elegant. Have you ever seen *Inspector Morse* on television?'

'Yes, of course.'

'His car—'

'Yes! A Jag. Was it like that?'

'No, dear. His car is red, isn't it? Well, maroon.'

'But the shape was similar?'

'Not in the least. What I'm trying to say is that on the front of Inspector Morse's car there's a sort of emblem.'

'The jaguar, yes.'

'Well, this one had something mounted on the bonnet, but it wasn't an animal.'

'The figure of a woman?'

'Oh, no. Definitely not a woman. A fish.'

'A *fish*?' Rose could think of no motor manufacturer who used a fish as a trademark. 'Are you sure?'

'That's what it appeared to be. I only caught a glimpse.'

'What kind of fish?'

'I'm sure I couldn't tell you. I'm no expert on the subject. A fish is just a fish to me.'

This was infuriating. 'Like a shark? A dolphin?'

'I don't think so. Not so exotic as those.'

'What colour?'

'Silver, I fancy. But don't hold me to that, will you?'

'You couldn't have confused it with something else?'

'Quite possibly,' Mrs Thornton blithely said. 'I'm just an old woman who knows nothing at all about cars or fish.'

'It's so bloody frustrating, Ada,' Rose told her companion on the way to the bus-stop. 'There's a fair chance that this white car was the one I was driven to the hospital in, but she can't tell me anything about it except that she thinks it had a fish mounted on the bonnet. A *fish*.'

'What's wrong with that, petal? A fish on a car is pretty unusual.'

'I'd say it is. Have you ever seen one?'

'Since you ask, no.'

'She's very vague about it and she only caught a glimpse, anyway.'

'Look on the bright side, ducky,' said Ada. 'Suppose she'd been a car expert and told you she saw a BMW five-series. You'd be no wiser, really. You could find hundreds of cars like that. If we can find a white car with a fish on it, we're really getting warm.'

Seven

Back at the hostel a message was handed to Rose. She was to phone Dr Whitfield as soon as possible.

'There you go,' said Ada with a told-you-so smile. 'Somebody cares. Just when you were saying that goddam hospital was only too pleased to be shot of you . . .'

'*You* said that.'

Rose used the payphone in the hall.

'How are you?' Dr Whitfield asked.

'No different. There's no change.'

'All in good time. Listen, I don't know if this is significant, but someone was asking after you this afternoon. A woman. She phoned the clinic. She wanted to know if you'd recovered consciousness.'

Rose's skin prickled. 'Did she mention my name?'

'No. She simply referred to you as the patient who was brought in unconscious on Monday evening.'

'Who is she?'

'She didn't identify herself. The call was taken by one of our least experienced staff, unfortunately.'

Biting back the rebuke that was imminent, Rose asked, 'What else was said?'

'The girl at our end told her you'd been discharged and were being cared for by the social services.'

'Did she tell this woman where to find me?'

The doctor said in a shocked tone, 'We wouldn't do that, particularly without knowing who the call was from. I'm afraid all we can tell you is that the voice sounded local. There was some of the West Country in it. It's odd that she didn't leave her name. None of this makes any sense, I suppose?'

'No sense at all,' Rose said, incensed that such a chance had been allowed to slip.

'The caller may well get on to the Social Services and trace you that way. I wanted you to be informed, just in case. How did you get on with Mrs Thornton?'

She controlled herself enough to tell him about the white car with the fish emblem. He said he hadn't any knowledge of such a vehicle.

'I wouldn't get too excited. Old people can get things wrong,' he told her. 'She could easily have made a mistake about the fish.'

When Rose replaced the phone her hand was red from gripping it. Through someone's incompetence a real chance had been lost. They should have traced that call. Dr Whitfield knew it and was covering up for the hospital. He was a right ruddy diplomat. How could she believe anything he said? All these promises about her memory being swiftly restored: how much were they worth from a man who told you what he thought you wanted to hear?

Up in their room she told Ada about the call. 'I want to strangle someone,' she said finally.

'Terrific,' said Ada. 'Just what I need to hear from the person I share my room with.'

Rose couldn't even raise a smile.

Ada asked, 'Who do you think she is, this woman who called the hospital?'

'That's the bind. I'll never know, will I, unless she gets in touch again? She could be one of my family, or a friend, or someone I work with.'

Ada shook her head. 'Think it through, petal. How could your nearest and dearest know you were in the Hinton Clinic? The only people who know you were in there are those pillocks who dumped you in the car park.'

Rose stared at her. Such was her anger that this simple point had not dawned on her.

Ada continued, 'It's my belief that this call was from the woman Mrs Thornton saw, the dark-haired dame in the car. She and Mr thin-on-top have you on their conscience. They needed to find out if you were dead.'

She had come to respect Ada's logic. 'You're saying the call was from the people who knocked me down?'

'Unless you can think of something better.'

'Bloody hell, it's so frustrating. And now they know I survived, will I hear from them?'

'No chance. What does every motor insurance company advise you to do after an accident? Admit nothing.'

Rose sank her face into her hands. 'Oh, shit a brick. What's to be done, Ada? Where do I turn for help?'

'Don't ask me,' said Ada.

She looked up. 'You're not giving up? I need your brain, Ada. Mine's seized up completely.'

'And I know why.'

'Yes?'

'You haven't eaten for hours. You can't think any more on an empty stomach. Me, too. Why don't we go down to Sainsbury's and liberate some fillet steaks?'

Rose stared at her in horror. 'I can't do that. I'm not a shoplifter.'

Ada's eyes glittered wickedly. 'How do you know?'

She stood as Ada's lookout at the end of the chilled meat aisle, trying to give the impression she couldn't decide between two portions of minced beef. She had one hand on a trolley containing two cartons of cereal and a bottle of lemonade. Her job was to keep watch for any member of the Sainsbury's staff who happened to come by. She was supposed to distract them by asking where to find the maple syrup. This would compel them (customer relations having such a high priority at Sainsbury's) to escort her to the far end of the store, leaving Ada to make a sharp exit at the other end of the aisle.

Even Rose, without any experience of this kind of crime, could tell that the strategy was flawed. Big supermarkets like this employed store detectives who weren't dressed in uniform. But then Ada had never claimed to be an efficient shoplifter. She grabbed two packs of meat and stuffed them inside her blouse while her accomplice watched, appalled. It was swiftly done and Rose could only suppose the extra bulges wouldn't show.

She wouldn't fancy the steak.

She had agreed to do this only from a sense of obligation. She felt she couldn't refuse after Ada had supported her at the Hinton Clinic. There was no risk in being the lookout, Ada had insisted. Ada Shaftsbury had never ratted on a friend, and you had to believe she was speaking the truth.

It was still nerve-racking, specially as Ada wasn't content with two packs. She grabbed two more and moved to another aisle to scoop up some vegetables. Rose went too, squeezing the handle of the trolley to stop her hands from shaking.

The plunder continued. Some loose runner beans and a number of courgettes went under the waistband of Ada's skirt. The fit was so tight that there was no danger of them falling through. Next, she acquired a handful of tomatoes and dropped them into her cleavage.

'Hello.'

Rose jerked in alarm.

'What are you doing?'

She turned around guiltily. But the voice was only a child's. A boy of about three, or perhaps a little older, in a Mickey Mouse T-shirt and blue shorts, was staring up at her.

She swallowed hard and told him, 'Just picking out some things.'

'What things?'

'I haven't decided.'

'Are you going to buy some biscuits?'

'I don't expect so.' She looked up and down the aisle. 'Shouldn't you be with your mummy?'

'She's over there.' He pointed vaguely. She could have been any one of a dozen women waiting for service at the cold meat counter.

'You don't want to get lost,' said Rose, wishing fervently that he would. She was supposed to be scouting for Ada, not humouring little boys. 'Why don't you go back to Mummy?'

He said, 'I like chocolate chip cookies. I like chocolate chip cookies best.'

'There aren't any here,' said Rose. 'This is fruit and vegetables here.'

'They're up there. Do you want me to show you?'

'No. I'm too busy.'

'They have got some here.'

'Is that so?' she responded without enthusiasm, still trying to keep Ada in sight.

'You got me some on the train,' said the child.

'What?' She frowned at him.

'Chocolate chip cookies. You remember.'

'*On the train?*'

'Yes. For being a good boy.'

Rose bent closer to his level. 'What train?'

'From Paddington. You remember, don't you?'

She glanced back. Ada was already moving towards the exit. The plan required Rose to go at once to the end of the aisle nearest the checkouts and create a diversion by dropping the lemonade bottle and smashing it while Ada made her escape. She should have started already. This couldn't be delayed.

She would be forced to leave the boy just as she was learning something vital.

'There are cookies in this shop,' he insisted. 'I've seen them.'

'What's your name?'

'Jeremy.'

Another glance. She dared not delay any longer. Ada depended on her. She was turning the corner at the end of the aisle.

She started moving. 'Jeremy what?'

He muttered something.

'Speak up.'

'Parker.'

Or was it Barker he said?

She couldn't wait to find out. She didn't want Ada to be arrested. She fairly raced towards the checkouts, fumbled in the trolley, pulled out the lemonade and let it drop. The bottle shattered. Splinters of glass slid across the floor in a pool of sticky lemonade.

'Oh, God!' said Rose with absolute conviction.

One of the supervisors was at her side almost at once to tell her it was no problem.

'I'm so sorry. It slipped out of my hand. Of course I'll pay,' Rose offered.

With the minimum of fuss the area was roped off and the glass swept up. She joined a queue. She looked along the length of the checkouts for Jeremy Barker (or Parker) and his mother. They were either still touring the shop, or they had slipped out. Rose decided not to linger. It was too dangerous. She paid for the few items she had, and left. Ada would be waiting for her in Green Park.

Ada liked her steaks cooked medium rare and she stood in the kitchen doorway to make sure Rose didn't leave them too long under the grill.

'They'd better be tender after all this trouble,' she said.

'Don't complain to me if they're not.'

Ada laughed heartily. 'Can't complain to Sainsbury's, either.'

While the cooking was going on, Rose gave Ada a less frantic account of what the boy Jeremy had said.

'Just a kid,' Ada said thoughtfully. 'How small did you say?'

'Under school age.'

'Three? Four?'

'Four, I'd guess.'

'You're wondering if you can rely on a little scrap like that? They're just as good at recognising someone as a grown-up is.'

'He was a bright little boy. I think he was sure he knew me,' said Rose.

'As someone who gave him chocolate chip cookies on a train?'

'From Paddington, he said. He had plenty of time to get a look at me. You're right, Ada. Kids are just as observant as grown-ups. More so, if they think they can get something out of them.'

'But did you recognise him? Watch those steaks, petal. When I said rare I meant it.'

Rose pulled out the grillpan and turned them over. The smell was appetising. She was changing her mind about eating one, even though it had been in such close contact with Ada. 'No. I didn't, but I wouldn't, would I?'

'Something's got to click some time. What did you say his name is?'

'Jeremy Barker. Or Parker.'

'Pity. There must be hundreds in the phone book.'

Presently Rose lifted the pan from under the grill and asked if the steaks would do.

She scooped some vegetables into a colander. They took everything upstairs on trays and sat on their beds to eat.

Ada said, 'Stupid of me. We should have liberated some wine. You shouldn't eat fine steak without wine. They do a superb vintage Rioja.'

'How do you smuggle out a bottle of wine?' Rose asked in amazement.

'With style, petal, and a piece of string.'

'*String*?'

'The best Rioja is always covered in fine wire netting. You thread the string through and hang the bottle under your skirt. It's bumpy on the knees, but you don't have to go far.'

Rose watched Ada start on her third fillet with the same relish she had shown for the others.

'You said you couldn't think on an empty stomach. Has this helped?'

'It's beginning to,' said Ada. 'What am I to think about – your problem?'

'It would help.'

'Things are becoming clearer, aren't they?' said Ada. 'If that kid in Sainsbury's had his head screwed on right, you were seen recently on a train travelling from London Paddington to Bath Spa. Some time since, you were in a tangle with a motor vehicle – and came off the worse for it. There's a good chance it was driven by a local couple who brought you to the Hinton Clinic and later phoned to enquire if you were still in the world of the living. Their car may have had a silver fish mounted on the bonnet. Fair summary?'

'I think you've covered all of it.'

'No, I haven't. There's yourself. A well brought-up gel, going by the way you talk. Southern counties accent, I'd say. Certainly not West Country. Anyway, that's a London haircut, in my opinion. True, you're a casual dresser, but none of the stuff you told me you were wearing is off the bargain rail. It all suggests to me that you work for a living, in a reasonably well-paid job that doesn't require grey suits and regular hours. And you're not a bad cook, either.'

'Thanks. But where do I go from here?'

'We could see if the Winemart down the hill is still open.'

'But I've got to be careful with my money . . .' Then she saw the gleam in Ada's eye and said, 'No way. I've taken enough risks for one day.'

They finished the meal in silence.

Eight

Ada was out of bed early. She muttered something about phoning a friend and then plodded downstairs.

Rose lay awake, but without moving, disappointed that another night had passed and no old memories had surfaced. Her known life still dated from less than a week ago. And now she was putting off doing anything else. She wasn't idle by nature, she felt sure. She hated the frustration of having no purpose for the day. She didn't want to spend it sitting in Harmer House or aimlessly wandering the streets of Bath. She wept a little.

What an opportunity she had missed by walking away from the little boy in Sainsbury's. She was certain in her mind that he really had seen her on the train. She should have asked him to take her to his mother. In a train journey of an hour and a half, she and the woman must have exchanged some personal information. Must have. Clearly they had been on talking terms, or she would never have bought cookies for the child. Two women of about the same age had things in common. At the very least they must have talked about their reasons for travelling to Bath.

If Ada hadn't involved me in the shoplifting, she thought, I might be lying in my own bed this morning.

Sod Ada.

She wiped away the tears, sat up awkwardly and examined her legs. The bruises had gone from blue to greenish yellow. Her ribs still hurt, but the body was recovering. Then why not the brain?

In this chastened mood, she speculated what would happen if her memory never returned. Unless she took drastic action, she was condemned to eke out her existence in places like this, or worse, dependent on welfare handouts.

She had no skills or qualifications that she knew of. The descent into self-neglect, apathy and despair would be hard to resist. That was how people ended living rough.

The sound of the stairs groaning under pressure blended in with her mood. Then her thoughts were blasted away by a spectacle almost psychedelic in effect. At nights Ada wore an orange-coloured T-shirt the size of a tent and Union Jack knickers. She seemed to relish prowling about the hostel dressed like that, startling the other inmates.

'I've got Hildegarde started on the cooking. She would have overslept. I said you'd probably want mushrooms with yours, am I right? She can't say mushrooms, but she knows what they are now.'

Rose started to say, 'I don't think I—'

'Yes, you do. Get a good breakfast inside you. We've got things to do.'

'Oh, yes – like another supermarket? No thanks, Ada.'

Ada made her feel mean by announcing that she'd been on the phone to a friend who had forgotten more about cars than she or Rose were ever likely to find out. If anyone in Bath knew about silver fish mascots, it was Percy. He had promised to see them in his used car mart on the Warminster Road at ten.

The overheads at Percy's Car Bargains were minimal. He had about eighty used vehicles lined up on a patch of gravel beside the A36 and his office was a Land Rover. Two tattooed youths were employed with buckets and sponges. They probably got paid in used fivers, with no questions asked about tax and National Insurance.

'My dear Miss Shaftsbury, my cup overflows,' Percy said in an accent that would not have been out of place in the Leander Club marquee at Henley. 'You *and* the young lady of mystery.'

'How do you know that?' said Ada.

'Well, unless I'm mistaken,' he said, pausing to scrutinise Rose as if she might be a respray job being passed off as new, 'you're the one who turned up at the Hinton Clinic the other night.'

Rose felt a sudden outbreak of goose-pimples.

Ada said, 'Percy, I didn't tell you that on the phone.'

'I saw it in last night's *Chronicle*, my dear. "Lost Memory Mystery" or some such. There was a photo of a stunningly attractive young lady, and I thought to myself that I wouldn't mind being introduced.' He turned to Rose. 'You had some injuries from a car – is that right? We're supposed to tell the plod if we can help.'

'I'm in the paper?' said Rose, appalled.

Ada clicked her tongue. 'Didn't I tell you it was a mistake to let them take pictures?'

'But no one asked my permission.' As Rose was speaking, she recalled the policewoman saying that her superiors would take the decisions.

Ada explained, 'Rose didn't want this. She wanted to deal with her own problem.'

Percy crowed his sympathy to the entire fleet of used cars. 'Bloody shame, my dear. You can't trust anyone these days, least of all the guardians of the peace, I'm sorry to say. I would have told you that myself, given the chance.'

Rose sighed deeply and looked away, across the rows of cars towards the trees, trying to compose herself.

'Percy knows exactly how you feel,' Ada said to Rose. 'He's a very understanding man. The world's most perfect gent. I haven't told you how we met. It was at Swindon Magistrates' Court.'

'So it was,' said Percy.

Ada continued to discuss her gentleman friend as if he wasn't present. 'I was up for shoplifting and he refused to believe I was guilty.'

'You're a magistrate?' said Rose.

'No, my dear,' said Percy, smiling. 'Like Miss Shaftsbury, I was waiting for my case to come up. Falsifying documents, or instruments, or some such nonsense, the sort of horse manure that is regularly dumped on a person in my profession. Well, we had an instant rapport, Miss Shaftsbury and I.'

'Percy, I do wish you'd call me Ada. He gave me his visiting card,' she told Rose, 'and he offered his services to my solicitor as a surprise witness. Petal, you should have been there. It was like one of those old Perry Mason films. Percy came into court and swore blind he was with me at a tea-dance at the time of the offence. A tea-dance, would you believe? He was brilliant. He said he partnered me in the square tango and it was etched on his memory for ever.'

Rose smiled, the image of Ada at a tea-dance temporarily pushing her other troubles into the background.

Percy frowned. 'Did I say that?'

'Don't tell me you've forgotten,' said Ada sharply. 'It was the nicest compliment anyone ever paid me. You said dancing with me was bliss.'

'She must be right,' said the world's most perfect gent. 'I must have said it.'

'Don't spoil it now,' Ada warned him. She turned back to Rose. 'He said he was a hopeless dancer normally and this was bliss because he could tell the minute we linked arms that there was no risk of treading on my feet. He said he would remember me anywhere.'

'Absolutely true,' said Percy.

'He offered to pick me out in an identity parade. He had the entire court speechless with laughter. Can you see me in a line-up? I don't know if they believed a word of it, but they had a ball and my case was dismissed.'

'And mine was deferred for two weeks,' said Percy. 'By which time I got myself better organised. Now, ladies, I'd like to invite you to sit down, but the best I can offer is the back of my Land Rover and I'm not sure if it's such a good idea.'

'That's all right, love,' said Ada. 'If I could squeeze inside, which is doubtful, I'd be sure to bust the suspension. We'll talk here.'

'I can offer something very agreeable from a flask if you don't object to paper cups.'

Ada insisted that they hadn't come for hospitality. 'This silver fish mascot I mentioned on the phone, Percy. Have you ever seen anything like it?'

'On a modern car? No, I can't say I have,' he said. 'Sorry to disappoint. Mascots of any sort are rare these days, with a few obvious exceptions. They were used to decorate the radiator cap originally. Like figureheads, which is what we call them in the trade. Common enough before the First World War and into the twenties and thirties. I've seen monkeys, dragonflies, dancers. They looked rather fetching on the front of a handsome vehicle. No offence, but the most popular by far were naked ladies. I *have* seen fish. But not mass-produced, if that's what you're asking.'

'We're not,' said Ada. 'All we want is to find this car.'

Percy's face twisted into a look of pain as he plumbed the depths of his memory. 'There was a leaping salmon designed by a firm in Birmingham. That was silver – well, chrome – but I haven't seen one in the last thirty years. A silver fish on a modern car . . . As I say, I don't believe any motor manufacturer uses a fish. All I can suggest is that it must be something the owner had fitted.'

'Custom made?' said Ada.

He nodded. 'You come across them once in a while. The most bizarre I heard of was the late Marquess of Exeter, David Burghley. He had a Roller, you know, a Rolls Royce, being one of the elite. Poor chap had terrible arthritis of the hips in middle age, which was sad considering he'd been a marvellous athlete in his time. Won the Olympic hurdles – that's how good he was. Remember *Chariots of Fire*, racing round the quad at Cambridge while Great Tom was chiming noon? That was based on one of his exploits. Anyway, he made light of his handicap. Had one of the early artificial hip replacement operations in the days when the things were metal, and when it was later removed, he had the stainless steel socket mounted on the front of his Roller in place of the Spirit of Ecstasy that you see on all of them. So, you see, it can happen. Some people go to exceptional lengths to personalise their cars.'

'You think we could be looking for something unique,' said Ada. 'That's got to be helpful.'

'If we can rely on our information,' said Rose, thinking how old Mrs Thornton was, and wishing her witness was more dependable.

'It seems to me,' Percy summed up, 'that you've got to look for an owner in some way connected with fish. An angler. Plenty of them in this part of the world.'

'Or somebody called Fish?' said Ada.

'Pike,' said Rose resignedly. 'Or Whiting.'

'Equally, this might be a chappie in the fish and chip business,' Percy suggested. 'It's got all kinds of connotations when you begin to think about it. There are tropical fish-keepers.'

'Don't go on, Perce,' said Ada. 'We've got the point. It's going to be easier to look for the car than work out who owns it.'

'I'll see if I can discover anything through the trade,' Percy offered. 'Ask around. That's the way to find things out.'

They rode back to the city centre in a minibus. Before climbing aboard, Ada got the usual dubious look from the driver. She needed the width of two seats, but nothing was said and she paid the same fare as Rose.

'He's a poppet,' said Ada, meaning Percy.

'Yes.' Rose was still weighing the morning's developments.

'He'll get weaving now. He's got all sorts of contacts.'

She responded flatly, 'Good.'

They got off at Cleveland Place and crossed the bridge to return to the hostel, for lunch, as Ada made clear.

Neither of them paid much attention to the line of cars outside Harmer House. Parked cars fitted naturally into the scenery in Bathwick Street. Only a space in the line might have merited some interest, for in this part of the city one vehicle always replaced another in a very short time.

Ada continued to talk optimistically of Percy's networking skills, while Rose heard without really listening.

They were passing the building next to the hostel when a car door opened somewhere near. Rose didn't even glance towards it, so she had a shock when a hand grasped her arm above the elbow. Turning, she looked into the face of a thin, youngish, black-haired man with a forced smile. 'Hello, love,' he said without raising his voice. 'You don't have to go in there after all. I've come to take you home.'

'What?' she said, startled. She didn't know him.

His grip on her arm tightened. 'The car's over there. Look lively.' He was still grinning like a doorstep evangelist. He needed a shave, but his clothes were passably smart.

'Who are you?'

'Come on, love. You know me,' he answered, tugging on her arm.

She was forced to take a couple of steps towards him.

Ada had barely noticed this going on, but now she turned and said, 'Someone you know, petal?'

Rose's fear came out in her voice. 'I don't remember.' She told the man, 'Let go of my arm, please.'

Ada asked him, 'What's this about? Who are you?'

He said, 'Keep out of this. She's going with me.'

'She isn't if she doesn't want to,' said Ada. 'Let's talk about this in a civilised way.'

Civility was not on this man's agenda. He tugged Rose towards him, wrapped his left arm around her back and hustled her across the pavement towards the open rear door of a large red Toyota. The engine was running and someone was in the driving seat.

Rose cried out in pain from the contact of the man's hand on her injured ribs. He leaned on her, forcing her to bend low so as to ram her into the car, at the same time pressing a knee against her buttocks. She tried to resist by reaching out and bracing her arm against the door-frame, but it was useless. Disabled by her injury, she was incapable of holding on.

She screamed.

Her face jammed against the leather of the back seat. She braced her legs and tried unsuccessfully to kick. He had grabbed her below the knees. Only her shins and feet were still outside the car and he was bundling them in like pieces of luggage.

Then Ada acted.

Excessive weight is mostly a burden, but on rare occasions it can be turned to advantage. Lacking the strength to pull the man off, Ada charged him with agility that would not have disgraced a sumo wrestler and swung the full weight of her ample hips against him. The impact would have crushed the man's pelvis if he had not turned instinctively a moment before the crunch. The car suffered the major damage, a dent in the bodywork the size of a dinner plate. The man caught a glancing thump and was thrust sideways. He bounced against the door so hard that it was forced past the restrainers on the hinges. Ada gave him a shove in the chest. He grunted, crumpled and hit the pavement.

They couldn't expect to hold him off a second time. Ada grabbed Rose by the belt of her jeans, scooped her out and swung her across the pavement towards the entrance to the hostel. 'In the house, quick!' she gasped.

Rose needed no bidding. She dashed inside and upstairs. Behind her, Ada stood between the stone gateposts ready, if necessary, to do battle again.

There was no need. The man picked himself up, crawled into the car and gasped something to his driver. They were on the move with the door still hanging open. It was unlikely if it would shut or if they cared.

'Take me a while to get my breath back,' Ada said when she rejoined Rose upstairs. She slumped on her bed.

Rose thanked her. She was stretched out fighting for breath herself.

They lay like that for some time, recovering.

'What was it for?' Rose said eventually. 'What was he going to do with me?'

'I wouldn't put money on a candlelit supper,' said Ada.

'Yes, but . . .'

'If he's really your bloke, you're better off without him until he calms down a bit.'

'My bloke? He isn't my bloke,' Rose shrilled. She was appalled that Ada should think it a possibility. 'I've never laid eyes on him.'

'How do you know, petal?'

She said, 'For God's sake, don't keep saying that to me, Ada. Look, I'm really grateful for what you did down there. I am, honestly. But if you think that gorilla had anything to do with me, you can't have much an opinion of me.'

'He must have had something to do with you, petal,' persisted Ada. 'Okay, he didn't treat you like precious goods, but he knew what he wanted. He was waiting there for you.'

'How did he know? Oh,' she said, answering herself, 'the paper. It was in the bloody paper. I suppose it said I was staying here.'

'Even if it didn't, any guy with half a brain could find out,' said Ada. 'There aren't that many hostels in Bath for drop-outs like you and me.'

'He started by calling me "love" and telling me he was taking me home,' Rose recalled. 'Trying to sweet-talk me into going with him.'

'Optimist,' said Ada.

'Bastard,' said Rose. 'One look at him told me he was phoney. That horrible grin. What is he – a maniac? He was trying to abduct me, Ada.' *Abduct*: the word sounded positively Victorian and the moment she spoke it she expected Ada to mock, but she didn't.

'No argument, petal, but I wouldn't put him down as a nutter. He had a driver in that car. Nutters are loners. They don't hunt in pairs.'

'It's not unknown.'

'This wasn't a casual pick-up. These two were organised. They must have been waiting there some time.'

Rose shivered. 'That's ugly.'

'Sinister.'

'Why, Ada? Why would anybody want to snatch some unfortunate woman who loses her memory and gets her picture in the paper?'

There was a longish pause from the other bed while Ada weighed the possibilities. Up to now, her advice had always been sensible except when it touched on kleptomania. 'If it was one bloke, I'd say he was after the usual thing. Two makes it different. There's got to be advantage in it. Money.'

'Kidnapping?'

'Here's one scenario. They – or someone they work for – saw your picture in the paper and recognised you. Let's say you come from a wealthy family. They could demand a good ransom. You're an easy target.'

'If my face is so well known, why didn't my own people come and find me?'

'Maybe they will. Let's hope so.'

Rose said, 'I'm going to go to the police. What happened just now was a crime, Ada. They could easily try again.'

Ada's reluctance to have any truck with the police was well known. She said dismissively, 'That's your decision, petal.'

'Well, I can't bank on you being there to beat off the opposition next time,' Rose pointed out.

'Is that what you think the fuzz will do? Supply you with a personal bodyguard?'

'No, but at least they'll pursue these thugs who attacked us. I can give them a description.'

'What description?' said Ada, becoming increasingly sarcastic. 'Some white guy between twenty and thirty, average height, with black hair, a grey suit and stubble, accompanied by someone else of uncertain age, height and sex, who can drive a car. I'm sure they'll comb the West Country looking for those two.'

'We know the colour of the car.'

'We know it was a Toyota, but I could point you out a dozen red Toyotas without walking five minutes from here. I didn't take the number – did you?'

Rose shook her head. 'But someone else might have noticed them waiting.'

'And taken the number?' Ada heaved herself into a sitting position. 'Listen to me, dreamer. All you have to do is change your address. Those goons won't know where to look for you.'

'How can I do that? I don't have any money.'

'But I have chums. I could find you a squat.'

One stage closer to sleeping rough. Rose didn't care for that one bit. 'I'll think it over,' she said.

'Feel any better now?' asked Ada.

'I'm not shaking so much, if that's what you mean.'

'Good. Let's eat. It's okay . . .' Ada held up her hands in mock self-defence. '. . . we don't have to go to the shops. I have a stack of pork pies in the fridge.'

Nine

Ada was right about one thing. To move out of Harmer House was Rose's top priority now. She had no liking for the place. She wanted to leave right away; but not to enter a squat, as Ada had suggested. She would ask Avon Social Services to relocate her. She called their office to make an appointment, and was told that Imogen was in court. The earliest she could manage was next morning.

After an uneventful night, she walked alone all the way down to the office in Manvers Street, nervously eyeing the stationary cars she passed, yet feeling better each step of the way for showing some independence. She was not ungrateful to Ada, who had offered to come in support, but this time it would not have been wise. Ada knew everyone at Social Services and boasted that she could get some action out of 'that lot who never get off their backsides except to switch on the kettle' – an approach that might have achieved results, but not the sort Rose hoped for. Besides, her own experience of Imogen was fine; she couldn't fault her. She had thanked Ada warmly and said she felt this was one matter she had to sort out for herself.

But she was reminded of Ada's remark when Imogen, seated in the office, said it was one of those days that sapped her energy. 'It's so heavy again. The air isn't moving.'

And neither are you, blossom, Rose found herself thinking as if by telepathy.

'Shall I make coffee?' Imogen suggested.

Rose told her not to trouble. She gave her account of the incident outside Harmer House.

Imogen became more animated, fingering her beads and saying, 'That's dreadful. Deplorable. What a brute. We can't have that happening to women in our care. You didn't know the man?'

'I hope not,' Rose answered. 'I really hope not.'

'You poor soul,' said Imogen. 'You still haven't got your memory back?'

Rose shook her head.

'What a bind.'

'You're telling me.'

'Look, there's got to be something wrong here,' said Imogen, shifting the emphasis in a way Rose was unprepared for. 'They were very confident at the hospital that you'd be all right in a matter of hours.'

'Well, it hasn't happened.'

'Harmer House was just an arrangement to tide you over. There was no intention you should become a resident there.'

'Can you find me somewhere else, then?'

'I can certainly try. More important than that, I think we should get some fresh medical advice, don't you?'

This wasn't what Rose had come for, yet she had to agree it was sensible.

Imogen picked up the phone and proved her worth by taking on the formidable appointments machinery at the Royal United Hospital and winning. 'Two-fifteen this afternoon,' she told Rose. 'Dr Grombeck. Cranial Injuries Unit. Would you like me to come with you?'

Rose said she could manage alone.

The desk sergeant at Manvers Street hailed Julie Hargreaves over the heads of the people waiting in line to report lost property, abusive beggars and complaints against their neighbours. 'Inspector Hargreaves, ma'am, can you spare a moment?'

She looked at her watch. She was about to slip out for a quiet coffee with Peter Diamond, away from the hurly-burly, as he called it, meaning John Wigfull and his henchmen. Diamond had asked for the canteen gossip and he would be waiting for it in the Lilliput Teashop at ten-thirty.

Julie had some sympathy for the sergeant. She had worked the desk in her time and knew the pressure. 'Just a jiffy, then.'

'It's the old problem. A tourist. No English at all. I don't know if she's lost, or what. Could you point her in the direction of the Tourist Information Office? They're more likely to speak her language than I am.'

The woman's eyes lit up when Julie approached her. Clearly she was as frustrated as the sergeant at the lack of communication. Before Julie had taken her across the entrance hall to a quieter position, she asked, '*Spricht hier jemand Deutsch*?', and Julie knew she would not be of much more use than the sergeant. She had a smattering of German, no more.

This was no schoolgirl looking for her tour-leader. She was about Julie's age, around thirty. Her worn jeans and faded grey tracksuit top were too shabby for a tourist. She could easily have come from the queue outside the job centre. The face, pale and framed by short brown hair, had deep worry lines. She was in a state over something.

Without much difficulty, Julie established the woman's name. Hildegarde Henkel. She wrote it down. But progress after that was next to impossible without a German/English dictionary. It wasn't even clear whether Ms Henkel wanted to report an incident or register a complaint. Sign language didn't get them far.

Julie ended up speaking to herself. 'I really think the sergeant is right. We've got to find someone who speaks your language.' She beckoned to the woman and walked with her to the Tourist Information Office in Abbey Chambers.

She left Hildegarde Henkel deeply relieved and in earnest conversation with one of the staff. It seemed to be about some dispute in the street the previous afternoon involving a car. The German-speaking information officer said she would phone the police station with the salient details.

More than ten minutes late for coffee with Diamond, Julie cut through York Street to North Parade. He was seated with his back to the Lilliput's bow window, making inroads into a mushroom omelette. 'You didn't see this,' he said when she got inside. 'I'm supposed to be watching my weight. Half a grapefruit and some toast for breakfast. I was fading fast.'

'A diet?' said Julie, surprised.

'Nothing so drastic.' He forked up another mouthful. 'Just being sensible. Doctor's orders.'

'I see.' Really, she didn't see at all. Diamond kept away from doctors. And missing his cooked breakfast was on a par with the Pope cutting Mass. She explained about the detour with the German woman.

'Probably wanting to find Marks and Spencer,' he said amiably. The omelette was improving his mood. 'They come over here and buy all their underwear at M and S, Steph informs me.' He wiped his mouth. 'Coffee and a scone, is it?'

'Just the coffee, thanks. She wasn't a tourist.'

'Student, then.'

'Different age group.'

Immediately the order had been taken, he dropped the subject of the German woman. 'What's the inside story on the dead farmer?'

'You're going to be intrigued. According to the blokes who drove out there, the place is really isolated. Only a few acres, a couple of fields. The farmhouse is a tumbledown ruin. He's lived there all his life, just about.'

'I got most of this from Wigfull,' he muttered.

'Don't shoot the pianist – she's doing her best,' Julie countered. 'There's something he didn't tell you.'

'What's that?'

'I'm coming to it. I haven't even got my coffee yet. The old man has lived at this dump all his life, just about. He used to work the land and keep a few animals, but he gave up the heavy work a few years ago, when he got arthritis of the hip. Now there are a few pathetic chickens, and that's all. The lads are not surprised he decided to end it all. They say there's no electricity or gas. Damp everywhere, fungus growing on the ceiling.'

'You don't have to be so graphic. I just had a mushroom omelette.'

'Some time last week, he sat in a chair, put the muzzle of his twelve-bore under his chin and pulled the trigger.'

'I know that. Did he leave a note?'

'No.'

'Any family?'

'They're checking. His name was Gladstone, like the old Prime Minister.'

'Before my time.' He leaned back as the waitress placed

a toasted teacake in front of him and served the coffee. When they were alone again, he said, 'But what's the ray of sunshine in this squalid story? What brought John Wigfull hotfoot from Bath?'

Julie added some milk to her coffee, taking her time. 'They only discovered that by chance. It was pretty overpowering in the house while the pathologist was doing his stuff. One of the constables, Mike James, felt in urgent need of fresh air.'

'A smoke, more like.'

'Anyway, he went outside and took a stroll across the field.'

'Found something?'

'As I said, the land hasn't been farmed for some years, so it was solid underfoot. He hadn't gone far when he noticed his feet sinking in.'

'Moles.'

'No, Mr Diamond. Digging had taken place.'

'Ploughing, you mean?'

She shook her head. 'This was definitely done with a spade.'

'The old boy buried something before he topped himself?'

'They're not sure. This was recent digging. It could even have been done *after the farmer's death.*'

He paused in his eating. 'Julie, is that likely?'

'You know what freshly dug soil is like,' she said, as if Diamond spent all his weekends in gumboots. 'After a few days the top hardens off and gets lighter in colour. Some shoots of grass appear. This wasn't like that. Anyway, with his arthritis the old man was in no condition to dig holes.'

'Are you saying there was more than one?'

'Mike found another patch, yes.'

She had his full attention now. 'I can't picture this, Julie. Is it just a spade's depth, like a gardener turning over the soil, or something deeper?'

'I'm only reporting what they said. I wasn't there. From the look of it, deep digging. Holes that had been dug and filled in.'

'What size?'

'I got the impression they were large. They think something could be buried there.'

'Or someone.' This was the head of the murder squad speculating.

Julie said, 'All I know is that when it was reported to John Wigfull he drove out especially to look.'

'If these are graves, I should have been told,' said Diamond.

A couple of heads turned at the next table. 'I think we should lower our voices,' Julie cautioned.

'What's Wigfull playing at, keeping this to himself?'

'Give them a chance. They haven't dug anything up yet. They've been too busy inside the house. There are only two of them. He's talking about sending some more fellows out with spades.'

'Sod that for a game of soldiers.'

Overhearing the sounds of displeasure, the waitress paused at the table and asked if anything was wrong.

'It is, my dear,' Diamond said, 'but it has nothing to do with the food. That was not a bad omelette, not bad at all.'

When the waitress was out of earshot, Julie said, 'Unless they find human remains, he's within his rights, surely. He is head of CID operations.'

'There's such a thing as consultation.'

Wisely, she refrained from comment.

'I might just take a drive in that direction when I get an hour to spare,' he said.

Some of the bored outpatients in the waiting area stirred and looked across with interest when Rose's name was called as 'Miss X', but she'd been through this before. She was past the stage of embarrassment.

She was required to give samples of blood and urine – not exactly the way she had visualised the day. Another hour went by before she got in to see Dr Grombeck.

He was not the earnest, bespectacled little man she anticipated from his name. He looked as if he had wandered in after driving from London in a vintage sports car. Young, ruddy-faced and with black, unruly curls, he had the sort of smile that would have made you feel good about being told you only had hours to live. He glanced up from the card in front of him.

'Well, Miss X, I don't know much about you, but it seems you don't know much about yourself.'

'That's right.' She told him about waking up in the Hinton Clinic and knowing nothing at all.

'This was when?'

'Last Tuesday morning.'

'That isn't long.' He asked her a series of questions to elicit information about her family, education and friends, and got nothing. But when he turned to matters of general knowledge like the names of the royal princes and the Rolling Stones, she supplied the answers with ease.

He enquired about her injuries and she told him about the cracked ribs and the bruising.

'Nothing to show on the head? No sore spots?'

'No.' She told him Dr Whitfield's theory that concussion can be caused by a sudden jerk of the head.

He didn't comment. He asked to examine her head. Probing gently with his fingertips, he said, 'You're quite certain you were unconscious when they brought you into the Clinic?'

'Well, I can't be certain.'

'Dumb question. Sorry.' He flashed that smile. 'That's what they told you, is it?'

'Yes.'

'Then there's no question that you spent some hours in coma. You're not diabetic – we tested. And presumably the Hinton tested you for drugs and found nothing. So we're back to this accident as the explanation.' He perched on the edge of his desk and rubbed his chin. The few known facts of her case seemed to perplex him. Finally he sighed heavily and told her, 'Miss X, I'm sorry. I don't think I'm the chap to help you.'

'Why not?' she said, feeling cheated. She'd pinned strong hopes on this man.

'I'd better explain about memory loss. For our purposes, there are two sorts. The kind we're used to dealing with in this place is known as retrograde amnesia. It's caused by an injury to the brain. The patient is unable to remember the events leading up to the injury. It's a permanent loss of a small section of memory – and that may well have happened to you. But it shouldn't have blocked out your long-term memory. It doesn't behave like that.'

She listened apprehensively. She didn't want to be a problem case. She wanted a simple solution.

'The amnesia you're displaying at this stage – the virtual loss of identity, the blocking out of all your personal memories – has to be different in origin. It's the other sort, and I have to say I'm doubtful if it came as the result of the accident.'

Rose was frowning. 'What is the "other sort"?'

He didn't answer directly. 'The good news for you is that the memories can be recovered.'

'How soon?'

'Hold on a minute. The point about your condition – if I'm right in my opinion – is that it has nothing to do with an injury to the brain. The cause is psychological.'

She stared, repeating the last word in her head.

'For some reason, your memory is suppressed. It isn't lost. Something deeply upsetting must have happened to you, some emotional shock that you couldn't cope with. You blot out everything, denying even your own existence. You won't recover your long-term memory until you're capable of dealing with the situation that faced you.'

'How will I do that?' Rose said blankly. This fresh theory had poleaxed her.

'Psychotherapy. Investigation.'

'Doctor, let me get this clear. You're telling me my loss of memory wasn't caused by the accident. Is that right?'

'Not completely. You may well have suffered some retrograde amnesia as well, but that isn't the problem you have right now.'

'That's a mental problem?'

'Yes, but don't look so alarmed. You're not losing your marbles. The cause must have been external, some event that happened in your life.'

'Recently?'

'We can assume so. You're sure you don't recall anything prior to waking up in the hospital?'

'Positive.'

'Then I reckon it happened the same day. Would you like to see a psychotherapist? We can arrange it.'

She came out of the hospital with an appointment card in her back pocket and a totally different diagnosis from the one she'd expected. *Something deeply upsetting . . . some emotional shock.* She took the bus back to the centre of Bath and stopped at a teashop called the Lilliput to collect herself before seeing Imogen again.

What could have caused a shock so momentous in her life? A break-up with a man? People were ending relationships all the time. They didn't lose their memories because of it. No, it had to be more traumatic, some terrible thing she had discovered about herself. A life-threatening illness, perhaps. Would that be enough to make one deny one's existence? She thought not. And she felt well in herself. Even the sore ribs had improved. Then was it a matter of conscience? Some deeply shaming act. Even a crime. Was that what she wanted to remove herself from?

Tea was brought to the table. She left the pot standing a long time. While people at other tables chatted blithely about their grandchildren and last night's television, Rose constructed a theory, a bleak, demeaning scenario. Far from being the victim of an accident, she was responsible for it. She pictured herself driving too fast along a country road, running over and killing a pedestrian. A child, perhaps, or an old person. Unable to cope with the shock and the upsurge of guilt, she suppressed it. Injured, but not seriously, she climbed out of the car and wandered the lanes in a state of amnesia. Eventually she blacked out and was found by the couple with the fish mascot on their car. They drove her to the Hinton Clinic. Because they didn't want questions asked about themselves (they were having an affair) they left her in the car park confident that she would soon be found and taken inside.

She poured some lukewarm tea and sipped it.

There were flaws. If there was an accident victim lying dead beside an abandoned car, why hadn't the police been alerted? They knew about her. They'd visited the Hinton Clinic the night she was brought in. They would surely have suspected a connection with the accident.

The tea was now too cold to drink. She left it, paid, and walked the short distance to Imogen's office.

The first person she saw was Ada. Ada was the first person you would see anywhere. She was in the general office wagging a finger at Imogen. She swung around.

'There you are at last, petal. We've waited the best part of two hours. Imogen's had it up to here with me.'

Imogen didn't deny this.

Rose said she didn't know she'd kept anyone waiting.

Imogen asked, 'How did you get on?'

'They want me to see a psychotherapist.'

'A nut doctor?' said Ada in alarm. 'Don't go, blossom. They'll have have you in the funny farm as soon as look at you.'

Imogen rebuked her with, 'Ada, that isn't helpful.'

'You haven't been on the receiving end, ducky,' said Ada. 'I have, more times than I care to remember. "Remanded for a further month, pending psychiatric reports." I've seen them all. The ones with bow-ties are the worst. And the women. Grey hair in buns and half-glasses. They're all alike. Stay clear.'

'The cranial injuries unit can't help me,' said Rose. She did her best to explain the distinction between the two sorts of amnesia.

'Any trouble a woman gets, if you're not actually missing a limb, you can bet they'll tell you it's psychological,' said Ada. 'And if you cave in and see the shrink, he'll send you barking mad anyway.'

Imogen disagreed. She urged Rose to keep the appointment.

'It's three weeks away,' said Rose. 'Three weeks – I hope I'm right before then.'

Ada remained unimpressed. 'We can get you right ourselves. Speaking of which, I have hotshit news for you, buttercup. Percy has struck gold. Well, silver, to be accurate. There's a bloke in Westbury with a silver fish on his car. I've got a name and address.'

'That's brilliant,' said Rose, transformed. 'Westbury – where's that?'

'No distance at all. We can get the train from here. There's still time.'

'I'm short of money.'

'Get it off Imogen. This is going to save them a bomb.'

'And I don't have anywhere to sleep tonight.'

Imogen solved both problems. She handed over thirty pounds from the contingency fund and she phoned a bed and breakfast place on Wellsway that took some of Avon's homeless. Ada said she would help Rose with the move. Imogen told Ada firmly that she wasn't to go prospecting for better lodgings.

'What do you think I am, always out for the main chance?' Ada protested.

'And don't you dare walk out with anything belonging to the house,' Imogen warned her, unmoved.

Ten

Prospect Road, Westbury, was a long trek, they discovered, south of the town under the figure of the white horse once carved, now cemented, into Bratton Down. They spent some of Rose's money taking a taxi from the railway station.

'This man Dunkley-Brown is well known in the area, Percy told me,' Ada started to explain, whereupon the taxi-driver joined in.

'If it's Ned Dunkley-Brown you mean, he were mayor of Bradford some years back. Powerful speaker in his time.'

'He doesn't mean that Bradford,' Ada said for Rose's benefit. 'Bradford on Avon is a dinky little town not far from here.' She asked the driver, 'Politician, is he?'

'Was. Don't get much time for politics no more. Too busy testing the ale.'

'Enjoys his bevvy, does he?'

'You could say that. Him and his missus. If we catch them at home at this time of day, I'll be surprised.'

He had no need to be surprised. No one came to the door of the large, detached house. Inside, a dog was barking. Ada said she would go exploring. She marched around the side as if she owned it. Presently, she called out from somewhere, 'Come and look at this.'

Rose found her in the garage, jammed into a space between the wall and a large white car, her hand resting on the silver fish figurehead. She said with pride, 'I knew we could bank on Percy.'

Rose's heart-rate stepped up. 'This *must* be the one.'

'Funny-looking fish,' Ada commented.

'What do you mean?'

'For a car, I mean. The fins stick up high. Not very streamlined.'

True, it was spikier than a trout, say, or a salmon. 'It's still a fish.'

'Definitely.'

'We'd better go,' said Rose, suspicious that Ada might be planning some housebreaking. 'We don't want to get caught here.'

They had asked their driver to wait, and he offered to take them to the pub the Dunkley-Browns frequented. It wouldn't have taken long to walk there, but Ada preferred travelling on wheels whenever possible. This had a useful result, because the driver once more picked up a point from their conversation.

'That fish on D-B's car? That's a gudgeon.'

'A what?' said Ada.

'Gudgeon. A freshwater fish. They're small. Good for bait. Not much of a bite for supper, though. You know why he has it on his car, don't you?'

Ada said, 'That was my next question.'

'Maybe,' he said slyly, 'but I asked it first.'

'He's a fisherman?' Ada hazarded.

'No.'

'He drinks like a fish?'

He chuckled. 'I like it, and it's true, but that ain't the reason. I told you he were mayor of Bradford once. Proper proud of that, he is. That fish is the official fish of Bradford. Gudgeon.'

'Like a symbol of the town?'

'Correct. You've heard the saying, haven't you, "You be under the fish and over the water"?'

'Can't say I have,' said Ada. 'Like a riddle, is it?

Rose asked what it meant.

'Local people know it. You know the Bradford town bridge, anywhiles?'

'Yes.'

Even Rose knew that, just as she knew the names of the Rolling Stones. The medieval nine-arched bridge over the Avon is one of the more famous landmarks in the West Country. Generations of artists and photographers have captured the quaint profile with the domed lock-up (once a chapel) projecting above the structure.

'On top of the lock-up, there's a weathervane in the form

of a gudgeon. So if you had some cause to spend the night in there . . .'

'We get the point,' said Ada. 'Mr Dunkley-Brown is proud of his time as mayor, and that's all we need to know, except where to find him.'

'No problem there,' said the driver.

He turned up Alfred Street and stopped in the Market Place opposite the Westbury Hotel, a Georgian red-brick building that looked well up to catering for an ex-mayor. Obviously it had an identity problem, because the gilt and wrought-iron lettering over the door still proclaimed it as the Lopes Arms and there was a board with a coat of arms to affirm it. Another board claimed a history dating back to the fourteenth century and yet another gave it four stars from the English Tourist Board. Mindful of a possible tip, the driver took the trouble to get out and look inside the bar. 'What did I tell you, ladies? Table on the left, party of six. He's the little bald bloke and his missus next to him.'

Ada heaved herself out of the back seat and thanked the driver. 'Do you happen to have a card? We might need to call you again.' She explained later to Rose that asking a driver for his card was the ploy she used when unable to afford a tip. It saved embarrassment because there was just the suggestion that the tip was being saved for the second run, which never happened.

The interior bore out the promise of gentility: a leather-clad bar, thick, patterned carpet, dark wood panelling and framed Victorian cartoons by Spy. The Dunkley-Browns looked well set for a long session, seated with four others in a partitioned section a step up from the main bar, their table already stacked with empties. Although their conversation didn't quite carry, the bursts of laughter did.

Rose would have started by going to the liveried barmaid and ordering something. Ada was more direct. She stepped up to the table where the Dunkley-Browns were and said, 'Pardon me for butting in, but you *are* the former Mayor and Mayoress of Bradford, aren't you?'

Ned Dunkley-Brown seemed to grow a couple of inches. Bright-eyed, short and with clownish clumps of hair on either side of his bald patch, he appeared friendly enough. 'As a matter of fact we are. Should we know you?'

Mrs Dunkley-Brown, beside him, cast a sharp eye over the newcomers. She was probably twenty years younger than her husband, with black, shoulder-length hair. She must have enlivened civic receptions in Bradford on Avon.

'No, we're visitors here,' said Ada. 'Ada Shaftsbury and – what do you call yourself, petal?'

'Rose.'

'She's Rose. Our driver pointed you out.'

'So you drove here?' said Dunkley-Brown, simply being civil with these people who may have appeared odd, but who had earned his approval for reminding his drinking companions that he had once been the top dog in Bradford on Avon.

'Not all the way,' said Ada. 'We took the train from Bath. We don't own a handsome car like yours.'

'You've seen my Bentley, have you?'

Someone in the party made some aside and the women – Mrs Dunkley-Brown excepted – giggled behind their hands.

'It's a motor you'd notice anywhere, a gorgeous run-about like that,' Ada said, unfazed. 'Specially with the figurehead.'

'The fish. You know about the fish?'

'The gudgeon of Bradford.'

'You are well-informed. Look, why don't you ladies join us? We're just having a few drinks with our friends here. What will you have?'

'A few private words will do. We didn't come to crash your party.'

'*Private* words?' said Dunkley-Brown.

'It's important,' said Ada.

He became defensive. 'But I've never met you before.'

Mrs Dunkley-Brown said, 'Just who are you?'

'I said – Ada Shaftsbury. We'd also like a word with you in a moment.'

Rose decided to soften the approach. Ada's tone was becoming abrasive. 'It's for my sake, actually. It's true you haven't met Ada before, but you may recognise me.'

The Dunkley-Browns looked at her fully and she was certain there was a moment of recognition. To her astonishment the husband said immediately in a hard, clipped tone,

'No, my dear. Never once clapped eyes on you. Obviously you're mistaken.'

Ada, braced for battle, said, 'Mistaken about your motor, are we?'

'Anyone could have told you about my car . . .' Dunkley-Brown started to say. Then he interrupted himself and said, 'All right, you're obviously mistaken, but for the sake of some peace, I'll talk to you outside. Fair enough?'

'Do you want me to come, Ned?' his wife asked.

Ada spoke up as if the offer were addressed to her. 'Thanks, but we'd rather talk to you later.'

She said, 'You sound like the police. What are we supposed to have done? Robbed a bank?'

'Gordon Bennett, we're nothing to do with the police,' said Ada, speaking from the heart.

Dunkley-Brown stood up. 'Let's sort this out, whatever it is. I'll step outside with you, but I'm not having my wife's evening disturbed.'

Ada led the way and they stood in the sparse evening light in the Market Place while Rose explained the connection. She set out the facts without guile, admitting that she had her information second-hand from an elderly woman, fully expecting her frankness to be matched by Dunkley-Brown's. He heard it all in silence, his eyes giving no hint of involvement.

Finally Rose asked him, 'Well, was it your car she saw? Did you bring me to the Hinton Clinic that evening?'

Dunkley-Brown overrode the last word. 'Absolutely not. You're mistaken. I was nowhere near Bath last Monday night and neither was my car. We spent the evening in Westbury. I can't help you.'

Ada couldn't contain herself. 'But the car was seen, a big white car with a fish on the bonnet. How many cars like that are there in these parts? Have you ever seen another one?'

He would not yield. 'There's no reason why someone else shouldn't have one.'

'The driver was a bald bloke.'

Ada spoke this as a statement of fact without regard to any sensitivity Dunkley-Brown may have had about his appearance. He didn't care for it at all. 'I've heard more than enough of this. I've made myself clear. I can't help you. Now allow me to get back to my friends.'

Ada was blocking his route to the bar door.

She remained where she was. However, she said with more tact, 'If you took the trouble to drive her to hospital, you must have been concerned.'

He said, 'Will you stand out of my way?'

'Please. We're not blaming you for anything,' said Rose. 'I just want to know what happened to me that night. You're the best chance I have – the only chance.'

'No, he isn't,' said Ada. 'There's his wife.'

Dunkley-Brown said through clenched teeth, 'You are not speaking to my wife.'

'She offered to come outside,' said Ada.

'There's no reason. She can't tell you a damned thing.'

'Then you have nothing to fear.'

'I've nothing to fear anyway. My conscience is perfectly clear.'

Ada turned to Rose. 'Why don't I stay out here with Mr Dunkley-Brown while you go and ask his good lady to join us?'

'This is outrageous,' said Dunkley-Brown. 'You can't detain me against my will. I'll complain to the police.'

Ada beamed at him. 'I bet you won't, buster. I bet my next dinner you won't.'

Rose went back inside and found that the bonhomie had been fully restored at the table. There was some ribald comment when they saw who had come from outside.

'Hullo, what's happened to Ned?' one of them said. 'Still at it?'

The other man said, 'With the big one.'

'Showing her his Bentley,' shrieked one of the women.

Ignoring them, Rose walked around the chairs and up to Mrs Dunkley-Brown. 'If you don't mind, we'd like you to help us after all.'

'Watch out, Pippa,' said the woman to her right. 'They might want you for a threesome.'

Pippa Dunkley-Brown glared at Rose. 'My husband said he could handle it. What do you want me for?'

'To support what he's saying.'

'He doesn't need me. He's well used to speaking for himself and being believed.'

'You were there. We want to know what happened.'

'Where? What *is* this about?'

'The Hinton Clinic last Monday night.'

After a pause, she said, 'I don't know a damned thing about the Hinton Clinic. I've never set foot inside the place.'

In her exasperation, Rose found herself pouring out words. 'Oh, come on, I don't mean inside. Just in the grounds. The car park, where I was found. I need your help. I'm not accusing you of anything. You probably saved my life, you and your husband. If you want to keep quiet about what you did, that's up to you, but please have some understanding for my position.'

The man across the table, the most vocal of the group, said, 'What's this about saving her life, Pippa? Have you and Ned been performing acts of heroism and keeping it from your old chums?'

She said tight-lipped, 'She's confused.'

'Yes, I am confused,' Rose said. 'I admit it. That's why I'm appealing to you for help.'

Pippa Dunkley-Brown drew herself up. 'Young woman, I'm becoming more than a little angry.'

The man opposite, well soused, seized the chance to goad her. 'Come clean, Pippa. What were you and Ned up to in this hospital car park that you don't want us to know about? Naughties in the back of the Bentley?'

She snapped, 'Don't be so bloody ridiculous.'

'Well, if it wasn't you with Ned,' he said with a grin at the other women, 'who was it?'

Pippa reddened.

One of the women, probably the man's wife, said, 'Knock it off, Keith, you stupid jerk.'

The rebuke had the effect of stinging Pippa rather than Keith, for it showed that these friends of hers were taking the suggestion seriously. The idea that her ageing husband might dally with another woman was more damaging than any threat represented by Rose and Ada. She couldn't allow it to pass unchallenged. She said in a low, measured voice, 'What are you on about, Keith?'

'Ignore him. You know what he's like,' said Keith's wife.

'No, I'm not having Ned smeared. If you've got something to tell us, Keith, you'd better say it, or apologise.'

Keith was grinning to cover his unease. 'Calm down, love,' he said. 'I was only pulling your leg.'

The other man tried clumsily to assist. 'Let's face it. Old Ned's a bit of a lad.'

'That's what you think, is it?' said Pippa, at the limit of her self-control. 'Right.' She made a fist with her right hand and thumped the table. 'I'm going to tell you all exactly what happened. I was with Ned all of last Monday, all of it. We were coming back from Bristol early in the evening, about six-thirty. We'd been to a garden centre to look at some ornaments and left a bit late to miss the worst of the traffic. We were on the motorway, the M4, as far as that junction that leads down into Bath.'

'Eighteen,' said the other man at the table to ease the tension. 'She means Junction Eighteen.'

'I suggested we got something from a Chinese takeaway. That's why we headed for Bath. We drove along there for about a mile.'

'The A46,' said the same man. 'You were on the A46.'

'Shut up, Frank,' said his wife.

Pippa continued, 'It was that difficult light between day and evening. Ned was driving. It's that stretch before you come to Dyrham Park. Just open country. I was thinking about other things. Suddenly Ned had the brakes on and I was jerked forward against the safety belt. What had happened was that this stupid woman – you.' She pointed at Rose. 'You had wandered into the road, right in front of us. Thank God Ned saw you a bit ahead, because you would have been dead meat now if he hadn't. He jammed on the brakes, as I said, and when we hit you we'd slowed right down. Good thing there wasn't anything close behind us. You still fell across the bonnet and you must have landed awkwardly because you were right out. It was terrifying. We got you off the front of the car and made sure you were still breathing and tried to revive you at the side of the road. Ned was in a state of shock, poor man. He knew he was in deep, deep trouble.' She looked across the room towards the door. 'He isn't coming, is he?'

Rose said, 'He won't get past Ada. Go on, please.'

'He's been caught before for being over the limit,' said Pippa. 'You all know that. One more would do for him. He'd had a couple of drinks in Bristol. It doesn't affect his driving, not that amount. I tell you, this wasn't his fault, but it would have been no good arguing. They'd have breathalysed him and taken his licence away, and if it was known he'd hit someone, he'd get sent down for a term. That's why we couldn't report it. I knew the hospital wasn't far away. There's a road sign along there.'

'I know it,' said Frank.

She looked up at Rose. 'We did what we could for you. We lifted you into the back seat. Cars and lorries were going by, but no one stopped, thank God. Then we drove to the Hinton Clinic, with Ned at the wheel and me beside you in the back seat.'

'What a nightmare,' said Keith's wife.

'Then we had this problem. We couldn't take you in as a casualty, or questions would have been asked. To have given false names would have made it worse. So I suggested we put you down in the car park where someone was sure to discover you and get you inside. That's what we did. We picked a spot under a lamp-post. Then we got the hell out of there.'

'That's all?' said Rose.

'Well, I called the hospital a couple of days or so later.'

'That was you. I see.' Now that the story was told – and told with enough detail to make it credible – Rose was gripped by overwhelming disappointment. She had learned some more about what happened that night, but the overriding question remained unanswered. 'When you first saw me, I was wandering in the road?'

'Yes.'

'In open country?'

'You came out of nowhere,' said Pippa. 'Look, Ned's going to go through the roof when he finds out I've told you all this. We were going to say nothing to anybody. I was just so incensed when Keith started hinting that Ned—'

'Pippa, darling, what are friends for, if we can't stand by you at a time like this?' put in Keith's wife. 'It could have happened to any of us.'

Rose turned away. She hadn't listened to the last exchange.

She wasn't interested in how Pippa made peace with her husband. The painstaking process of reconstruction, from Mrs Thornton to Percy the car-dealer, to the Dunkley-Browns, had crashed with that devastating phrase: 'You came out of nowhere.'

Eleven

On Westbury station, Ada found the chocolate-bar machine and subjected it to a series of expert thumps.

When seated with the resulting heap of Cadbury's bars in her lap, she remarked to Rose, 'I wouldn't want to be Pippa when he gets her home.'

Rose hadn't given a thought to Pippa. Her mind was occupied trying once more to find a way out of her predicament.

Ada chuckled a little and said, 'While her old man was refusing to admit to anything, she was singing like the three tenors.'

'It wasn't like that,' said Rose, snapping out of her thoughts and turning to face her.

'Get away. Have some choc.'

'She didn't set out to tell me anything. It was only because her friends started winding her up, hinting that her husband was having an affair.'

'Which he very likely is,' said Ada. 'And she very likely knows it.'

'How do you work that out?'

Ada answered with conviction, 'They must have got horribly close to the truth. Much more of it, and she would have cracked, and all her friends would know she couldn't hang on to her decrepit old goat of a husband. Bloody humiliating for a woman as pretty as Pippa.'

'Maybe. But instead she told them how he knocked me down and failed to report an accident. That's worse than humiliation. That's a crime, Ada.'

'That crowd are boozers themselves, petal. They won't shop him.'

All of this rang true, but none of it helped Rose. 'I'm not

much further on, am I? We now discover that I wandered onto a main road and was lucky not to be killed. What was I doing there?'

Ada ripped open another bar of chocolate. 'Buggered if I know. If that's the stretch I'm thinking of, it's desolate up there.'

'Really?'

'No trees, no houses, nothing.'

'Ada, I'm going to have to go there and see the place for myself.'

'What use is that?'

'I want to find out what I was doing there.'

Ada's flesh rippled with amusement. 'A date with a little green man?'

'Get serious, will you?' said Rose. 'It could spark off a memory.'

'Shut up and eat some chocolate.'

'I've really got to go there.'

'Tomorrow, petal. Tonight you move into your new place on Wellsway. Remember?'

First, they returned to Harmer House to collect Rose's few possessions, automatically quickening their steps on approaching the line of parked cars outside. This time they reached the front door without incident. 'You don't have to help me with the move,' Rose said as they started up the creaking stairs. 'You've given up so much of your time already, and I'm really grateful, but I can do this by myself.'

'Try and keep me away,' said Ada.

Rose thanked her.

Ada said, 'Don't get ideas. I want to see if it's a better drum than this.'

Rose knew it wasn't in Ada's nature to admit to being helpful. 'I've really enjoyed your company. I don't know how you feel about keeping in touch. I'd like to stay friends if you would.'

They went up four or five more stairs before Ada reacted. 'Give me a five.'

'What?' said Rose.

'Your hand.'

'Oh.' She held out her palm and Ada slapped hers against it in agreement.

'Whatever, wherever.'

'Whatever, wherever,' repeated Rose.

Ada stopped suddenly and lowered her voice. 'Can you hear anything? I think there's someone in our room.'

Rose listened. Without question there were voices coming from the bedroom. 'It sounds like Imogen.'

'At this time?'

They crept to the top. The door had been left ajar. Rose was right. Imogen's well-bred drawl was coming through clearly. The other voice was female also.

Rose looked at Ada, who shrugged.

They pushed the door wide and stepped in.

'Goodness, you surprised us,' said Imogen.

Ada, close behind Rose, said, 'Can't think why. Believe it or not, this is our room, ducky.'

'Yes, it's an intrusion. I'm sorry, but there was nowhere else to wait,' said Imogen. 'And something very special . . .'

. . . was interrupted by something very unexpected. The other woman opened her arms wide, said, 'Darling, where have you been?' and stepped forward to embrace Rose in a hug that squeezed a high note out of her like a Scottish piper starting up.

Ada cried out, 'Watch it – she's busted her ribs.'

The woman released Rose. 'Oh, my God, I had no idea.'

Actually the discomfort was mild, for the pressure had been cushioned by a substantial bosom. The woman was sturdy, though sylphlike compared to Ada. She was about Rose's age or younger, with fine brown hair, worn in a ponytail. Her get-up was strangely chosen for visiting a hostel for the homeless. She looked as if she had spent the last hour having a make-over in a department store. She was in a white silk blouse that hung loose over black leggings. An expensive-looking coat was draped over a chair-back.

Imogen said, 'This is your sister Doreen. Don't you recognise her?'

Rose felt as if lightning had struck. 'My *sister*?'

'Stepsister, to be accurate,' said the woman. 'Roz, it's me.' She took one of Rose's hands and clasped it between both of hers. 'It's all over, love. I've come to take you home.'

Pulses buzzed in Rose's head and none of them made any helpful connections. She took a step away, releasing her hand.

Imogen said, 'When Miss Jenkins called the office, I just had to bring her here. I know it's late and obviously we've taken you by surprise.'

Rose said flatly, 'I don't know her.'

'You don't *recognise* her,' Imogen corrected her. 'You don't recognise her because you still haven't got your memory back.'

'But if she's my own sister . . .'

'It doesn't mean that your memory will suddenly switch on.' She turned to the woman. 'You'll have to make allowances, I'm afraid. It's like a shutter in her brain. She can't see anything behind it.'

Rose went white with anger. Imogen had no right to discuss her as if she were some dead laboratory animal pinned out for dissection. She was intelligent, for God's sake. She could hear what was being said.

Before she opened her mouth to object, Ada said, 'The point is, we can't be too careful. Yesterday, some gorilla claimed to know Rose and then tried to force her into a car. I was there. We both had to fight to get away.'

Imogen quickly said, 'It's all right, Ada. There's no question of any deception here. Miss Jenkins has satisfied me that she's Rose's sister. She has proof. Photos.'

Doreen Jenkins picked her handbag off the back of a chair, unzipped it and opened a pigskin wallet. And she had enough tact to address Rose directly. 'Here's one of you with Mummy in the garden at Twickenham.' She handed across a standard-size colour print of two women arm in arm in front of a lavender bush.

Rose had to steady the photo from shaking in her hand. Here was a large, smiling middle-aged woman in a print dress. The other was younger, slimmer, dark-haired, with the face she saw in mirrors, the face she had learned to accept as her own. Sharply focused and in a good light, the likeness couldn't be dismissed. 'This is me with my mother?' she said, frowning.

'Yes, and she's my mummy, too, of course,' said Doreen Jenkins, smiling. 'Look at some others.' She handed across two more. 'They're more recent. I don't know where they were taken. Probably on holiday. I didn't take them. I got them from you.'

Imogen, suddenly at Rose's side and squeezing her arm, said, 'There isn't any doubt, is there? It's you.'

A detail in these extra pictures clinched it. Both were shots of Rose alone, one seated on a drystone wall, the other standing in a doorway. In each she was wearing the belt she had been found in and was wearing now, its large steel buckle unmistakable. Probably the jeans were the same designer pair she had damaged in the accident.

Ada came over to look. 'Pity,' she said. 'We were shaping up nicely as sleuths, weren't we, petal?'

Rose turned to the woman she now had to accept as her stepsister. She had to force herself to speak. 'Did I hear right just now? Did you call me Roz?'

Doreen nodded. 'That's your name. Rosamund.'

Imogen said in a self-congratulating tone, 'I wasn't far out, calling you Rose.'

'What's my surname – Jenkins?'

'No,' said Doreen. 'You're Rosamund Black. You and I had different fathers. Mummy got a divorce in 1972. It's so peculiar having to tell you this.'

It was more peculiar listening to it, struggling to believe it. 'Rosamund Black,' she repeated as if the name might trigger some reaction in her brain. She ought to feel genuine warmth for this woman who was her stepsister and had gone to the trouble of finding her. Instead she felt like running out of the room. Now that the uncertainty was removed she was panicking. She wasn't sure that she could face any more truth about herself.

Imogen said, 'When you've had a chance to take it in, everything will fall into place.'

Doreen said, 'I'm going to take care of you.'

'I'm not sick,' Rose snapped back, then softened it to, 'I can take care of myself, now that you tell me who I am. How did you find me?'

'We tracked you down,' Doreen answered. 'Mummy was worried. You always phone her Sunday nights, wherever you are, and you missed last week. When she tried you, there was no answer. You can imagine the state she was in, with her imagination. She's always reading stuff in the papers about women disappearing. Remember the fuss she made about your trip to Florida? I suppose not. Well, you still managed to call her from the States at the usual time. What with Mummy going spare, I promised to make some enquiries. Jackie – your friend, Jackie Mays – thought you'd said something about a weekend in Bath. Some hotel deal. She didn't know which one. I phoned a few without success, and then Jerry said he'd got a week owing to him so why didn't we go down and stay at a bed and breakfast. The first or second person we asked said there had been a report in the local paper about a woman who'd lost her memory. It was you – my own sister! When I saw your picture, I phoned the social services and here I am.'

'Who's Jerry?'

Doreen gave her a surprised look. 'My bloke.'

'Does he know me?'

'Of course he does. I've been living with him for the last three years. You're going to stay with us tonight. I insist, and so does Jerry. There are spare rooms in the place where we are out at Bathford. It's a lovely spot and it'll do you good.'

Rose said – and it must have sounded ungrateful, but she refused to be swamped by all the concern – 'I'd rather get home if you'd tell me where it is.'

Imogen said quickly, 'That might not be such a good idea. You'd be better off with your family until your memory comes back.'

Doreen took Rose's hand and said, 'We can help you remember things. Between us we'll soon get you right. You'll be home in no time. Promise.'

She tugged her hand away. 'For God's sake, will you all stop treating me like a four-year-old?'

She was angry with herself as much as them, playing the spoilt brat and insisting they treated her with respect. She felt guilty giving bad reactions to this well-meaning sister who wanted to take her over. There was no way she could explain the degree of alienation seething within her.

She asked, 'Where do I live?'

'Hounslow,' said Doreen. 'Quite close to Mummy. We'll

take you back in a day or two. Now that Jerry's here, he'd like to see a little more of Bath. It *is* his holiday.'

'Tell me the address. I'm perfectly able to travel.'

'We wouldn't hear of it,' said Doreen, taking a more assertive line. 'What if you had another blackout? Look, I know you want to be independent. So would I. We're like that, aren't we, you and I? Believe me, Roz, you need someone to keep an eye on you, at least until we know you're back to normal.'

'Doreen's right,' Imogen weighed in, in her role as social worker. 'There's nothing like the support of one's family.'

Doreen said, 'You must speak to Mummy as soon as possible and put her mind at rest. We can ring her from the place where we're staying.'

Imogen said, 'You can call from here. There's a payphone downstairs.'

'Let's do it now,' said Doreen.

All this had happened at a pace too fast for Rose – or Roz – to take in. She didn't yet feel comfortable with this stepsister who wanted to take her over and she balked at the prospect of phoning a mother she didn't recognise. Naively she had imagined being reunited with her family would solve her problems, restore the life she had been severed from, but she was discovering that she didn't want to be claimed by these people she still regarded as strangers. She needed more time to adjust.

She said to Doreen, 'You call if you like. I'd rather not speak to her yet.'

'Why not?'

'I'd feel uncomfortable and it would show in my voice. You can tell her what happened. Say I haven't got my memory back yet.'

Doreen's expression tightened. 'I think you ought to speak to her.'

Imogen was nodding.

Ada backed her friend. 'Jesus, if it was my Mum, all she'd want to know is that I was alive and kicking. But if I sounded like a zombie on the end of the line, she'd go bananas.' She told Doreen, 'You cover for your sister, love. Phone's on the wall at the bottom of the stairs. You can't miss it.'

Ada's air of authority succeeded. Doreen Jenkins sighed, shrugged and left the room.

Ada asked Rose, 'What's up, kiddo? You ought to be over the moon. Don't you take to your long-lost sister?'

'That's immaterial,' said Rose.

'In other words, she's a right cow.'

'Ada, I didn't say that!'

'The trouble is, we can't choose our families,' said Ada. 'We're stuck with the beauties we've got. I can talk. The Shaftsbury mob could teach the Borgias tricks. You managed to escape yours for a bit, and now they've caught up with you.'

Imogen, as usual, tried to compensate for Ada's outspokenness. 'I found her pleasant to deal with, and there can't be any doubt. She's made a special trip from London to find you.'

'I know.'

'The photos clinch it, don't they?'

Rose folded her arms. 'It's hard to put into words the way I feel. I'm sure she's doing this from the best motive. I suppose I'm panicking a bit. Or pig-headed. Part of me doesn't want to be taken over. You see, I feel perfectly well in myself. I could manage. I can manage, here, with Ada.'

'What you're overlooking,' said Imogen, with a hard edge to her voice, 'is that you've been managing with the help of Avon Social Services. That was fine while you were homeless and without family. Now, you see, the rules have altered. I can't let you stay here when your own people are willing to take you back.'

'You're kicking me out, in other words.'

'I've got my job to do.'

'Tonight?'

'Why put it off until tomorrow? Your sister's offering you a comfortable room somewhere.'

Ada put a beefy arm around Rose's shoulders. 'Life's a bummer. Like we said, petal, whatever, wherever. Let me know when you get home. Directly, right?'

Rose nodded.

'In fact, I'll give you one of my cards.' Ada went to the cupboard beside her bed.

'Your *what*?' said Imogen.

Ada had been full of surprises from the start, but the idea of a homeless woman having cards to hand out was the most incredible yet.

The expression on Imogen's face was priceless.

'You can have one, too, if you like,' Ada said. 'I've got about two thousand.' What she had was a handful of postcards. 'Aerial views of Bath. Lovely, aren't they?'

Imogen said, 'Ada, you're the limit.'

Ada gave her a disdainful look, 'They're legit. I got them out of a skip, sweetie. They're all fuzzy. Some cock-up with the printing. They were being chucked out. How many do you want?'

Imogen shook her head.

Rose told Ada, 'You've been more than a good friend. You've kept me sane.'

'Send me one of these as soon as you get back to Hounslow, right?' said Ada, putting a bunch of them in her hand. 'And when you've got yourself together again, come and see me. I'll be here if I'm not doing another stretch – and if I am I'd still appreciate a visit.'

Rose couldn't speak any more. She picked a Sainsbury's bag off the back of a chair and started putting her few possessions into it.

Twelve

The farm 'at Tormarton' turned out to be closer to Acton Turville than Tormarton, Diamond only discovered after cruising the lanes for three-quarters of an hour. This was a corner of the county he seldom visited, unless you could call racing through on the motorway a visit. On this bleak October afternoon, contending with patches of mist, he concluded that if any stretch of countryside could absorb a three-lane motorway without appreciable loss of character, it was this. The two people he met and asked for directions said they couldn't help. Locals both, they hadn't heard of a farmer called Gladstone. When eventually he found the farm (luckily spotting a police vehicle at the end of a mud track) he had no difficulty in understanding how the body had lain undiscovered for up to a week. The stone cottage looked derelict. The outbuildings were overgrown with a mass of soggy Old Man's Beard, its hairy awns, silver in high summer, now as brown as if the Old Man smoked sixty a day.

The remoteness of the place meant that he could not in all conscience tell Wigfull that he merely happened to be passing. Instead he gave no explanation at all when he hailed the party of diggers.

'Any progress, John?'

If Dracula himself had stepped out of the mist Wigfull could not have been more startled.

'I said how's it going?'

'What are you . . . ?'

'Is there any progress?'

'If shifting half a ton of soil is progress, yes,' Wigfull succeeded in saying.

'But you haven't found anything?'

'If you insist on standing there,' said Wigfull, 'you'll get your shoes dirty.' It sounded more like a threat than a warning. He was more sensibly clad than Diamond, in gumboots and overalls.

Diamond took a step back. Perhaps to make the point for Wigfull, one of the men at work in the hole deposited a chunk of soil where the big detective had been standing.

Pre-empting the next question, Wigfull said, 'It's an exploratory dig. We're keeping an open mind.'

'Sensible. How deep do you intend to go?'

'When we come to the end of the loose stuff, we stop.'

'Sounds as if you're almost there.'

'Possibly.' Alerted to the fact that this was the critical point in the excavation, Wigfull bent over the hole and instructed the two diggers to take care.

Diamond, too, stepped closer and peered in. The depth was a little over four feet. 'Difficult to see. You want some lighting on a day like this.'

Wigfull didn't respond.

The spades were definitely scraping on the bedrock. One of the diggers climbed out and the other asked for a rake. It was increasingly obvious that nothing so bulky as a corpse was buried there. Diamond stepped away from the trench and took a few paces across the field. 'There's another hole here, by the look of it,' he reported.

'We know,' said Wigfull with ill-concealed annoyance. 'There are three, at least.'

'I'll see if I can find some more for you.' Why, he thought after he'd spoken, did Wigfull bring out the worst in him?

In a penitent mood, he took a slow walk around the boundary of the late Farmer Gladstone's land, in truth not looking for more evidence of recent digging. The methodical Wigfull could be relied on to find anything suspicious. Instead, he mused on the purpose of the holes. If they weren't used to bury things, what were they for? A search? There was the stock story of the recluse who leads a frugal life and secretly has a hoard of money that he buries. Had someone heard of the old man's suicide and come shifting earth on the off-chance? Three trenches suggested rather more confidence than an off-chance.

The neglected field was a conservationist's ideal, the

hedge bristling with small trees and shrubs, with mud-slides showing evidence of badgers along the far side. He stopped and looked over the hedge at the deep ploughing that presumably indicated someone else's land. What had the neighbours to say about old Gladstone? he wondered. And had they noticed anyone digging on his land in recent days?

Having toured the field, he approached the house, which was open. The SOCOs had long since collected all the forensic evidence they wanted, and now it was in use as a base for the police. Some attempt had been made that afternoon to get a fire going in the range. He used the bellows on the feebly smouldering wood and soon had a flame, though he doubted if it would give much heat to the kettle on top. The range stood in what must once have been the open hearth, and the section where they had started the fire was intended for coal, but he didn't fancy exploring the outhouses in search of some.

Here, as the fading afternoon gave increasing emphasis to the flickering fire, he felt a strong sense of the old man shuffling around the brown matting that covered most of the flagstones, seeing out his days here, cooking on the range, dozing in the chair and occasionally stepping outside to collect eggs from the hen-house, or to wring a chicken's neck. His bed was against the wall, the bedding amounting to a pair of blankets and an overcoat. Thanks to the work of the SOCOs, the place was very likely cleaner at this minute than it had been in years.

The chair – presumably the one the body had been found in – stood in a corner, a Victorian easy chair with a padded seat, back and wooden armrests. He saw the chalkmarks on the floor indicating the position it had been found in. There, also, were the outlines of the dead man's footprints and of a gun.

A shotgun is not the most convenient weapon for a suicide, but every farmer owns one and so do many others in the country, so the choice is not uncommon. Methods of firing the fatal shot vary. Gladstone's way, seated in the chair, presumably with the butt of the gun propped on the floor between the knees, and the muzzle tucked under the chin, was as efficient as any. With the arms fully extended along the barrel, both thumbs could be used to press down on the trigger. The result must have been quick for the victim, if messy for those who came after. Diamond looked up and noticed on the ceiling a number of dark marks ringed with chalk. He recalled the rookie constables in their face masks assisting the police surgeon and was thankful that his 'blooding' as a young officer had not been quite so gruesome.

For distraction, he crossed the room to a chest of drawers and opened the top one. An immediate bond of sympathy was formed with the farmer, for the inside was a mess, as much of a dog's breakfast as Diamond's own top drawer at home. This one contained a variety of kitchen implements, together with pencils, glue, a watch with a broken face, matches, a pipe, a black tie, some coins, a number of shotgun cartridges and thirty-five pounds in notes. The presence of the money was interesting. This drawer, surely, was an obvious place any intruder would have searched for spare cash. The fact that it had not been taken rather undermined his theory that the digging outside had been in search of Gladstone's savings, unless the digger had been too squeamish to enter the cottage and pick up what had been there for the taking.

The lower drawers contained only clothes, so old and malodorous that the sympathy was put under some strain. He closed the drawer, blew his nose, and looked into the cottage's only other room, a musty place that could not have been used for years. It was filled with such junk as a hip-bath, a clothes-horse, a shelf of books along a window-ledge, a wardrobe, a roll of carpet, a fire-bucket and other bits and pieces surplus to everyday requirements.

Diamond sidled between the hip-bath and a bentwood hat-stand to get a closer look at the books, all of which had suffered water-damage from a crack in the window behind them. They told him little about the man. There was a county history of Somerset and two others on Somerset villages; an *Enquire Within Upon Everything*; several manuals on farming; one on poultry-keeping; and a Bible.

When he picked the Bible off the shelf, the cloth cover flapped away from the board where the damp had penetrated. A pity, because it was clearly an antique. In the end-paper at the front was inscribed a family tree. It went

Gabriel Turner = 1794 Ethel Moon

Gabriel	*John*	*Sarah*	*Joan*	*William*	*Jabez*	*Ann*	*Louise*	*Maud*
1795	*1797*	*1798*	*1799*	*1802*	*1808*	*1806*	*1807*	*1808*

= 1824 Sarah Smith

Edward
1834

= 1861 Mary Booth

John George
1870

= 1899 Sarah Ann Catt

David William
1900

= 1921 Jane Higgins

May
1924

= 1943 Daniel Gladstone

(St Mary Magdalene, Tormarton)

back to 1794, when one Gabriel Turner had married Ethel Moon. Gabriel and Ethel's progeny of nine spread across the width of two sheets and would surely have defeated the exercise if a later architect of the tree had not decided to restrict further entries to one line of descent, ending in 1943, when May Turner married Daniel Gladstone in St Mary Magdalene Church, Tormarton.

So far as Diamond could discern from the handwriting and the ink, all the entries had been made by two individuals. It appeared that the originals had been inscribed early in the nineteenth century, with the object of listing Gabriel and Ethel's family; and the later entry was post-1943, to provide a record of May's link through the generations with her great-great-grandparents. Daniel, presumably, was the suicide victim.

Sad. Now the old farmer would probably be buried in the church where he and his bride had married over half a century ago. Even more touching, the Bible also contained a Christmas card, faded with age, and inside it was a square black and white photo of a woman with a small girl. A message had been inscribed in the card: *I thought you would like this picture of your family. God's blessing to us all at this time. Meg.*

Odd. He turned back the pages to check. The writing was clear. Daniel Gladstone had married May Turner, not Meg.

A second marriage? If so, the message seemed to suggest that it was a marriage under strain.

Hearing someone enter the cottage, he replaced the Bible and its contents where he had found it. John Wigfull heard him and looked through the door, his hair and moustache glistening from exposure to the mist.

'Digging around?'

'I thought that was the order of the day,' Diamond answered.

'We've given up. It's too dark to see a damned thing and the mist is coming down.'

'You're right. I was getting eye-strain looking at his books,' said Diamond. 'Not much of a reader, apparently. What an existence. No papers, no telly. I'm not surprised he decided to end it. Did you find any personal papers?'

'There was a deed-box. I've got it at Manvers Street. Birth certificate and so on. It establishes clearly who he was. We can't trace a next of kin, so a health visitor will have to do the formal identification for us. At least Social Services were aware of his existence. Not many round here were.'

'You've talked to neighbours, then?'

'They scarcely ever saw him. There was some friction. I think the fellow on the next farm made several offers to buy him out when he stopped working the land, but he was a cussed old character.'

'Aren't we all, John?'

Wigfull was reluctant to bracket himself with the farmer or his rival. 'What I was going to say is that no one could stand him for long. He married twice and both women divorced him.'

'Any children?'

'If there were, they didn't visit their old dad.'

Diamond explained why he asked the question. He picked the Bible off the shelf again and showed the Christmas card and photo to Wigfull.

There wasn't much gratitude. 'Could be anyone, couldn't it? There's nothing to prove these people were his family. I mean, the Bible looks as if it belonged to the wife. It's her family tree in the front, not his.'

Diamond didn't pursue it. Wigfull was discouraged by the digging and even more discouraged by Diamond's visit.

'So will you come back tomorrow?'

'No chance,' answered Wigfull. 'I've got to get the body identified before we can fix a post-mortem. These lonely people who kill themselves without even leaving a note are a pest to deal with. For the present, I've seen more than enough of this God-forsaken place and I'm chilled to the bone. I might send a bunch of cadets out to turn over the other trenches. I don't expect to find anything.'

'Any theories?'

'About the digging? No. If we'd turned up something, I might be interested.'

'There must be some explanation, John. It represents a lot of hard work.'

'You think I don't know? Anyway, I'm leaving. If you want to stay, be my guest. There are candles in the kitchen.'

Thirteen

Doreen had a taxi waiting outside Harmer House. She opened the rear door for Rose, helped her in with the two carrier bags containing all her things, and got in beside her.

The driver turned to Doreen and asked, 'All right, my love? All aboard and ready to roll?'

Visitors to the West Country are sometimes surprised by the endearments lavished on them. Doreen answered with a nod.

Rose was looking back at the hostel. She felt no regret at leaving the place, only at being parted from Ada, who had been a staunch friend. She was sure Ada would not let the parting get her down, and neither would she, if she could help it.

'At least you'll have a room to yourself tonight,' Doreen said, trying to be supportive.

'Will I?'

'It's like a furnished flat. Your own bathroom, kitchen, everything. I've done some shopping for you. Hope you don't mind pre-cooked meals.'

'I'll eat anything, but I don't have much cash to pay for it.'

'Forget it, darling. We're family.'

They drove past the fire station at the top of Bathwick Street and over Cleveland Bridge.

'Did you walk along here while you were staying at the hostel?'

'No. It's new to me.'

Doreen smiled. 'Different from Hounslow High Street.'

The joke was lost on Rose. The street they had just joined, with its tall, terraced blocks with classical features, might as well have been Hounslow for all she knew.

The taxi moved across the city at a good rate into some

more modern areas built of imitation stone that looked shoddy after the places they had left. But presently they drove up a narrow street into a fine, eighteenth-century square built on a slope around a stretch of garden with well-established trees.

'Your temporary home.'

'Aren't you staying here as well?'

'Just around the corner in a bed and breakfast. You don't mind having the place to yourself?'

Truth to tell, Rose preferred it. She was drained by the effort of accepting as her sister this woman she had no recollection of meeting before. They got out at the lower end of the square. Doreen had a hefty fare to settle: she counted out six five-pound notes and got a receipt, which she pocketed. Then she escorted Rose to the door. 'There are shops along there, in St James's Street, newsagent and grocer combined, deli, launderette, enough for all immediate needs,' she said, sounding like a travel guide. 'Oh, and a hairdresser's.'

'Does it look that awful?'

'Of course it doesn't, but if you're like me, you get a lift from having your hair done. If not, there's the pub.'

From the arrangement of doorbells, Rose noted that the house was divided into flats with a shared entrance.

'Hope you won't mind the basement,' Doreen said apologetically, when she had let them in. 'That's all I could get at short notice.'

They stood in a clean, roomy and impersonal hall without furniture except a table for the mail.

'You must have been confident of finding me to have fixed this up.'

'More than confident, my dear. I knew. Saw your picture in the paper, you see. It said you were being looked after by the Social Services, so it was just a matter of establishing who I was.'

'And who I am.'

'Well, yes.' Doreen led the way downstairs and turned the key in the door. They stepped inside a large room that must have faced onto the square. All you could see through the window was the outer wall of the basement well and, high up, a strip of the street with railings.

'The living room. Better than the hostel?'

'I don't think the hostel had a living room.'

Affectionately Doreen put her arm around her. 'So this will do?'

'Home from home.'

In reality, it was just another strange setting for Rose to get used to. She was impatient to get back to her own place, whatever that turned out to be. She hated being under an obligation to people. Unfortunately, there was nothing she could do while Doreen and her partner Jerry chose to linger in Bath.

Fitted green carpet, two armchairs, glass-topped table, bookshelf with a few paperbacks: it would do. The only thing she disliked was having to keep the light on during daytime, a fact of basement life.

'I'm going to make us a cuppa,' said Doreen, crossing to the kitchen.

Rose looked into the bedroom. Clean, if rather spartan. Two divan beds with the mattresses showing. A sleeping bag had been arranged on the nearer one. Fair enough, she thought. I could hardly expect them to go to the trouble of buying a full set of bed linen. She put her carrier bags on the spare bed. Unpacking wouldn't take long.

Back in the kitchen, Doreen showed her the food shopping she had done. There was enough for a couple of days at least. 'Didn't know whether you'd gone back to your vegetarian phase, so it's rather heavy on veggies,' she said.

'If I have, it's all gone by the board in the last few days. I simply don't remember if I'm supposed to be a vegetarian.'

'You were always taking up new diets. I could never keep track of them.' Doreen poured hot water into the teapot and swirled it around. 'But you like your tea made properly. The pot has to be warmed.'

'It's so strange being told these things. I'm wanting to know everything about myself, of course, but it's still like talking about another person. If I make tea for myself, I suppose I'll go to the trouble of warming the pot now that you've told me I always do it, but it's the strangest feeling – as if I'm trying to be someone I'm not.'

'It will all start coming back, I expect,' Doreen said, 'and then it will make more sense. Did the doctors give you any idea how long you'll be like this?'

'Not really. All I was told is that I'll get that part of my memory back. It isn't like concussion, when you lose a small chunk of your life for ever. I may have had concussion as well, of course.'

'You have had a time of it.'

'I'll be all right soon.'

'But it's still horrid for you while it lasts.'

'Yes.'

'How will it come back, all at one go, or in little bits?'

'I've no idea.'

'You haven't noticed anything stirring at the back of your mind?'

'I wish I could say I had. You said my real name is Rosamund. I didn't even know that.'

While the tea was brewing, they sat on two stools facing each other across the kitchen table. People with impaired sight or hearing sometimes develop their other senses more sharply. Rose, deprived of so much of her memory and experience, found she was becoming acutely observant of the way others behaved towards her. She could detect insincerity as if with a sixth sense. For example, she had found Imogen, the social worker, friendly, but unwilling to get involved beyond the limits of her job. She carried out her duties without really throwing herself into them whole-heartedly. Ada, on the other hand, had come across as totally committed, dependable and sympathetic, however brash her utterances were.

She could tell that Doreen's motives were more complex. Doreen had a strong, honest concern, though it came out less obviously than Ada's. Maybe that was only the difference between family and friends. No doubt Doreen was trying to reconcile different loyalties, to their mother, her partner, Jerry, and to Rose. The important thing, Rose concluded, was that Doreen clearly had her welfare at heart. She might appear manipulative, bossy, even, but she had gone to all the trouble of arranging this flat, and it was done with Rose's interests clearly in mind.

She was trying her best to warm to Doreen.

'Will I meet Jerry soon?'

'Jerry?' There was hesitation, as if Doreen's mind had been on other things. 'You threw me for a moment. It won't be a case of meeting him. He knows you almost as well as I do.'

'Sorry. You'll have to make allowances. Remind me what he's like.'

Doreen blushed a little. 'I think he's special, or I wouldn't have moved in with him and shocked the family. They've accepted him now, even Mother.'

'Good-looking, then?'

'I think so, anyway.'

'You live at his place?'

'Yes, but we don't crowd each other. Today I told him I didn't want him with me when I called at the Social Services place. Jerry can be a bit abrupt with people like that. It called for some tact and persuasion, if you know what I mean. So he's doing his own thing, which probably means test-driving a new car at some posh garage. You'll see him soon enough.'

'Tonight?'

'I thought you'd want an evening at home. Nice bath, chance to put your feet up and relax.'

Rose took this to mean that her sister wanted dinner out somewhere nice with her partner. And why not? This was their short break in Bath.

'About tomorrow,' she thought it right to say. 'If you two want to spend the day together, sightseeing or something, I don't need to tag around with you. There are plenty of things I can do.'

Doreen ventured no immediate response. She went to the fridge and took out a carton of milk. 'Is semi-skimmed all right?'

'Fine.'

When the tea was poured, Doreen said, 'Look, I don't want to alarm you or anything, but you've got to be on your guard.'

'Why?'

'Oh, come on, darling. Someone tried to force you into a car yesterday.'

So much had happened since that Rose had put it out of her mind. She shrugged and said dismissively, 'I don't know what that was about. You get some weirdos these days. I suppose he saw my picture in the paper. He knew my name, the name I'm using, anyway.'

'Good thing your friend Ada was there to help you.'

'And how!'

'I think you should keep your head down now,' Doreen continued the sisterly pressure. 'That's why I didn't tell the social worker exactly where we're staying. I told her Bathford, which is on the other side of town. You don't want too many people knowing.'

Rose didn't have much patience with the cloak and dagger stuff. 'I don't think Imogen goes round talking to all and sundry about her clients.'

'All I'm saying is better safe than sorry. You'll be all right here. You wouldn't think of going out tonight, would you?'

Rose giggled at that. 'It isn't the back streets of Cairo out there.'

'But you'll stay in? Promise me.'

'Your hotel is nearby, isn't it?'

'Hotel?' Doreen said with a pained expression. 'I keep telling you it's only a private boarding-house. Yes, it's very near, just around the corner in Marlborough Street, in fact. What's that got to do with it?'

'What's it called if I need you?'

She was evasive. 'Look, you won't need me if you do as I say and stay in tonight. I'll show you where we're staying tomorrow.'

'Why the mystery?'

'No mystery at all. I feel responsible for you, right? Look, this may sound high-handed, but I think I'd better hold on to the keys of this place. Then you won't be tempted to go for an evening walk if you know you wouldn't get back in.'

Rose reddened and said, 'That's absurd.'

'Not after all the trouble I've been to for your sake, it isn't.'

They finished the tea. At Doreen's suggestion, they explored the central heating system and succeeded in getting the boiler going. Rose, trying her best to be appreciative, said she was looking forward to a bath.

Before leaving, Doreen showed her the spyhole in the door and urged her to use it if anyone called. 'It should only be me, anyway, and I won't be back before ten tomorrow. Don't open the door to anyone else, will you?'

Rose assured her that she would not.

'If your bell rings, ignore it. Nobody knows you're here except for me.'

'Hadn't I better have the keys? What if there's a fire?'

'You open the door and walk out. You don't need a key to get out.'

'All right.'

'And there's a chain on this door.'

Rose rolled her eyes upwards. 'All these precautions. I should be so lucky – strange men beating a path to my door.'

'Use it. Promise.'

Reluctantly, she said, 'All right, I promise.' She smiled at Doreen. 'Just my luck.'

'What's that?'

'To have Bossyboots for a sister.'

At about this time a woman called at the Central Police Station at the top of Manvers Street and handed over a sheet of paper. She explained that she was from the Tourist Information Office and she had been asked to translate something a German woman had wanted to tell Detective Inspector Hargreaves. It was about an incident in Bathwick Street the previous day. The desk sergeant glanced through it, thanked her, and had it taken upstairs to Julie's desk.

The same evening a phone message reached the sergeant with responsibility for missing persons. He noted the details and turned to the computer operator on the adjacent desk. 'When you get a moment, you can close the file on this one. She's one of the Harmer House women, the one found wandering on the A46 suffering from loss of memory. Her family have surfaced now. Taking her back to Hounslow, where she lives. The name is Rosamund Black.'

'Nice when there's a happy ending,' the computer operator said.

Fourteen

A bell was ringing intermittently and the sound fitted into a dream Rose was having. After the third or fourth time, she wriggled down in the sleeping bag and covered her exposed ear. Then the idea penetrated that this had to be a real sound. But if it's the doorbell I'm supposed to ignore it, she told herself, remembering enough of yesterday's instructions to justify her sloth. Fine. She felt so drowsy she could sleep for another six hours. Soon, surely, the bloody thing would stop.

Through the padded sleeping bag she could hear the ringing almost as clearly as before. Please give up and go away, she silently appealed to it.

Now the sound changed to knocking. Whoever it was had no consideration. Angrily she freed one arm and felt for the small digital clock on the shelf by the bed.

10.08.

She sat up and took in the scene, registering that she was in a strange room and that it was daylight and that her head felt like a butterfly farm.

The doorbell started up again.

Her surroundings began to make sense – the twin divans, the chipped tallboy, the wardrobe with a door that wouldn't close properly – a job-lot of second-hand furniture to fill a flat. She remembered being brought here by her sister Doreen. Squirming out of the sleeping bag, she put her feet to the floor, padded through the living-room and looked through the spyhole. Doreen was out there, alone.

Rose released the safety-chain.

'I thought you'd never come,' Doreen said as she entered.

'Asleep. Sorry.'

'Why don't you swish some cold water over your face and wake yourself up?'

'Sadist.'

'I did say I'd be here by ten. I'll make coffee.'

Still light-headed in a way she didn't like or understand, Rose went into the bathroom. The sensation of the water against her face helped a little. She took a shower and then remembered there was no bath-towel. After the bath last night she'd had to improvise. Fortunately the kitchen-roll she had used was still here and there was enough left, just. The coarse feel of the paper against her goose-pimpled skin did more to waken her than the shower. She slipped the nightdress over her head again. She could smell bacon cooking when she stepped into the living-room.

'I'm getting you some breakfast,' Doreen called out from the kitchen. 'One egg or two?'

'One's enough. I feel just as if I took a sleeping-tablet.'

'You did, darling. I popped a sedative into your tea last night.'

There was a second of shocked silence.

'You didn't?' She went to the kitchen door and looked in, to see if the remark was serious.

Doreen said without looking away from the frying-pan, 'It's always difficult sleeping in a strange place, so I helped you out.'

'You had no right.' If she had not felt so muzzy, she would have objected more strongly. 'I'm trying to get my brain working properly, not make it even more woolly.'

'I guessed you'd say something like that. Get some clothes on and don't be too long about it. This'll be ready in five minutes.'

She didn't feel alert enough to stand there arguing, but she would later, she would.

Over breakfast, she registered another protest about the sedative, but Doreen dismissed it. 'That was only something herbal that I take myself. It might have a very good effect on your amnesia.'

'I don't know how.'

'Relaxing you.'

She made it as clear as she could that she didn't want any more sedatives secretly administered. 'Look, if we're going to stay on speaking terms, there's got to be some trust between us.'

Doreen started to say, 'I was only doing it—'

'. . . for my own good? Well, I'd rather decide for myself what's good for me.'

Doreen suggested a walk. The sun was out, she said, and they should make the best of it.

They strolled around St James's Square and left at the north-west end to make their way up the hill in search of a good viewpoint.

Rose asked, 'Are you and Jerry planning anything today?'

'Planning anything?'

'Sightseeing.'

She sounded relieved. 'Oh, I see what you mean. No plans. Jerry's not feeling too good. Last night's wine, I wouldn't be surprised.'

'Where did you go?'

'Some little Italian place in the centre of town. I didn't even look at the name. We made the mistake of ordering a bottle of the house wine. Jerry had most of it. The taste put me off.'

'Is it a headache, or what?'

'Tummy. He doesn't dare go out. I don't think you'll be seeing him today, poor old thing.'

'I'm sorry.'

'Well, I'm assuming it was the wine. We don't want our holiday ruined.'

'How many days are left?' Rose asked.

Doreen frowned. 'What do you mean?'

'Of the holiday. When do we all go home?'

'Oh. Tuesday or Wednesday.'

Rose wondered if she could hold out so long. 'Wouldn't it be simpler all round if I took a train home this afternoon? You wouldn't have to pay for the flat and you two could enjoy your holiday without bothering about me.'

'I thought we'd been through that,' Doreen said in her brisk, assertive way. 'We couldn't possibly enjoy ourselves in the knowledge that you've gone off again. You're in no state to cope on your own. Besides, you don't know where you live.'

'Hounslow, you said.'

She gave a smile that said she could trump anything. 'Yes, but I didn't tell you the address, did I? And I won't, just in case you get ideas of wandering off.'

'Don't bother,' Rose said with a glare. 'I haven't got enough for a train ticket.'

They toiled right up to Lansdown Crescent by way of Somerset Place. The panorama of the city, the limestone walls gleaming in the thin autumnal sunshine, was worth the climb. Against all her inclinations, Rose had to concede that you could do worse than pass a few days here.

Doreen took a wallet from her handbag and handed across two ten-pound notes. 'Take it. Really. You may want to do some shopping. Tomorrow we'll go into town together and get some more food in. Make a note of anything you need. Would it suit you better if I came in the afternoon?'

She came alone again. Jerry, she said, sent his apologies. He was still quite poorly. Rose found herself unkindly wondering if Jerry's upset stomach might bring a premature end to the holiday.

The possibility didn't seem to have crossed Doreen's mind, because she insisted on buying Rose a set of towels and three days' supply of groceries. They had tea and pastries in Jolly's department store.

'How did you spend yesterday evening?'

'Reading.'

'One of those books in the flat?'

'An old Georgette Heyer. I don't want anything more demanding.'

'You're still blocked – your memory, I mean?'

'Unfortunately.'

They were so laden with shopping that Doreen suggested a taxi. She was less bossy today, and Rose quite enjoyed her company. They emerged into Milsom Street to discover that this was the Bath version of a rush hour and all the cabs coming down from George Street were occupied. They stood uncertainly, watching the steady one-way flow of traffic.

'Perhaps we should start walking.'

'There are buses. We'd better find out if any of them go up to the Square,' said Doreen.

Unexpectedly, a driver flashed his headlights.

'Look, someone's seen us,' Rose said elatedly. She lifted a bag in salute and started towards the car. He had braked and was holding up the traffic.

Behind her, blocked by other people, Doreen shouted her name. Urgently. It came out almost as a scream. At the same time, Rose got a clear sight of the driver, and she knew him.

He was the man who had tried to grab her outside Harmer House. She recognised his wide, fixed, unfriendly grin, and it petrified her. He was flapping his hand, beckoning to her.

She felt her coat grabbed from behind and for a moment she thought she was about to be forced into that car again, but it was Doreen tugging her away, shouting, 'What's wrong with you? Come on!'

The man swung open his door and stepped out.

Rose dropped her shopping, shattering something in the bag and spreading a stream of liquid across the pavement. She turned and let Doreen force her through the door of the nearest shop, which was Jolly's. They dashed through the cosmetics section, rattling the merchandise. Rose glanced fearfully behind her and a display of perfumes on a glass-topped table narrowly escaped destruction. She veered left, past bemused shoppers, and was confronted by the theatrical-looking double staircase that dominates the centre of the store.

Behind her, Doreen said, 'Not the stairs.'

They cut to the right, around the staircase and into the menswear department, all jackets on hangers, up a few steps and into an area enclosed on three sides which turned out to be the suit-room. Down more steps to the level they'd just left, past a jigging blur of socks and shorts, and back to where they had just come from. A silver-haired shop assistant snatched up a phone and spoke into it, his alarmed eyes on them.

Rose was losing all confidence. The place was a maze. She fully expected to come out at Milsom Street again. The only untried way ahead was to the left and up a different staircase, with the risk of getting trapped on a floor that led nowhere.

Doreen spoke the obvious. 'We've got no choice.'

The stairs had two right-angled turns and brought them up to the household section, which looked depressingly like another dead end until they turned left and saw a way through.

'The restaurant's up here somewhere,' Doreen confidently claimed. 'There are some back stairs if we can only find them.'

Finding the restaurant was not so simple, and that was not the only problem. They started along one aisle, only to be confronted by a uniformed security man hunched like a wrestler. But their immediate about-turn brought them face to face with the exit sign and the stairs Doreen had spotted earlier.

Through the door they dashed, and down what felt like far too many stairs, but with promising glimpses through the windows of a narrow road that was definitely not Milsom Street. Expecting to find a way out at the bottom, they found themselves instead among displays of women's raincoats and hats.

But Doreen pointed to a door at the end.

They emerged in the street at the back of the store. It was narrow and quiet, with antique shops of the sort you never see anybody go into.

'This way. Don't slow up now.'

'It was him,' Rose said. 'That thug who tried to grab me the other day. I nearly got in his car before I saw who it was.'

'You prat. After all the warnings I gave you.'

'I thought it was some bloke being helpful.'

'Didn't I warn you to be on your guard? Didn't I?'

'I'm bloody scared, Doreen.'

'*You're* scared? How do you think I feel?'

They had stopped running. They were both short of breath, but nobody was in sight behind them.

'Did he follow us into the store?' Rose asked.

'If he did, we shook him off.'

The road came out at the corner of a vast square with a grotesque obelisk at the centre partially hidden by some mighty plane trees. The two women looked nervously at the traffic moving clockwise around the margin.

'Over there,' said Doreen.

Rose's heart thumped again. 'What?'

'Taxis. Outside the hotel.'

One taxi moved away from the entrance to the Francis just as another with a passenger drew up. Doreen made a reckless beeline across the road, shouting, 'Taxi!'

Rose was on the point of following. She looked at the flow of cars, trying to spot a gap. One flashed its lights and she nearly had heart failure, but the driver was a woman, and she was signalling that it would be safe to cross.

She made it to the other side. Doreen had already secured the cab. They collapsed into the rear seat. The taxi moved off.

She grasped Doreen's arm. 'Thank God for that.'

Doreen did not respond. She had turned and was staring out of the rear window.

'What is it?' Rose asked, alarmed again.

'Nothing.' Doreen turned to face the front, flicking the loose hair from her face. 'Just my nerves.'

Not entirely believing her, Rose took a look herself. There was only a blue mini behind them, followed by a white van. It was a red car she dreaded seeing. A big red Toyota.

'The way he looked at me,' she said aloud, with a shudder.

When they drew up outside the house in St James's Square, there was no other car behind them.

'You'll come in, won't you?' Rose insisted.

Doreen nodded whilst finding her money for the fare.

Rose waited, looking sharply left and right. Just then a red Toyota saloon nosed into the Square from the St James's Street side.

'Doreen!'

Doreen heard the shout and guessed what it meant. She didn't wait for change from the note she'd given the driver. Without even a glance along the street, she stepped to the front door, unlocked and ushered Rose inside and slammed the door.

'I think it was him.'

'Darling, red cars are two a penny.'

They went down the stairs to the basement. 'How are you doing? I'm shattered,' said Rose.

'Me, too. I'll make tea. Calm our nerves.'

'Don't you dare put anything in it. He's out there somewhere and I want to be alert.'

'Now cut the crap, Rose. You're safe with me.' For the normally demure Doreen, this was strong talk.

Over tea, they assessed the position. Rose insisted she had seen the red car entering the Square as they were getting out of the taxi. Doreen pointed out that even if it were the same car – which was unlikely – and even if the driver had spotted them going into the building – which she doubted – he had no way of entering without a key and he didn't know which flat they were using. There was someone else's name against the doorbell, two names, in fact, left by the previous tenants.

'Could I move in to your boarding house?'

'Not possible,' said Doreen. 'All the other rooms are booked.'

'Is it nearby?'

'Of course. Just round the corner, in Marlborough Street. I was going to show you, wasn't I, but we missed the chance.'

'It isn't safe here any more. I'm going back to Hounslow.'

'We've been through that, Rose. You're not going anywhere without us, and Jerry's in no state to travel. I'll tell you what I'll do. In the morning, I'll ask at the tourist office. They may have another flat on their list. But you'll be lucky to get a place as nice as this.'

To her credit, she stayed for over an hour.

'Got a grip on your nerves?' Doreen asked.

'I'm not nervous,' Rose retorted. 'I can assess my situation, can't I?'

'You still want to move out?' Doreen enquired before leaving.

'Definitely.'

Left alone, she admitted to some qualms, putting out the living-room light in case it could be seen through the high, barred windows at the front. After fixing the safety-chain, she went into the bedroom and tried to interest herself in Georgette Heyer's regency romance. Another night in this regency basement exercised her imagination much more.

A few times she heard other tenants use the front door of the building and hoped that they closed it properly behind them. There seemed to be people living in the two top flats, but she'd heard nothing from the ground floor above her.

After an hour or so, more to occupy herself than because she fancied food, she went into the kitchen and selected a meal from the packets Doreen had stacked in the fridge. The yoghurts, the apple juice and half a dozen eggs hadn't made it back to the flat; they must have been in the bag she had dropped outside Jolly's. A happy find for someone, or a nice gooey mess, she thought, trying to smile.

In the twenty minutes it took to heat a quiche, she prepared a salad, taking her time, washing each leaf and chopping everything finely, humming to drown the silence. She had no liking for television, but if the flat had contained a set, it would have provided some background sound.

When it was ready she had only a little of the food, sitting on a stool facing the window over the draining-board. She could be reasonably confident that the grinning man wouldn't appear on that side of the house. The kitchen was at the rear of the terrace, overlooking an enclosed yard. And since the house was built on a sloping site, the window was a good ten feet above the ground outside. Even so, she glanced at it from time to time.

She threw most of the meal away, washed up and returned to the bedroom to read the book. The evening was passing. In a while she would change into her night clothes. I slept here last night, she told herself, and I can do it again. But you were given a sedative last night, another inner voice reminded her.

She made a pledge with herself that she would read one more chapter before undressing. The clock showed 9.45.

She turned the page and her doorbell rang.

She went rigid.

Be sensible. Think this through. Doreen is the only person who knows you're here. It's not that late. Very likely she's had her evening meal and decided to call in and make sure you're all right.

She got off the bed and went into the living-room without switching on the light.

But Doreen has the keys, her panicky inner voice reminded

her, so she has no need to ring. She could let herself in through the front door.

On the other hand, Doreen may have rung as a kindness to me, just once, to let me know she's out there, and coming in.

It rang again. Rose's heart gave such a thump it was painful.

Not Doreen, then. It has to be a mistake, someone pressing the wrong button in the dark. Ignore it. They'll find the right bell in a moment. Or they'll give up and go away.

They did neither. There was a pause of about half a minute and then she heard a new sound, of footsteps crossing the pavement. Heavy steps. Surely a man. The visitor had given up ringing and was walking off.

Or was he?

Instead of getting fainter, the steps increased in strength, coming closer. Then she realised why the sound appeared so close. Level with the top pane of the living-room window was a section of the street. Against the railings right outside the window she could see his shoes and the part of his trousers below the knees, caught in the street light. And as she watched, petrified, the legs bent like a drawbridge. First a hand appeared, dangling below the level of the knees, and then a face, at an angle, straining to see into the room.

The grinning man.

She reacted by taking a step backwards. The back of her leg touched a chair and she cried out in terror. The light was off, so it was unlikely he could see her, but she could see him. She dared not move again.

He shone a torch into the room.

The beam picked out the bits of furniture, flicking up and down. Then it found her feet and moved up her body, dazzling her.

She bolted through the door.

He had seen her for sure.

There were iron bars across the living-room window, so he could not possibly get into the flat that way, she told herself, standing in the kitchen, shaking, her hands clasped in front of her.

The bell rang again.

Some chance.

Then she heard a sound like an echo, a fainter ringing, somewhere else in the house. He must have pressed someone else's doorbell.

It sounded again, faintly, higher in the house.

Then there were footsteps on the stairs. One of the other tenants was coming down to open the door. This was a danger that hadn't crossed her mind. She had to stop them. They were quick, light steps, still descending.

She ran to the door of the flat and felt for the handle. The door would open only a fraction because the safety chain was in place. She fumbled with the chain in the darkness, wasting precious seconds. When she managed to release it and look out, she was too late. The person from upstairs was at the front door, opening it. She heard him say, 'Yes?'

She tried slamming her door, but it came to a grating stop – the dangling safety chain caught between the edge and the frame. With a cry of terror, she abandoned it and ran through the flat to the kitchen. There was no back door to this basement. The only means of escape was through the window over the draining board. She didn't hesitate. The fastening was stiff, but her strength was superhuman at this minute. She thrust the window open, climbed on the draining board and jumped into the dark back yard.

Part Two

Either by Suicide

Fifteen

Ten days after his hypertension due to underwork was diagnosed, Diamond did something about it. He went to work on a Sunday morning. The average Sunday in a police station is busier than outsiders realise. The rowdies and the drunks emerge from a night in the cells and Saturday night's alarms and indiscretions are sorted out. Occasionally a serious incident needs investigating. On the other hand, the phone rings less and the top brass are not around. Or not expected to be. Diamond was surprised, not to say shocked, to have the new Assistant Chief Constable walk into his office. On a Sunday morning a man of his rank ought to be sitting in the Conservative Club knocking back malt whisky.

The ACC parked himself in the armchair and said as if he had just discovered the origin of the universe, 'Have you ever noticed that people here get depressed?'

Diamond frowned. 'Can't say I have.' In case the question was meant personally, he stopped frowning and put on a cheerful front.

'It's something to do with the air quality,' the ACC explained, 'the fact that we're surrounded by hills. The air gets trapped. People get listless. Lethargic. Haven't you ever felt that you needed to get away?'

'Every day around four-thirty.'

'Because of the air, I mean.'

There was a thoughtful silence.

Diamond then asked, 'Are we going to get air-conditioning?'

'Lord, no.'

The ACC was pussyfooting. Diamond could guess what was coming. His best efforts to occupy the murder squad on a couple of unsolved killings from four years ago were not succeeding. Too many of the stupid gumbos were being seen at the snooker table in the canteen.

The ACC tried again. 'It would be fascinating to know if the suicide rate is higher here than in other parts of the country.'

It might fascinate *you*, matey, but I'd rather watch my toenails growing, thought Diamond as he said a faint, 'Yes?'

'Mind you, other factors play a part. The papers are full of gloom and doom. People being laid off work, businesses failing, the homeless on the streets.'

'So it's not the air,' said Diamond. 'It's the press.'

'That isn't what I'm saying, Peter.'

'You mean we need some good news?'

'We've got quite a log-jam of suicides,' said the ACC, getting closer to the point.

'On the force?'

'For God's sake, no. On our patch.' He went on to itemise them. The farmer, up at Tormarton two weeks ago. A foreign student found yesterday in a garage, killed by exhaust fumes from his car. And – this very morning – a young woman in her twenties who had chosen the spectacular way, leaping off the balustrade of the Royal Crescent.

'Looking on the bright side,' said Diamond after this catalogue of tragedies, 'at least we have the bodies. The ones who disappear take up most time.'

The ACC made a dismissive gesture. 'Be a good man, Peter. You're not fully stretched on the murder squad. John Wigfull discovered that the farmer wasn't the simple matter he appeared to be at first. We still haven't had the post-mortem.'

'You want me to take it over?' he said, trying not to sound over-eager.

'No. John will see it through. It's just a matter of contacting people now, and he's good at that. Help him out by taking a look at one of the other two, you and your team.'

'It would be no hardship, sir. The farmer, I mean. I visited the scene at the time.'

'No point. Wigfull has it buttoned up.'

His offer spurned, Diamond mentally compared the

remaining two suicides. If taking a look was meant literally, he thought the asphyxiated student might be easier on the eye than the high diver. 'Any particular one?'

'Talk to John. He's co-ordinating this.'

His knee behaved as if someone had hit it with a rubber hammer. 'In charge, you mean?'

'I said co-ordinating.'

'Co-ordinating what? There's no connection, is there? Serial suicides?'

This new ACC had no sense of humour. 'I don't think I follow you.'

'Where's the co-ordinating?'

'Just the manpower, Peter. Co-ordinating the manpower.'

'Wigfull is not co-ordinating me. I out-rank him.'

'We know that. You can handle this with your well-known tact.'

A look passed between them. No more was said.

The desk sergeant buzzed him. 'I've got a lady here, sir, asking to see the senior detective on duty.'

'What about?'

'Suspicious circumstances, she says.'

'Concerning what?'

'Hold on a minute, Mr Diamond.' There was a pause, then: 'A possible abduction.'

'What of – a child?'

'A woman friend of hers.' Some angry shouting could be heard at the end of the line. The sergeant's voice dropped to a confidential mutter. 'She's been here over an hour, Mr Diamond. She won't speak to anyone else. She's a right pain, sir.'

'In what way?'

'Mouthing off about how bloody useless we are.'

'So she is speaking to other people.'

'Everyone who comes in. Even the postman copped an earful.'

'Get someone to take a statement and I'll look at it. I'm on a suicide right now.'

'I tried that. She wants to see the top man, she says.'

Over the background noise came a shout: 'I said the head dick, dickhead.'

He thought he recognised the voice. This was not turning out to be much of a day. 'Do you know this woman?'

'No, sir, but she seems to think I should. I'm new here. I'm normally based at Yeovil.'

'You don't need to tell me that, laddie. What's her name?'

'Just a sec.'

Diamond pressed the earpiece closer, but it wasn't necessary. He heard the name clearly.

The sergeant started to say, 'She's—'

'Just now I said I was on a suicide,' Diamond cut him off. 'That was wrong. I'm on three suicides.'

'So can't you see her right now, Mr Diamond?'

'Right now, sergeant, I'd rather see my dentist standing over me with the needle.'

Ada Shaftsbury's treatment of police officers was a well-known hazard at Manvers Street. She had a stream of abuse worthy of a camel-driver. Rookies and recent arrivals would bring her in for shoplifting and suffer public humiliation. When Ada was in full flow the older hands would leave their offices to listen.

'Too busy?' said the sergeant, near desperation.

'Ask her to put it in writing.'

'Sir, I don't think she'll go away.'

'Maybe so, but I will, sergeant.' He put down the phone.

Detective Chief Inspector John Wigfull wasn't his favourite person by any stretch of the imagination, but compared to Ada he was a baa-lamb. On entering Wigfull's office, Diamond caught the end of his briefing of three detectives who looked straight out of school. '. . . and I don't want to hear anyone use the word "suicide". This is a suspicious death until proved otherwise, do you understand? Get to it, then.'

Before the trio were out of the door, Diamond said, 'Morning, John. I'm told you've got *three* suicides now.'

Wigfull sat up even taller and grasped the edge of his desk. His moustache, less perky these days, was into a Mexican phase that hid most of his mouth. 'I'm assuming nothing.'

'So I heard.'

'Then shall we get our terminology straight?'

'Before we do,' said Diamond. 'I'm quoting the ACC. He asked me to take over one of these . . . suicides.'

'Oh.'

'If it's all the same to you, I was thinking about the fellow found in the garage.'

'Chou.'

'*Ciao*?' The Mexican phase was confirmed.

'Yes, Chou,' said Wigfull. 'From Singapore. A final-year student of engineering. Found last night. He left a note. Very organised. If it's all the same to you, I'd value your help more on the case at the Royal Crescent.'

Diamond played the phrase over in his mind. 'Value your help' was Wigfull at his most diplomatic. And the organised engineering student did sound dull, even though he was less messy. 'What's the story, then?'

'This was also last night. We don't know her name yet. The start of it was when two couples won the lottery. When I say "won", they had four numbers up. They watched the draw in the Grapes in Westgate Street – that pub that's always full of music and young people – and of course there were celebrations and soon it transferred to the Crescent, where they live.'

'Four numbers isn't the jackpot,' said Diamond.

'Any excuse, isn't it? The word went round the pubs that some lucky blighter had won and was giving a party, and in no time half young Bath was making a beeline for the house. It was out of control. People who didn't know the tenants were letting in other people. There wasn't much drink, but there was music. At ten-thirty or thereabouts, one of the neighbours complained about the noise. Two of our lads went in and tried to find the tenants. They got the volume turned down a bit and left. By this time, the discos in town were open and quite a few were leaving. We thought the problem was over. Around seven-thirty this morning we had a call to say a woman was lying dead in the basement yard, apparently from a fall.'

'That's certain, is it?'

'The fall? The injuries bear it out.'

Diamond said as if to a child, 'What I mean, John, is was it a fall or did she jump?'

'How would I know?' Wigfull said with irritation. 'That's what we've got to find out. All we know is that at some point after eleven – eleven the previous evening, I mean – a couple who were leaving heard a sound, looked up and spotted a figure on the roof.'

'The roof?'

'You know the Crescent, Peter. It's three storeys high with a balustrade at the level of the roof. You reach it from the attic windows. The witnesses saw her sitting on the balustrade with her legs dangling.'

'In the dark?'

'There's a street lamp right outside.'

'What did they do about it? Bugger all?'

'No. They showed some responsibility. Went back to tell someone, and by degrees the message got to the tenants, who went to look, they think about eleven-thirty. There was no sign of her there. The attic window was still open, but they assumed she'd gone inside the house again.'

'No one checked downstairs?'

'The body wasn't found until this morning.'

'Who by?'

'A paper-boy on his round. What happened was that the woman fell into the well of the basement – the coalhole, as it would have been originally – in shadow and out of sight of people leaving the party unless they had some reason to look over the railings. She must have died instantly. The skull was badly impacted. It was a fall of sixty feet or so.'

The injuries were all too easy to imagine in full colour.

'Where's the body now?'

'At the Royal United. We had the police surgeon on the scene quite fast. If you'd like to go up to the Crescent now, you can still see where the head met the flagstones.'

Diamond backpedalled. 'Are you sure you wouldn't like me to take on the Chinese student instead? This one could run and run. Did she fall, did she jump or was she pushed?'

'I don't think there's any question of pushing,' said Wigfull, with a sudden twitch of the eyebrows.

'I thought your line was that these are unexplained deaths.'

'Well, yes.'

'Got to keep an open mind, then.' Artfully, knowing how Wigfull's mind worked, he said, 'We can't rule out murder.' After a pause to let that sink in, he enquired, 'Wouldn't you prefer to deal with this yourself, John?'

'Sorry. I'm committed to the farmer. Those lads I sent out . . .'

'They looked half-baked to me.'

'They are. That's why I've got to take a personal interest.'

For once, Diamond had been outflanked by Wigfull.

An unexplained death may be a misfortune, but it may also be someone else's opportunity. This was the first solid job in months for Diamond, even if it was not his first choice. Generously he opted to share it with Julie Hargreaves. He phoned her at home and asked if she would sacrifice whatever she was doing for a crack at an unexplained death. She said she was cooking the Sunday roast, but if this was action stations, she would have to ask Charlie to take over. In that case, Diamond said, hand the apron to Charlie and he would expect her in the next half-hour.

Every tourist worthy of the name makes a pilgrimage north-west of the city to see the Royal Crescent. Without question John Wood the younger's spectacular terrace with its hundred and fourteen columns was the crowning achievement of Georgian architecture, but oddly, Diamond's work rarely took him past the place. So this morning the sweep of the great curved monolith outlined against a powder blue sky above the lawns of Royal Victoria Park still made him catch his breath. Or so he convinced himself, unwilling to accept that the bumping from the cobbled roadway may have winded him.

'Take it easy, Julie. Nobody's expecting us.'

The house where last night's party had been was towards the Crescent's west end.

Police tape had been used to cordon off an area in front. On emerging from the car, Diamond and Julie were approached by an official-looking man with a clipboard.

Diamond took him to be one of the scene of the crime team – until he spoke in an accent that would have made a Viceroy feel inferior.

'I say, you there.'

Sensing trouble, Diamond did his deaf act.

'Yes, you in the trilby hat. Are you connected with the police?'

He sighed and turned round. 'We are.'

'Then be so good as to tell me, will you, when you propose to remove these unsightly tapes and restore the place to normal? I've been here with my crew and some very distinguished actors since eight this morning and we haven't shot a single frame of film.'

'You're filming the Crescent?'

'I *ought* to be. It's Sunday morning. The light is perfect. We went to no end of trouble and expense arranging for all the residents to park elsewhere – and here we are, faced with one house sectioned off with ghastly black and yellow tape, not to mention two police vans and now another eyesore in the shape of your car.'

Diamond turned his head to take in the full majestic panorama of the building. 'Can't you point your camera at the other end?'

'My dear sir, the camera is over there by the trees. The whole object is to capture the entire frontage in one establishing shot.'

'What's the film?'

'*The Pickwick Papers.*'

'So is the Crescent mentioned in *The Pickwick Papers*?'

'Is it mentioned? Mr Pickwick took rooms here. Several chapters are set in Bath. He visits the Pump Room, the Assembly Rooms—'

Diamond put up his hand. 'Then I suggest you take your cameras down the road to the Assembly Rooms and keep your actors busy there. These tapes are staying as long as I want them, and I've only just arrived.'

The film director reddened. 'We're not scheduled to be at the Assembly Rooms today.'

'And I'm not scheduled to be here, sir. I'm scheduled to be in my office having a nice cup of coffee and a chocolate biscuit. The best laid plans—'

'You obviously know as little about filming as you do about *The Pickwick Papers.*'

'Right, sir,' said Diamond. 'I'm wery much afeard you're right.' He lifted the barrier tape for Julie and they went inside.

At Diamond's request, the uniformed sergeant at the door gave them a rundown of the use of the building. A couple called Allardyce had the top floor and the attic. The first and ground floors were tenanted by Guy Treadwell, ARIBA, Chartered Architect, and Emma Treadwell, FRICS, Chartered Surveyor (the card above their doorbell stated). The basement flat was vacant. The Allardyces and the Treadwells were on good terms, the sergeant said, and were at this minute together in the upper apartment.

Diamond took his time in the entrance hall, taking stock of the artwork displayed on the walls, a set of gilt-framed engravings of local buildings and a number of eighteenth-century county maps. Predictable for people in architecture, he reflected. You wouldn't expect them to decorate their hall with Michael Jackson posters. Entrance halls were all about making the right impression. He nodded to Julie and moved on.

Litter from the party lay all over the staircase. After picking their way up two flights through beer-cans and cigarette-ends, they were admitted by Guy Treadwell. In case the card downstairs was not enough to establish his credentials, Treadwell wore a bow-tie, a black corduroy suit, half-glasses on a retaining-cord and a goatee beard – bizarre on a man not much over twenty-five.

'The state of the whole house is disgusting, we know,' this fashion plate said, 'but your people gave us strict instructions to leave everything exactly as it is.'

'Just the ticket,' said Diamond with a glance around the Allardyces' living-room. Just about every surface was crowded with mugs, glasses, cans, empty cigarette packs, half-eaten pizzas and soiled tissues. The pink carpet looked like the floor of an exhibition stand at the end of a busy Saturday. His eyes travelled upwards. 'I like your ceiling.'

'We're not really in a mood for humour, officer,' said Treadwell in a condescending tone meant to establish the pecking order.

When it came to pecking, Diamond had seen off better men than Guy Treadwell. 'Who said anything about humour? That's handsome plasterwork. What sort of leaves are they around the centre bit?'

'In the first place it isn't my ceiling, and in the second I've no idea.'

'Let's hear from someone who has, then. Your ceiling, is it?' said Diamond, switching to the other young man in the room.

'We're the tenants, yes,' came the answer, 'but eighteenth-century plasterwork isn't our thing.'

'You don't recognise the leaves either? I'm sure the ladies do.'

'Acanthus, I believe,' Julie Hargreaves unexpectedly said.

Surprised and impressed, Diamond held out his hands as if to gather the approval of the others. 'If you want to know about your antique ceilings, ask a policewoman.'

Treadwell tried a second time to bring him to heel by pointing out that they were not introduced yet.

'Detective Inspector Julie Hargreaves,' said Diamond, 'my ceiling consultant.'

Stiffly, Treadwell introduced his wife Emma and his neighbours the Allardyces. They had the jaded look of people badly missing their Sunday morning lie-in. Sally Allardyce, a tall, willowy black woman with glossy hair drawn back into a red velvet scrunch, offered coffee.

Diamond thanked her and said they'd had some.

Her husband William apologised because there was no sherry left in the house. It was a poor show considering he was employed in public relations, he said with a tired smile, but everything in bottles had gone. William Allardyce was white, about as white as a man can look whose heart is still pumping. He had a white T-shirt as well, with some lettering across the chest that was difficult to read. He was wearing an old-fashioned grey tracksuit, baggy at the waist and ankles, and the top was only partially unzipped. The letters IGHT were all that could be seen.

Guy Turnbull added, 'They even drank our bloody cider-vinegar.'

'It was a nightmare,' said Emma Treadwell, large-eyed, pale and anxious. She must have showered recently, because she was still in a white bath-robe and flip-flops and her head was draped in a towel. 'Three-quarters of the people were strangers to us.'

'Including the woman who fell off the roof?' asked Diamond.

'Guy says we didn't know her. I didn't go out to look. I couldn't bear to.'

'Total stranger to me,' said her husband.

'And you, sir?' Diamond asked William Allardyce. 'You went to look at the body as well, I gather. Had you ever seen her before?'

'Only briefly.'

'So you remember seeing her at the party?' Julie asked.

Allardyce nodded. 'We discussed that just before you came in. I'm the only one who remembers her. She was sitting on the stairs with a fellow in a leather jacket. Large, dark hair, drinking lager.'

'Our lager,' stressed his wife.

'You mean the *fellow* was large, with dark hair?' asked Diamond.

Allardyce took this as humour and smiled. 'The man, yes.'

'How large?'

'They were seated, of course, but anyone could see from the width of his shoulders and the size of his hands that he was bigger, say, than any of us.'

'Drinking lager, you say. Lager from a can?'

Treadwell said in his withering voice, 'It wasn't the kind of party where glasses were handed out. The blighters helped themselves.'

Allardyce was more forgiving. 'Let's face it, Guy. Most of those people were under the impression that we'd won a fortune and opened our house to them.'

'Was the woman drinking, too?' Diamond asked.

Allardyce answered, 'I believe she had a can in her hand.'

'And how was she dressed?'

'A pink top and dark jeans. She had short brown hair. Large brown eyes. Full lips. One of those faces you had to notice.'

'You did, obviously,' said his wife with a sharp glance.

'I'm trying to be helpful, Sally.'

'Good-looking, you mean?' said Diamond.
'Attractive, certainly.'
'Jewellery?'
'Can't remember any.'
'Let's come to the crunch,' said Diamond insensitively, considering the nature of the incident. 'When did you learn that someone was on the roof?'
Emma Treadwell spoke up. 'Getting on for midnight. Eleven-thirty, at least. Someone who was leaving told me they'd looked up and seen a woman up there, sitting on the stonework, dangling her legs.'
'They came back especially to tell you?'
'Well, wouldn't you? It was bloody dangerous,' said Guy Treadwell.
Allardyce said, 'Most of the people there were decent folk. If you saw someone taking a stupid risk, you'd want to do something about it.'
'Who was it who told you?' Diamond asked Emma.
'A stranger. A man in his thirties, with a woman about the same age. He must have known I lived here because I was trying to protect my things, asking people to use the ashtrays I'd put out.'
'He found you especially?'
'Yes. I told Guy . . .'
Treadwell nodded. 'And I spoke to William.' He looked over his half-glasses at Allardyce.
Diamond said, 'And you investigated and found nobody?'
The PR man blushed. 'I went straight upstairs to check. The window was open—'
'This is the attic window?'
'Yes. But nobody was out there. I was too late. At the time, I had no idea, of course. I thought she must have come to her senses and gone downstairs. It didn't enter my mind that she'd jumped.'
'Did you step outside, onto the roof?'
'I leaned out.'
'But you didn't step right out?'
'No.'
'Could you see enough from there?'
'It was a dark night. A new moon, I think. But the street-lamp helps. I could see nobody was out there.'

Diamond thought about challenging this assumption and then decided there was more of value to be learned by moving on. 'You viewed the body this morning?' he asked Allardyce.

'This morning, yes. What happened was that the paperboy found her first. He knocked on Guy's door—'

'Repeatedly, about seven-fifteen, when I was feeling like death myself,' Treadwell pitched in, unwilling to have his part in these events reported second-hand. 'When I got up to look and saw her lying there, it was obvious that she was past help. I called the police and then went up to tell William.'

'I came down and we were together when your patrol car arrived,' Allardyce completed it.

'So you both saw the body?'

Treadwell answered for them, 'We were asked by your people to go down the basement stairs and look. Not a pleasant duty when you're totally unused to the sight of blood. We confirmed that we don't know who the poor woman is.'

'Other than my seeing her on the stairs with her friend the evening before,' Allardyce added. 'But as to her identity, we can't help.'

Diamond nodded to register that he'd digested all of that. 'We'd like to see how she got onto the roof. I expect our people have already been up there?'

'I think half the police force have been up there,' Allardyce said. 'The access is from the attic room, which is above the room we sleep in. I'll show you. You'll have to excuse the chaos. We haven't even had time to make our bed.'

'There were people in here while the party was on?' Diamond asked in the bedroom, a vast high-ceilinged room with pale blue drapes on the wall above a kingsize bed.

'They were everywhere. You can't imagine how crowded it was. When we finally came to bed, there were beer-cans scattered about the room. We pushed them to the edges, as you see. I don't like to contemplate what else we'll find when we begin to clear up properly.'

'But you won't do that until I give the word,' said Diamond.

'Save your breath. We've had our instructions.' Allardyce escorted them across the room to the door leading to the attic. He offered to show them up.

Diamond said there was no need. He and Julie went up the stairs to what must once have been a servant's room. Now it was a junk room largely taken up with packing-cases and luggage. The window was open and it took no great effort for Diamond to shift his bulk across the sill and stand outside.

'Fabulous view,' said Julie as she joined him.

'That isn't why we're here.'

'But it is terrific, you must admit.'

He gave a nod without actually facing the view. 'Where did you learn about eighteenth-century plasterwork?'

'I didn't. We've got an acanthus in our garden.' She leaned over the balustrade. Quite far over. 'It is a fair drop.'

'I wouldn't do that, Julie.'

She drew herself back and gave a faint smile with a suggestion of mockery. 'Do you have a fear of heights, Mr Diamond?'

'No, no. Not at all.'

'It's nothing to be ashamed of.'

'I said I'm all right. I only spoke because . . .'

'Yes?'

'Your skirt's undone.'

'Oh, hell.' Blushing deeply she felt for the zip and pulled the tab over a small white 'v' of exposed underwear.

Diamond was tempted to make some remark about the view, but for once he behaved impeccably. 'The woman was seen sitting here on the ledge, apparently. It doesn't suggest she was forced over.'

'She could have been pushed.'

'True. But she'd got herself into a dangerous position. The odds are that she meant to jump.'

'Or fly.'

He let that sink in. 'You're thinking drugs?'

'It was a party.'

'We'll see what the blood shows.'

'The other possibility is that she fell by mistake,' said Julie. 'She could have been sitting here to show off, made braver by a few drinks, and then lost her balance. Easy to do.'

They returned to the living-room where the shocked tenants sat in silence.

'How much did you win?' Diamond asked no one in particular.

'Win?' said Sally Allardyce.

'The lottery.'

'We don't know yet,' said Treadwell. 'It won't be much. The mob who descended on us seemed to think we'd won the jackpot.'

'Four numbers should get you something over fifty pounds,' said Diamond. 'Maybe as much as a hundred. Enough to get your carpets cleaned.'

'Not enough to pay for the food and drink we were robbed of last night. Where did we go wrong?'

Treadwell's wife reminded him, 'Our problems are nothing beside the tragedy of the young woman's death.'

Treadwell grasped how insensitive his remark had been. 'What a fatal chain of circumstances. If we hadn't shouted about our winnings in a public bar, she'd still be alive.'

'We were all looking out for the numbers on the TV,' said Sally. 'We couldn't have kept quiet, Guy.'

'Who picked the numbers?' Diamond asked.

'Guy,' said Sally. 'We all have faith in Guy. He's one of those amazing people who win things all the time.'

'That's an exaggeration,' Treadwell pointed out.

'Have you won the lottery before, then?'

'It was our first time as a syndicate.'

'First time winners. You should do it again.'

'No way,' said Emma.

Diamond adopted a sagelike expression and commented, '"He who can predict winning numbers has no need to let off crackers."'

'What are you on about?' said Treadwell.

'I was quoting from Kai Lung.'

The relevance of the saying – if relevant it was – escaped them all.

'So how does this lucky streak manifest itself, Mr Treadwell?'

There was a huff of impatience from the lucky man.

Sally said, 'Own up, Guy. There was that inheritance that came out of the blue. Five grand from a cousin in the Channel Islands you hadn't even met. And that Sunday paper that featured you as the architect of the nineties. A big spread in the colour supplement.'

'That wasn't luck,' said Treadwell.

Emma chimed in, 'The lucky bit was that you went to the same Cambridge college as the editor.'

He snapped back, 'So are you inferring it wasn't in the paper on merit?'

'Of course not. We're saying you're a winner, and you are. You go on your digs and you're the only one who finds anything all weekend.'

'What's this,' said Diamond. 'Archaeology?'

'A pastime, at a very amateur level,' said Treadwell.

'You found those gorgeous old bottles on the river bank,' said Emma.

'They're nothing special,' said Treadwell.

'Admit it, Guy. You get all the breaks.'

Allardyce said gallantly, 'And your luckiest break of all was getting hitched to Emma.'

Emma blushed at the compliment, but her churlish husband said nothing.

Sally added for Diamond's benefit, 'He'll go on denying he has a charmed life, but just don't get into a poker game with him.'

Diamond asked what time the gatecrashers had started arriving and was told they first appeared around 9pm and soon it became unstoppable. The pressure only eased about 10.30, after the two policemen had called, following the complaint from a neighbour. By that time all the drink was gone and the clubs and discos were opening in town.

'And some remained?'

'Plenty,' said Sally. 'For hours.'

'But you had no knowledge that anyone was on the roof?'

'Not until we were told.'

Diamond went downstairs and talked to the sergeant at the door, a grizzled man with a face you could have struck a match on. 'Do you have a personal radio?'

'Yes, sir. Want to use it?'

He might as well have invited Diamond to perform brain surgery. 'No. Has there been any word about the victim? Has anyone reported her missing?'

'Nothing's come through to me, sir.'

'Were you here when they took her away?'

'I helped put her on the stretcher, sir.'

'In that case, you can tell me what she was like.'

'A right mess, to tell you the truth. The crack in her head—'

'Yes, I know all about that,' Diamond firmly cut him off. 'I was wanting some idea of her normal appearance.'

'She was a brunette, sir. Quite short hair actually. Good figure.'

'Clothes?'

'She was covered with a blanket when I arrived.'

'But you helped lift her onto the stretcher, right? What did you take hold of? Her arms?'

'The legs. Well, the feet. She had black jeans, white socks, black and white trainers. Only one trainer, in point of fact. One was missing.'

'Fell off, you mean?'

'I suppose so.'

'Was it in the yard? Did anyone pick it up?' Diamond's voice had an edge of urgency that produced a nervous response from the sergeant.

'Em . . .'

'Think, man.'

'I couldn't say, sir.'

The missing trainer had galvanised Diamond. 'Get on that radio of yours and find out if anyone has the shoe. Tell Manvers Street from me to contact everyone who was here at the scene, including the SOCOs, the police surgeon, the mortuary. If we have the shoe, I want to know exactly where it was found, on the roof, in the basement, or any other place. Do it now, Sergeant.'

Sixteen

Early the same afternoon, the filming of *The Pickwick Papers* was abandoned after two minibuses joined the other police vehicles in front of the Royal Crescent and a dozen officers emerged. The director said he would be consulting lawyers.

Inside the house the reinforcements began a 'sweep'; collecting, bagging and labelling each item discarded by the party-goers the previous night. The residents took turns to make tea and coffee, and tried without much conviction to behave as if it were a normal Sunday. Diamond had asked them to remain indoors until the sweep was over. Complications could occur, he said darkly, if people weren't present when their house was being checked for evidence. To encourage co-operation, he asked Julie to stay there. Any hope she had of lunch with Charlie had long since been abandoned.

The big man himself made a reluctant appearance at the Royal United Hospital mortuary. The corpse of the young woman, still in her bloodstained clothes, was wheeled out for his inspection.

He held his breath, but the injuries were less disfiguring than he had prepared himself for. The back of her skull had taken the main impact. Blood had congealed and encrusted in a patch not strikingly different from the dark brown of her hair. The unmarked face had the look of wax. Its serenity was an appearance, not an expression, confirming the melancholy truth that a detective's job is doomed to be unsatisfying, for the best it can do is reconstruct facts and determine what happened and who was responsible. Nothing he could discover or deduce, however brilliant, would diminish the tragedy of a young life lost.

He stepped away for a moment, and the attendant asked if he'd finished.

'Far from it.' He approached the other end of the trolley and spent some time examining the black and white Reebok trainer on the left foot and the white sock on the right. The remaining shoe was fairly new, with little wear. It fitted snugly and was laced and tied with a double bow. The sock on the other, shoeless foot had been tugged down a little, so that the heel was hanging slackly. He attached no importance to this. It could easily have been done as the body was being moved. But he was intrigued to find the underside of the sock perfectly clean.

'What it shows clearly,' he told DCI John Wigfull in his Manvers Street lair, 'is that she didn't put her foot on the ground without the shoe. The dirt runs off the roof and collects in the gully behind the balustrade. You can't avoid stepping in muck.'

'What did she do, then? Hop?'

Diamond shot him a surprised look. Sarcasm wasn't Wigfull's style. He was about as waggish as a Rottweiler.

'I suppose she kicked the shoe off as she jumped,' Wigfull said, more soberly.

'But where is it? That shoe is missing. I've checked with everyone. No sign of it, on the roof or down in the basement yard.'

'The adjoining basement?'

'My lads aren't amateurs, John. I said it's missing.'

Wigfull's unappreciative gaze rested on Diamond for a moment. 'You have a theory, I suppose?'

'Someone picked up the damned shoe and took it away.' Having delivered this startling opinion, Diamond paused. 'You're going to ask me why.'

A sound very like a snort of contempt escaped from under the Mexican moustache. 'I wouldn't give you that satisfaction.' Wigfull was definitely getting uppish.

'Suit yourself.'

'Before you dash off, I think I'm entitled to know what you're doing about this woman up at the Crescent.'

'She isn't up at the Crescent any more. She's down at the RUH.'

'This missing shoe. What does it mean, in your opinion?'

A grin spread across Diamond's face. 'I thought you weren't going to ask. There are two questions, aren't there? How did the shoe get parted from her foot, and where is it?'

'Well?'

'Question One, then. If you take it from me that she didn't put her foot to the ground, then the shoe must have come off while she was sitting on the balustrade. She was seen up there some time around eleven-thirty to midnight, "dangling her legs", so I was told. If her legs were visible, she was facing outwards looking at the lights of Bath. Of course, she *may* have dangled so energetically that it simply . . .'

'Slipped off her foot?'

'Yes. Or, more likely, she struck her heel against one of the stone things underneath. What are they called?'

'Balusters.'

'Against one of the balusters, loosening the shoe, in which case it dropped to the ground, or the basement.'

'But you said it hasn't been found.'

'Don't rush me, John. Something I didn't say is that the other trainer, on the left foot, is securely tied, laced with a double bow.' He paused. 'Now, you were saying . . . ?'

Wigfull was not so laid-back now. In fact, he was hunched forward. 'Where is the damned shoe?'

'Thank you. That's my Question Two. It isn't there any more, so – as I said a few minutes ago – it must have been removed from the scene.'

'But who by?'

'This is just a theory. Someone else was up there on the roof. The woman hears something and turns, feeling vulnerable. The other party goes to her and there's a struggle in which the shoe is tugged off. The victim falls to her death.'

Wigfull's brown eyes widened. 'Peter, you're talking murder now.'

'I didn't say the word.'

'You were about to.'

'Hold on,' said Diamond, deliberately playing down the obvious. 'The second person could have been trying to *prevent* the victim jumping off. It could have been a rescue attempt that didn't succeed.'

Wigfull was unconvinced. 'Why would the rescuer want to get rid of the shoe?'

Diamond didn't offer a theory.

'The only certain thing,' said Wigfull, 'is that she fell to her death – or was pushed.'

'No, there is another certain thing, and that's that her shoe is missing.'

'Quite true, and that's difficult to reconcile with a rescue attempt.'

'Agreed.'

Diamond, forceful by reputation, was rather relishing this softly-softly approach with his old antagonist. He wasn't going to thump the desk and say this stood out as a case of murder.

Wigfull said, 'Do you really think someone else is involved?'

'Allowing that the shoe went missing, yes. Otherwise, where is it?'

Wigfull sank back into his chair and said with an air of martyrdom, 'God, why didn't I ask you to take on the student?'

'I offered.'

'I know. You're saying because the shoe is missing someone else must be involved. What do they gain from disposing of the shoe? What are they worried about? Prints? Fibres?'

'You know what forensic say: every contact leaves its traces.'

'Which makes murder a strong bet. But why? Why attack her at all?'

Diamond spread his hands wide, like Moses arriving at the Promised Land. 'That's all to be discovered.'

'You don't even know the victim's name. Is anyone reported missing?'

'What time is it?' asked Diamond.

'Two-thirty.'

'Most of that crowd who were partying last night will be scarcely out of bed. And when they are, a lot of them won't know whose bed it is. To expect them to notice someone is missing is asking a lot, John.'

'What was she like, this woman?'

'Mid-twenties. Dark, with shortish hair. Average height and build. Brown eyes. Dressed for an evening out, in a pink sweater and black jeans.'

'White socks and one Reebok trainer,' Wigfull made a point of completing it for him. He liked his reputation as a stickler for detail.

'She was seen at the party sitting on the stairs with some bruiser in a leather jacket.'

'And he hasn't come forward?'

'Not yet.'

'Is that the best description you've got?'

'Of the victim? I could do better. I could circulate a picture if we're serious about murder. This is what I wanted to talk to you about. Unless she's identified, the post-mortem will have to be delayed, just like it is for your farmer. I'm about to put out a press statement asking for information. Do you want a hand in it?'

Wigfull sighed. If he'd known this unexplained death would shape up as a murder inquiry, he'd have grabbed it for himself. Now that he'd handed the job to Diamond, the official head of the murder squad, he could hardly claim it back.

He conceded bleakly, 'This one is yours.'

At his own desk Diamond cleared a space with a swimmer's movement and started drafting the press release, a task he would have handed to Julie if she were not still at the Crescent. Julie was good with words – only she was also a model of tact, the ideal person to have in charge at the scene of the incident, keeping the tenants from getting stroppy. She'd radioed in to say that the sweep through the house was complete. Nothing of obvious significance had been found, certainly no Reebok trainer.

He had radioed back and ordered a search of the building, a specific search this time, for the missing trainer. Yes, a search, he emphasised to Julie. A different exercise from the sweep. This time the team would open cupboards, look into drawers, between layers of bedding, under loose floorboards. When Julie pointed out that they had no search warrant, Diamond told her brusquely that a DI with her experience ought to have the personal authority to carry through an exercise like this. It wasn't as if anyone was under suspicion of hiding drugs or stolen goods. It was a pesky shoe they were looking for. Julie, caught in the trap familiar to female police officers – the suggestion that they lack assertiveness – bit back her objections and went off to supervise the search.

The press release.

He wrote in his bold lettering, *A woman aged between twenty-five and thirty died, apparently from a fall, at a party at number ??* [He'd need to check the number again] *The Royal Crescent, Bath, late on Saturday night. Police are anxious to identify the woman and trace witnesses who may have seen her before the incident. She was wearing . . .* Then he looked up.

A sergeant had come through the open door, embarrassment writ large across his face. Before any words were spoken, the reason was clear. Apparent behind the sergeant, too large to be obscured by his merely average physique, followed Ada Shaftsbury.

The sergeant started saying, 'Sir, I did my—'

Ada elbowed him aside and advanced on Diamond. This female lacked nothing in assertiveness. 'Here he is, the original shrinking violet. Just who do you think you are – the Scarlet sodding Pimpernel? I spend half the day sitting on my butt waiting for a sight of you and you don't even get up to shake hands. What are you afraid of – that I'll get mine around your throat?'

Diamond had nothing personal against Ada. In small amounts, and at the right time, he enjoyed listening to her. As a senior officer, he had tried once or twice to stop her causing mayhem in the charge room and quickly came to appreciate her sharp humour and agile brain. Also the strong moral values that, ironically, many habitual criminals possess. Her morality happened to be a little out of kilter with the law, that was all. It allowed her to shoplift with impunity, but never to steal from individuals.

'Ada, if I had the time . . .' He waved the wretched sergeant away. 'I can give you three minutes. It's red alert here.'

'It always bloody is,' she said, tugging a revolving chair from the desk Julie used and sinking onto it with a force that would forever impair its spring mechanism. 'I've waited all the frigging morning to see you, Mr Sexton bloody Blake, and now you're going to listen. They asked me to make a written statement. What use is that? I know what happens to bits of paper in places like this. I've seen it.'

'What's your gripe, Ada?' Diamond asked.

'No gripe.'

'Apart from being kept waiting.'

A brief smile escaped. 'Well, that. I'm bothered something chronic about my friend, that's the problem. I live in one of them social security hostels, Harmer House, up Bathwick Street. Do you know it?'

He gave a nod.

'A couple of weeks ago – it was on the Wednesday – a social worker brought in this girl who'd lost her memory – all of her memory, up to when she was dumped in some private hospital grounds, with broken ribs, bruising, all the signs of an accident. She couldn't remember a sodding thing, not even her name. Seeing that she wasn't a paying patient, this hospital patched her up and passed her on to Social Services, which is how she came to us. She's in your records. Your people photographed her and everything. Don't know what you called her. She was Rose to us in the hostel. I shared a room with her.'

Diamond warned her, 'I said three minutes, Ada.'

'I'm keeping it short, Kojak. Rose was desperate to get her memory back and no one seemed to care. The best hope the hospital could hold out was sending her to a shrink, and she'd have to wait weeks – just to be made even more confused. Not bloody good enough, I said, and rolled up my sleeves and did something about it – what you lot should have been doing – tracking down the old lady who found her in the hospital grounds, and the car that brought her there and the toe-rags who knocked her down.'

'You did all this, Ada?' he said in a flat tone, thinking with resignation of the chain of false assumptions and mistaken identities that it probably represented.

'Yes, and there's more to it than a road accident, I promise you. We was coming back to the hostel – Rose and me – in broad daylight, when some yobbo jumped out of a car and grabbed her. He talked like he knew her. Said he was taking her home. She told me later she'd never clapped eyes on him before. He'd just about bundled her into the back seat before either one of us caught our breath. There was another oik driving and they would have got clean away if I hadn't taken a hand. I managed to hook her out in time.'

'You saved her?'

'I can knock the stuffing out of most men.'

'What did they do about it?'

'Drove off like it was the bloody Grand Prix.'

'What did he look like?'

'Think, dark-haired, early twenties. A hard case. I'd know him again.'

'And is this what you've waited all day to tell me?'

'I haven't come to the main part,' said Ada, moving on without pausing for breath. 'Like I said, we found these people who ran into Rose in their car. This happened early one evening way up the A46, between that poncy great house that's open to visitors – what's it called?'

'Dereham Park?'

'Between there and the motorway. They said she stepped out of nowhere, right in front of their car. Could have killed her. As it was, they managed to brake and she wasn't hit too hard.'

'Did they report it?'

'Get wise, Mr Diamond. They wouldn't have left her lying dead to the world in the hospital grounds if they'd reported it, would they?'

'You say they admitted all this? You're quite sure they didn't say it under duress?'

'Duress? What's that when it's at home? Listen, we were on track, Rose and me, steaming along, getting to the truth, when – boom! – we ran into a buffer. We got back to the hostel right after seeing these two, to find the social worker in our room with some woman claiming to be Rose's sister, or stepsister, or something. She seemed to know all about her. Brought out some photos that were definitely Rose with some old woman she said was their mother, at Twickenham. Where's that?'

'West London.'

'She said Rose lived in Hounslow.'

'Not far from Twickenham,' said Diamond.

'This woman said her name was Jenkins, Doreen Jenkins. She said she'd come to Bath with her boyfriend especially to look for Rose. Mind, Rose didn't seem to know her.'

'But Rose had lost her memory.'

'Right.'

'So she wouldn't have recognised her.'

'Let me finish, will you? I could see Rose was really unhappy. She wouldn't have gone with the Jenkins woman, I'm sure, but that silly cow Imogen forced the issue.'

'Imogen?'

'The social worker. The case was closed, in her opinion. Her office wasn't responsible no more. Rose had been claimed. So she had to go. Rose was cut up about it, I can tell you. Now this is the worrying bit. She promised to keep in touch whatever happened. We both promised. I gave her a postcard specially. She was going to write to me directly she got back to Hounslow. I've heard sod all, Mr Diamond, and it's been the best part of two weeks.'

'Is that it?' he asked.

Ada thrust out her chin. 'What do you mean – "Is that it?"'

'You've come to us simply because you haven't had a card from your friend? Ada, she had a lot on her mind. People forget.'

'I never liked the look of that sister,' said Ada.

'You're wasting my time.'

'Wait,' said Ada. 'I tried writing to her – Miss Rosamund Black, Hounslow, and the letter came back yesterday with "return to sender" written on it.'

'What do you expect? There are probably thirty or forty people called Black in Hounslow. The postman isn't going to knock on every door.'

'I looked in the phone book and there's no Miss R. Black in Hounslow.'

'Maybe she doesn't have a phone. Ada, I said three minutes and you've had ten.'

'She's been abducted.'

'Oh, come on. You just told me what happened and it was her choice.'

'Hobson's bloody choice. What about the bloke who tried to drag her into the car?'

'Ada, that was another incident. You're not suggesting the sister had any connection with him? She behaved properly. She went to Avon Social Services. They were satisfied she was speaking the truth.'

Ada was outraged. 'Rose could be dead for all you care, you idle slob. If you're the best Bath can afford, God help us all. You don't know sheepshit from cherrypips.'

He stood up. 'Out.'

'Dorkbrain. Something's happened to my friend, and when I find out the truth you'll wish you hadn't been born, you . . . you feather-merchant.'

Before drafting the rest of the press release, he sent one of the police cadets shopping. The recent extension in Sunday trading was a lifesaver to anyone whose eating arrangements were as makeshift as Diamond's.

When he returned to the house in the Crescent at the end of the afternoon, he was holding two plastic carriers. Julie met him in the entrance hall, which was now restored to something like a respectable state. She told him the search squad had left a few minutes before with a vast collection of rubbish.

He set the bags down on a marble-topped table. 'No shoe?'

'We went through the place with a small-tooth comb, the attic to the basement. I'm positive it isn't here.'

'Outside?'

'I had six men out there for two and a half hours.'

He ran his fingers through what remained of his hair. 'I'm mystified, Julie. I can think of three or four ways the shoe may have come off. I'm trying to think of one good reason why anyone would wish to remove it from the scene.'

She shook her head and shrugged. 'One shoe's no use to anyone.'

'If it incriminated someone, I'd understand,' he said. 'But how could it? Let's take the extreme case, say she was murdered, shoved off the balustrade after a struggle in which the shoe came off. What does her killer do with the shoe? He'd sling it after her, wouldn't he, down into the basement? Then we'd assume it got knocked off her foot when she hit the ground. It would still look like an accident, or suicide. Keeping it, hiding it, disposing of it, is self-defeating. It announces that someone else was involved.'

'People aren't always rational,' Julie pointed out. 'This killer – if there is one – may have been drunk.'

'Could have been.' Diamond didn't say so, but he thought it unlikely that a drunk would bother to pick up a shoe and smuggle it out of the house.

'Have we finished here?' she asked.

'Where are the tenants – still upstairs?'

'Yes.'

'How are they taking it?'

'They're not happy, but would anyone be? They couldn't understand the reason for the search. They're just ordinary people – well, not all that ordinary, or they wouldn't be living at an address like this – but you know what I mean. They were really unlucky the way this party came about.'

'Or unwise.'

Julie didn't agree. 'I doubt if anyone could have prevented what happened.'

He showed his disagreement with a sniff. 'If you won the lottery, you wouldn't shout it out in a pub.'

'I might. Anyway, their luck was really out when the woman was killed. You can't dispute that.'

'You've obviously come to like these people.'

'They've been helpful, making tea and things. I'm hungry, though.'

His eyes slid away, to a framed print of John Wood's 1727 plan of Queen Square. 'The Treadwells are architects, right?'

'Yes, and making a good living at it, I get the impression. They have an office in Gay Street. He designs those enormous out-of-town supermarkets. She's the surveyor. Knows all about maps and land use and so on. She sizes up the site and he draws the plans.'

'Cosy.'

'I think they're doing all right. Not much of the building

industry is booming these days, but supermarkets are going up everywhere.'

'Red-brick barracks with green-tiled roofs.' Diamond had no love of them, whatever their design. He knew them from the inside, as a trolley-man in his spell in London. 'It's a cancer, Julie, scarring the countryside and bleeding the life out of the city centres. So the geniuses who design them choose to live in a posh Georgian terrace and work in a building that was here when Beau Nash was alive. I bet they don't drive out of town to do their shopping.'

'They don't have a car.'

'There you are, then.'

She hesitated. 'Does it matter how they make their living?'

'They've won you over, haven't they?'

'I take people as I find them, Mr Diamond.'

He was forced to smile. She'd scored a point. Here he was, ranting on again, no better than a feather-merchant, whatever that was. Thank God there were people like Julie to nudge him out of it. 'And you find them more agreeable than your boss?'

She blushed deeply. 'Actually, the couple upstairs are the friendlier ones. Mr Treadwell is still angry about having his house invaded and I think his mood rubs off on her, although she does her best to sound civilised. The Allardyces seem to take a more fatalistic view of the whole weekend.'

'It was fatal for someone, anyway. They're the people in public relations, aren't they?' He held up a pacifying hand. 'All right, Julie, I won't give you my views on public relations. Remind me of their first names.'

'Sally and William.'

'And they're still approachable, after having their house turned over? It beggars belief.'

'It's in the breeding. Grin and bear it.'

'Let's go up and pay our respects to these models of restraint.' He picked up his shopping. He was feeling chipper. Not a hint of hypertension.

Sally Allardyce admitted them to the living-room that featured the acanthus-leaf ceiling. Both couples were present. The lights were on and a simulated fire was flickering yellow and blue in the grate. A game of cards was in progress at the round table at the end nearest the main casement window.

Emma Treadwell had changed from her bath-robe into a pale blue dress. Made-up, bright-featured and pretty, she still showed some strain, fingering the ends of her long, dark hair.

Diamond glanced at the way the cards were arranged. 'Whist?'

'Solo whist, actually,' said William Allardyce. His tracksuit top was unzipped lower than before and the lettering entirely revealed. Aptly for the man Julie had found the more friendly, it read MR RIGHT.

'Finish the hand, then,' Diamond urged them. 'You can't stop in the middle. Is someone on an abundance?'

'*Misère*,' said Treadwell, without looking up from the cards in his hand. 'It's me, and it just about sums up the weekend.'

Sally Allardyce said, 'We were only filling in time. Your inspector – Julie – said you'd be along soon. I'll make some fresh tea.'

Diamond seized his opportunity to earn some goodwill. He became masterful. 'No, you won't. You'll take your place at the table and give Mr Treadwell the chance to glory in his *misère*. Where's the kitchen? Through there?'

'What exactly . . . ?'

'Julie and I will prepare – what is it you call it in all the best circles? – high tea. I heard you were cleaned out by all your visitors, so I brought some food in. Is anyone game for scrambled eggs on toast? My speciality.'

After some hesitation, it was agreed. They would finish the game and take their chances with Peter Diamond's speciality.

In the kitchen, he grabbed an apron off the back of the door and tied it on. 'I'm a clumsy bugger,' he explained to Julie as if it were news to her. 'This is my best suit. There's a cut loaf in the bag. Why don't you get some toast and tea on the go and leave the eggs to me?'

Mastering the cooker was the first challenge. It was electric and easy and he popped in half a dozen plates, informing Julie that nothing was worse than serving a warm meal on a cold plate. The gas hob proved less amenable. The spark wouldn't ignite the burner for some seconds, and when it finally did with a small explosion, there was a distinct whiff of singed hair. He rubbed the back of his right hand.

Sally Allardyce called out from the card-game, 'Are you managing all right?'

Julie answered that they were and Diamond began robustly cracking eggs into a large bowl and tossing the shells across the room, aiming for – and not always reaching – the sink. 'You need a dozen for a party this size, so I got some extra in case of accidents,' he informed Julie with a wave of his sticky hand covered in bits of broken shell. But he seemed to know what he was doing. When she offered to pass him the milk he said, 'Never use milk in scrambled eggs. Cream, if you want them rich. But I prefer to serve them fluffy. A little water, that's the secret. The whole thing will be light as air.' He found an old-fashioned whisk and attacked the mixture vigorously. 'How's the toast?'

'Almost there.'

'The tea?'

'Will be.' Julie hesitated. 'What's *misère*, Mr Diamond?'

'A call in solo. You have to lose every trick.'

'And then what?'

'You make your *misère* – and the others pay up. Being a total loser isn't so easy as you think.'

'Guy Treadwell should be all right. He's supposed to be the lucky one.'

He worked with two frying pans and generous knobs of butter, tipped some of the mixture into each and worked it into the right consistency with a wooden spatula. At this moment the cooking took priority over police work. He was absorbed. 'I hope to God they've finished the hand. Timing is everything.'

Some deft work from Julie ensured that six portions of approximately equal size were carried steaming into the living-room. Place mats and cutlery were quickly produced.

'They're going to like this,' he murmured to Julie.

Until they see the state of their kitchen, she thought.

'Did you get it, Mr Treadwell?' Diamond asked after compliments had been paid to the scrambled eggs on toast.

Treadwell looked up inquiringly.

'The *misère*.'

'He got it,' said his wife. 'With a hand like that he could have made *misère ouverte*.'

'When the cards are exposed on the table,' Diamond explained to Julie. 'Do you tip horses, Mr Treadwell?'

A sour-faced shake of the head.

'I only wish William were half so lucky,' said Sally. 'He's never found a blessed thing on his country walks. Not so much as a bad penny.'

The attention of the CID shifted to Allardyce. 'You're one of those ramblers I see out with their trousers tucked into their socks?'

William Allardyce smiled. 'Nothing so ambitious as that. Just a Sunday afternoon walk when I can get it. It's good to get out after a week in the office.'

'Public relations – what does it come down to?'

'It doesn't come down to anything – ever. If PR is doing what it should, it's rising. We raise the profile of our clients by increasing the goodwill and understanding they achieve with their customers.'

'Through the media?'

'Much more than that. We're concerned with the entire public perception of the client and his product.'

'The image?'

'If that's what you choose to call it, yes.' Mindful of his own public perception, he raked his fingers through his dark hair, tidying it.

'You buff up the image?'

'We begin by examining what they've achieved already in public esteem, if anything. Good opinion has to be earned. Then we suggest how it may be enhanced. We don't distort, if that's what you mean by polishing.'

'You're freelance?'

'A consultancy, yes.'

Diamond turned to Sally Allardyce. 'And are you in the firm?'

'No,' she said. 'I work in local television.'

'So you must be a useful PR contact.'

'Not really. I'm in make-up.'

'Useful with the grooming of the clients?'

She smiled in a way that told him it was a damn-fool comment. That avenue was closed.

Diamond turned back to the husband. There was still some mileage in this topic. He hadn't brought it up simply to make conversation. 'I was wondering what PR could do for me – assuming the police could afford your fees and I was a client. Would you change my image?'

Allardyce smiled uncertainly and looked down at his empty plate. 'I'd, em, I'd need to know a great deal more about you and the nature of your work. All I know is that you're a detective superintendent.'

'I'm head of the murder squad.'

The statement had the impact Diamond expected, some sharp intakes of breath and a general twitching of facial muscles. Across the table, Treadwell tugged at his bow tie as if it was suddenly uncomfortable.

His wife rested a hand on his arm. 'Surely there's no suggestion that this woman was murdered?'

'That's all we wanted to hear,' said Treadwell, grinding his teeth.

'It was an accident,' said Sally Allardyce. 'She was playing about on the roof and she fell.'

'I wish we could be certain of that, ma'am,' said Diamond. 'It's my job to consider all possibilities. To come back to my image, Mr Allardyce . . .' He got up from the table and executed a mannequin-like half-turn. '. . . I suppose you'll tell me I should get a sharp new suit and a striped tie.'

'I wouldn't presume to advise you as to clothes,' said Allardyce, his voice flat, unwilling to continue with this.

Julie told Diamond, 'But I will. You should definitely leave off the apron.'

The head of the murder squad looked down at the butcher's vertical stripes and smoothed them over his belly. 'Ah. Forgot.'

The tension eased a little, but Treadwell continued making sounds suggesting his blood pressure was dangerously high.

Allardyce made an effort to recoup. 'I suppose a detective needs to blend in easily with his surroundings.'

'Should I lose weight?'

'No, I was about to say that there's a paradox. If there is such a thing as a detective image, you don't want it, or you give yourself away.'

'Fair comment, sir – except that I don't often go in disguise. No need to make a secret of my job. I don't *always* announce myself at the outset, but sooner or later people get to know who I am – the murder man.'

That word again. In the short pause that followed, Diamond picked a volume off the bookshelf and flicked through the pages. It was a book of local walks. Whilst pretending to take an interest in the text he studied the contrasting reactions of the two couples. The Allardyces were flustered, but staunchly trying not to show it, whereas the experience of the night before and this day's infliction of policemen seemed to have reduced the Treadwells to red-faced gloom, certainly the husband. *Misère* was right.

On balance, the Treadwells' reaction was easier to understand.

'I'd like to get a couple of things clear in my mind and then we'll leave you in peace, Julie and I,' said Diamond. 'Which pub was it last night?'

'The Grapes,' said Sally Allardyce.

'Down in Westgate Street? Long walk from here.'

'It has a TV. Not so many pubs do.'

'And when your numbers came up . . . ?'

'There was rejoicing, obviously. People started asking if it was drinks all round. We bought a round, but if we'd remained we'd have been cleaned out.'

'So you left the Grapes and came back here and got cleaned out at home.'

'They just assumed it would be open house here.'

'Are you sure you didn't invite people?'

'A few friends – but only a few friends,' Allardyce admitted. 'We were misunderstood. These things happen.'

'Did you walk back?'

'What?'

'Mr Allardyce enjoys a walk.'

'For God's sake,' said Treadwell in a spasm of anger. 'Are you trying to catch us out on drunk driving? Look, only one of us has a car, and that's William, and his bloody car was sitting in Brock Street all evening. We took a taxi. Satisfied?'

'I'm getting the timing right in my head,' said Diamond, who wasn't noted for fine calculations. 'The lottery is announced about eight. You buy a round. At let's say eight-fifteen, or eight-twenty, you decide to return here. You go out and look for a taxi – or did you find one?'

'They line up in Kingsmead Square. We got one there.'

'And were back here by – what? – eight-thirty?'

'Later than that. We stopped at the off-licence and picked up some booze.'

'It *was* planned as a party, then?'

'Drinks for a few friends,' said Treadwell with disdain. 'I don't call that a party.'

'The trouble is, the rest of Bath did,' said his wife.

The daylight was fading when Diamond and Julie emerged from the house.

'Do you do the lottery?' she asked.

'Do I look like a winner?' he said. 'We tried a few times. Nothing. Then someone told me a sobering fact. No matter who you are, what age you are, what kind of life you lead, it's more likely you'll drop dead by eight o'clock Saturday night than win the big one. So I don't do it any more.'

'If you did drop dead and won, you'd be given a lovely send-off.'

He didn't comment.

'So are we any wiser?' she asked.

'About what?'

'The dead woman.'

He ignored the question – more interested, apparently, in the scene in front of the Crescent. 'Something's different.'

'Well, the cars are back,' said Julie. 'Or a lot of them are.'

'Cars?'

'The film crew wanted them out of sight by this morning. The residents got twenty pounds a car for the inconvenience.' She studied his face to see if a joke would be timely. 'Not many Mercedes in *The Pickwick Papers*.'

'You're right. That was why Allardyce's car was parked in Brock Street last night.' He shook his head, chiding himself. 'I should have asked when he moved it and what he drives.'

'About six-thirty last evening,' said Julie. 'Before they went out to the pub. And it's a pale blue BMW.'

Not for the first time, he had underestimated Julie. Her hours stuck in this house with the tenants had been put to good use. He received the information as if it went without saying that she would have discovered such things, but she may have seen his eyebrows prick up.

He glanced along the rank of parked cars. 'Then it isn't back yet.'

'He hasn't been out,' said Julie. 'None of them have.' She waited a moment before asking, 'Are you suspicious of him?'

'Wouldn't put it as strongly as that, but there's something. Got to be suspicious of a man with MR RIGHT written across his chest.'

'He is in public relations.'

'Mm.' He got into the passenger seat of the car. 'Drive us out of the Crescent and stop in Brock Street. We'll wait there for a bit.'

Seventeen

This being Sunday evening, Julie had no trouble in finding space to park on the south side of Brock Street, the road that links the Royal Crescent to the Circus. She took a position opposite a wine shop, facing the entrance to the Crescent. Anyone approaching would be easily spotted under an ornate lamp-post that from there looked taller than the far side of the building, just visible across the residents' lawn. In the next ten minutes five individuals came by. Three collected their cars from Brock Street and returned them to the front of the Crescent. William Allardyce was not among them, though his blue BMW was parked in the street, opposite an art gallery.

'What are you expecting to see exactly?' Julie asked when the clock in the car showed they had been there twenty minutes.

Diamond took exception to the last word. '*Exactly*? I wouldn't put it as strongly as that. "Possibly" is more like it.'

'Possibly, then?'

'There's a possibility that we may see Allardyce come round that corner and walk to his car. There's a chance – and I wouldn't put it higher than that – a chance that he'll have the shoe with him.'

'I don't see how. We covered every inch of that house.'

'And every inch of the tenants?'

'Come off it, Mr Diamond,' said Julie, reddening. 'We had no authority to make body searches. Besides, you can't hide something as big as a shoe . . .' Her voice trailed off and she stared at him with wide, enlightened eyes. 'The tracksuit. William could have been carrying it around all day in the tracksuit.'

'Baggy enough to hide a shoe, I'll grant you,' he said as if the idea were hers.

'But that would mean he . . .'

'Yes.'

But it seemed to Julie that on this occasion the magus of the murder squad had picked the wrong star to follow. Inspired as he may have been in the past, his record wasn't perfect. And now he waited smug as a toad for her to tease out the arcane reasoning that had them sitting there. She leaned against the head-restraint and composed herself. She was not too proud to put a direct question to him. Others might balk at the prospect. Not Julie. 'What makes William Allardyce a suspect?'

As if marshalling his thoughts, he was slow to answer. 'The missing shoe is the key to it. She was wearing it when she sat on the balustrade. Must have been. Her sock was perfectly—' He didn't complete the sentence.

Someone had just come into view around the railings fronting the end house of the Crescent, a man of Allardyce's height and build. He was wearing a cap and raincoat and carrying a plastic bag that clearly contained an object whose general shape and solidity demanded their whole attention. Neither Diamond nor Julie spoke. They watched the man cross the cobbles to a shadowy area at the edge of the lamp-post's arc of light, close to the residents' lawn. There he halted. After glancing right and left, he stooped, as if to examine the low stone ridge that supported the railings. Still crouching, he took the object from the bag and they saw that it was not a shoe, but a trowel. Next he scraped at the ground with the trowel and shovelled something into the bag. Then he gave a whistle and a large dog bounded out of the shadows and joined him. With his dog, his trowel and the contents of the carrier bag, he walked back with pious tread towards the Crescent.

That was not William Allardyce.

Diamond resumed without comment. 'That shoe disappeared, so we can assume that someone is concealing it. Are you with me?'

After the day she had spent exploring every inch of that house, she thought his 'Are you with me?' was the bloody limit.

'I kept asking myself why,' he said, oblivious. 'If we are dealing with a killer here, what's his game? The fact that the shoe is missing is what gives rise to suspicion. If it had been found beside her, you and I wouldn't be here, Julie. We'd have thought it came off when she hit the ground. An accident: that's what we'd have taken it to be. So why didn't our killer chuck the shoe where the body was? I think I have the answer.'

She stared impassively ahead. She'd had about enough of Peter Diamond for one day.

'Theoretically,' he said in the same clever-dick tone, 'any one of the scores of people who crashed the party could have shoved her off the ledge. They didn't. This has to be one of the tenants, and I'll tell you why. The killer didn't realise that the shoe had come off until it was too late to do anything about it. The next morning. If you recall what happened, the paper-boy discovered the body and knocked on the door of the house. Treadwell came out. He alerted Allardyce, who also came to have a look. That was the moment when one of them – and it must be Allardyce for a reason I shall explain – saw to his horror that the dead woman was missing one shoe. It had come off in the struggle and was still lying somewhere on the roof.' Diamond turned to face her and stepped up his delivery. 'What can he do? It's too late now to plant it beside the body. The police are on the way and two witnesses have viewed the scene. He belts upstairs and finds the shoe, maybe with a torn lace, scuffing, signs of the struggle she put up. So he hides it, meaning to dispose of it later.'

Julie saved him the trouble of explaining why Allardyce was preferred as the suspect. 'As the Allardyces live upstairs, he could get up to the roof without arousing any suspicion.'

'Right, and this links up with another moment. Let's backtrack to the party. When someone reported the woman on the roof, who was it who went up to investigate, but the master of the house, the caring Mr Allardyce?'

He paused for some show of admiration, but he didn't get it.

Beginning to sound huffy, he picked up the thread again. 'If you're still with me, Allardyce claims he saw no one on the roof. He'd like us to suppose the woman must have fallen or jumped in the interval between the people spotting her and the moment he looked out of his attic window. He states that he didn't climb out of the window to check. He just leaned out and saw no one on the balustrade and assumed she'd given up and come down. That's his version. Have I given it fairly?'

He got a curt nod from Julie.

Outside, the darkness had set in and the grey mass of the Crescent appeared to merge at the top with the night sky. Unusually for such a well-known building there was no floodlighting. The reason was that it was residential, and residents in their living rooms have no desire to be in the spotlight to that degree. So the only lighting was supplied by those pseudo-Victorian lamp-posts painted black and gilt, with their iron cross-pieces supposedly to support the lamplighter's ladder.

'He claims not to have climbed onto the roof for a thorough look,' Diamond went on. 'Why not? We climbed out ourselves. You'll agree with me that it's as easy as getting into a bath. In spite of what he suggests, there are parts of the roof you can't see from inside the attic. She could have been up on the tiles behind him. Or she could have moved along the balustrade over one of his neighbours' houses. Wasn't he interested enough to check?'

'You can't blame him for that,' Julie found herself saying in the man's defence. 'His house had been taken over. He was concerned about what was going on inside.'

'Fair point,' Diamond admitted. 'There's some good stuff there. Antique ornaments. Period furniture. A beautiful music centre in the living-room with hundreds of CDs. If it had been my house full of strangers whooping it up, I'd have been going spare.'

'Perhaps he was. He can afford to be cool about it now it's over.'

He turned to her again. 'Julie, you're so right. He's not making an issue of what happened, as Treadwell is. He's incredibly blasé. What happened was okay by Allardyce, perfectly understandable. That's the impression I got. Did you?'

'Well, yes, now it's over.'

'But was he so happy at the time, I wonder? There's a ruthless young man behind that smooth exterior. You don't get results in business simply by being charming. Public relations is dog eat dog.'

'Being tough in business is one thing. Murder is something else,' she said, far from convinced.

'Hold on. I doubt if this would stand as murder,' he told her. 'Manslaughter, maybe. This wasn't premeditated. It was an impulse killing. What I picture is Allardyce made angry by events – extremely angry – in complete contrast to the PR front he was presenting this afternoon.'

'Mr Right as Mr Raving Mad?' she said, meaning it to be ironical.

He seized on that. 'Spot on. He's all fired up. He goes up to the attic and sees the woman seated on the balustrade. He has a wild impulse to push her. He climbs out of the window and starts towards her, but she hears him. She half-turns. Instead of giving her one quick shove in the back, he has a fight on his hands. That's when the shoe falls off. He doesn't notice that, of course. He's totally involved in forcing her over the edge. Nobody has seen him and luckily for him the woman falls into the well of the basement. It's a dark night, and she isn't noticed by any of the people leaving the house. It's daylight before she is found. The rest I've explained, his problem with the shoe, and so forth. Is it plausible?'

She could almost feel the heat of his expectation. 'So far as it goes, I can't see any obvious holes. The only thing is . . .'

'Yes?'

'This vicious side to his character is difficult for me to picture.'

'You called him Mr Raving Mad.'

'Just picking up on what you were saying. I didn't agree with it.'

'So he's Mr Nice Guy, is he?'

'Mr Right, anyway.'

'You must have been out with men on their best behaviour who suddenly turned nasty when you didn't let them have their wicked way.'

'Not homicidal.'

'I'm glad to hear it.'

She said after an interval for reflection, 'My experiences with men have got nothing to do with this.'

'Just making a point,' he said. 'We're all prisoners of our hormones – you know that.'

'Bollocks.'

'Those, too.'

She was forced to smile. 'Am I mistaken, or is the window steaming up?'

He rubbed it with the sleeve of his coat. 'Well, it's all speculation up to now. Unless we catch him with that ruddy shoe, we've got nothing worth making into a prosecution. Even then, I doubt if it will stick. A half-decent barrister would get him off.'

'So are we wasting our time here?'

'Not at all.'

But as it turned out, they were. After almost two hours of waiting, he radioed Manvers Street and asked for someone to take over.

And the blue BMW stayed where it was in Brock Street until Monday morning, when Allardyce drove to work.

Monday morning in Manvers Street Police Station brought John Wigfull to Diamond's office. And when the two detectives had finished discussing every facet of the Royal Crescent incident, they were forced to agree that little more could be achieved until they had a post-mortem report on the victim.

The priority was to identify her. Diamond's press release appealing for information had been distributed, but because the local news machine grinds to a virtual halt on Sundays, a response couldn't be expected until the story broke at midday in the *Bath Chronicle* and on local radio and television.

'It's strange that nobody who was at the party has come forward,' Wigfull commented. 'Word must have got around the city that someone was found there. The papers may not have been printed yesterday, but the pubs were open, and most of the people at the party were only there because they happened to hear about it in a pub.'

'They haven't had the description,' Diamond said.

'What *is* she like, then?'

'Apart from dead? Dark-haired with brown eyes, about thirty or younger, slim build, average height.'

'Good-looking?'

'Do you know, John, it must be something lacking in me, but I find it hard to think of corpses as good-looking. She had one of those trendy haircuts, shorn severely at the sides, and with a thick mop on top that soaked up quite a lot of the blood from the head wound. Is that good-looking? Oh, and she painted her fingernails. They were damaged, some of them, whether from hitting the ground or fighting off an attacker I wouldn't know.'

'We could publish a photo if all else fails.'

'And put it out on TV about six-thirty when people are just sitting down in front of the box with their meat and two veg. Isn't it marvellous what they find to show you about that time? Mad cows, magnified head-lice and battered old ladies appear on my screen night after night, so why shouldn't we show them a face from the morgue? But do me a favour and choose a night when I'm not at home.'

Wigfull had never been able to tell when Diamond was serious. He said, 'That dead farmer I'm investigating is no picnic.'

'Your farmer at Tormarton? Haven't you put that one to bed yet?'

'Just about.' Wigfull hesitated in a way that told Diamond the Tormarton farmer had *not* been put to bed. 'Virtually, anyway. The post-mortem hasn't been done yet.'

'What's the hold-up?'

'Identification. I was trying to get a relative, but we haven't traced anyone yet. It looks as if we'll be using his social worker and maybe one of the meals-on-wheels people. He didn't have much to do with his neighbours. Nothing is ever as simple as it first appears, is it?'

Diamond said, 'Surely there's no question that the corpse *is* Daniel Gladstone?'

'You know me by now, Peter. I don't cut corners.' Wigfull brought his hands together in a way that signalled he wanted an end to the discussion.

'Speaking for myself, I like to get on with things,' said Diamond. 'I don't want a delay on the Royal Crescent woman. Full publicity. Someone who knows her will read about her in the paper and we'll get a PM this week.'

'Speaking of people coming forward . . .' Wigfull said in a tentative manner.

'Yes?'

'Ada Shaftsbury was here again first thing, raising Cain about this friend of hers who she says is abducted.'

'Ada?' The hypertension kicked in again. 'Look, Ada and I are not on the best of terms. She was practically at my throat yesterday morning. She called me – what was it? – a feather-merchant. Now, I haven't yet discovered what a feather-merchant is or does, but it doesn't make me want to spend more time with Ada.'

'This is only a suggestion,' said Wigfull. 'If someone could sort Ada's problem, he'd do us all a service.'

'It's a non-existent problem. Her friend left Bath a couple of weeks ago and hasn't written to Ada since. That isn't a police matter, John.'

'I was only passing it on.'

'Consider it passed on, then.'

As the sound of the chief inspector's steps died away, Diamond found himself remembering a saying of Kai Lung he had read in bed the previous night: 'Even a goat and an ox must keep in step if they are to plough together.' Shaking his head, he got up and went to look for Julie.

She was in the canteen finishing a coffee, watching two of the murder squad perfecting their snooker. She asked Diamond if anything fresh had come up at the Royal Crescent and he made a sweeping gesture that disposed of that line of conversation. He commented that this was early in the day for coffee and Julie said she needed one after meeting Ada Shaftsbury as she arrived for work.

'You, too?' he said. 'Wigfull had a blast this morning and I had a basinful yesterday.'

Julie said she knew about his basinful because Ada had referred to him.

'That's a delicate way of phrasing it, Julie.'

She laughed. 'We agreed on one or two things, Ada and I.'

'Thanks.'

She said, 'I don't know if it crossed your mind, but when

she was talking about this Rose or Rosamund, the woman who hasn't been in touch, I couldn't help comparing her description with the woman who was killed at the party.'

'Really?' The word was drained of all interest the way he spoke it.

'Some of the details do compare,' she pressed on. 'The age, the colour and length of the hair, the slim figure.'

'All that applies to thousands of women. Could easily be a description of you.'

'Do you mind? I paid a bomb for these blonde highlights.'

'You can't deny it's short.' He made a pretence of swaying to ride a punch. 'Fair enough, I was ignoring the highlights. They look, em, good value. Would you like your coffee topped up?'

She shook her blonde highlights.

'A fresh one, then?'

Conscious that he had some fence-mending to do, he also offered to buy her a bun. When he returned with a tray and two mugs and set them on the table Julie had chosen, well away from the snooker game, she remarked, 'I still think you ought to speak to Ada. One of the things she goes on about is that some man tried to grab her friend Rose outside the hostel and force her into a car.'

'She told me.'

She mopped up some of the coffee he'd slopped on the tray. 'Well, it isn't a fantasy. It really happened. Remember a week or so ago, the morning we met at the Lilliput, I was late because of a German woman I had to take to the Tourist Information Office? That afternoon I was given a statement in English of what she said, and it turns out that she was a witness to this incident in Bathwick Street. She lives in the hostel and she happened to be right across the street when the bloke tried to snatch Rose.'

'I didn't say it was a fantasy, Julie.'

'I'm just passing on my thoughts about Ada. I know it doesn't interest you particularly, but she's in a fair old state about her friend.'

He sighed. 'Tell me something new, Julie.'

She wasn't giving up. 'Ada may be a chronic shoplifter, but she's not stupid. If she thinks there's something iffy about the woman who collected her friend, she may be right.'

He admitted as much with a shrug. 'But it isn't my job to investigate iffy women.'

Julie's blue eyes locked with his. 'You could take Ada down to the RUH and give her a sight of the corpse.'

'What use would that be?'

'Who knows – it could be her friend Rose in the chiller.'

'No chance.'

'Yes, but it might get Ada off your back.'

'Now you're talking.' A slow smile spread across his face. 'What a neat idea.'

Eighteen

Ada was so stunned that she stopped speaking for about five seconds. When she restarted, it was to ask in a faltering voice for a drop of brandy. Most of the morning she had been sounding off to all and sundry that her friend could easily be dead by now. She was not expecting this early opportunity to find out. She said her legs were going.

She was guided to a chair and something alcoholic in a paper cup was placed in her plump, trembling hand. Peter Diamond, prepared to do a deal, told her gently that if she didn't feel able to accompany him to the mortuary, nobody would insist. She could leave the police station and nobody would think any the worse of her – provided she stayed away in future. As for the likelihood of the dead woman turning out to be her friend, it was extremely remote. 'A shot in the dark,' he said – an unfortunate phrase that caused Ada to squeeze the cup and spill some of the drink. Hastily he went on to explain that he doubted if Rose, or Rosamund, last heard of returning to Hounslow with her stepsister, had come back to Bath and fallen off the roof of the Royal Crescent on Saturday night. There were just the similarities in description, all superficial, and the importance Ada herself attached to Rose's well-being. If Ada cared to go through the points with him now, she would probably find some detail that didn't match and save herself a harrowing experience.

He read the description to her. She asked for more brandy. A short while later, he drove her to the hospital.

From the back seat, Ada confided to him that she had never seen a dead person. 'They said I could look at my poor old mother after she went, but I didn't want to.'

'You're in the majority,' he said. 'I get queasy myself.'

'But you've seen this one?'

'Oh, yes. Looking very peaceful. You wouldn't know she'd, em . . . Well, you wouldn't know.'

She said in a shaky voice, 'I want to tell you something, Mr Diamond.'

He leaned back in the seat, trying to be both a good driver and a good listener. 'What's that?'

She said huskily into his ear, 'If this does turn out to be Rose, and you tossers could have saved her, I'll push your face through the back of your neck and wee on your grave.'

The mortuary attendant was a woman. Diamond took her aside and asked if a chair could be provided for Ada. 'The lady is nervous and if she passed out I doubt if you and I could hold her up between us.'

With Ada seated and shredding a tissue between her fingers, the trolley was wheeled out and the cover unzipped to reveal the features of the dead woman.

'You may need to stand for a moment, my dear,' the attendant advised.

Ada got to her feet and glanced down at the face. She gave a gasp of recognition, said, 'Strike a light!' and passed out.

The chair collapsed with her.

He phoned Julie from the mortuary.

'Was Ada any help?' she asked.

'She was, as it happens. She recognised the body. Gave her a real shock. She passed out, in fact. But it isn't her friend. Not that friend. It's someone else she knew from Harmer House, someone you've met, a German woman called Hildegarde.'

Nineteen

Julie Hargreaves was still at Manvers Street, at work on a computer keyboard, when Diamond looked in. She was logging her report on a phone call to Imogen Starr, the social worker responsible for Hildegarde Henkel, the woman who had fallen to her death at the Royal Crescent.

'Aren't you just kicking yourself?' he said.

'What for?' she asked.

'For not paying more attention to this woman when she tapped you on the arm that morning she appeared downstairs.'

'She didn't tap me on the arm, Mr Diamond. The desk sergeant asked me to help him out. I gave her all the attention I could considering she hardly spoke a word of English. I walked with her personally all the way to the Tourist Information Office and left her in the care of someone who did speak her language. If there's something else I should have done, perhaps you'll enlighten me.'

He muttered something about not going off the deep end and said he would need to take a close look at the statement, but he'd need some background first.

'Can you give it to me in a nutshell?' he asked. 'I was supposed to be home early tonight.'

Barely containing her irritation, Julie said, 'I could have a printout waiting on your desk tomorrow morning if you're in that much of a hurry.'

'I'll have it now.'

She stared at the screen. 'Well, she's German, from Bonn. A drop-out from school who lost touch with her people. Got friendly with a young English guy working as an interpreter at the British Embassy and married him. Soon after, they moved to England. He turned out to be a fly-by-night and was away in a matter of weeks. This poor girl found herself jobless and without much knowledge of the language.'

'Couldn't she have gone back to Germany?'

'Didn't want to. Her life was a mess. She'd walked out on her parents. As the wife of a British subject she was entitled to remain in Britain, and that was her best hope, she thought. She soon used up what little money she had, lived rough for a while, got treated for depression and ended up as one of Imogen's case-load at Avon Social Services. That's it, in your nutshell.'

'The husband. Was his name Henkel, then?'

'Perkins, or something like that. She wanted to forget him, and no wonder, poor girl.'

'Wanted it both ways. Wipe him out of her life and use him to qualify as a resident.'

Julie's eyebrows pricked up. 'That's harsh, isn't it?'

'Don't know about that. Your version sounded a shade too sisterly for my taste.'

'Well, she is dead, for God's sake. Aren't we allowed any pity at all in this job?' She switched off the machine, rolled back the chair and quit the room.

With a sigh, he ran his hand over his head. He held Julie in high regard. Out of churlishness, he'd upset her just to make a point about some woman he had never met except on a mortuary trolley.

Exactly how unfortunate the upset was became clear presently, when he went to his desk to look at the messages. On top was a note from the local Home Office pathologist stating that now that formal identification had taken place, he proposed carrying out the post-mortem on Hildegarde Henkel at 8.30am the next morning. Normally Diamond would have found some pretext for missing the autopsy. It was the one part of CID work he tried to avoid. At least one senior detective on the case was routinely supposed to be present, listening to the pathologist's running commentary and discussing the findings immediately afterwards. The only possible stand-in was Julie, who had deputised on several similar occasions.

A call to Julie at home?

Even Peter Diamond didn't have the brass neck for that.

* * *

He did not, after all, get home early. He drove over Pulteney Bridge, ignoring the ban on private vehicles, and up Henrietta Street to Bathwick Street, to call at Harmer House. He had two objectives. The first was to examine Hildegarde Henkel's room. The second was to call on Ada Shaftsbury, a prospect he didn't relish, but against all reason he felt some sympathy for Ada after the shock she had suffered. True, she had not had to endure the ordeal of watching a pathologist at work, but by her own lights she had gone through a traumatic experience and it had been at his behest.

He found her in her room eating iced bun-rings. Her voice, when she called out to him to come in, was faint, and he prepared to find her in a depleted state. It transpired that her mouth was full of bun.

'You,' she said accusingly. 'You're the last person I want to see.'

For a moment the feeling was mutual, and he almost turned round and left. She presented such a gross spectacle seated on her bed, her enormous lap heaped with paper bags filled at the baker's.

'I called to see how you are – after this morning.'

'Shaky,' said Ada. 'Very shaky.'

'I didn't expect it to be someone you knew. I can honestly tell you that, Ada.'

'She was a true mate of mine,' said Ada, starting on another bun-ring. 'She cooked my breakfast every day, you know. She was wonderful in the kitchen. Germans are good learners, and I showed her what an English breakfast should be. I don't know what I'm going to do without her.'

'Did you talk to her much?'

She managed a faint grin. 'Quite a bit. But she didn't say a lot to me. Her English wasn't up to it. I taught her a few essential words.'

'So you wouldn't know about her state of mind? If she was depressed, say?'

'You can tell a lot just by looking at people,' said Ada. 'Take yourself, Mr Diamond. I can see you're on pins in case I mention my friend Rose again. You can't wait to get out of here.'

He ignored the shrewd and accurate observation. 'And Hildegarde?'

'She was happier here than she'd been for a long time. She wasn't suicidal.'

'Any friends?'

'Don't know. I never saw her with any. Not here. She used to go out evenings sometimes. Maybe she knew some German people. They stick together. I can't think how she got to that party at the Crescent unless she was with some people.'

Diamond pondered the possibility and it seemed sensible. 'If she was with anyone, they haven't come forward yet.'

'Maybe I'm wrong, then. She could have just followed the crowd. Germans are more easily led than us, wouldn't you say?'

He gave a shrug. These sweeping statements about the Germans left him cold. He was interested only in Hildegarde's individual actions.

'Do you want a bun?' Ada offered. 'There's plenty for both of us.'

He was hungry, he realised. 'Just a section, then. Not the whole ring.'

'You look as if you could put it away, easy. You and I are built the same way.'

'Oh, thanks.'

She missed the intended irony. 'Got to keep body and soul together.'

'I'm eating later.'

'I could make tea if you like.'

'This is fine. Really.'

After a pause for ingestion, Ada said, 'Help yourself to another one. Do you think she jumped?'

'I can't answer that,' he said. 'I didn't know her. You did.'

'Someone else's house is a funny place to choose to end it all,' Ada speculated. 'But if she wasn't planning to kill herself, what was she doing on the ledge? Had she taken something?'

'We haven't heard from the lab yet. It's possible. I'm going to look at her room presently.'

'She didn't leave a suicide note, I can tell you that.'

'You've been in to check, I suppose?'

'It's open house here, always has been,' Ada said, unabashed. 'Are you going to talk to that ball of fire, Imogen, her social worker?'

'I expect so.'

'Hildegarde was on her list, same as Rose was. Imogen keeps shedding clients, have you noticed? Dropping them faster than a peep-show girl.'

'You can't blame the social worker.'

'Try me, ducky. Rose didn't know the woman who came to collect her, but did it cross Imogen's tiny mind that it might be a try-on? Not on your nelly.'

Here we go, thought Diamond.

She went on, 'I've been thinking about those photos. They didn't *prove* this woman was Rose's stepsister. The only thing they proved is that she'd brought in some photos of Rose with some old woman. If there had been a picture of the step-sister with Rose, the two of them in one picture, I'd shut up, but there wasn't. And I still haven't had that postcard.'

'Her memory was dodgy,' said Diamond.

'Her short-term memory was spot on.'

'You won't let go, will you? Look, when I speak to the social worker I'll check on your friend Rose as well, right? Now point me towards Hildegarde's room.'

Ada escorted him downstairs, still griping about Rose. After she'd thrust open a door, he thanked her and said he would examine the room alone. He had to repeat it before she left him in peace.

Had she remained, she would have told him, he was certain, that Germans are very methodical. Everything in sight in the room – and there was not much – was tidily arranged. It was rather like entering a hotel room. The bed, unlike Ada's, was made without a loose fold anywhere. Hildegarde's few items of make-up and her brush and comb were grouped in front of the mirror on the makeshift dressing-table consisting of two sets of plastic drawers linked by a sheet of plate glass.

He started opening drawers and the contrast with the sights and smells he'd recoiled from in Daniel Gladstone's cottage could not have been more complete. Everything from thick-knit sweaters to knickers and bras was arranged in layers and each drawer had its bag of sweet-smelling herbs in the front right-hand corner.

The room was conspicuously short of the personal documents that Hildegarde Henkel must have possessed: passport, wedding certificate and social security papers. Their absence tended to confirm his view that she had carried them in a handbag that some opportunist thief had picked up at the party in the Royal Crescent. He doubted if Ada had taken anything from the room. As far as he knew she never stole from individuals.

Anything of more than passing interest he threw on the immaculate bed. At the end of the exercise he had a photo of a dog, two books in German, a German/English dictionary, a packet of birth control pills, a set of wedding photos, a Walkman and a couple of Oasis tapes and a bar of chocolate. No suicide note, diary, address book, drugs. He scooped up the lot and replaced them in a drawer.

In sombre mood, he drove home.

Twenty

Peter Diamond's moods may have been uncertain to his colleagues, but his wife Stephanie reckoned he was transparent ninety-nine per cent of the time. This morning was the one per cent exception. His behaviour was totally out of character. After bringing her the tea that was her daily treat, he rolled back into bed and opened the *Guardian* instead of going for his shower and shave and starting the routine of grooming, dressing, eating and listening to the radio that he'd observed for years. When he finally put down the paper, he went for a bath. A bath. He simply didn't take baths in the morning. There was never time. He preferred evenings after work, when he would linger for hours with a book, topping up the hot water from time to time by deft action with his big toe against the tap.

She tapped on the bathroom door. 'Are you all right in there?'

'Why? Are you waiting to come in?' he called.

'No, I'm only asking.' She was more discreet than to mention his blood pressure. 'As long as you know how the time is going.'

'Sixty minutes an hour when I last heard.'

'Sorry I spoke, my lord.'

She'd finished her breakfast and was on the point of going out when he came downstairs.

The sight of him still in his dressing-gown and slippers evoked a grim memory and her face creased in concern. 'Peter, should you be telling me something? You haven't resigned again?'

He smiled and reached for her hand. The two-year exile from the police had been a rough passage for them both. 'No, love.'

'And they haven't . . . ?'

'Given me the old heave-ho? No. It's just that I don't have to go in first thing. I'm supposed to be down at the RUH.'

'Oh?' White-faced, she said, 'Another appointment?'

'A post-mortem.'

A moment of incomprehension, then, as the light dawned, 'Oh.'

'You know, Steph, it never occurred to me when we bought this place that it was just up the road from the hospital. When we lived on Wellsway I could say I'd been sitting in a line of traffic for ages and be believed. That little wrinkle isn't much use now I live in Weston and can walk down to the mortuary in five minutes. If I want a reason for not showing up on time I've got to think of something smarter.'

'And have you?'

'I'm giving it my full attention.'

'Do you really need to be there?'

'Need? No. But it's expected. This one is what we term a suspicious death. The pathologist points out anything worthy of note, and discusses it with CID. I'm supposed to take an active interest, or one of us on the case is.'

'Isn't there someone else, then? I mean, if you're practically allergic, as we know you are . . .'

'Not this time. I had a bit of a run-in with Julie last night.'

'Oh, Pete!'

'Can't really ask her a favour. No, I'll tough it out, but I don't have to watch the whole performance, so long as I appear at some point with a good story.' He rolled his eyes upwards, trying to conjure something up. 'We could have a problem with the plumbing. Water all over the floor. Or the cat had kittens.'

'A neutered male?'

'Surprised us all. There's no stopping Raffles.'

'I'd think of something better if I were you.'

'Such as?'

'Such as your wife, finally driven berserk, clobbering you with a rolling-pin. No one would find that hard to understand.'

* * *

Eventually he drove into the RUH about the time he judged the pathologist would be peeling off his rubber gloves. He parked in a space beside one of the police photographers, who had his window down and was smoking.

'Taken your pictures, then?' Diamond called out to him matily and got a nod. 'Are they going to be long in there?'

'Twenty minutes more, I reckon,' came the heartening answer.

He made a slow performance of unwrapping an extra-strong peppermint. He thought he might listen to the latest news on Radio Bristol before getting out of the car, just (he told himself) to see if anything new had come up. Then they played a Beatles track and he had to listen to that.

Finally he got out and ambled towards the mortuary block just as the door opened and Jim Middleton, the senior histopathologist at the RUH, came out accompanied by – of all people – John Wigfull. Well, if Wigfull had represented the CID, so be it. He was welcome to attend as many autopsies as he wished.

Middleton, a Yorkshireman, still wearing his rubber apron, greeted Diamond with a mock salute. 'Good to see you, Superintendent. Nice timing.'

'Family crisis that I won't go into,' Diamond said in a well-rehearsed phrase. 'Why do they always blow up at the most awkward times? I dare say John can fill me in, unless there's something unexpected I should hear about at once.'

'Unexpected?' Middleton shook his head. 'The only thing you won't have been expecting is that we switched the running order. I've just examined Mr Wigfull's farmer. All done. Your young woman is next, which is why I said your timing was nice. We're on in ten minutes or so, after I've had some fresh air.'

No one needed the fresh air more than Diamond. His eyes glazed over. 'I had a message that it was to be eight-thirty.'

'I know, and we were ready to go, but we didn't like to start without anyone from CID. Isn't it fortunate that Chief-Inspector Wigfull phoned in to find out what time he would be needed for the farmer? "As soon as you can get here," I told him.'

Wigfull didn't actually smirk. He didn't need to.

There was no ducking it now. In a short time, Diamond stood numbly in attendance in the post-mortem room with a scenes of crime officer, two photographers and a number of medical students. First the photographs were taken as each item of Hildegarde Henkel's clothing was removed. It was a slow process. A continuous record had to be provided.

Jim Middleton clearly regarded all this as wearisome and unconnected with his medical expertise, so he filled the gaps with conversation about the previous autopsy. 'Poor old sod, lying dead that long. It's a sad comment on our times that anyone can be left for up to a week and nobody knows or cares.'

He stepped forward and loosened the dead woman's left shoe and removed it. The sock inside was as clean as the other. 'Double bow, securely tied. Yes, he was far from fresh. An interesting suicide, though. I don't think I've heard of a case where the gun is fired from under the chin. A shotgun, I mean. All the cases I've seen, they either put the muzzle against the forehead or in the mouth.'

'Why is that?' Diamond asked, happy to absent himself from what was going on under his nose.

'Think about it. It's bloody difficult firing a shotgun at yourself anyway. You've got to stretch your arm down the length of the barrel and work the trigger. I haven't tried it and I hope I never will, but I imagine it just adds to the difficulty if you can't see what you're doing.'

Unnoticed by anyone else, Diamond mimed the action, jutting out his chin like Mussolini making a speech, and at the same time holding his right arm rigid in front of himself and making the trigger movement with his thumb. Middleton had made a telling point. The victim couldn't possibly have seen his finger on the trigger without moving the muzzle into the mouth or against the front of his face. But would it really matter to someone about to kill himself? Wouldn't he be content to grope for the trigger?

Middleton continued to find the farmer's death more interesting than that of the woman in front of him. 'It's not unknown for shotgun suicides to take off their shoe and sock and press the trigger with their big toe. That didn't happen in this case.'

The words were lost on Diamond. Mentally he was yet another remove from here, up the A46 and across the motorway at Gladstone's farm. The scene in the cottage came back vividly. He pictured the position of the chair and the chalked outlines of the farmer's feet. How he wished he had seen it before the body was taken away. He made a mental note to look at the photos, for he had thought of another problem with the suicide. He brooded on the matter for a long time, going over it repeatedly, pondering the way it was done. If you are about to blow your brains out, do you choose the most simple way? In that state of mind, are you capable of taking practical decisions?

Such was his concentration that he didn't get much involved in the activity at the dissecting table.

When he emerged from the reverie, he heard Middleton saying, '. . . nothing inconsistent with a fall from a considerable height. Obviously we'll see what Chepstow have to say about the samples, but them's me findings for what they're worth, ladies and gentlemen, and unless you have any questions I recommend an early lunch.'

The early lunch was part of the patter, a pay-off that the pathologist took a morbid pleasure in inflicting. Judging by the queasy looks around the table it would be a long time before his audience could face anything to eat.

Before returning to the nick, Diamond called at Avon Social Services at Lewis House in Manvers Street. Having heard about Imogen from Ada and Julie, he was intrigued to meet the lady. He knew most of the social workers. This one couldn't have been long in the job.

She came out to reception specially and extended a slim hand with silver-painted nails. 'Is it about poor Hilde Henkel? I heard the news from your Inspector Hargreaves.' She seemed genuinely troubled, with worry lines extending across her pale features. 'Why don't you come through to my office?'

He followed her, wondering if the bouncy blonde curls and willowy figure could be in any degree responsible for Ada's contempt.

'Before we start,' he said when they were seated, 'how long have you been with Avon, Miss, em . . . ?'

'Starr.' She went slightly pink. She must have taken some leg-pulling for that name in the past. 'Just over a year actually.'

'And before that?'

'University. If you're thinking I haven't had much experience, you're right. This is the first tragedy I've had among my clients.'

'They're all tragedies in a sense, aren't they?' he said. 'I know what you mean, though. I'm not a knocker of social workers and I don't blame you for being inexperienced. Got to start somewhere. If it's anything like the police, you're new so you get lumbered with some of the hardest cases.'

She said, 'I didn't think of Hilde as a hard case. There are others I'd have thought more at risk.'

'You have a file on her?'

She reddened again. 'I can't let you see it.'

'But she's dead now.'

'The notes are personal to me.'

'I don't mind if you consult them and give me a summary. How many times have you met her?'

She went to the filing cabinet in the corner and withdrew a tabbed file.

'You don't keep your case-notes on computer, then?' he commented.

She said, 'These are people. I think they deserve the fullest confidentiality. I don't trust computers.'

'Miss Starr, I totally agree.'

She asked him to call her Imogen, as everyone else did. 'You were asking how many meetings I had with Hilde. Six altogether. Do you know the story, how she got onto our list?'

He pretended he had not, so as to hear it directly from her.

'This depression she had,' he said when she had finished. 'Didn't you think it serious?'

She said, 'Difficult to judge. I thought it came from her situation, being homeless in a foreign country and abandoned by her husband. Once she was in Harmer House she seemed to improve in spirits.'

'Her life looked up, her present life?'

'Well, she went out in the day and in the evenings

sometimes. Mind you, she didn't have money to spend. Precious little, anyway.'

'Did she mention any people she met in Bath?'

'Not to me.'

'She didn't know anyone in the Royal Crescent?'

'I've no idea.'

'On the night of the party someone saw her sitting on the balustrade, high up on the roof, dangling her legs. It sounds as if she was having a wild time.'

She digested this. 'It's difficult to picture. The people I see here are in a formal situation. It's impossible to tell what they're like in party mood.'

'After a few drinks or drugs?'

'That's speculation, isn't it?'

'Yes,' he said. 'I'm waiting for the blood test results. You didn't ever notice a devil-may-care side to Hilde's character?'

'It may have been there, but I wasn't likely to see it.'

He'd heard nothing from Imogen that Julie hadn't already reported, but there was another matter he'd promised to raise. 'While I'm here, I want to ask about another young woman at Harmer House, who was also one of yours – Rose, is it, or Rosamund?'

She shifted in her chair and he noticed that her hands came together and were clasped tight. 'Rosamund Black. She's no longer there. She lost her memory, but her people came for her. They took her back to West London a couple of weeks ago.'

'Have you heard from her since?'

'No, but I wouldn't expect to.'

'You have an address for her, though? We'd like to get in touch with her.'

Imogen got up and returned to the filing cabinet. Presently she said, 'It's Twelve Turpin Street, Hounslow.'

'And the people who came for her? Where do they live?'

'Somewhere near, I gathered. The mother is in Twickenham.' She gave a sigh, chiding herself as she stared at the notes. 'I didn't get their address. Their name is Jenkins. The stepsister is Doreen Jenkins.'

'How exactly did this lady, Doreen Jenkins, get to know about Rose?'

She closed her eyes in an effort to remember. Something else wasn't in the notes. 'She heard from someone, a friend of Rose's, that Rose had gone to Bath on a weekend hotel break. When Rose didn't make her regular phone call, the old mother got worried, and the following weekend the stepsister and her partner came to Bath to try and get in touch with her. They saw a piece in the paper about a woman who had lost her memory and recognised the picture as Rose.'

'And was it a happy reunion?'

'Rose didn't seem to know her sister, if that's what you're asking, but her memory still wasn't functioning. She went with them of her own free will.'

'You satisfied her that they were definitely her family?'

'They satisfied her. And they satisfied me as well. They had photos with them, of Rose, alone and with the mother. There wasn't any doubt.'

'I'm not suggesting there is.'

Imogen's lips tightened. 'This is Ada, isn't it? She's been agitating because Rose hasn't written to her. I keep telling her not to make waves. Rose will write in her own good time if she wishes to. She's got enough on her plate trying to get back to normal.'

'Quite probably. What is normal? Did you find out? Did the stepsister have anything else to say about Rose's life in Hounslow?'

'I can't recall anything, except that Rose had been on a trip to Florida some time and still managed to phone her mother.'

The mention of the phone gave him an idea. 'Do you have a set of London phone directories in this place?'

'Behind you.'

He picked the first one off the shelf and looked up the name Black. 'Hounslow, you said. Miss R.Black, 12 Turpin Street.' Slowly he ran his finger down the columns. 'Can't find it here, Imogen.'

'Perhaps she's ex-directory.'

He replaced the directory. Beside it were a number of street atlases, including a London A-Z, which he picked up to study the index. 'Turpin Street. You're quite sure of that?'

'I suppose it could have been Turpin Road.'

'Doesn't matter. There's only one Turpin in this book and that's Turpin Way in Wallington, a long way from Hounslow. I hate to say this, my dear, but it looks as if you've been given a fast shuffle by this woman. Ada may be onto something after all.'

Twenty-one

It was 'Be Nice to Julie' day. 'In case you're waiting for me, I'm afraid I've got to work through,' he thoughtfully told her. 'But you can go off as soon as you like. Take your time. You've earned it twice over.'

Julie suppressed a smile. She knew why the old gannet couldn't face lunch. She'd heard about his belated arrival at the mortuary only to discover that the autopsy on Hildegarde Henkel had been rescheduled, forcing him to watch the whole thing.

'So don't let me stop you, if you want to go down to the . . .' he said, the voice trailing off, unable to articulate the word 'canteen'.

She told him she'd eaten earlier. She asked if there was anything new on the case.

'Depends which case you mean.' The awkwardness between them was not only due to his nausea.

She said, not without irony, 'I was under the impression we were working on Hildegarde Henkel.'

'No progress there.'

'Nothing came out of the post-mortem?'

'Nothing we don't know already.'

He was unwilling to say more than the minimum and she had no desire to pump him for information. People of his rank were supposed to communicate.

She waited.

Finally he felt compelled to speak. 'We ought to put things right between us, Julie. Some straight-talking. That wasn't very professional yesterday.'

'Do you mean your sexist remark, or my reaction to it?'

'Sexist, was it?'

'No more than usual. The difference was that you made it personal.'

'I can't even remember what I said.'

'I'll tell you, then,' she said. 'I made some sympathetic remark about the dead woman and you said I was being a shade too sisterly for your taste, which I thought was bloody mean considering how much I take from you without bitching.'

'Hold on,' he said. 'It was a light-hearted comment. I wasn't attacking you.'

'It was sarcasm.'

'Yes, and I know what they say about that, but I thought you had enough of a sense of humour to take it with a smile.'

'Spare me that old line, Mr Diamond.'

He gave a twitchy smile. 'Look, it was only because you're not one of those die-hard feminists that I made the remark. You call it sarcastic: I meant it to be ironic. I didn't expect to touch a raw nerve. You and I know better than to fall out over a word, Julie.'

She said, 'We'd have fallen out long before this if I'd objected to words. It's the assumption behind them. You make snide remarks about my so-called feminist opinions as if I ride a broomstick and put curses on men. I'm another human being doing a job. I don't ask for any more consideration than the men get. It's about being treated as one of the human race instead of a lesser species.'

'I've never thought of you as lesser anything,' he told her.

She rolled her eyes upwards and said nothing.

'Look at me,' Diamond went on. 'Would a fat, arrogant git like this choose anyone less than the best for a deputy? I rate you, Julie. I'm not going to turn into a New Man overnight, but I'm big enough to say that I rate you – and I wouldn't say that about many others in this God-forsaken nick, male or female.'

She held his gaze. It was the nearest thing to an apology she was likely to get. Nothing more was said for an interval. Finally she looked away and told him, 'God help you if you ever meet a real feminist.'

The air was not entirely clear, but it had improved.

He nearly ruined it by the lordly way he extended his hand towards a chair. With a sigh, she sat down.

Normal business resumed. 'You asked about progress,' he said. 'I'm not sure if this fits the heading, but I discovered that Ada Shaftsbury may be right after all in raising the alarm about her friend, the one who lost her memory and hasn't been in contact.'

'Rose.'

'I just called at Social Services. The people who collected her gave a bogus address.'

'She isn't living there?'

'The street doesn't even exist.'

Their minds were working in concert now. 'Then the woman really is missing.'

'She can't be contacted, anyway.'

Julie weighed the implications. 'If something dodgy happened, it's quite a coincidence that Hildegarde was staying in the same hostel.'

'Or quite a connection.'

'One woman dead and one missing out of how many staying there?'

'Only three, as far as I can make out. Ada is the only one left.'

'Then she does have reason to be concerned,' said Julie. 'We've been treating her like the boy who cried "Wolf!"'

Diamond introduced a note of caution. 'On the other hand, people like these – living in a hostel, I mean – are more unstable than your average citizens.'

'Meaning what? That one suspicious death and one abduction are par for the course?'

He smiled. 'No, but it's not impossible that two people at the same address turn out to be victims of different crimes.'

'But are they different crimes?' said Julie. 'We don't know what happened to Rose. She could be dead, the same as Hildegarde.'

He shook his head. 'Not the same at all, Julie. There's no evidence that Hildegarde's death was planned. How could it have been, when the party at the Royal Crescent was a surprise even to the tenants? Compare it to the planning that seems to have gone into the abduction of Rose Black, or whatever her name may be.'

She thought it through and grudgingly concluded that he had a point. The abduction of Rose, if it was an abduction, must have involved some sophisticated planning. To have gone to the Social Services claiming to be her family and producing photographs as evidence was a high-risk operation that could only have worked if it was carried through with conviction. She spoke her next thought aloud: 'But is it right to assume something sinister just because the woman gave a false address to Social Services? Could there be a reason for it?'

He said flippantly, 'Like winning the lottery and wanting no publicity?'

Julie treated the remark seriously. 'In a way, yes. I was thinking that the family knew something they wanted to keep to themselves. Suppose they discovered that Rose lost her memory in a car accident she caused, killing or maiming someone. They'd have reason enough for whisking her away and leaving no traces.'

Diamond's eyebrows pricked up. 'That's good. That's very good.' He leaned back in his chair, confirming that her theory made sense. 'If I remember right, she was found wandering on the A46 by some people from Westbury.'

'Some people Ada is being cagey about in case we prosecute them,' said Julie.

'Prosecute them – why?'

'Oh, come on, Mr Diamond. Rose stepped into the road and their car struck her and knocked her out. They drove her to the Hinton Clinic and dumped her in the car park.'

'Then they damned well should be nicked.' But he allowed that trifling thought to pass. 'Why was she wandering in the first place? That's the nub of it. You've got a point. An earlier incident, on the motorway perhaps. It's not unknown for people in shock to walk away from an accident. Do we know the date she was found?'

'It's on file,' Julie reminded him. 'The clinic notified us when she was brought in. There are photographs of her injuries. If you'd care to see them—'

'Not now,' he said quickly. He'd seen enough gore for one day.

Julie added, 'We checked at the time for road accidents

on the motorway and every other road within a five-mile radius. There weren't any that fitted the circumstances.'

'There weren't any we heard about. That's not quite the same thing, Julie.' He drummed his fingertips on the chair-arm. 'Look, by rights this could be farmed out to one of Wigfull's people.'

She listened with amusement, confident of what was coming.

'But it could be argued that Harmer House provides a link with the Royal Crescent case, so I think we'll take this on board, Julie. See what you can do with it. Have a talk yourself with Imogen Starr, the social worker, and see what she remembers of Doreen Jenkins, the woman who collected Rose. Then check every detail of the story for accuracy. Find out where Jenkins was staying in Bath. See if there really was a man in tow, as she claimed. Check Hounslow, Twickenham. Check the mother, if you can.'

'Do you want me to involve Ada at this stage?'

'Personally,' he said, 'I don't feel strong enough. It's up to you.'

She got up. At the door she turned and asked, 'Will you be concentrating on Hildegarde Henkel's death?'

'Someone has to,' he said with a martyred air.

But the first move he made after Julie had left was to the room where items of evidence were stored, and the item he asked to examine had not belonged to Hildegarde Henkel.

'A shotgun,' he told the sergeant in charge. 'Property of Daniel Gladstone, deceased.'

There was some hesitation. 'That's Mr Wigfull's case, sir.'

'You think I don't know whose case it is, sergeant?'

'Mr Wigfull is very hot on exhibits, sir.' And so was this sergeant, a real stickler for procedure.

'I'm sure he is, and he's right to be. He and I are working hand in hand on several cases, as you heard, no doubt. The gun has been seen by forensic, I take it – checked for prints and so on.'

'I believe it has, sir.'

'It's bagged up, then? Bagged up and labelled?'

'Yes, sir.' Said with a note of finality.

'Good.' Diamond grinned like a chess-player who has watched his opponent make the wrong move. 'Just what the doctor ordered.'

'Is it, sir?'

'Because I won't need to disturb the bag. I can examine it without breaking the seal, and no one need get uptight.'

'Mr Diamond, I don't wish to be obstructive—'

'Nor me, sergeant, nor me. So I'll save your reputation by coming round the back and checking the item here on the premises. It won't have left your control. Just lift the flap for me, would you?'

Minutes after, the sergeant was privy to the bizarre spectacle of Detective Superintendent Diamond seated on a chair, with the shotgun in its polythene wrapping poised between his legs, the butt supported on the floor, the muzzle under his chin, while his fingers groped along the barrel towards the trigger guard.

'Be a sport, sergeant, and keep this to yourself. There are things a man wouldn't like his best friends to know about.'

With his mind still on Farmer Gladstone, he drove out to Tormarton to have another look at the farm. Crime-scene tape was still spread across the gate and the front door. He left the car in the lane and lifted his leg over the tape.

There were several large heaps of earth in the field outside. He went over to one of the pits and looked inside. They had dug to the bedrock.

He detached the tape from the front door of the farmhouse and was pleased to find that he could open it. He went through the kitchen to the back room. The Bible he had found was still on the window-sill, obviously of no interest to John Wigfull. He picked it up and glanced at the family tree in the front, the long line of male descendants ending with a female, May Turner, who had married Daniel Gladstone here in Tormarton in 1943. Then he let the pages fall open at the old Christmas card. He wanted another look at the photo inside, of the woman and child, and the wording on the card, concise, touching and yet remote: '*I thought you would like this picture of your family. God's blessings to us all at this time. Meg.*' Was it really meant to bless, he wondered, or to damn?

He closed the Bible and slipped it into his coat pocket, trying not to feel furtive.

Outside, he made a more thorough tour of the outhouses than before. They had been ravaged by the winds endemic in this exposed place, and patched up from time to time with tarpaulin and pieces of corrugated iron. They should have been torn down long ago and rebuilt. Someone, he noticed, had recently fed and watered the chickens. It was one of life's few certainties that whenever there were animals at a crime scene, you could count on one of the police seeing to their needs. He scraped away some straw in the hen-house in case there had been recent digging underneath, but the surface was brick-hard.

Then he returned to his car and drove through the lanes to Tormarton village, a cluster of grey houses, cottages and farm buildings behind drystone walls. Rustic it may have appeared, yet there was the steady drone of traffic from the motorway only a quarter of a mile to the south. The inhabitants must have been willing to trade the noise for the convenience. It didn't take a detective to tell that many were escapees from suburban life. The old buildings remained, but gentrified, cleaned up and adapted to a car-owning population. The Old School House no longer catered for children. The shop and sub-Post Office had been converted into a pub. The Cotswold Way, another modern gloss on ancient features, snaked between the cottages and across the fields.

He parked opposite the church and called at Church Cottage nearby. A woman answered, rubbing her hands on a towel. She smiled as if she knew why he was there. The fragrance of fried onions gusted from behind her, causing Diamond some unease over his still-turbulent stomach. He explained who he was.

'You're looking for the vicar, are you?' The woman grinned. 'Don't worry. You're not the first to make that mistake. Our vicar lives at Marshfield. We have to share him with two other parishes.'

'Is there a church warden in the village, then?'

'There is, but if you want the vicar, he may be in the

church, still. There was a funeral earlier.' Her gaze shifted from Diamond. 'No, get your skates on – there he goes, at the end of the street.'

'Thanks.' He gave a shout and stepped out briskly after a tall, silver-haired man in the act of bundling his vestments into the back seat of a car.

The vicar straightened up and looked round. Diamond introduced himself.

'You're a detective? This is to do with poor old Gladstone, I suppose.'

'Can you spare a few minutes, sir?'

The vicar said that he doubted if he could help much, but he would answer any questions he could. 'Have you had lunch? The Portcullis has a rather good bar menu.'

Diamond patted his ample belly. 'I'm giving it a miss today.'

'Then why don't we talk inside the church?'

'Whatever suits you, sir.'

St Mary Magdalene, the vicar explained as they approached it, was pre-Conquest in origin. There were Saxon stones in the structure of the tower. The priest of Tormarton, he said, was mentioned in Domesday.

'So you're one of a long line, sir?' Diamond commented, willing to listen to some potted history in exchange for goodwill and, he hoped, the local gossip.

'Yes, indeed. The line probably goes back two or three centuries earlier than that. There are various theories about the origin of the name of our village. The first syllable, "Tor", may refer to "torr", a hill, or the pagan deity Thor, or it may derive from a thorn tree. But there's no dispute about the second part of the name. The derivation is "macre tun" – the farm on the boundary, or border. We stand, you see – and it's rather exciting – on the ancient border of the Kingdoms of Mercia and Wessex.'

'Mercia and Wessex,' Diamond said without sharing the excitement. There was a danger of the history over-running.

'But the present church is basically late Norman, as you must have noted already.'

'Certainly have, sir. Must take a lot of upkeep. Do you have a good-sized congregation?'

'It depends what you take to be a good size. I suppose

we do reasonably well for these times.' The vicar opened the wooden gate and led the way up a small avenue of yew trees, through the genteel end of the churchyard, where a high complement of raised tombs blackened by age stood at odd angles. The main entrance was round the right-hand side of the church.

'Was Daniel Gladstone one of your flock?'

'They all are,' said the vicar. 'But I know what you're asking. He didn't join in the worship. He didn't join in anything much. Quite a solitary figure.' He paused, then sighed and said, 'The manner of his death is on all our consciences. And it was too long before he was found, far too long.'

'Several days, anyway.'

'Dreadful. Every parish priest has a few like that, insisting on going on in their own way, shutting the world out. It's a dilemma. I called on him occasionally and he was barely civil.'

'No family?'

'Not in the neighbourhood. Both his marriages failed. It was a hard life, and I don't think the wives could take it.'

'So there were two marriages?' said Diamond.

They stepped into the small arched porch and the vicar turned the iron ring of the church door and parted the red curtains inside. 'Two, yes. He was married here the first time during the war, long before I came. She wasn't a local girl, I understand. From London, I think, to escape the bombing. Old Daniel must have been more sociable in those days. Young and carefree. His father would have owned the farm, then.'

They had paused in front of a sculptured wall monument to one Edward Topp, who had died in 1699. The Topp coat of arms consisted of a gloved hand gripping a severed arm, the soggy end painted red. Diamond thought of the post-mortem, took a deep breath and switched his gaze to a floor brass of a figure in a long garment, with all his limbs intact.

'Fifteenth century. John Ceysill, a steward. Note the pen and inkhorn at his waist,' the vicar informed him. 'The Gladstones are one of the village families from generations back. If you're looking for their name on the memorials

– of which we have some fine examples – you will be disappointed. Ordinary folk were not commemorated like the gentry.'

'Unless they're on the war memorial.'

'Good point. The two world wars had slipped my mind.'

'Easily done.'

'But there are many fine features here in St Mary's.'

Diamond's gaze had already moved up to the fine feature of the timbered roof, not to admire it, but to work out how to stave off a lecture on its history. He produced the Bible from his pocket, an inspired move.

It was enough to stop the vicar in his tracks. True, they were in the right place, but policemen didn't usually carry the Good Book.

'So was old Daniel the last of the line?'

'To my knowledge, yes.'

'His first wife was only nineteen.'

Then Diamond opened the inside page with the family tree and passed it across.

'I didn't know he possessed a Bible,' said the vicar, quick to understand. 'This evidently came from the wife's family, the Turners. Ah. May Turner married Daniel Gladstone, 1943, St Mary Magdalene's.'

'But it didn't last long, you say?'

'That was my understanding. They separated quite soon and she must have left her Bible behind. I heard that she left suddenly. Can't tell you when.'

'If there was a second marriage . . .'

'There must have been a death or a divorce,' the vicar completed it for him. 'I can't tell you which. His second marriage would have been in the nineteen-sixties. She was another very young woman, the daughter of the publican, I was told.'

'Would her name have been Meg?'

'Meg?' He sounded doubtful.

'Short for Margaret.'

'Well, we can check in the marriage register, if you like. I keep that in the safe with the silver. How did you discover her name?'

'If you look in the Book of Psalms . . .'

He peered over his glasses at Diamond, deeply sceptical

that anyone called Meg was mentioned in the Psalms. 'Ah.' He had let the Bible fall open at the Christmas card. 'Now I see what you mean. Bibles have so many uses, not least as a filing system.'

'Look inside the card,' said Diamond.

The vicar opened it and found the photo of the woman and child and read the writing on the card. 'How very moving. It's coming back to me now. I did once hear that there was a daughter of the second marriage. This must be Margaret with her little girl. If you're thinking of returning the Bible to them, I don't know how you'd make contact. She left him when the child was very young. Let's check the marriage register, shall we?' He returned the Bible to Diamond and led him through a passageway (that he couldn't resist naming as yet another feature of St Mary's, its ambulatory) to the chancel and across the aisle to the vestry.

'You said he was a loner – a solitary man.'

'In his old age, he was.' The vicar smiled. 'I see what you mean. For a loner, two wives isn't a bad achievement. He must have been more sociable in his youth, wouldn't you say?'

'Did something happen, I wonder, that turned him off people?'

'I wouldn't know about that.' The vicar took the keys from his pocket and unlocked a wall-safe.

'Was there any gossip?'

'I'm not the right person to ask. Not much Tormarton gossip reaches me at Marshfield. There were stories that he was miserly, sleeping on a mattress stuffed with money, and so on, but almost any old person living alone has to put up with that sort of nonsense.'

'Some small amount of cash was found in the house.'

'That's a relief – that anything was left, I mean. I shouldn't say this, but I know of one or two locally who wouldn't think twice about robbing the dead.' He lifted a leather-bound register from the safe and rested it on the table where the choir's hymn-books were stacked. 'There were not so many weddings in the sixties, before they built the motorway. This shouldn't take long.'

He found the year 1960 and began turning the pages.

'So many familiar names.' He stopped at 1967. 'Here we are. *15th July. Daniel Gladstone, forty-four* – no spring chicken – *widower, farmer.* That's one question answered, then. The first wife must have died. *Margaret Ann Torrington, twenty, spinster, barmaid.*'

'Do you have the record of Baptisms? While you've got the books out, I'd like to see if we can find the child's name.'

They started on another register and eventually found the entry for Christine Gladstone, baptised 20th February, 1970. 'They stayed together this long, anyway,' said the vicar. 'What is it – two and a half years?'

Diamond thanked him for his trouble, still wondering if there was more to be discovered here about Gladstone's death. 'Who are the neighbours? Were they on good terms with the old man?'

'You've put your finger on one of the problems,' said the vicar. 'The adjacent farm, Liversedge Farm, changed hands a number of times in recent years. It's much larger in acreage than Gladstone's. His is no more than a smallholding, as you've seen, and the way it is placed is just a nuisance to the neighbours. If you took an aerial view, you'd see it's in the shape of a frying pan, slightly elongated – the handle being the access lane – almost entirely surrounded by Liversedge land. He was approached a number of times about selling up, but he refused.'

'Who are the present owners?'

'A company. One of these faceless organisations. They do rather nicely out of the European farm subsidies. Much of their land isn't being farmed at all.'

'"Set-aside"?'

'Yes. The rationale is beyond me, paying farmers not to grow things when much of the world is starving.'

'Some of their land must be in use.'

'For grazing, yes. Low maintenance. Nice for the shareholders.'

Diamond had a bizarre mental picture of some portly shareholders on their knees nibbling the grass. 'Isn't it good land for farming?'

'Not the easiest. Remember we're six hundred feet high up here, being on a scarp of the Cotswolds, but it's all there is.'

'A time-honoured occupation, like yours and mine.'

'Indeed. Farming has gone on here for thousands of years. There has been human occupation in the area since the mesolithic period. Stone Age flints are picked up from time to time. Why, only as recently as 1986, when some work was being done in a barn, a stone coffin was excavated containing the skeleton of a child aged about five. They estimated it as 1,800 years old.'

Another disturbing mental image. Having just looked at the photograph of Gladstone's daughter Christine with her mother, Diamond had no difficulty picturing a small, dead girl of about that age. 'There's evidence of recent digging on Gladstone's farm. Quite recent. Since his death, I mean. Would you know anything about that?'

The vicar closed the safe and locked it. 'I heard that you policemen were busy with spades. Everyone in the village has a theory as to what you will unearth. I hope they're wrong.'

'It's all but finished now. We found nothing.'

'That's a relief.'

'But we'd like to know who disturbed the land in the first place, and why.'

'I've heard nothing about that.'

'No stories of people digging?'

'Not until you folk arrived. I wonder who they were. Do you think someone had a theory that the old man had buried his money there?'

'That's one possibility.'

'It's very peculiar. Whatever the purpose of the digging was, they must have known he was dead, or they wouldn't have started digging. Why didn't they notify anyone if they knew poor old Daniel was lying inside the farmhouse?'

'They wouldn't, would they, if they were nicking his savings?'

'Good thinking,' said the vicar. He smiled. 'Perhaps I should stick to preaching and leave the detecting to people like you.'

The drive back to Bath found Diamond in a better frame of mind. He had made real progress over the mystery of the farmer's death. Pity it was the one case he had no business investigating. John Wigfull would not be happy. But then Wigfull had virtually written off the farmer as a suicide victim. And as Diamond had decided there was a strong suspicion of murder, it would be out of Wigfull's orbit.

He had not driven far along the A46 when he recalled that this was a significant stretch of road, the long approach to Dyrham where Ada's friend Rose had wandered into the path of an approaching car. Some way short of the Crown Inn, he pulled off the main carriageway and got out to look around.

It was a bleak, windswept spot, one of those vast landscapes that made you feel insignificant. Miles of farmland lay on either side of the road and a row of power-lines on pylons stretched almost to infinity. The traffic sped by, oblivious, intent on reaching the next road-sign. He had often driven through himself without ever noticing anyone on foot along here.

Where had she come from that night? There were only two possibilities he could think of: one was that she had been set down at the motorway junction and walked this far, the other that she had made her way from the nearest village, perhaps a mile and a half back along the road. And that village was Tormarton.

Twenty-two

On his return to Manvers Street Police Station, Diamond was handed a message from the Forensic Science Lab. Tests on the blood sample taken from the dead woman found at the Royal Crescent on Sunday morning had proved negative for drugs and so low for alcohol that she could not have drunk much more than a glass of wine. He gave a told-you-so grunt. Hildegarde Henkel had not fallen off that roof because of her physical state.

The phone had been beeping steadily since he came in. He picked it up and heard from the desk sergeant that 'some nerd' had come in an hour ago in response to the appeal for information about the party up at the Crescent.

'What do you mean – "some nerd"?'

'A member of the public, then, sir. Sorry about that.'

'Sergeant, I'm not complaining. I only want to know what makes him a nerd.'

'The impression I got, Mr Diamond. I could be mistaken.'

'You could, but now that you've dumped on this public-spirited person, you'd better be more specific.'

'Well, I think he's harmless.'

'A weirdo?'

'That's a bit strong.'

'A nerd, then.'

'That about sums it up, sir.'

'Wasting our time?'

'I wouldn't know that.'

He said with a sigh, 'Have him brought up. I'll see him now.'

'Not possible, sir. He wouldn't wait. There was no one here to see him at the time, Mr Wigfull being out and DI Hargreaves as well.'

'So you didn't even get a statement?'

'He said he'd be in the Grapes if you wanted to talk to him.'

Diamond made a sound deep in his throat that mingled contempt and amusement in equal measure. 'That's why he couldn't wait. Urgent business at the Grapes. This isn't a nerd, Sergeant, it's a barfly. What name does he go under?'

'Gary Paternoster.'

'God help us. What's that – South African?'

Before going out, he phoned the pathologist, Jim Middleton.

'You got those blood-test results, then,' Middleton's rich Yorkshire brogue came down the line, confident that he knew the reason for the call.

'On the woman, yes,' Diamond said.

'So did I. No drugs and very little alcohol, which greatly simplifies your job, doesn't it?'

'This isn't about her. If you don't mind, I've got a question about the other PM you did this morning.'

'The old farmer? Fire away.'

This required tact from Diamond; the medical profession don't like laymen giving them advice. 'I was thinking over what you said, about it being unusual in suicides, aiming the muzzle under the chin.'

'This one was the first I've come across,' Middleton confirmed, 'but there's always something new in this game.'

'He must have had a long reach. I had a look at the gun earlier. The distance from muzzle to trigger is twenty-eight inches.'

'Actually, he was on the short side.' A pause. 'You've got a point there, my friend.' The tone of that 'my friend' rather undermined the sentiment. 'I'd better check my measurements.'

'When the body was found, there wasn't any sign that he was tied to the chair,' Diamond started to say.

'Hold on,' said Middleton. 'What the fuck are you suggesting, inspector?'

'Superintendent.'

'What?'

'Peter will do. Is it conceivable that this was set up to look like a suicide when it was something else?'

There was another awkward silence before Middleton said, 'I found no marks of ligatures, if that's what you're suggesting.'

'He was in a wooden armchair,' Diamond said. 'If his arms were pinioned in some way to the chair, he'd be helpless. He was in his seventies.'

'I said I found no marks.'

'He was wearing several layers of clothes: jacket, pullover, shirt and long-sleeved vest. If a ligature was over the clothes, would the pressure marks show through?'

'You're bloody persistent, aren't you? It depends how tight this theoretical ligature was, but, no, it need not. This was a corpse after a week of putrefaction. We're not dealing in subtleties at that stage. What are you suggesting – that he was trussed up for slaughter and then untied after death?'

Twenty minutes and a brisk walk later, Diamond entered the pub in Westgate Street where the Allardyces and the Treadwells had begun their celebrations on the fateful Saturday night. Not many were in. Six-fifteen this Tuesday evening was too early for the youthful regulars who nightly turned the Grapes into Bath's hottest drinking spot. The sound from the music system was well short of the decibels it would reach later, but still loud for a man whose peaks of listening came on Radio Two.

He sauntered through the narrow low-beamed bar with its low-watt electric lights masquerading as oil-lamps. The dark wood panelling and antique paintings lived up to the claim, inscribed along a crossbeam, that the present façade dated from the seventeenth century; the fruit machines on every side undermined the impression. He saw the TV set at the far end of the bar that must have given the Treadwells and the Allardyces the news of their lottery success. There were bottled drinks he'd never heard of on display behind the bar. A man of his maturity stood out in this place, he thought. Anyone expecting a visitor from the police ought to give him a second glance. No one did. He strolled the length of the bar eyeing all the lone drinkers. He was beginning to take against Gary Paternoster before having met him, which was stupid. This one might be a nerd, and a barfly into the bargain, but he had gone to the trouble of calling at the nick. He could be about to provide the information that would nail a killer.

So quit racing your motor, Diamond told himself. Watch your blood pressure.

He asked a barmaid for help.

'Dunno, love, but it could be him over there, under the fish.'

The fish was a *trompe l'oeil*, a pike carved in wood to look as if it was in a showcase. It was mounted on the wall near the door. Alone at a table, a youth sat like a more convincing stuffed specimen, staring ahead with glazed eyes. He was in a suit, a businessman's three-piece, navy blue with a faint white pinstripe. He had an old-fashioned short-back-and-sides and owlish glasses. When Diamond spoke his name, he jerked and stood up.

'Take it easy,' Diamond told him. 'What's that you're drinking?'

'Lemonade shandy.'

A pained expression came over Diamond's features. It was a long time since he'd come across anyone drinking shandy. The very notion of mixing good beer with lemonade . . .

In his innocence Gary Paternoster added, 'But one is enough for me, thank you, sir.'

Diamond went back to the bar and collected a pint of best bitter for himself, a chance to focus his thoughts. This wasn't the class of nerd he'd expected. This was a throwback to some time in the dim past when kids in their teens respected their elders and stayed sober and wore their Sunday best for talking to the police. Did it matter? Not if the boy was reliable as a witness.

At the table again, he perched uncomfortably on a padded stool with his back to a fruit machine called *Monte Carlo or Bust* and said, 'Didn't you want to wait at the nick, Mr Paternoster?'

A nervous smile. 'To be honest, they made me a little uncomfortable. Not the police officers. Some of the people who came in.'

'I don't blame you. They give me the creeps. So you offered to wait here. More relaxing, eh?'

They were sitting under a throbbing loudspeaker that

didn't relax Diamond much, but the music did guarantee that their conversation wasn't overheard.

'This was the only place I could think of. It's mentioned in the newspaper.' The boy took a cutting from his top pocket and passed it across the table. 'They said you were out making inquiries. They couldn't tell me where.'

Diamond left the cutting where it was. 'I see. You thought I might be here.'

'I thought I'd come and see.'

'Local, are you?'

'Yes, sir.'

'From Bath, I mean?'

'Great Pulteney Street, actually.'

'Very local, then. Nice address.'

'It's my mother's.'

He lived with his mother, and who would have guessed, Diamond cynically thought. 'And are you in a job?'

'I work at the Treasure House.'

'What's that – a Chinese restaurant?'

Gary Paternoster blushed scarlet. 'No. It's a shop in Walcot Street, for detectorists.'

'Oh, yes?' Diamond's confidence in his star witness plunged another fathom. 'Like me, you mean?'

'Are you a detectorist?'

Save us, he thought. 'Detective Superintendent. Will that do?'

The young man blushed again. 'I don't think you understand. I'm talking about people who use metal detectors.'

Normally Diamond was quick, but it took a moment for the penny to drop. 'What – treasure-hunters? The guys you see on the beach with those probe-things looking for money and watches other people have lost?'

Gary Paternoster swallowed hard and said with disapproval, 'Those people get us a bad name. Real detectorists aren't interested in lost property – well, not modern lost property. You'll find us in a ploughed field looking for ancient relics.'

'Do you do it?'

'Quite often, yes.'

'Detectoring, you call it?'

'Yes.'

'Ever found anything?'

'Plenty.' Self-congratulation lit the boyish features for a moment.

Diamond pretended not to believe. 'What – horseshoes and nails and bits of barbed wire?'

'No. Medieval bronze buckles. Roman coins. Brooches and things. You learn a lot about history.'

'Lonely hobby, I should think, for a young man like you.'

This gentle goading was not wasted. Faint glimmers of a personality were emerging from behind the shop-assistant's manner. 'I find it very satisfying, actually.'

'And profitable?'

'Not yet, but you never know what you might find – and profit isn't really the point of it. We're uncovering the past.'

Uncovering the past summed up Gary Paternoster. He was a relic looking for relics.

'But you weren't out with your metal detector last Saturday night,' Diamond said in an unsubtle shift to the matter under investigation.

He looked at Diamond as if the question did him no credit. 'It's no good going out after dark. You wouldn't find a thing.'

'Mr Paternoster.'

'Yes, sir?'

'I'm inviting you to tell me what happened.'

'Oh.' He fastened a button on his suit. 'I was up at the Royal Crescent, at that party.'

Surprised, for Gary Paternoster didn't look like a party-goer, Diamond said, 'By invitation?'

'Not in point of fact. It was open to everyone, wasn't it? The shop was open late that evening, being Saturday. I was on my way home, about nine, I suppose, when I met some people I knew in Northgate Street. One of them was at school with me, quite a forceful personality. They were all on their way to this party and they asked me to join them. They said things I'm too embarrassed to repeat, about getting . . . getting . . .'

'Laid?'

'I was going to say getting lucky with girls. I didn't really want to, and I said I wasn't invited, but they said none of them were. I'm not very good at standing up to people like that.'

'So you tagged along.' Now he understood. The kid had been press-ganged.

'I thought I'd slip away as soon as I got a chance. Parties make me tense. There seemed to be dozens going up there. They said someone here – in the Grapes – had won the lottery and thrown their house open for a party. That was what I heard and I think it's true. When we got to the house, the door was open and we just walked in. There was loud music and beer. It seemed to be on several floors. We went upstairs to the first floor and that was where I saw the young lady who was killed.'

'Already dead?'

'No, at this point she was alive.'

'You're sure it was her?'

'She's the one whose picture is in the paper today. She was German, wasn't she? She had a pink jumper thing and jeans – black or dark blue. A pretty face with dark hair, quite short. My friends seemed to know her from the pub – this place. She used to come here most evenings. It turned out that she didn't know any English, because they were talking about her, making fun of her, saying suggestive things to her face.'

'Such as?'

'Stupid stuff, like she was desperate for . . .' He cleared his throat. Simply couldn't bring himself to say the word.

'Sex?'

Paternoster took an intense interest in his shandy. 'And they tried to embarrass me by telling her I wanted to go upstairs with her. She didn't understand.'

'She must have guessed what was going on,' said Diamond. 'She must have known what it was about from the sniggering. How did she take it? Was she upset?'

'She ignored it. She seemed to be thinking about other things. She kept looking away, across the room.'

'What at?'

'The door, I think. She wasn't looking at people. After a short time she just turned her back and moved off. They told me to go after her. They said she wanted me to follow her. I didn't really believe it, but they were making me very embarrassed, so I went, just to get out of the room, really.' He paused. 'I don't want you to think I had anything to do with her falling off the roof.'

'It hasn't crossed my mind,' Diamond said in gospel truth. 'Did you see where she went?'

'Upstairs to the top flat. It was open. The party was going on there as well.'

'And you followed?'

The young man took a deep, audible breath through his mouth. 'On the stairs she looked round to see who was following. I was at the bottom of the stairs, and our eyes met. I'm not very confident with girls as a rule, and I didn't really expect anything, but the look she gave wasn't unfriendly. It was kind of amused, as if she'd expected one of the others to be coming after her and was pleased to find it was me instead. I knew she was foreign and couldn't speak the language and that was a help actually because I get tongue-tied when I talk to them. She was older than me by a few years and that was nice. Girls my age seem more hostile. Older women like my mother's friends say I'm nice. She wasn't as old as Mum's friends, but she was in her twenties, I should think.'

'So you began to fancy your chances?'

He fingered his tie. 'No, don't misunderstand me. I was pleased because she'd noticed me and hadn't pulled a face or something. I followed her upstairs. There were quite a number of people in the top flat, drinking and talking. I think some of them were dancing. It's quite a big room.'

'I've seen it. What did the woman do?'

'She stood for a bit, watching. She went into the kitchen, I think, and came out.'

'Was anyone with her?'

'No.'

'Are you certain of that? Did you notice a tall man in a leather jacket and jeans?'

'I wasn't looking much at the other people there. I was watching her.'

'Try and remember. It's important.'

Paternoster frowned. 'How tall do you mean?'

'Really big. Well over six foot. Large hands, wide shoulders.'

'No. I don't remember anyone like that.'

'Do you remember anyone at all, any of the guests who stood out?'

'There was a black lady, but she was talking to people as if she belonged there.'

'You're probably right about that. Sally Allardyce is black and she lives in the top flat. You said she was talking to people. Can't you picture any of them?'

'No. They must have been friends. They seemed to know each other.'

'Perhaps she was with the Treadwells, from downstairs.'

'Not Mrs Treadwell. I know her and she wasn't with them. I saw her downstairs. She was definitely downstairs.'

'You know Mrs Treadwell?'

'I've seen her in our shop.'

'She's a detectorist?'

He smiled. 'No. I know all the people in Bath who do it seriously. She came in out of interest one afternoon and looked at some books and magazines. A lot of people drop in just to see what it's about. I think they expect us to have some treasure on view.'

'How did you find out her name?'

'Saw a picture of her in the paper almost the next day with her husband. In the business section. Something about a supermarket they designed. I remembered her face.'

Diamond returned to the more pressing matter of Hildegarde Henkel. 'You were telling me how you watched the German woman.'

'Yes. She was there some time, getting on for half an hour, I'd say, and I was trying to pluck up the courage to go over to her.'

'I know the feeling.'

He was unsettled by Diamond's comment. 'Oh, but I was only wanting to let her know that not everyone in the place was unfriendly. I kept trying to catch her eye and smile or something, only she didn't look my way. Like I said before, she didn't seem to be looking at people. Then I got distracted – someone dropped a glass, I think – and when I looked up, she'd gone. I knew she hadn't left the flat, because I was by the door and, believe me, I would have noticed if she'd come that close.'

'I believe you,' Diamond said. 'So what did you do about it?'

'Well, there was a small passageway at the end with two doors leading off it. One was the bathroom. I'd heard the toilet flushing as people came out. The other room had to be the bedroom. I assumed she'd gone to the bathroom. I waited some minutes to see if she would come out, but when the door opened, it was a man. So . . . so I guessed she'd gone into the bedroom.'

'Did you follow?'

He eased a finger between his collar and his neck. 'In the end, I did.'

Diamond was almost moved to remind this wimp that he was not his mother and didn't give a damn whether he followed a woman into a bedroom at a party.

The confession resumed. 'It was dark inside. I couldn't really see much, just the shape of a large bed, and I could hear people on it. From the sounds it was obvious that they were . . .'

'Hard at it?'

'Yes. Me being there didn't make any difference to them. I was amazed.'

'That they ignored you?'

'No. What surprised me was that it happened so fast. The man must have been in there waiting for her. I haven't the faintest idea who he was.'

He had put the wrong construction on this altogether. Diamond said, 'So what did you do?'

'I came out. Left them to it. That's all I can tell you, because I walked downstairs and out of the house at that point.'

Having made the first bold decision of his life by stepping into that bedroom, the boy had been cruelly disillusioned. Humiliated, he had quit the scene. It was easy to imagine, and it rang true.

Diamond had heard all he needed. He could have thanked young Paternoster and arranged for someone else to take the statement. But some inner prompting, the memory, probably, of his own adolescent rebuffs, made him merciful. 'I think you should know that there's a second door in that bedroom. It's on the far side. You wouldn't have seen it unless you were looking for it, but I know it's there because I've seen it. You said the German woman wasn't looking at people. She'd worked out that there was an extra room – the attic room – upstairs. She looked everywhere else, and decided that the access to the attic had to be from the bedroom. I believe she found it and went up the stairs and eventually onto the roof.'

'But . . . the people on the bed.'

'Some other couple. You and I know what parties are like, Gary. We wouldn't choose someone else's house for a legover, but there's always some randy couple who will.'

'She wasn't there?'

'When you came in, she'd already found the door and gone up to the attic.'

Diamond's statement acted like a reprieve. The boy's posture altered. His face lit up. 'That never occurred to me.'

Diamond nodded. 'I'm going to get you a beer, son. A regular beer.'

He remained with the lad for some time, talking of the high expectations of women and how even a man of his experience could never hope to match their dreams. 'That's their agony, Gary, and ours. We're all trying to make the best of what we've got. They have to accept that you're not Elvis, or Bill Gates, or Jesus Christ, and if you keep talking, make them laugh a little, show them you're neither a rapist nor a rabbit, you may find one willing to stretch a point and spend some time with you.' The boy said he lacked confidence. Talking more like a best mate than the father he had not been, Diamond pointed out that the party hadn't been the personal disaster it seemed. To have faltered at the bedroom door would have been a failure. The lad had proved to himself that he was man enough to go in. Now it was just a question of some fine tuning. Trendy clothes. A different haircut. Drinking beer was a good start.

The time had not been wasted.

Twenty-three

'John, I'm setting up a murder inquiry.'

Wigfull stiffened and pressed himself back in his chair. 'This German woman?'

'No.'

'Who, then?'

'The farmer.'

'*Gladstone*?'

In a pacifying gesture, Diamond put up his palms. 'It was your case, I know, and you had it down as a suicide.'

Wigfull snatched up a manila folder. 'It's here, ready for the coroner.'

There was a moment's silence out of respect for all the work contained in the manila folder. 'As you know,' Diamond resumed, 'I was out at Tormarton the afternoon you were there. I've been back since.'

The Chief Inspector's face turned geranium red. 'You had no right.'

Diamond went on in a steady tone, neither apologetic nor triumphant, 'The first test of suicide is to make sure that the death wound was self-inflicted. I've looked at the shotgun, in its wrapper. I measured it. Have you seen it? The length, I mean. I tucked it under my chin and tried the position he is supposed to have used to blow his own brains out. I'm a larger man than old Gladstone was and I tell you, John, my fingers can't reach the trigger with my arms fully stretched. If the muzzle was in my mouth, yes, I could fire it, just. If it was against my forehead, easier still. But the cartridge went through his jaw from underneath. The little old man was physically incapable of doing that.'

Wigfull was unwilling to be persuaded. 'We found his prints on the breechblock and on the barrel.'

'But you would. The gun was his.'

'There were no other prints.'

Diamond gave him a long, unadmiring look. 'If you were handling a murder weapon, would you leave your prints on it?'

'The gun was found beside him.'

'To make it look like suicide.'

'Are you saying I'm incompetent?'

'John, for pity's sake, listen. This was set up as a suicide. It looked cut and dried. Dead man in a chair with his shotgun beside him. You saw it yourself before forensic removed the body from the scene. Difficult to reconstruct later, of course. That's the fault of the procedure. We store the gun in one place and the corpse in another and it's easy to overlook the mechanics. I'm not getting at you personally. Any of us.'

'Except you,' Wigfull said with ill-concealed resentment.

'But do you see what I'm driving at?'

'What put you onto it?'

The question signalled that Wigfull was listening to reason, and Diamond treated it with restraint. 'I couldn't understand why the ground was disturbed at the farm after Gladstone's death.'

'I knew all about that,' Wigfull waded in again, still making this an issue of personal rivalry. 'In fact I was the one who told you about it.'

'Perfectly true.'

'And I wouldn't pin too much on it,' he added, seeing a possible flaw in Diamond's reasoning. 'What was it – five days the body lay there? You can bet some evil bastard noticed that the old farmer wasn't about. Maybe they looked in and thought this was an opportunity. There were rumours Gladstone was miserly. Someone could have thought he buried his savings. If they dug a few holes, it might make them trespassers and thieves, but it doesn't make them murderers.'

'Fair point,' said Diamond. 'You may still be right about the digging. But you wanted to know what put me onto homicide as a possibility, and I'm telling you. When I see signs of a third party at the scene, I automatically think murder. It's my job. I asked myself if Gladstone's death could have been caused by the person or people who dug his land. Ran it through my mind as a faked suicide. Looked at the scene and checked the weapon. And unless the old boy had arms like an orang-utan, I'm right.'

Wigfull resigned the contest. The moustache hung over his downturned mouth like the wings of a caged vulture. 'So what was the motive? Theft?'

'That isn't clear yet. But I have a suspect.'

He sat forward, animated again. 'You do?'

Diamond's bland expression didn't alter. 'But if you don't mind, John, I'll sleep on it. Tomorrow we'll set up an incident room and a squad and I'll take them through the evidence. I expect you'll want to be in on it.'

He went to look for Julie.

She had not returned, so he ambled down to the canteen for some supper. Baked beans, bacon, fried eggs, chips and toast, with a mug of tea. 'You're a credit to us, Mr Diamond,' the manageress told him.

'Stoking up,' he said. 'Heavy session in prospect.'

It was almost eight when Julie got back to the nick.

'Have you eaten?' he asked her first.

'Not since lunch.'

'Why don't we go across to Bloomsburys? I don't think I can face the canteen tonight.' Coming from a man who was a credit to the police canteen, it was a betrayal. What a good thing the manageress didn't hear him.

Julie said, 'On one condition: that you stay off the beer.' Seeing his eyes widen at that, she explained, 'No disrespect, but you've had enough for one day if you're driving home after.'

'How do you know that?'

Her slightly raised eyebrows said enough.

Bloomsburys Café-Bar was their local, just across the street from the nick, a place with bewildering decor that amused Diamond each time he came in. Pink and green dominated and the portraits of Virginia Woolf and members of the Bloomsbury Set co-existed with non-stop TV and plastic tablecloths, lulled by rock ballads and the click of billiard balls from the games room behind the bar.

They chose a round table in a window bay. Diamond circled it first, assessing the fit of the chairs. On previous visits he'd discovered a variation in size, although they were all painted pale green. A big man had to be alert to such things. While Julie started on a chicken curry with rice and poppadom, he sampled the apple pie and custard, stared at the Diet Coke in front of him and brought her up to date on his long afternoon, recalling how he handled the shotgun, examined the church registers at Tormarton and gave advice on women to a detectorist. Unusually, he went to some trouble to explain how each experience had an impact on their investigations. In total, he said, it had been a satisfactory afternoon – and how was it for her?

Less exciting, she told him. She had started, as per instructions, by visiting Imogen Starr, the social worker, and questioning her about Doreen Jenkins, the woman who had collected Rose. In Imogen's opinion, Jenkins was an intelligent and well-disposed woman, concerned about Rose and well capable of caring for her.

'Ho-hum,' commented Diamond. 'Did you get a description from her?'

'A good one. I'll say that for Imogen: she'd make a cracking witness. She puts the woman's age at thirty or slightly younger. Height five-eight. Broad-shouldered. Healthy complexion. Regular, good-looking features, but with large cheek-bones. Good teeth, quite large. Brown eyes. Fine, chestnut brown hair worn in a ponytail. She was beautifully made-up, face, nails, the lot. White silk blouse, black leggings, black lace-up shoes. Oh, and she had a mock-leather jacket that she put on at the end and one of those large leather shoulder-bags with a zip.'

'Accent?'

'Home counties. Educated.'

'Your memory isn't so bad either. I take it that Imogen hasn't changed her opinion about this elegant dame?'

'She still believes Rose is in good hands.'

He clicked his tongue in dissent. 'And I told her myself that the Hounslow address is false.'

'She thinks it quite feasible that the family wanted to protect Rose from the press.'

'Talk about Starr. Starry-eyed,' he said.

'Inexperienced,' said Julie.

Doreen Jenkins's integrity had unravelled as Julie had got

on the trail, phoning around and checking the information. None of it had stood up to examination. Nothing was known of the family in Twickenham or Hounslow, nor of Jackie Mays, the friend who had been mentioned. Rose's mother was supposed to have got a divorce and remarried in 1972. A check of all the marriages that year of men named Black had failed to link any with a woman whose surname was Jenkins.

Doreen Jenkins and her partner Jerry were supposed to have been staying at a bed and breakfast place in Bathford. Not one of the licensed boarding houses could recall a couple staying that week and being joined later by someone of Rose's name or description.

'Ada Shaftsbury was right all the time,' Julie summed up. 'This woman was lying through her teeth.'

'Except for the photos,' he said. 'They must have been genuine to have convinced Ada as well as Imogen. They definitely showed Rose with an older woman.'

'I'd be more impressed if they'd shown Doreen Jenkins in the same picture.'

'You doubt if she's the stepsister?'

'Having spent this afternoon the way I did, I doubt everything the bloody woman said.'

Hunched over the drink, which he was taking in small sips like cough medicine, he said, 'Why then? Why all the subterfuge?'

Julie shook her head, at a loss. 'I spent the last two hours with Ada, going over everything again.'

'With Ada?'

She nodded.

He shook his head. 'You need a socking great drink.'

'And some.'

'I'll join you.' He closed his eyes and downed the last of the Diet Coke.

'In that case,' she said, 'make it Diet Cokes for both of us.'

His mouth may have turned down at the edges, but he didn't protest. Meekly he stepped back to the bar and when he returned with the drinks he told her, 'Yours has vodka added.'

She said, 'They look the same to me.'

'Colourless, isn't it?' He took a long swig of his. 'Now, Julie, I want to try out a theory on you. If it holds up, we may have a suspect for Gladstone's murder.'

Rain turning to sleet, sweeping in on an east wind, rattled the metal-framed windows of the Manvers Street building as Diamond briefed the murder squad. It was nine-twenty on Wednesday morning. Sixteen of them had assembled, most in their twenties, in leather and denim, the 'plain-clothes' that is almost a CID uniform, their hair either close-cropped or overlong. John Wigfull, the only suit in the room, sat slightly apart, closest to the door. Behind Diamond was a display board with a map of north-east Avon showing Tormarton Farm marked with a red arrow. There were several eight-by-ten photos of the scene inside the farmhouse, the corpse slumped in an armchair, the back of the head blown away, the shotgun lying on the floor. That same gun in its transparent wrapping lay across a table. Already this morning Diamond had demonstrated the impossibility of Daniel Gladstone's 'suicide'. He had talked about the digging on the farm at Tormarton and the possible motive of theft. Now he turned to another incident.

'Monday, October 3rd, about six-thirty. An elderly couple called Dunkley-Brown are driving back from Bristol to Westbury on the M4. At Junction Eighteen . . .' He took a step towards the map and touched the point. '. . . they decide to take a detour through Bath to collect a Chinese takeaway. They start down the A46 and after maybe three-quarters of a mile – before Dyrham, anyway – they are forced to brake. A young woman has wandered into the road. They can't avoid hitting her, but they think they've avoided a serious accident. She fell across the bonnet. But when they go to help her it's clear that she's lost consciousness. They try to revive her at the side of the road. This is a real dilemma for them because the man has endorsements for drunk driving and he's had a few beers during the day. They don't want to be identified. What they do is this: drive her to the nearest hospital, a private clinic, here . . .' He touched the map again. '. . . the Hinton Clinic – and dump her unconscious in the car park. But they are seen leaving the hospital and they have a Bentley with a distinctive mascot, and that's how we know as much as we do.

'The woman is found and taken into the hospital still in a coma and at this point it becomes a police matter. We send someone to the Hinton, but without much result, because although the patient is nursed back to consciousness, she is apparently suffering from a total loss of memory about her past, everything leading up to and including the accident. However, her physical injuries amount to no more than a cracked rib and some bruising and she's handed over to Bath Social Services. We send a photographer to get some pics of the damage. Screen, please.'

One of the squad unfurled the screen on the front wall. Diamond switched on a slide-projector and the back view of a naked woman appeared and was hailed with approving noises by the largely male audience. Julie Hargreaves shook her head at the juvenile reaction, but they quietened down when Diamond pointed out the cuts and bruising on the thighs and legs. The next slide, a frontal shot, still got a few rutting sounds, if more muted than before. The woman on the screen had attractive breasts and a trim waist, yet her discomfort at being photographed was evident in the pose.

'That's the end of the floorshow, gentlemen.'

Some good-humoured dissent was heard.

Diamond slotted in another slide, a close-up of the woman's face, and left it on the screen while he told the story of Rose's short stay at Harmer House, eventually concluding it with: '. . . and after she is collected by the woman claiming to be her stepsister, we hear no more of her. Nobody hears a dickybird, not Social Services, not Ada, not the Old Bill.'

The room had gone silent except for the steady drumming of the rain. To a murder squad, the disappearance of a woman is ominous.

'What is more,' Diamond added, 'nothing holds up in the stepsister's story. Julie spent most of yesterday checking.' He paused and looked at the tense, troubled face on the screen. 'It's already two weeks since she was collected. We thought we knew her name and background, but we can't be sure of it any more. We'll continue to call her Rose. Take a long look. She's top priority. We've got to find her.'

He made eye contact with Julie. 'DI Hargreaves is in charge of the search.'

He turned back to the map. 'Now, look at this, the point on the A46, here, where she wanders into the road out of nowhere, the first anyone has heard of her. It's not a great distance from Tormarton, is it? Not a great distance from Daniel Gladstone's farm.' He spanned it roughly with his outstretched forefinger and thumb. 'Two miles at most. Think about that, will you? And think about when it happened, Monday, October 3rd. Curious, isn't it, that the Friday previous is the pathologist's best estimate of the old farmer's date of death?'

'You think she killed him, sir?' someone asked.

Diamond faced the screen, saying nothing.

'How could she?' one of the younger detectives asked. 'You'd need two people. One to pull the trigger and the other to hold the old bloke still.'

Another chipped in. 'Bloody risky, holding his head over a shotgun. I wouldn't do it. You could get your face blown away, easy.'

'What you do,' said Keith Halliwell, the longest-serving member of the squad, 'is tie him to the chair first.'

'You think a woman trussed him up?'

'No problem. He was seventy-plus. Did you look at her physique?'

'Well . . .'

'Keith did,' said a mocking voice. 'Keefy likes 'em beefy.'

Diamond swung around, glaring at the unfortunate who had spoken. 'Oh, dead funny. Why don't you come up here and do your act from the front? We'll all club together, buy a red nose and a whoopee cushion and get you into show business.' With silence reinstated, he said, 'Someone asked if I think Rose killed the farmer. I was coming to that.' He let them stew for another interval while he walked across to the window and looked at the rain. 'Yes. It's a possibility. She was in the area at approximately the time he was killed. Very approximately. The pathologist will tell you we're dealing in rough figures here. A couple of days either side. So let's not get carried away. However—' He paused to wipe some condensation from the window. '—if the loss of memory is genuine, it will have been caused by some deeply stressful, traumatic event. And not just concussion from the accident. That's different. You don't lose your long-term memory from a bump on the head. This woman is suffering from acute neurosis. The scene in that farmhouse was scary enough to throw anyone's mind off beam. True, it seems to have been a cold-blooded execution, but the effect of that shotgun blasting the back of old Gladstone's skull off may have been more of a shock to the killer than she expected. Enough to suppress her memory and wipe out her own identity. And for those of you thinking I know sod-all about traumatic disorders, I did consult a couple of textbooks. There have been cases like it.

'And now you're going to ask me about a motive and I can't tell you one because I don't know who the woman is. But the possibilities are there. You can say she hates him because of something evil he did in the past, like abusing her when she was a child, or raping her mother. Or she could be the cold-blooded sort, after his savings. She may be mad, of course.'

'She may have no connection with the case,' said Julie unexpectedly.

Diamond stopped for a moment as if Julie's words were being played back to him. Then he turned to face her. 'I thought I made that clear. This is just a hypothesis.'

'So long as we don't lose sight of it,' she said.

The strains were showing. 'So you think she's a red herring?'

'No, Mr Diamond, I'm agreeing with you that she's got to be found. She may be dangerous, as you say, more dangerous than she herself realises. Or she may be *in* danger. I spent most of yesterday checking out the woman who took her away and finding everything she said is bogus, so you'll understand why I see it this way. I got used to thinking of Rose as a victim, not a villain. Just another hypothesis.'

He drew himself back from the brink. He'd given Julie the job yesterday, the kind of research she did so well, systematically uncovering the deception. Moreover, she'd been exposed for a couple of hours to Ada's anxieties about the missing woman. Was it any wonder that she took a different line?

'Thanks, Julie. Point taken.' He pitched his voice to the entire room again. 'I propose to bring in the press at this stage. I'm issuing this picture of the missing woman with the few real facts we know about her. For public consumption we're appealing for information because there's concern for her safety. Understood? Julie, you'd better warn Social Services to be ready for some flak over this.' He crossed the room and switched off the projector. 'We'll also go public on the killing of Daniel Gladstone. It's going to make large headlines, I'm afraid. The execution-style killing of an old man is sure to excite the tabloids. For the time being we'll treat the incidents as unrelated. Let's see what the publicity brings in. And of course it's all systems go on the murder inquiry. Keith, would you set up the incident room here? Frank, you're in charge of the hunt for Rose Black. Jerry, the farmer's background is your job. His life history – family, work, the state of his finances, the lot. I can give you some pointers if you see me presently.' He went on assigning duties for several minutes more. This had always been one of his strengths, instilling urgency into an inquiry.

After Diamond had left the room, Keith Halliwell put a hand on Julie's shoulder. 'You've got more guts than the rest of us, kiddo, speaking out like that.'

She shook her head. 'I knew what was coming. Had more time to think it over.'

'What do you reckon?' he asked. 'Has the old buzzard flipped?

'In what way?'

'Picking on this woman as a suspect. Can you see a woman trussing up an old man and firing a shotgun at his head?'

'I don't see why not,' she answered, sensitive to the discrimination. 'Any fit woman is capable of it.'

He shrugged. 'But would they carry it out? Don't you think it's too brutal?'

'It's a question of motivation.'

'Unlikely, though.' He stretched and yawned. 'He made such a brilliant start, too, all that stuff about the shotgun. No one else in CID would have sussed that it was murder. John Wigfull didn't, and he was supposed to be handling the case.'

Julie declined the invitation to rubbish Wigfull.

Halliwell continued to fret about Diamond's startling theory. 'I mean, all he's got on the woman is that she was in the area – well, a couple of miles away – at the time of the killing, give or take a few days.'

'Behaving strangely.'

'Okay. Give you that.'

'With loss of memory. And then she gets spirited away by someone telling a heap of lies.'

He laughed. 'I should have known you'd back the old sod.'

'The thing is,' Julie said, 'he's not often wrong.'

Part Three

a Bag of Gold

Twenty-four

John Wigfull was pencil thin and a brisk mover, so Diamond was breathless when he finally drew level on the stairs.

'A word in your ear, John.'

Wigfull stopped with one leg bent like a wading bird. He didn't turn to look.

Diamond spoke more than a word into the ear. 'I didn't mention this in the meeting, but I need to take over any exhibits you picked up at the scene. Gladstone's personal papers. Prints, fibres, hairs. Can I take it that the Sellotapers went through the farmhouse?'

'Sellotapers?'

'The scenes of crime lads.'

'SOCOs.'

Diamond nodded. Something deep in his psyche balked at using the acronyms accepted by everyone else in the police. 'I was sure you must have called them out, even though it looked like a routine suicide.'

'A suspicious death. I know the drill.'

'I never doubted.'

There was a glint in Wigfull's eye. 'Forensic had a field day. The place hadn't been swept or dusted in months. The bloodstains alone are a major task. So if you're looking for results, you may have to wait a while.'

'I'll check with them.'

'You could try.'

'Is the rest of the stuff with you?'

'Yes. You can have it. Is that all?' The bent leg started to move again.

'Not quite. There's the question of the other inquiry, into Hildegarde Henkel's death.'

Wigfull turned to look at Diamond. 'What about it?'

'Difficult for me to manage at the same time as the Tormarton case.'

Wigfull's eyebrows reared up like caterpillars meeting. 'You want me to take it back?'

'I do and I don't. It could well be another murder.'

'Work under your direction?'

'I know. You'd rather have a seat in a galley-ship. Listen, all I want is a watching brief. You tell me what progress you make and I won't interfere. We've had our differences, but, sod it, John, you ran the squad when I was away.'

'I'm not saying I couldn't do it.'

'Shall we square it with the boss, then?'

'Would you give me a free hand?'

Diamond swallowed hard.

'And a team?'

'The pick of the squad, other than Keith and Julie.'

Thoughtfully Wigfull preened the big moustache. This was an undeniable opportunity.

'I could have taken on that job,' said Julie when he told her.

'I know.'

'Well, then?' Her blue eyes fixed him accusingly.

'I need you on this one.'

'Nobody would think so.'

'Why do you say that?'

'You assigned responsibilities to practically everyone else.'

'I don't want you tied down. That's the reason.'

She was unconvinced, certain he was punishing her for speaking out of turn in the meeting. He always expected her to back him, or at least keep quiet. He was so pig-headed that he didn't know most of the squad agreed he was way off beam when he linked Rose Black to the murder.

Oblivious to all this, he said, 'These stories that the old man had money tucked away – I'd like to know if there's any foundation for them. Would you get on to it, Julie? Find out if he had a bank account. He must have received the Old Age Pension. What did he do with it?'

In front of him was the deed-box that Wigfull had removed from the farmhouse. 'There's precious little here. His birth certificate. Believe it or not, his mother gave birth to him in that squalid house.'

'Perhaps it wasn't so squalid in the nineteen-twenties. Do we know when the parents died?'

'There's nothing in here about it. Some Ministry of Agriculture pamphlets he should have slung out years ago. Remember the Colorado Beetle scares? A parish magazine dated August, 1953. Instructions for a vacuum cleaner – much use he made of that. And some out-of-date supermarket offers.'

'I expect the parents are buried in the churchyard.'

'Probably. Is that any use to us?'

'I suppose not. May I see the box?'

Diamond pushed it across to her. 'Be my guest. I want to put a call through to Chepstow. It's high time I fired a broadside at forensic.'

While he was on the phone demanding to be put through to the people carrying out the work on the Tormarton samples, Julie sifted through the papers. She took out the old parish magazine and skimmed the contents. The Church was St Mary Magdalene, Tormarton. In a short time she discovered why Daniel Gladstone had kept this copy. Towards the back was a section headed 'Valete', a list of recent deaths, and among them appeared Jacob Gladstone, 1881–1953. A few lines recorded his life:

> Jacob Gladstone, farmer, of Marton Farm, passed away last January 8th, of pneumonia. A widower, he lived all his life in the parish. For many years he served as sidesman. In September, 1943, Mr Gladstone unearthed the Anglo-Saxon sword known as the Tormarton Seax, and now in the British Museum. He is survived by his beloved son Daniel.'

Julie read it again. She leaned back in her chair, absorbing the information. If Gladstone's father had made an archaeological find during the war, perhaps it had some bearing on the case. Eager for more information, she scanned the rest of the magazine and found only a piece about the meaning of Easter, written by the vicar, and reports on the Mothers' Union and the Youth Club.

Diamond was still sounding off to Chepstow about the urgency of his inquiry. Through sheer bullying he had got through to someone actually at work on the case. He stressed several times that this was now upgraded to a murder, and surely it warranted a higher priority. 'Can't you even give me some preliminary findings?' he appealed to the hapless scientist on the end of the line. 'Like what? Well, like whether anything so far suggests the presence of someone else in the farmhouse. You don't have to tell me it was a Welsh-speaking Morris-dancer with size nine shoes and a birthmark on his left buttock. I'll settle for anyone at all at this stage.' He rolled his eyes at Julie while listening. 'Right, now we're getting somewhere,' he said presently. 'Two, you say, definitely not the farmer's. What colour? . . . Brown? Well, you could have told me that at the outset. Male or female? . . . How long? . . . Yes, I understand . . . No, we won't. We're not exactly new in this game . . . Thanks. And sooner if you can.' He slammed down the phone.

Julie looked up.

'They have two hairs from the scene that didn't belong to the victim,' he summed up. 'Brown, three to four inches. They warned me that there's no way of telling how they got there. They could have come from some visitor weeks before the murder. They're doing some kind of test that breaks down the elements in the hair.'

'NAA,' said Julie.

'Come again.'

'Neutron Activation Analysis.'

'Sorry I asked.'

'It was part of that course I did at Chepstow last year. You can find up to fourteen elements in a single inch of hair. If you isolate as many as nine, the chance of two people having the same concentration is a million to one.'

'Could be that,' he said grudgingly. 'But it's the usual story. What it comes down to is that whatever the result it's bugger-all use without a hair from the suspect to match.'

She shrugged. 'We can hardly expect them to analyse a hair and tell us the name of the person it came from.'

He grinned. 'Take all the fun out of the job, wouldn't it?'

She showed him the piece in the magazine and it was as

if the sun had just come out. 'Good spotting,' he said when he'd studied it. 'His old dad had his fifteen minutes of fame, then. The Tormarton Seax.'

Julie said, 'Thinking about those holes—'

'Yes,' he said. 'I was thinking about them. If there was a sword buried on the site, there could have been more stuff. And someone may have done some excavating.'

'Wouldn't they have organised a dig in 1943 when it was found? I can't imagine anything of interest would be left.'

'Of value, Julie. Bugger the interest.' He glanced at the page again. 'Well, this was the middle of the Second World War. People had other things on their minds than Anglo-Saxon swords. I reckon archaeology took a back seat.'

'But later, when the war ended, wouldn't they have wanted to explore the site?'

'Possibly. It seems nothing else was found, or it would have got mentioned here. I just don't know. What happens if the landowner doesn't want a bunch of university students scraping at his soil for weeks on end? By all accounts, Daniel Gladstone wasn't the friendliest farmer in these parts. If his dad was equally obstructive, it's quite on the cards that nobody ever followed up the find.'

'Until just recently.'

'Right.'

'It could explain the digging.'

'It could, Julie.' He closed the magazine and tossed it back into the deed-box. 'Do you know, I've thought of someone who may throw some light on this.'

Down in the reception area, the desk sergeant was under siege.

'If you won't let me through,' Ada Shaftsbury told him, 'I'll go straight out to the car park and stand on top of his car. I know which one it is. He'll soon come running when he looks out the window and sees his roof cave in.'

'Mr Diamond isn't dealing with it any more,' the sergeant explained for the second time. 'He's on another case.'

'Don't give me that crock of shit.'

'Madam—'

'Ada.'

'Ada, if you've got something material to say, I'll make a note of it. There are other people waiting now.'

'If gutso isn't dealing with it, who is?'

'Another officer in CID.'

'Well, is it a secret, or something?'

'I don't suppose you've heard of him.'

'Try me. I know everyone in this cruddy place. I spend half my life here.'

'I know that, Ada. Chief Inspector Wigfull has taken over.'

She grimaced. 'Him with the big tash. God help us!'

'Now if you'll kindly move aside . . .'

'I'll have a word with Wigfull, then.'

'We'll tell him you called.'

'You won't. You'll take me to see him pronto. I have important information to impart.'

At this sensitive moment the interior door opened and Peter Diamond stepped into the reception area on his way out.

'Mr Diamond!' Ada practically embraced him.

'Can't see you now, Ada. I'm on an emergency.'

'Is it true you're off the case?'

'What case?'

'The missing woman, my friend Rose.'

He said with deliberate obtuseness, 'I'm dealing with a murder. An old man. Right?'

Ada said bitterly, 'Nobody bloody cares. You've written her off, haven't you? She's off your list. They moved a new woman in last night. It's like she never existed. And how about poor little Hilde?'

He crossed the floor and went through the door, leaving Ada still defiantly at the head of the queue. She would presently get upstairs to torment Wigfull, he thought with amusement. Offloading the Royal Crescent case had been a wise decision. But halfway up Manvers Street he grasped the significance of something Ada had said. If they had moved a new woman into Rose's room at Harmer House, they must have vacuumed it and changed the bed-linen. Any chance of obtaining a sample of Rose's hair from that source had gone. The smile vanished.

*   *   *

Young Gary Paternoster was alone behind the counter in the shop called the Treasure House when Diamond entered. He dropped the book he was reading and stood up guiltily. He was still wearing the suit, but a yellow tie with a palm tree design held promise that some of the previous day's man-to-man advice had sunk in.

It was Diamond's first experience of a detectorists' shop. They had designed it to excite the customer with murals of gold and silver objects half submerged in sand. There was a real wooden chest open in one corner and filled with fake treasure picked out by a spotlight. But most of the space was taken up with metal detectors with their special selling-points listed. 'Silent search', 'deep penetration' and 'accurate discrimination' were the qualities most touted. You would need to make some major finds to justify the prices, Diamond decided. There was also a stand with books, magazines and maps.

'Relax, Gary,' Diamond told the quaking youth. 'I'm not here to make an arrest. I want to tap your expert knowledge. Have you ever heard of the Tormarton Seax?'

The question took some time to make contact. Mentally, Paternoster was still in the bedroom at the Royal Crescent. 'It's a sword, isn't it? In the British Museum.'

'Right. I don't expect you to have its history off pat. It was found in the war by a farmer up at Tormarton, north of where the motorway is now.'

'I know,' he said. 'It's a place where detectorists go.'

'The farm?'

'Not the farm. No one's ever been allowed on the farm. I mean the general area. It was the border between two ancient kingdoms, Mercia and Wessex, so there were skirmishes. And there was the great battle in the sixth century.'

Where had he heard this, about Mercia and Wessex? From the vicar, explaining the derivation of Tormarton's name. 'What great battle?'

'Between the Saxons and the Britons. The Saxon army was fighting its way west for years, across the Berkshire Downs and to the south as well. This was the decisive battle. Hardly anybody knows about it these days, but it was just as important to our history as Hastings. It was the one that made modern England. If you've got a minute, there's a book on the stand.'

Diamond wasn't sure how much he needed to know of sixth-century history, but he was going to get some. Young Paternoster was fired up.

'Here it is. "As the Anglo-Saxon Chronicle tells us, in 577 Cuthwine and Ceawlin fought against the Britons and killed three kings, Conmail, Condidan and Farinmail, at the place called Dyrham, and they captured three of their cities, Gloucester, Cirencester and Bath."'

'At Dyrham, it says?'

'A mile or so south-west of Tormarton, actually. "The West Saxons, under the command of their king, Ceawlin, cut the Bath to Cirencester Road, the A46, as it is now, and camped a little to the west, at Hinton Hill Fort."'

'Hinton, I've heard of.'

'"The Britons had assembled three armies, two from the north and the other from the south, and they sensibly combined forces, but this required strenuous manoeuvres to avoid being picked off separately by the Saxons. It is likely that their fighters were exhausted and dispirited before the battle. Moreover, they made the tactical error of trying to attack the well-defended Saxon army by pushing up the hill. They suffered a massive defeat. Wessex was established in the south-west, and the Britons retreated to Cornwall and Wales."'

'Stirring stuff,' said Diamond. 'So what can you tell me about the Tormarton sword? Was that thrown down by some unlucky fellow who copped his lot?'

'I doubt if it was ever used in battle. I think it was partly made of silver, with some precious stones inlaid in the hilt, the kind of sword a nobleman owned as a symbol of his power. I guess it belonged to an important Saxon. Let's see if there's anything about it in these other books. *Anglo-Saxon Artefacts* should mention it.' He took another book off the stand and turned to the index.

'It's here. With a picture.' He found the page and handed Diamond the book.

It was a colour photograph of a short, single-bladed sword with its scabbard displayed beside it. 'The Tormarton Seax, unearthed on farmland in North-West Wiltshire in 1943,' the caption read. 'This Frankish design came into use in England during the seventh century. The pommel is decorated with garnets set in silver, probably worked by a Frankish silversmith. The scabbard is also of silver. Acquired by the British Museum.'

'Handsome,' said Diamond.

'But seventh century,' Paternoster pointed out. 'Well after the Battle of Dyrham. By then Tormarton was firmly in Saxon hands.'

'So what do you reckon, Gary? How did it get in the ground?'

'Difficult to say. Sometimes when people were being invaded or attacked, they buried valuable things to keep them safe, meaning to dig them up again later. If that was what happened, the sword should have been declared Treasure Trove, and the British Museum would have paid the farmer its market value. If it was buried in a grave, it belonged to the landowner. He might sell it to the Museum, but he could bargain for a better price than the valuation.'

'Either way, he makes some money.'

'Unless he decided to keep the treasure. If it isn't Treasure Trove, he's entitled to hang onto it.'

'How do they decide?'

'By inquest, so it's up to the coroner and his jury. They have to try and work out why it was buried. If it's found in a situation that is obviously a grave, there's no argument. It belongs to the landowner.'

'How can anyone tell? I suppose if it's lying beside a skeleton.'

'Archaeologists can usually tell. The difficulty comes with isolated finds.'

'Was this an isolated find?'

Paternoster shrugged. 'I've never heard of anything else turning up there. But to my knowledge the farm has never been searched or excavated. If the owner doesn't want you there, there's nothing you can do, and he's said to be dead against us. He's been asked many times. People like me can't wait to get up there with our detectors.'

'How does it work?' Diamond asked.

'Detectoring?'

'I understand the principle, but what do you do exactly?'

The young man started to speak with genuine authority. 'First you have to get the farmer's permission, and like I say that isn't so easy. I offer fifty-fifty on any finds, but we're still just a nuisance to some of them. Obviously I wouldn't ask if the field has just been sown. And a freshly ploughed field isn't ideal because of the furrows, you see. It's better when the soil is flatter, because more coins lie within range of your detector. So I like a harrowed field to work in.'

'Do you find much in fields?'

'Not so much as in parks or commons where people go more often, but what you find is more interesting.'

'Such as?'

'Silver medieval coins. My average is one every two or three hours. I've also found ring-brooches, buckles and bits of horse-harness.'

'In bare fields?'

'You've got to remember that in centuries past hundreds of people worked those fields. It was far more labour-intensive then than it is these days, with so much farm machinery.'

Diamond picked up one of the detectors and felt its weight. 'What's your most powerful model?'

'The two-box. This one over here. It's designed for people searching for hoards, rather than small items like single coins.' He picked up a contraption with two sensors separated by a metre-length bar. 'It can signal substantial amounts of metal at some depth, say six feet. The trouble is, you have to be prepared to do an awful lot of digging and possibly find something no more exciting than a buried oil-drum or a tractor-part.'

The two-box was a source of much interest for Diamond. He could see a plausible explanation for the digging at the farm. If some treasure-hunter had ambitions of finding a hoard, the most promising site, surely, would be one that had already yielded a famous find, and the best machine for the job was the two-box. And if the site-owner was a stubborn old farmer who steadfastly refused to allow anyone on his land, the first opportunity would have come after his death.

Was it, he wondered, sufficient motive for murder?

'Have you sold any of these things in the last year or so?'

'Two-boxes? No. This hasn't been in the shop long.'

'Can people hire them?'

'I suppose we might come to an agreement, but we haven't up to now.'

'You just have, Gary. I'll send someone to collect it.'

Twenty-five

'Up and running,' Keith Halliwell announced with some pride.

Nobody was quicker than Halliwell at furnishing an incident room. Phones, radio-communications, computers and filing cabinets were in place. The photos and maps from the briefing session were rearranged on an end wall. Two civilian computer operators were keying information into the system. Having ordered all this, Diamond could not allow himself to be intimidated by it, even though he was a computer-illiterate. He mumbled some words of appreciation to Halliwell and even dredged up a joke about hardware: he hadn't seen so much since his last visit to the ironmonger's. The younger people didn't seem to know what an ironmonger's was, so it fell flat. Then he spotted Julie sitting with a phone against her ear. He went over. Telephones he could understand.

'Who are you on to?'

She put her hand over the mouthpiece. 'Acton Turville Post Office. Gladstone used to collect his pension from there. They're checking dates.'

'When you come off . . .'

She nodded, and started speaking into the phone again.

In the act of moving towards the sergeant who was handling press liaison, Diamond caught his foot under a cable and cut off the power supply to the computers.

'Who the blazes did that?' said one of the civilian women when her screen whistled and went blank. She was new to the murder squad.

'I did, madam,' he told her. 'I almost fell into your lap. Next time lucky.'

'You great oaf.' Clearly she had no idea who she was addressing.

Halliwell zoomed over to prevent a dust-up. 'I should have warned you, sir.'

'About this abusive woman?'

'About the cable. It needs a strip of gaffer tape.'

'Bugger the cable,' said Diamond. 'She thinks you should tape the gaffer.'

'His mouth, for starters,' said the woman, before it dawned on her who this great oaf was.

With timing that just prevented mayhem, Julie finished on the phone and called across, 'He last drew his pension on September 18th.'

'In cash?'

'He used to cycle in to Acton Turville once a week. He'd do some shopping and then cycle back.'

Stepping more carefully than before, he moved between the desks to where Julie was. 'Didn't anyone notice when he stopped coming in?'

'Sometimes he would let it mount up for two or three weeks. People do.'

'How would he manage for shopping?'

'Tinned food, I suppose. The chickens supplied him with eggs. And another thing, Mr Diamond. I've called all the local banks and building societies and none of them had any record of him as an account-holder.'

He glanced up at the clock. 'What time is my press conference?'

'Two-fifteen, sir,' the press liaison sergeant told him. 'The hand-outs are ready if you want to see them. Everyone gets a head-and-shoulders of Rose.'

He scanned the press release. 'Fine.' He turned back to Julie. 'There's time for you to drive me out to Westbury. A pub lunch with the double-barrels.'

'The who?'

'Dunkley-something. The people who ran into Rose on the A46. Oh, and there will be another passenger, a scene of crime officer.'

The ex-mayor and his lady were, as Diamond anticipated, having a liquid lunch at the Westbury Hotel. The barmaid pointed them out at one of the tables under the Spy cartoons, a grinning, gnome-ish man opposite a dark-haired woman wearing enough mascara for a chorus-line.

'We'll leave you here at the bar,' Diamond said quietly to Jim Marsh, the SOCO he had recruited for this exercise. 'What are you drinking?'

'It had better be a grapefruit juice, sir.'

'God help us. What are you – a blood-pressure case?'

'I'm working, sir,'

The affable mood at the table changed dramatically when Diamond announced who he was and introduced Julie.

The gnome, Ned Dunkley-Brown, reddened and said, 'I told you we hadn't heard the last of it, Pippa. All that malarkey about things spoken in confidence.'

His wife said, 'Ned, I think we should hear what they have to say.' She gave Diamond a patronising stare. 'My husband is an ex-mayor of Bradford on Avon. He served on the police committee.'

'But that was Wiltshire County,' said Dunkley-Brown. 'These officers are from Bath.'

'Avon and Somerset,' she corrected him.

'Now we've got that straight,' Diamond said, under some strain to stay civil with this couple, 'I'd like to hear about the evening you had the accident on the A46. That's inside our boundary, by the way.'

'Accident?' shrilled Pippa Dunkley-Brown, folding her thin arms.

'Don't say another word,' Dunkley-Brown commanded his wife. 'No comment.'

Diamond took a long, therapeutic swig of beer. 'We're not from Traffic Division, sir. We're CID. People's mistakes at the wheel are someone else's pigeon.'

The Dunkley-Browns exchanged looks.

'We're investigating the young woman you met that evening. Called herself Rose.'

'Oh, yes?' said Dunkley-Brown in a faraway tone.

'She's a mystery all round. Lost her memory, or so she claimed. And now she's missing.'

Pippa Dunkley-Brown was still coming to terms with an earlier statement. 'What do you mean – "mistakes at the wheel"? There was no question of a mistake.'

'Leave it,' said Dunkley-Brown through his teeth. The training in local politics took over as he diverted along the safer avenue. 'Missing, you say. But she was in here speaking to us, with a large woman.'

'Ada Shaftsbury, yes. Rose hasn't been seen since the day you spoke to them.'

Julie put in quickly, 'We're not accusing you of anything.'

'I should damned well hope not!' said the wife.

Indifferent to the mood of mild hysteria, Diamond explained patiently, 'We're retracing Rose's movements, as far as they're known. It all started with you meeting her on the road and transporting her to the hospital. We don't know anything about her before that evening.'

'Nor do we,' said Dunkley-Brown. 'She was unconscious.'

'Unconscious when she walked into the road?'

'Not then, but after. We didn't get a word out of her. We took her to the nearest hospital.'

'Hospital car park.' In spite of his efforts Diamond was getting increasingly irritated with this couple.

Julie said, 'Did she appear to be waving you down?'

'She put up her arms,' said Dunkley-Brown, 'but she was out in the road by then.'

'Lunacy,' said his wife.

He added, 'Anyone would raise an arm if a car was bearing down on them.'

'We weren't speeding,' said she.

'It's dark along that stretch,' said he.

'So you slammed on the brakes,' said Diamond.

'And tried to avoid her,' said the husband. 'We skidded a bit to the right. By the time we hit her, the car was virtually at a standstill. It nudged her off balance and I suppose she took a bump on the head.' He made it sound like an incident in a bouncy-castle.

'She was unconscious,' Diamond reminded him.

'Yes, so we did our best to revive her at the side of the road, and when it was obvious that we weren't going to be successful, we lifted her into the car—'

'The back seat?'

'Yes.'

'Lying across the seat?'

'Propped up against one corner really.'

Diamond sat forward, interested. 'Which side was her head? The nearside?'

'The left, yes. After that we drove her to the Hinton Clinic. She was very soon taken in, I understand.'

'But you'd already pissed off out of it.'

'That's offensive,' said Pippa.

'Pippa phoned a day or so later to enquire about her,' Dunkley-Brown was anxious to stress. 'The people at the hospital said she was so much better that she'd been discharged. We assumed she'd made a full recovery.'

'Very reassuring.'

'We didn't know about her loss of memory.'

Diamond finished his beer. 'We'd like to look at your car. Is it back at the house?'

The colour drained from Dunkley-Brown's face. 'But you said you weren't here to inquire into the accident.'

'As a traffic offence, it doesn't concern me, sir. As an incident involving a missing person, it does. Do you see the tall man at the bar drinking fruit juice? He's trained to look for evidence. He can back up your story by examining the car.'

'But we've been perfectly frank.'

'No problem, then. Shall we go?'

'Do you use it much, Mr Dunkley-Brown?' Diamond asked after the Bentley had been backed out of the garage for inspection.

'Not a great deal these days. If we go to the pub, we tend to walk. It's exercise, which is good at our age, and we can enjoy a couple of drinks without being breathalysed.'

'Shopping?'

'We do use the car for that, but it's only a trip to the local supermarket.'

'We'll join you presently, then,' Diamond said. 'DI Hargreaves wouldn't mind a coffee if your wife would oblige.' When Dunkley-Brown was out of earshot he told the SOCO. 'If nothing else, find me some long, dark hairs on the nearside of the back seat and you're on for a double Scotch.'

* * *

When Jim Marsh came in to report that he'd finished his examination of the car, he didn't have the look of a man who has just earned a double Scotch.

'No joy?' said Diamond.

'It's been vacuumed inside,' said the SOCO, 'and very thoroughly.'

Diamond turned to look at Dunkley-Brown. 'Is that a fact?'

A shrug and a smile. 'There's no law against Hoovering one's car, is there?'

'I know why you did it.'

'You may well be right, Mr Diamond. We'd have been fools to have left any evidence of the girl there.'

'May we see your Hoover?'

'Certainly, only at the risk of upsetting you I'd better admit that we emptied the dust-bag right away. It was collected by the dustmen the same week.'

Diamond was not at his best during the drive back to Bath. Not a word was said about the abortive search of the Bentley's interior. Nothing much at all was said. Each of them knew how essential it was to find a sample of Rose's hair. Diamond's far-from-convincing theory linking her to Gladstone's murder could only be taken seriously if the hairs found at the farmhouse were proved to be hers. The idea behind the trip to Westbury had been an inspiration, but unhappily inspirations sometimes come to nothing.

He rallied his spirits for the press conference, held in a briefing room downstairs at Manvers Street. He needed to be sharp. His purpose in talking to the media was simply to step up the hunt for Rose. He didn't intend to link her disappearance to any other crime. However, he was meeting a pack of journalists, and the modern generation of hacks were all too quick to make connections. Their first reaction would be that the head of the murder squad wouldn't waste time on a missing woman unless he expected her to be found dead. From there, it was a short step to questioning him about other recent deaths: Daniel Gladstone and possibly Hildegarde Henkel. These same press people had reported the finding of the bodies. It was all too fresh in their memories.

He handled the session adeptly, keeping Rose steadily in the frame. It was obvious from the questions that Social Services would be in for some stick. They were used to being in the front line. Poor buggers, they came in for more criticism than any other organisation.

He was about to wrap up when the inevitable question came, from a young, angelic-featured woman with a ring through her right nostril. Nothing made him feel the generation-gap more than this craze for body piercing. 'Would you comment on the possible connection with the death of the German woman, Hildegarde Henkel, at the Royal Crescent?'

He was ready. 'I'd rather not. That case is being handled by another officer.'

'Who is that, please?'

'DCI Wigfull.'

'But you were seen up at the Crescent at the weekend. You made more than one visit.'

'That's correct. I'm now on another case. If that's all, ladies and gentlemen . . .'

She was persistent. 'It may be another case, Mr Diamond, but you must have taken note that the missing woman Rose was staying in Harmer House at the same time as Ms Henkel.'

'Yes.'

'There were only three women staying in the hostel,' she said evenly, watching for his reaction, 'and one of them is missing and one is dead.'

'I wouldn't read too much into that if I were you. Harmer House is used as a temporary refuge for people in the care of Social Services. Some of them are sure to be unstable, or otherwise at risk.'

She had thought this through. 'There was a superficial similarity between Rose and Hildegarde Henkel. Dark, short hair. Slim. Aged in their twenties. Is it true that there was speculation at the weekend that the body at the Royal Crescent was that of Rose?'

'If there was,' answered Diamond evenly, 'it was unfounded. I don't really see what you're driving at.'

'I thought it was obvious. You've made no announcement about the cause of Ms Henkel's death.'

'She fell off the roof.' The slick answer tripped off his tongue, but even as he spoke it, he knew he shouldn't have. Several voices chorused with questions.

'I'm answering the lady,' he said, and provoked some good-natured abuse from her professional colleagues.

She was not thrown in the least. 'The fall is not in doubt, Mr Diamond. The question is whether she fell by accident or by design, and when I say by design I mean by her design or someone else's. In other words, suicide or murder.'

He gave a shrug. 'That's for a coroner's jury to decide.'

'Come on,' she chided him. 'That's a cop-out, if ever I heard one.'

This scored a laugh and cries of 'cop-out' from several of the press corps.

He wanted an out and he couldn't find one without arousing universal suspicion that he hadn't been honest with them.

She wasn't going to leave it. She said, 'If it was murder, have you considered the possibility that Ms Henkel was killed by mistake because she resembled Rose, the other woman, and they lived at the same address? If so, you must be extremely concerned, about the safety of Rose.'

The opening was there, and he took it. 'Of course we're concerned, regardless of this hypothesis of yours. That's why I called this conference. We're grateful for any information about Rose. The co-operation of all of you in publicising the case is appreciated.' He nodded across the room, avoiding the wide blue eyes of his inquisitor, and then quit the room fast.

'Who was she?' he asked the press sergeant.

'Ingeborg Smith. She's a freelance, doing a piece on missing women for one of the colour supplements, she says.'

'If she ever wants a job on the murder squad, she can have it.'

He sought out Julie, and found her in the incident room. 'When you spoke to Ada yesterday, did she say anything about the press?'

'She may have done. She did go on a bit.'

'She went on a bit to a newshound who goes under the name of Ingeborg Smith, unless I'm mistaken.'

'What about?'

'The possibility that Hilde was killed in error by someone who confused her with Rose.'

Julie said, 'It sounds like Ada talking, I agree.' She picked up the phone-pad. 'There's a large package waiting for you in reception.'

'That'll be my two-box. I'll leave it there for the present.'

'Your what?'

'Two-box.'

'It sounds slightly indelicate.'

'Wait till you see it in action. Has anything else of interest come in?'

She made the mistake of saying, 'It's early days.'

'What?' His face had changed.

'I mean all this was only set up a couple of hours ago.'

'All this?' He flapped his arm in the general direction of the computers. 'You think this is going to work some miracle? We've got a corpse that was rotting at the scene for a week and you tell me it's early days. The only conceivable suspect has vanished without trace. Forensic have gone silent. Julie, a roomful of screens and phones isn't going to trap an old man's killer.'

'It can help.'

He turned and looked at the blow-up of Rose's face pinned to the corkboard. 'What I need above all else is to get a hair of her head. One hair.'

Julie said nothing. They both knew that the best chance had gone when Rose's room at the hostel was cleared for another inmate. Dunkley-Brown's car had been a long shot that had missed.

He wouldn't leave it. 'Let's go over her movements. She's driven to the Hinton Clinic in the Bentley, but we know that's a dead pigeon. The people at the Clinic put her to bed.'

'Three weeks ago,' said Julie. 'They'll have changed and laundered the bedding since then – or it's not the kind of private hospital I'd want to stay in.'

'Two dead pigeons. They send her to Harmer House, and that's another one.'

'Just a minute,' said Julie. 'How did she get there?'

'To Harmer House? That social worker – Imogen – collected her.'

'In a car?'

'Well, they wouldn't have sent a taxi. Funds are scarce.' His brown eyes held hers for a moment. 'Julie, I'm trying not to raise my hopes. I think we should contact Imogen right now.'

Imogen was not optimistic. 'I don't recall Rose combing her hair in the car, or anything. I doubt if you'll find a hair.'

'People are shedding hair all the time,' Diamond informed her. 'She wouldn't have to comb it to leave one or two in your car.'

'In that case, you're up against it. I've given lifts to dozens of people since then. I'm always ferrying clients around the city.'

'We'd still like to have the car examined.'

'Suit yourself,' she said. 'How long does it take? I wouldn't want to be without wheels.'

'We'll send a man now. Collecting the material doesn't take long. It's the work in the lab that takes the time.'

'I don't like to contemplate what he'll find in my old Citroën. Some of my passengers – you should see the state of them.'

'Just as long as you haven't vacuumed the interior recently.'

'You're joking. I have more important things to do.'

He asked Julie to drive him out to the farm to check the mobile operational office, or so he claimed. She suspected he wanted to try out his new toy.

The van was parked in the yard and manned by DS Miller and DC Hodge, the only woman of her rank on the squad. They were discovered diligently studying a large-scale Ordnance Survey map, no doubt after being tipped off by Manvers Street that Diamond was imminent. What were telecommunications for, if not to keep track of the boss?

When asked what they were doing they said checking the

locations of nearby farms. Someone had already called at the immediate neighbour and spoken to a farmhand called Bickerstaff who was the only person present. He had confirmed that the owners were a company known as Hollandia Holdings, based in Bristol. Bickerstaff and his 'gaffer', a man from Marshfield, the next village, worked the land for the owners. It was a low-maintenance farm, with a flock of sheep, some fields rented out to the 'horsiculture' – the riding fraternity – and some set-aside. Bickerstaff had heard about old Gladstone's death and was sorry his body had lain undiscovered for so long, but expressed the view that local people couldn't be blamed. Gladstone had long been known as an 'awkward old cuss' who didn't welcome visitors.

'Have you got a fire going in the house?' Diamond asked Miller.

'Yes, sir.'

'Good. I'm going in there to put on my wellies.'

Julie and the sergeant exchanged glances and said nothing.

He was back in a short time shod in green gumboots and carrying a T-shaped metal detector with what looked like a pair of vanity cases mounted at either end of the metre-length crosspiece. 'You'll want a spade, Sergeant.'

'Will I, sir?'

'To dig up the finds.'

'Old coins and stuff?'

'No, this super-charged gizmo is too powerful for coins unless they're in a pot, a mass of them together. It ignores small objects. I'm after bigger things. It works at quite some depth, which is why you need the spade. Julie, there's a ball of string in the car with some skewers. You and the constable can line and pin the search area. We don't want to go over the same bit twice. Follow me.' He clamped a pair of headphones over his ears and strode towards the edge of the field. Clearly he had spent some time studying the handbook that came with the two-box.

'What does he expect to find?' Cathy Hodge asked Julie.

'Treasure, I think,' said Julie, 'if there's any left.'

'Has someone else been by?'

'Get with it, Cathy. You must have seen the evidence of recent digging. We don't know how thorough they were, or how much of the ground they covered.'

Diamond was already probing the field with the detector, treading an unerring line towards the far side. Julie sank a skewer into the turf, attached some string and started after him. 'Put more skewers in at two-foot intervals,' she called back to Hodge.

They completed about six shuttles of the field before something below ground must have made an interesting sound in Diamond's ear-phones. He stopped and summoned Sergeant Miller, who at this stage was watching the performance from the comfort of the drystone wall. 'I don't know how deep it is, but I'm getting a faint signal. Get to it, man.' Then, with the zest of a seasoned detectorist, he moved on with the two-box in pursuit of more finds.

Julie was beginning to tire of the game. She wasn't wearing boots and the mud was spattering her legs as well as coating a passable pair of shoes. 'Your turn with the string,' she told young Hodge.

'Ma'am, you said we don't know how much of the ground was searched by whoever did that digging.'

'Yes?'

'I just thought I ought to tell you that someone has marked this up before. If you look along here, there's a row of holes already.'

Julie saw for herself, circular holes in the earth at intervals of perhaps a metre, along the length of the hedge.

'Should we tell Mr Diamond?' Hodge asked. 'I mean, he could be wasting his time.'

'Tell him if you're feeling strong,' said Julie. 'I'm not.'

On consideration, nothing was said at that stage. Julie strolled over to the farmhouse, removed her shoes, went inside, filled a kettle and put it on the hotplate. A reasonable heat was coming up from a wood fire. There was a teapot on the table, with a carton of milk and some teabags and biscuits. The two on duty had wasted no time in providing for creature comforts. She found a chair – not the armchair – and sat with her damp feet as near the iron bars of the fire as possible.

She had always lived in modern houses, so the cottage range was outside her experience. She saw how it was a combination of boiler, cooking fire and bread oven. A great boon in its time, no doubt, with everything positioned so neatly around and over the source of heat: hot plate rack, swing iron for the meat, dampers and flue doors set into the tiled back. This one must have been fitted some time in the nineteenth century; the farmhouse was two or three hundred years older. Earlier generations would have cooked in the open hearth where the range now stood. She reckoned from the width of the mantelpiece over the hearth that in those days the fireplace must have stretched a yard more on either side. The 'built-in' range had been installed and the spaces filled in. It was obvious where the joins were.

Presently she got up and tapped the wall to the right of the oven and had the satisfaction of a hollow sound. An early example of the fitted kitchen unit. The water was simmering, the kettle singing in the soothing way that only old-fashioned kettles in old cottages do. She went back to the door and looked out. They hadn't finished, but the light was going. Sergeant Miller was hip-deep in the pit he had dug, a mound of soil beside him.

She went to look for more cups.

When they came in, Diamond looked in a better mood than was justified by the treasure-hunt. 'Tea? That's good organisation, Julie. It's getting chilly out there.'

'No luck?'

'Depends what you mean by luck. We didn't find you a Saxon necklace, if that's what you hoped for.'

'I wasn't counting on it.'

'But Sergeant Miller dug up a horse-brass.'

'Oh, thanks.'

'Finally,' said Miller as he slumped into the chair.

'It proves that the two-box works. And it also tells us that there ain't no Saxon treasure left in the ground.'

'Do you think any was found where the digging took place?'

'Don't know. My guess is that they used a two-box just as I did and got some signals. They could have found a bag of gold, or King Alfred's crown – or more horse-brasses.'

Julie poured the tea and handed it around. 'Just because a sword was found here fifty years ago, is it really likely that anything else would turn up?'

'You do ask difficult questions, Julie. I'm no archaeologist. Let's put it this way. I understand that people in past centuries buried precious objects like the Tormarton Seax for two reasons: either as part of the owner's funeral or for security. A grave or a hoard. Whichever, it's more than likely that other objects would be buried with them. So there's a better chance here than in some field where nothing has turned up.'

'Don't you think old Gladstone, or his father before him, would have searched his own land?'

'I'd put money on it, Julie, but let's remember that metal detectors weren't around in 1943, not for ordinary people to play with. They started going on sale in the late sixties. By that time the Gladstones must have dug most of their land many times over and decided nothing else was under there.'

'They missed the bloody horse-brass,' said Miller, with feeling.

'And they could have kept missing a Saxon hoard,' said Diamond. 'A ploughshare doesn't dig all that deep. There are major finds of gold and silver in fields that have been ploughed for a thousand years.'

'You're beginning to sound like a metal detector salesman,' said Julie.

A high-pitched electronic sound interrupted them.

'What's that?'

'My batphone,' said Sergeant Miller. He had hung his tunic on the back of the door. He picked off the personal radio and made contact with Manvers Street.

They all heard the voice coming over the static. 'Message for Mr Diamond. We have a reported sighting of a woman he wants to interview in connection with the Rose Black inquiry. She is called Doreen Jenkins. Repeat Doreen Jenkins. She was seen in Bath this afternoon.'

'Give me that,' said Diamond. He spoke into the mouthpiece. 'Who by?'

'You've pressed the off button, sir,' said Miller.

He re-established contact. 'This is DS Diamond. Who was it who saw Doreen Jenkins in Bath?'

'Miss Ada Shaftsbury. Repeat Ada—'

He tossed it back to Sergeant Miller and said to Julie, 'Ada. Who else?'

Twenty-six

'Where?'

'Rossiter's,' said Ada. 'That big shop in Broad Street with the creaky staircases.'

'What were you doing in Rossiter's?' asked Julie, thinking that Bath's most elegant department store would have been alien territory for Ada.

'Looking for the buyer.'

'You had something to *sell* them?'

'Postcards. Two thousand aerial views of Bath I'm trying to unload. Rossiter's have all kinds of cards. The ones I've got came out kind of fuzzy in the printing, but the colours are great, like an acid trip. A swanky shop like that could sell them as arty pictures, couldn't they? Anyway, it was worth a try. I went into the card section and I was running an eye over the stock, checking the postcards, when I heard this voice by the till. Some woman was asking if they sold fuses – you know, electrical fuses, them little things you get in plugs? This young assistant was telling her to go to some other shop. Telling her nicely. He was being really polite, giving her directions. I was pottering about in the background, not paying much attention.'

'Your mind on other things?' said Diamond, meaning shoplifting.

'If you want to hear this . . .'

'Go on, Ada. What happened?'

'It was her voice. Sort of familiar, la-de-dah, going on about fuses as if every shop worth tuppence ought to have them.' She stretched her features into a fair imitation of one of the county set and said in the authentic voice, '"But it's so incredibly boring, having to look for electrical shops." The penny didn't drop for me until she was walking out the shop. I went in closer, dying to know if I'd seen her before, and stone me I had, and I still couldn't place her. You know what it's like when you suddenly come eye to eye with some sonofagun you're not expecting.'

'Did she recognise you?'

'She almost wet herself.'

'When did you realise who she was?'

'Just after she left the shop. She was off like a bride's nightie. Jesus wept, that was the Jenkins woman, I thought. I turned to follow her, and I was almost through the door when the young bloke came round the counter and put his hand on my arm and asked to look in my plastic carrier.'

'Too quick,' said Diamond, who knew the law on shoplifting. 'He should have waited for you to step out of the shop.'

She glared at him. 'Listen, can you get it in your head that I wasn't working? I told you, I was there to sell stuff. Told him, too. Showed him the cards in my bag. He got a bit narked and so did I and by the time I got outside, she was gone.'

Diamond sighed.

Ada said, 'Look, she could have gone ten different ways from there. I had no chance of finding her. No chance.'

'What time was this?'

'Around four, four-fifteen. I came straight here.'

'You're positive it was the same woman who claimed to be Rose's stepsister?'

'No question. Look, I may have form, Mr Diamond, but I'm not thick.'

She seemed to expect some show of support here, so he said, 'No way.'

'She's supposed to come from Twickenham, so what's she doing in Bath?'

He reached for a notepad. 'Let's have a description, Ada. Everything you can remember.'

She closed her eyes and tried to summon up the image of the woman. 'Same height as me, more or less. Dark brown hair. Straight. The last time I saw her, she was wearing a ponytail. This time it was pinned up, off the neck, like some ballet-dancer, except she was a couple of sizes too heavy for the Sugar Plum Fairy. I'd say she's a sixteen, easy.' She opened her eyes again. 'Big bazoomas, if you're interested.'

If he was, he didn't declare it. 'Age?'

'Pushing thirty. Pretty good skin, what you could see of it. She lashes on the make-up.'

'Eyes?'

'Brown. With eye-liner, mascara, the works.'

'And her other features? Anything special about them?'

'You want your money's worth, don't you? Straight nose, thinnish lips, nicely shaped. Now you want to know about her clothes? She was in a cherry-red coat with black collar, black frogging and buttons. A pale blue chiffon scarf. Black tights or stockings and black shoes with heels. Her bag was patent leather, not the one she had when I saw her in the Social Security.'

As descriptions go, it was top bracket. He thanked her.

'So what are you going to do about it?' she demanded to know when he had finished writing it down.

'Find her.'

She regarded him with suspicion. 'You wouldn't farm this out to whatsisname with the tash?'

'DCI Wigfull? He's busy enough.' He got up from behind the table, signifying that the session was over.

But Ada lingered. 'When you find her, you'll put her through the grinder, won't you? She's evil. I don't like to think what's happened to Rose by now.'

'We've appealed for help,' he told her. 'Rose will be all over the front page in the paper tomorrow.'

'God, I hope not,' she said, misunderstanding him.

After Ada had gone, muttering and shaking her head like a latter-day Cassandra, Diamond commented to Julie, 'Don't ask what we're going to do about this. It's a terrific description, but next time the Jenkins woman goes out she's not going to be in cherry-red, she'll have her hair down and be wearing glasses and a blue trouser suit. She won't go within a mile of Rossiter's.'

'Because Ada recognised her?'

He nodded.

Julie said, 'It's a definite sighting – and in Bath.' She hesitated over the question that came next. 'Do you think Rose could still be in the city?'

'Hiding up?' He pressed his mouth tight. His eyes took on a glazed, distracted look.

Julie waited, expecting some insight.

Eventually he sighed and said, 'Rossiter's. I haven't been in there since they closed the restaurant. Steph and I used to go for a coffee sometimes, of a Saturday morning, up on the top floor. Self-service it was. You carried your tray to a deep settee and sat there as long as you liked, eating the finest wholemeal scones I've tasted in the whole of my life.'

She was lost for a comment. This vignette of the Diamond domestic routine had no bearing on the case that she could see.

'That was bad news, Julie,' he said.

She looked at him inquiringly.

'When Rossiter's restaurant closed.'

It seemed to signify the end of his interest in Ada's sensational encounter. Maybe it was his way of telling her not to expect insights.

They returned to the incident room to find that a message had been left by Jim Marsh, the SOCO. He had collected no less than seventeen hairs from Imogen Starr's Citroën Special and the lab were in process of examining them. There was no indication when a result might be forthcoming.

'Seventeen sounds like a long wait to me.'

'Most of them belong to Imogen, I expect,' said Julie.

'One of Rose's would be enough for me.'

He ambled over to Keith Halliwell and asked what else had been achieved.

'You asked us to check on the neighbouring farm at Tormarton, the one that wanted to swallow up Gladstone's little patch.'

'Yes.'

'It's owned by a company called Hollandia Holdings Limited.'

'We know that already, Keith.'

'We checked with Companies' House and got a list of the directors. It's here somewhere.' He sorted through the papers on his desk. 'Four names.'

Diamond looked at them and frowned.

Patrick van Beek (MD)
Aart Vroemen (CS)
Luc Beurskens
Marko Stigter

'Dutch?'

'Well, it is called Hollandia—'

'Yes. And we're all in the Common Market and the Dutch know a lot about farming. What are the letters after the names. Is van Beek a doctor?'

'Managing director.'

'Ah.' He grinned self-consciously. Abbreviations were his blind spot and everyone knew it. 'Do we have their addresses?'

'Just the company address, a Bristol PO number. PO – short for Post Office,' said Halliwell.

The grin faded. 'Thank you, Keith.' He turned to Julie. 'What's your opinion, then?'

She said, 'They're not locals, for sure. Can we check if they own other farms in this country?'

'We already have. Two in Somerset, one in Gloucestershire,' said Halliwell. 'The company seems to be kosher.'

The two of them looked to Diamond for an indication where the inquiry was heading now. He stood silent for some time, hunched in contemplation, hands clasped behind his neck. Finally he said, as if speaking to himself, 'There was just this chance that the neighbours were so set on acquiring the farm that they did away with Gladstone. We know he was made an offer more than once and refused, but that's no justification for blowing the old man's head off. It was a piddling piece of land. There had to be a stronger motive. The only one I can see is if they believed more Saxon treasure was buried there. The Tormarton Seax was well known. There might have been other things buried, but Gladstone was an obstinate old cuss who wouldn't let anyone find out. That's the best motive we have so far.' He paused and altered his posture, thrusting his hands in his pockets, but still self-absorbed. 'The idea of some faceless men, a company, greedy to grab the land and dig there, had some appeal. Now I'm less sure.'

'Somebody did some digging – quite a lot of it,' Julie commented.

He said sharply, 'I'm talking about the company, this Hollandia outfit. We know who they are now. Not faceless men. Keith gets the names from Companies House without any trouble at all. Mr van Beek and his chums, a bunch of Dutchmen with holdings in other farms as well. We can check them out – we *will* check them out – but I don't see them as killers. If they went to all the trouble of buying the farm next door, employing locals to work the land, if that's the planning, the commitment, they made to acquire this treasure, would they be quite so stupid as this?'

'It almost got by as a suicide,' said Halliwell.

'But it didn't. And we know their names. Check their credentials, Keith. Find out if the other farms they own are going concerns, how long they've been investing here. I think we'll discover these Dutchmen are more interested in turnips than treasure.'

'Now? It's getting late to phone people.'

'Get onto it.' Next it was Julie's turn to feel the heat. 'You just brought up the digging. Have you really thought it through?'

Experience of Diamond told her he wouldn't need a response.

'I said, have you thought it through? Has it crossed your mind at any point that the digging could be one bloody great red herring? People all around Tormarton knew about the Saxon sword. It was common knowledge that old Gladstone wouldn't let anyone excavate his land. He was lying dead in that house for a week and we're given to believe nobody knew. But what if some local person did find out, looked through the farmhouse window, saw the body and thought this is the chance everyone has waited fifty years for? Do you see? Your enterprising local lad comes along with a metal detector and spade and gets digging. If so, the murder and the digging are two separate incidents.'

'So are you suggesting we look for another motive?' said Julie, now that the discussion was becoming rational again. 'Why else would anyone have wanted to kill the old man?'

'What do we know about him, apart from the fact that he lived here all his life?'

'And was unfriendly to archaeologists?'

He talked through her comment. 'Who did we put onto researching the victim's life history? Jerry Hansen.'

'Sir?' The quiet man of the squad, Jerry, got up from his desk and came over.

'Where are we on Gladstone?'

'Piecing his story together, sir, from local knowledge and documentation. It's still patchy.'

'Let's have what you've got.'

Jerry launched smoothly into it. Nobody was better at ferreting for information. 'The Gladstone family have been at Marton Farm for generations. He was born in 1923, the only child of Jacob and Esther, and went to school in Tormarton. Left when he was fourteen, and worked for his father. Seems to have joined in village life in those days.'

Diamond gave a nod. 'Young and carefree, according to the vicar. That's a tearaway in the language you and I speak.'

'Well, he certainly married young, at nineteen, in 1943. In fact, they were both nineteen. She was May Turner, a London girl who was living in the village during the war.'

'It was her family Bible I found.'

'Yes, sir, that was helpful.'

'How about war service?'

'He was exempt. Farming was a reserved occupation. They rented rooms in a house in Tormarton. But the marriage wasn't happy. He seems to have been difficult all his life.'

'Unfaithful?'

'I don't know about that, but unbearable, it's fair to say,' said Jerry. 'This is gossip, but several elderly people in the village told us the same things. He was constantly picking on her, complaining of this and that. And he worked her hard. His mother died in 1944, so he and May moved into Marton Farm to care for the old father, who couldn't even boil an egg. May took on the job, but she didn't last long. She died two or three years after the marriage. We don't have the date yet.'

'What cause?'

'Bronchial pneumonia. The locals insist that she was ill before they moved to the farm. The lodgings were never heated properly. He would only buy so much paraffin.'

The detail opened a small window into the short, tragic marriage.

'Any children?'

'Not by the first wife.'

'And after she died, father and son fended for themselves?'

'Until 1953, when old Jacob passed on. Daniel managed the farm alone for some years. He married for the second time in 1967, to the local publican's daughter, Margaret Torrington, known as Meg. A child, a daughter, came along in 1970.'

'Christine. I saw her entry in the Church Register.'

'Yes. Soon after that, they separated. Life on the farm must have been hard.'

'Life with the farmer, more like. Do we know what became of Meg and her child?'

'We're piecing it together. Her parents have long since gone from the village to manage other pubs. No one knows where they ended up.'

'You could try the brewers.'

'We did. No joy. And none of the family kept in contact with anyone else in Tormarton. There was just the photo you found, and the message in the Christmas card.'

Diamond repeated the forlorn words, '"I thought you would like this picture of your family."'

'But it's not a total blank. Someone in the Post Office reckons they moved to London.'

'London's a big place, Jerry.'

'I was going to add Wood Green.'

'Better.'

'They also heard that Meg – the second wife – died of leukemia in January. We checked the registers and it seems to be true. A married woman called Margaret Gladstone died in St Ann's Hospital, Harringay – that's close enough to Wood Green – on January 28th, aged forty-nine.'

'Is that all?'

Jerry's face clouded. Clearly he thought he had done a reasonable job.

Diamond said, 'Her age, Jerry. I mean forty-nine is no age at all.'

'I see what you mean.'

'And he outlived her.'

Jerry said hesitantly, 'I found it rather a sad touch that on the death certificate she is still described as a barmaid.'

'You're too sentimental for a young man,' Diamond told him. 'She probably enjoyed working in bars. Do you know what I'm about to ask you?'

'The daughter Christine?'

'Spot on.'

'There is something to report. I contacted the hospital for Mrs Gladstone's next of kin. They confirmed the name on their file as Christine Gladstone, daughter, and gave me an address in Fulham. Gowan Avenue. I asked the Met to check and I'm waiting for a call.'

'We'll all be waiting,' said Diamond, rubbing his hands. 'God, yes. How old would this young woman be now?'

'We have the date of her baptism as February, 1970, so assuming she was baptised soon after birth she's about twenty-seven.'

'Near enough for me.'

No one else spoke. Each of them had made the connection. If it emerged that Christine Gladstone had been missing from home for the past four weeks, then it was a fair bet that she was the young woman known to them as Rose. And Diamond's insistence that Rose was the principal suspect suddenly looked reasonable.

Twenty-seven

'Pete!'

Diamond drew back, shocked by the panic in his wife's voice. A steel kitchen knife was in his hand.

Stephanie Diamond moved fast to the electric point and switched it off.

'You damned near electrocuted yourself, you great ninny. What were you thinking of?'

Thinking of using the knife to prise out the piece of toast stuck in the toaster and starting to smoke? Or not thinking?

With her slim fingers Steph picked out the charred remains and tossed them into the sink. 'Leave it to me. I'll cut you a fresh piece. You've never been able to cut bread evenly.'

He said, 'If we used a cut loaf . . .'

'You know why we don't,' she said, trimming off the overhang he had left on the loaf. 'What's the matter with you? I nearly had a corpse of my own to deal with.'

'Thinking of other things.'

She cut an even slice and dropped it into the toaster and switched on again. She didn't ask any more. If he wanted to tell her, he would. 'Other things' probably meant the details of his work that Steph preferred not to know. On the whole she was happier being given gossipy news of the Manvers Street staff: Wigfull, the ambitious one Peter called 'Mr Clean', making it sound like a term of abuse; or 'Winking, Blinking and Nod', the three Assistant Chief Constables; and Julie Hargreaves, the plucky young inspector who smoothed the way, dealt with the murmurings in the ranks and made it possible for her brilliant, but testy and brutally honest boss to function at all.

'I'm sleeping better, Steph.'

'You don't have to tell me that.'

'I reckon the tension isn't hyper any more. Things are humming nicely again.'

'You're doing an honest day's work?'

'Tell me this, if it doesn't ruin your breakfast. Why would a woman murder her father of seventy-one who she hasn't seen since she was a small child?'

Ruin breakfast? Lunch as well, she thought. But he seemed to need her advice. 'This is the one whose picture is in the local paper?'

He nodded.

'Insanity?'

His eyebrows popped up. 'That's a theory no one has mentioned up to now.'

'She looks confused.'

'She is. She lost her memory, allegedly. But people who met her say she's rational.'

'And you think she shot that old man at Tormarton?'

Now he looked at her in awe. She'd just made a connection it had taken him days to arrive at. 'Crosswords getting too easy, are they? You're having to read the rest of the paper?'

She smiled faintly.

'You're spot on,' he said. 'She's the daughter and she was found wandering a mile or so from the scene on the day of the murder. Today I expect to get the proof that she was present in the farmhouse. I'm still uncertain as to her motive. What does it take for a woman to tie her father to a chair and fire a shotgun at his head?'

'Did he abuse her as a child?'

'Don't know.'

'That's something you might consider,' Steph said. 'Anger surfacing after many years.'

'She's supposed to have lost her memory.'

'That could be due to repression. She blocks it all out after killing him. She wants to cleanse herself. The mind can act as a censor. Is it a possibility here?'

'Could be. The mother left him only a few years after they married.'

Steph spread her hands. 'If the mother found out . . .'

'But then she sent him a Christmas card with a photo of herself and the child. "I thought you would like this picture of your family. God's blessings to us all at this time." Would an angry mother do that?'

She thought for a moment and said, 'I doubt it. Maybe she never knew of the abuse.'

He tried his own pet theory on Steph. 'This woman, the mother. She died in January of leukemia. This is speculation, but I wonder if Rose, the daughter, sorting through her mother's things as she would, being next of kin, found something, a letter, say, or a diary, that revealed some family secret.'

'Such as?'

'Cruelty to her mother is the best bet. A history of violence or meanness that outraged her when she discovered it. She'd watched her mother die prematurely, at forty-nine. Now she discovered things that made her angry enough to find the old man and kill him.'

'You could be onto something there.'

'You really think so?'

'But you're not going to know the answer until you find her.'

'True.'

'Instead of trying to work out why she killed him, isn't it better to focus on finding her?'

'You mean she'll roll over and tell all? I guess you're right, as ever.'

He spread marmalade on his beautifully even piece of toast and left for work soon after.

The Metropolitan Police confirmed overnight that Christine Gladstone had not used her flat in Gowan Avenue, Fulham, since at least the last week in September. They had found a heap of unopened mail waiting for her. Her landlord knew nothing about her absence because she paid her rent by banker's order. The people in the other flat thought she was on a foreign holiday.

Diamond handed the fax back to Halliwell. 'We're closing in, Keith. I'll get up to London today and look at the flat. Julie can drive me. You're in charge here, at the cutting edge.'

Halliwell grinned. 'Expecting results from our press conference?'

Diamond was determined to be upbeat. 'I said we're closing in, Keith. It's all coming together. For example, I'm about to get the latest from Jim Marsh.'

But Jim Marsh, the pathologist, wasn't about. He wasn't at the lab, either.

Undaunted, Diamond asked the exchange to get his home number.

'Who'zzz zizzz?' The voice of a man on Temazepam. Or gin.

'Shouldn't you be in work like the rest of us? I'm sitting here like a buddha waiting for results from you.'

'Gave them to Ju – Ju—'

'Julie?'

'Couldn't get hold of you last night. Called her at home.'

'She isn't in yet. Have we come up trumps?'

Marsh was becoming more coherent, and he didn't sound like a man with a winning hand. 'Worked until bloody late. Three of us.'

'And?'

'I took a sleeper when I got home. If I work late I can't get off to sleep.' He was off on a tangent.

'What about the hairs, Jim?'

'Hairs?'

'The tests you were doing.'

'Tests, yes. I told you I found how many specimens of hair?'

'Seventeen.'

'Seventeen. Eleven from the owner of the car.'

'Imogen Starr.'

'That left . . .'

'Six.'

'Six, and when we analysed them, they came from three subjects. You're going to be pissed off, Mr Diamond. None of them matched the two hairs we found in the farmhouse.'

He couldn't believe it. 'You drew a complete blank?'

'It doesn't prove a thing either way. She could have sat in the car without losing a hair.'

'What do I do now?'

'Find the lady, I reckon.'

'Oh, cheers!'

'We still have the two hairs from the scene,' Marsh reminded him. 'That's the good thing about NAA. We don't destroy the evidence in the test. Those hairs will be useful at the trial.'

'What trial?'

After he'd slammed the phone down, he realised he had not actually thanked Marsh and his team for working overtime. For once he remembered his manners, pressed the redial button and rectified that.

Marsh listened and said, 'Mr Diamond.'

'Yes?'

'Would you get off my phone now?'

He gave the disappointing news to the others in the incident room, and then added, 'It's not all gloom and doom. With the Met's help, we've confirmed that Christine Gladstone, alias Rose Black, the victim's daughter, has been missing from home since the end of September. I'm off to London shortly to search her flat. Meantime, Keith will take over here. Since we went public yesterday, a number of possible sightings have come in.'

Halliwell summed up the paltry results. Seven reported sightings and two offers of help from psychics. The missing woman had apparently shopped in Waitrose and Waterstone's, cycled down Widcombe Hill, eaten an apricot slice in Scoff's, appeared at a bedroom window in Lower Weston, studied Spanish in Trowbridge and walked two Afghan hounds on Lansdown. One of the psychics thought she was dead, buried on the beach at Weston-super-Mare, and the other had a vision of her with a tall, dark man in a balloon. All of it, however unlikely, was being processed into the filing system, and would need to be followed up.

The squad heard the results in silence. Appeals for help from the public had predictable results. You had to hope something of substance would appear. As yet, it had not.

'Do we go national now?' Halliwell asked.

'No. We knock on doors in Tormarton,' said Diamond.

'House-to-house?'

'Someone up there knows about the digging, if nothing else. There were seven large holes, for God's sake, and they didn't have a JCB. It took days. They were tidy. They filled in after. Covered over any footprints. Get a doorstepping team together, Keith, and draw up some questions that we can agree.'

'Is it worth targeting the metal-detector people, the guys who spend their weekends looking for treasure?'

He snapped his fingers. 'Of course it is. Good. Send someone to Gary Paternoster, the lad who runs the shop in Walcot Street, the Treasure House, and get a list of his customers, plus any clubs that function locally. Julie and I are off to London shortly to . . .' He looked around the room. 'Where the hell is Julie?'

'Hasn't been in yet,' said Halliwell.

'Any message?'

Halliwell shook his head.

'What time is it?' Diamond asked. 'She would have called in by now if she's ill.'

Shortly after nine that morning, William Allardyce came out of the house in the Royal Crescent and looked for the blue BMW. It was not in its usual place. Then his attention was caught by a fat man dressed in eccentric clothes and behaving oddly and he was reminded of the filming of *Pickwick*. All the residents had been paid to park elsewhere the previous night. His BMW was in the Circus.

Annoyed with himself, he set off at a canter along Brock Street. He didn't like being late for appointments and he hadn't allowed for the extra ten minutes this would add to his short journey. He was due to meet an important client at the Bath Spa Hotel.

When he reached his car it was already 9.15. He unlocked and got in. The moment he sat down he realised something was wrong, a crunch, a solid sensation when the springs took his weight. He got out. As he feared, he had a flat, one of the rear tyres. He kicked it and the casing gaped. This wasn't a simple puncture. Some vandal had slashed it. So far as he could see, other cars nearby had not been damaged. His was singled out.

There was no time to change the tyre and he was without his mobile phone. The nearest taxi rank was at the bottom of Milsom Street. He decided to return home and phone the hotel to say the earliest he could manage was 9.45. And while he was waiting for a taxi he would also phone the police.

Julie's non-arrival at the incident room was the result of a night without much sleep. Late last evening, Jim Marsh had called her at home to report the disappointing result of the hair analysis. People who knew Diamond's volatile moods tended to take the soft option and give Julie the bad news and ask her to relay it to him. She had decided to save it for the morning. About 1.30am, her brain churning over the day's events for the umpteenth time, still fretting at the lack of progress, she reached for the light-switch and sat up to read, hoping some science fiction would engage her mind more than hair samples that didn't match. Charlie was away, on duty in Norfolk. She opened *Dune*, a book she was re-reading and enjoying even more the second time. Soon the chill in the room got uncomfortable. She reached for a drawer and took out a thick cardigan and wrapped it around her shoulders. As she brought the sleeves across her chest she happened to notice a hair attached to the ribbing. Automatically she picked it off and dropped it over the edge of the bed. She carried on reading. Some minutes passed before this unthinking action was replayed in her mind. Then an idea came to her that kept her from sleeping for another two hours.

In the morning it still seemed worth following up. She hoped she could deal with it before Peter Diamond got into work. By nine she was at the Social Services office, just along the street from the nick. Unluckily, Imogen Starr had also had a disturbed night and didn't turn up until almost nine-thirty.

Julie told her that the hair samples from the car had proved negative. 'We're still hoping to find one of Rose's, and I had a thought last night. When you brought her back from the hospital what was she wearing?'

'Her own things,' said Imogen.

'The clothes she was found in?'

'They were stained and torn, but they were all she had.'

'So did you fit her out with fresh clothes?'

'Yes.'

'Where from?'

'From our stock. Here. We keep some basic clothes for emergency use. I brought her in before we went to Harmer House and we found a shirt and some jeans. They weren't new, but they were clean and in better condition than the ones she had.'

Tensely Julie asked, 'And what happened to the old clothes?'

'They were really no use to her.'

'Did she take them with her?'

'No, she discarded them. There was nothing left in the pockets, if that's what you were thinking.'

'What happened to them?'

Imogen lifted her shoulders in a dismissive way. 'I suppose they were thrown out with the rubbish. Well, the shirt was, for sure. We may have kept the jeans. They were hanging open at the knee, but that's fashionable, isn't it? We don't like to throw anything out that might come in useful.'

'Where would they be if you kept them?'

'The storeroom.'

'Can we check?'

'I don't want to dash your hopes, if you're hoping to find a hair on them, but they've probably been washed by now.'

Julie felt a flutter of despair.

'We wait for a reasonable load and then someone takes them to the launderette.'

'But I'd like you to check, please,' Julie insisted.

In the storeroom she helped Imogen rummage through black plastic sacks of musty-smelling clothes.

'Most of these haven't been to the laundry.'

'Yes, we've obviously been stockpiling.'

Eventually, Imogen looked into a bag and said, 'This could be them.'

'Careful,' Julie warned. 'Don't lift them out.'

'How can we tell if they're hers if we don't lift them out?'

'Look at them in the sack. Spread it open. Keep your head back if you can. We don't want to catch one of your hairs.'

Imogen found the rip in the knee she remembered.

Resisting the temptation to see if she'd really got lucky, Julie tied a knot in the top of the bag and carried it through the street to the police station.

She went in search of Jim Marsh.

Eventually, she arrived at the incident room at 10.20. The meeting was over and people were going about their business with a quiet sense of purpose, so each word of what followed was heard by most of the squad.

'It looks nice,' Diamond said in his heavy-handed way.

'I beg your pardon.'

'The do. Been to the hairdresser's, have you?'

There was an awkward interval. Then Julie said, 'Obviously I should have called earlier, but I didn't think it would take so long.'

'The highlighting?'

She'd had enough. 'Will you listen? I don't fix personal appointments in police time. As a matter of fact, the last time I was due to have my hair done, you put me on overtime, so I had to cancel. If you want to know where I was first thing this morning, it was on police business, on my own initiative. Is that allowed?'

'All right, I'm out of order,' he said without sounding as if he meant it. 'Where were you?'

She told him about her last-ditch idea of tracking down Rose's rejected clothes, and of locating the jeans in the storeroom.

His entire approach altered. 'I hardly dare ask. Have you shown them to Marsh yet?'

'That's why I'm so late. He was still at home.'

'I know. But did he find anything?'

'He said it had to be examined in a controlled situation, or some such phrase.'

'Here?'

'In the SOCOs' section, I think.'

He picked up a phone and pressed the internal number. He was through to Marsh directly.

'You have? With what result? . . . Brilliant! . . . I know, I know, you don't have to tell me that. Just rush it to the lab and see if we're in business, will you?' He put down the phone and smiled at Julie. 'One dark hair, nine centimetres long. You may have cracked it this time, Julie.'

She didn't trust herself to say anything.

Allardyce was surprised to be shown into Chief Inspector

Wigfull's office. 'I expected to speak to Superintendent Diamond. He's the one I saw previously.'

'Mr Diamond is on another case,' said Wigfull in a lofty tone. 'I've taken over the handling of the incident at your house.'

'It's just that we haven't seen you there.'

'It's mainly paperwork at this stage. The on-site investigation is complete.'

'What conclusion did you reach – or am I not supposed to ask?'

'That will be up to the coroner. We simply present the evidence. You'll be notified about the inquest in due course, sir. You'll be called as a witness. As to this other matter, the damage to your car, we'll investigate, of course, but—'

'The tyre was slashed. It had to be reported.'

'You're absolutely right, sir, but if it's any consolation, it may not have been personal,' Wigfull said, confirming a melancholy truth. 'Casual vandalism is quite common even in Bath, I'm sorry to say. If we had more officers to patrol the streets . . .'

'If it wasn't personal, why was my car picked out? None of the others were touched.' He was genuinely puzzled and hurt.

'You said it's new. Sometimes that can be a provocation.'

Allardyce gave a shrug and a smile. 'What are we supposed to do? Never drive a new car?'

Wigfull shifted in his chair. He was beginning to feel sympathy for this young man. 'Why else should it have been picked out? You tell me, sir.'

'I've no idea.'

This justified leading the witness a little. 'I suppose it comes suspiciously soon after the publicity about the young woman's death in your house.'

'Are you serious?'

'Any vandalism is taken seriously, sir.'

Allardyce ignored the empty phrase. 'I mean what does that poor woman's death have to do with this?'

'I don't know. If they decided you were responsible in some way . . .'

'Me?'

'I'm trying to see it from their point of view.'

'Who are you talking about?'

'Some friend of the deceased.' Even as he spoke, an uncomfortable idea was stirring at the back of Wigfull's brain.

'I don't follow your thinking.'

'But it's well known that you weren't to blame for what happened,' Wigfull affirmed, not wanting to grapple with the dire thought now forming. 'Your house was taken over by young people wanting a party. There was a tragic consequence. No fault of yours.'

'If that's the way you see it . . .' said Allardyce, beginning to be swayed.

'Besides,' said Wigfull, 'it wasn't as if your car was parked outside your house. Anyone wanting to get at you personally would have to know which car it was and where you parked it last night.'

'True.'

'We'll follow this up and let you know if we have a result, but my money is on some kid out of school who doesn't know your vehicle from anyone else's,' he lied, to bring this to a close. He got up from his chair and showed Allardyce to the door. 'Your neighbour – Mr Treadwell. Does he have a car?'

'No. Wise man. He works in Bath and doesn't need to travel so much.'

Alone in his office again, Wigfull sat brooding like a Thomas Hardy hero on the malign sport of the fates. Finally he sighed, pressed the intercom and spoke to the control room. 'Send someone round to Harmer House, would you, and bring in Ada Shaftsbury. Yes, I repeat: Ada Shaftsbury.'

Twenty-eight

Somewhere east of Reading on the M4, Diamond said to Julie, 'We've got some fences to repair, you and me.'

She didn't speak, so he amended it.

'I've got some fences to repair.'

They drove another half-mile in silence.

'I said I was out of order, didn't I? Meant it, too. You know me by now, Julie. Things start going wrong and I get stroppy. That's all it was back there. Jim Marsh had just been on the line telling me his tests were negative.'

She was driving as if she had a sleeping cobra on her lap.

'There's the difference between you and me,' Diamond talked on. 'I take my disappointment out on other people, anyone in the firing line, while you get on and sort out the problem.'

Not a flicker.

He opened the glove compartment. 'There were some Polos in here last time I looked. Fancy a mint?'

She mouthed the word 'no' without even a glance towards him.

This was becoming intolerable. He said, 'Well, if you want to cut me down to size, now's as good a time as any.'

'You mean in private,' she ended her silence, 'where the rest of the squad can't overhear us?'

'I don't follow you.'

'What really got to me,' Julie went on in a level tone that still managed to convey her anger, 'is that you put me down in front of the rest of them, people I outrank. You do it time and again. I don't mind taking stick. I don't even care if it's unjustified. Well, not much. But I really mind that you don't respect me enough to save it for a private moment. That's what you demand for yourself. Here, in the car with no one listening, you invite me to cut you down to size. Big deal. I'd rather save my breath.'

She had blown him away and she was talking of saving her breath. Like this, she was more devastating than Ada Shaftsbury turning the air blue with abuse.

He had no adequate response. All he could think to say was, 'Point taken.'

In the silence, he dredged his brain to think of something even more conciliatory, but Julie seemed to sense what it would be. 'Don't make promises you can't keep. You'll do the same thing again and I'll get madder still with you next time. Yes, I will have a Polo now.'

The traffic ahead was slowing. The motorway narrowed to two lanes as they approached Chiswick. Excuse enough to sink their differences for a while and consult over the route.

Just before the Hammersmith Flyover they peeled off and joined Fulham Palace Road. Diamond opened the *A-Z* and read out the names of the streets on the left. Gowan Avenue came up in a little over a mile, long, straight and dispiriting, the kind of drab terraced housing that obliterated the green fields of West London in the housing boom at the start of the twentieth century.

The landlord had been tipped off that they were coming and had the door open. He was Rajinder Singh, he told them, and his property was fully registered, documented and managed in accordance with the law of the land.

Diamond put him right as to the purpose of their visit and asked if he knew his tenant Christine Gladstone personally.

'Personally, my word yes,' Mr Singh said, eager to please. 'We have very close relations, Miss Gladstone and I. She is living in my house more than two years, hand in glove. Very charming young lady.'

Diamond thought he knew what was meant. 'Pays her rent by banker's order, I understand?'

'Midland Bank, yes. The Listening Bank. No problem.'

'Does she work nearby?'

'I am thinking she does. In shop.'

'You wouldn't know which one?'

'No, sir.'
'Does she drive a car?'
'Miss Gladstone? I do not think so.'
There was a pile of mail on a chair just inside the hallway, all addressed to Christine Gladstone. Diamond riffled through it. Mostly circulars and bills. A couple of bank statements from the Midland. The earliest postmark was 29th September.
'When did you last speak to her?'
'August, maybe. Some small problem with loose tile on roof. I am fixing such the same day.'
'She lives upstairs, then? Shall we go up?' When the door at the top of the stairs was unlocked for them, Diamond added, 'We'll be taking our time over this, sir. No need for you to stay.'
Mr Singh brought his hands together in the traditional salute of his race, dipped his turbaned head, and left.
'Don't know about you, Julie,' Diamond said when he had stepped inside, 'but I've lived in worse drums than this.'
They were in a small, blue-carpeted living-room, with papered walls, central heating, television, a bookcase and a pair of brown leather armchairs. Large framed posters of Venice lined one wall.
Julie picked a photograph off the bookcase. 'Her mother, I think.'
He studied it. The improbably blonde, gaunt woman must have been twenty years older than she had been in the picture he had found in the Bible in the farmhouse. The eyes were more sunken, the lines either side of the mouth more deeply etched. The leukemia may already have taken a grip, yet the smile had not changed.
'No question.'
His attention was caught by some cardboard cartons stacked along the wall below the posters. The first he opened contained pieces of used china and glass wrapped in newspaper, presumably treasured pieces brought from Meg Gladstone's house after she died.
Julie had gone through to the bedroom. 'More photos in here,' she called out.
'Any of the father?'

'No. Mummy again, and one of Rose arm-in-arm with a bloke.'

He looked into another box. Cookery books. The boxes were not so interesting after all.

Julie announced, 'There's a folder by the bed with a photocopy of the will inside. And other things. Solicitors' letters. Her mother's death certificate.'

He walked through to the bedroom and looked at the contents of the folder. It was a simple will leaving everything to 'my beloved daughter, Christine'. The Midland Bank were named as executors. No mention of the husband.

'She seems to have travelled a lot,' said Julie, running a fingertip along a bookshelf beside the bed. 'France, Switzerland, Iceland, Italy, Kenya, Spain. Maps, too, that look as if they've been used more than once.'

'She ought to have some personal papers. Income tax forms, passport, birth certificate.' He started opening drawers. The clothes inside were folded and tidily stacked. Then he found a box-file. 'Here we are. The dreaded Tax Return. *Trade, profession or vocation.* Any guesses?'

'Courier?'

'Not bad. Travel agent employed by Travel Ease. Fulham High Street. We'll call there, Julie. See if they know what her plans were.'

He returned the box to the drawer and took a more leisurely look at the bedroom, getting an impression of its user. It was without the frills and furry toys often favoured by single young women. A distinct absence of pastel pink and blue. The duvet had a strong abstract design of squares in primary colours. Against the window, the dressing-table was long, white and clinical, with a wide, rectangular mirror. A few pots of face-cream, more functional than expensive, a brush and comb and a small hand-mirror suggested someone not over-concerned with her appearance.

He picked up the photo of Rose (he couldn't get into his head that she was Christine) with the young man. More relaxed than in the police picture, her dark hair caught by a breeze, she looked alive, a personality, intelligent, aware and enjoying herself.

'If we could find an address book, we might learn who

the boyfriend is.' He unclipped the photo from its frame, but nothing was written on the reverse.

'She may use a personal organiser.' Seeing the uncertainty in his eyes, Julie said, 'You know what I mean? One of those electronic gadgets that tell you where you live and when you were born and when to take your anti-stress pills? John Wigfull has one.'

And he would, Diamond thought.

'If so,' she said, 'it probably went with her. She'll have taken her basic make-up as well. I noticed you check the dressing-table drawer.'

'Did I?'

'No lipstick, eye-liner, mascara.'

'So you think she packed for some time away?'

'I didn't say that. If you want my opinion, it's unlikely. She isn't a heavy buyer of clothes and there's still quite a stack of underwear in the drawers.'

'So?'

'Women always pack more knickers than they need.'

'The things you learn in this job.'

'That's why I tag along, isn't it?' She'd scored a nice point and she allowed herself a smile, the first in hours. 'I could be totally wrong. She must possess some luggage and I haven't come across any yet.'

'It ought to be obvious.'

'Unless it's stored somewhere else in the house. Should we check with Mr Singh?'

He pondered the matter. 'But would you pack a suitcase if you were going to Tormarton to murder your father?'

She didn't attempt an answer.

Diamond wrestled with his own question. 'Even if she did, and took a travelling bag with her, what happened to it? She wasn't carrying one when she was found.'

'She wasn't even carrying a handbag.'

He looked at her with approval. 'Good point. Why hasn't the handbag turned up?'

Julie shook her head.

Almost without thinking, Diamond stepped into the bathroom and made a telling discovery. He came out holding up a toothbrush. 'I think she was planning to come back the same day.'

But Julie had already moved into the small kitchen. She called out, 'I'm sure you're right. She left out a loaf and – ugh!'

'What's up?'

'A portion of uncooked chicken in the fridge. That's what's up. Well past its sell-by date.'

The smell travelled fast. He tugged open a sash-window in the living-room. Julie joined him there. The petrol fumes from the street were primrose-sweet at that moment.

'That's put me off chicken for a week.'

'Did you shut the fridge?'

'Yes, but you wouldn't believe I did.'

When the air was clearer they began a more thorough sweep of the shelves, cupboards and drawers in each room. Rose was unusually tidy and well organised, but things still came to light in unexpected places. Two tickets (under a candlestick on the chest of drawers) for a symphony concert at the Barbican in mid-October. A chocolate box containing opera programmes from La Scala, Milan, and Rome. A copy of a typed letter to Mr Singh complaining about a damp patch in the ceiling. A couple of gushing love-letters from someone called James; they were tucked into one end of the bookcase.

'I wonder why James hasn't been round to see her in all this time?'

'Take a look at the dates,' said Julie. 'September and October, 1993. He's history.'

'Why didn't she bin them, then?'

'Women don't get love letters all that often. She may want to keep them.'

'Or she forgot they were there.'

'Cynic.'

He didn't challenge her. He was taking one more look at the manila folder containing the will and death certificate. Diligence was rewarded. Trapped inside, out of sight along the inner fold of the pocket, was an extra piece of paper. He pulled it out. An envelope, torn open. On it was written: *To Christine, to be opened after my death.*

'Frustrating,' he said. 'This is her mother's handwriting. It matches the writing on that photo.'

'Isn't the letter in the folder?'

'No.'

'Then she must have it with her.'

'Unless she destroyed it.'

'The last letter she ever received from her mother?' said Julie on a high note of disbelief. 'Besides, if she kept the envelope, she means to keep the letter.'

He conceded the sense of this with a nod.

Julie added, 'Do you think the letter could have a direct bearing on the case? If it was only to be read after Meg Gladstone's death, it may have revealed some information Rose wasn't aware of, a family secret. Some reference to the old man's shabby treatment of them?'

'I don't know about that,' he commented after a moment's thought. 'It would be too negative. It's more likely to be a last request, some service the mother wanted Rose to perform for her.'

'A bit of unfinished business. Like visiting her father?'

'Possibly. You see, she delayed several months before going to see him. No doubt she was busy sorting things out for some time after her mother's death in – when was it? – January. She probably wanted to get down to Tormarton before the end of the year. That's my feeling about it – but of course it's all speculation without the damned letter.'

They spent another half-hour in the flat before he called time. On their way out, downstairs in the hall, they were treated to the sight of Mr Singh's scarlet turban behind a door that was drawn shut as they approached.

'Good day to you, landlord,' Diamond called out.

The door opened again and he looked out. 'All satisfactory, is it?'

'Thanks, yes.'

'She is in trouble, Miss Gladstone?'

'We hope not. If she comes back, you'll inform us, I expect.'

'Indeed, yes, sir, I will.'

'You live downstairs, do you, Mr Singh?'

'No, no.' He emerged fully from behind the door and held it open. 'This is store cupboard. I live across river. Detached house. Putney Hill. Five bedroom. I show you if you like.'

The store cupboard held more interest for them than Mr

Singh's detached house. 'This is where the tenants keep their luggage?'

'Just so.' He flicked on a light and they saw a stack of suitcases. One uncertainty, at least, had been cleared up.

Travel Ease, where Rose was employed, was crowded with people booking winter sunshine. It was not easy attracting the attention of the manager, and even when they got to his desk he assumed they were planning a holiday together. Diamond disillusioned him with a few pithy words and asked about Miss Gladstone.

'Yes,' the young man said, 'I have been concerned about Christine. She hasn't been in for weeks. I wrote letters and tried phoning with no result. It's so out of character. She's always been reliable up to now.'

'Did she say if she was going away?'

'She said nothing. You can ask any of my staff. She simply didn't turn up after one weekend. You don't think something dreadful has happened to her?'

They got back to Bath soon after four. Diamond commented to Julie that the incident room had all the fevered activity of a town museum on a hot day in August. One civilian computer operator was on duty. She said she thought Inspector Halliwell might have slipped out to the canteen. Only just, she added loyally.

They spotted Halliwell taking a shot at the snooker table. Someone alerted him and he put down the cue and snatched up a cup and came to meet Diamond and Julie midway across the canteen floor. 'I missed my lunch,' he said in mitigation. 'We've been overstretched. Most of them are out at Tormarton on the house-to-house. How did it go?'

'Has anything new come in?'

'A couple more sightings, but I wouldn't pin any hopes on them. Oh, and we've got a list of the treasure-hunters. I had no idea this is such a popular thing. Getting on for fifty names, and clubs in Bath, Bristol and Chippenham. Do you think it pays?' He was trying manfully to appear untroubled at being caught out.

'No word from Jim Marsh?'

'About the hair Julie found? No.'
'Have you called him?'
'Not yet.'
'You finish your break, then,' said Diamond. After a pause of merciless duration, he added, 'Your lunchbreak, I mean.'
On the way upstairs they met Ada Shaftsbury of all people. 'What idiot let her in?' he muttered to Julie. Then, to Ada, with an attempt at good humour, 'You're out of bounds, you know. This is strictly for the Old Bill.'
Ada twitched her nose, a dangerous sign. She also took a deep breath before sounding off. 'Do you think I'm here out of choice? Don't you know what's going on in your own festering nick? Well, obviously you don't. You're the bullshit artist who wouldn't listen when I came in about my friend Rose. She's all right, you said, talking down your nose at me. All done through Social Services, so there can't be nothing wrong. What do I see now? Rose's picture all over the papers. Missing woman. "Grounds for concern, says Superintendent Peter Diamond." Pity you didn't show some bleeding concern when I told you she was in trouble.'
'Ada, this isn't helping her. What are you doing here anyway?'
'Like I said, you don't even talk to each other, you lot. I was brought in. You grab an innocent woman off the street and throw garbage at her for the fun of it. Just because I'm homeless you think you can walk all over me. I'm going straight from here to see a lawyer. I'm going to get on television and tell my story.'
'What exactly is the trouble, Ada?'
'False arrest is the trouble. Invasion of civil liberties. Getting me in an arm-lock and forcing me into the back of one of your poky little panda cars, so I got bruises all over my body, and dragging me up here and strapping me about things I wouldn't do if I was paid.'
'What things?'
'Only vandalising a car, like I'm some hopped-up kid, that's what.'
'What did you do – lean on it?'
'Piss off. I didn't do nothing. Haven't been near the place. Stupid berk.'

'Who are you talking about now?'

'Him with the face-fungus. Wigwam.'

'Chief Inspector Wigfull?'

'I told you it was barmy letting him take over. He's got sod-all interest in how my friend Hilde died. All he cares about is a frigging flat tyre. Bastard. Well, he's got egg all over his mean face now, because I had a copper-bottom alibi, didn't I? I was doing my night job.'

'You've got a job?'

She sniffed and drew herself up. 'Two nights a week, ten till six. I sit in a shabby little office in Bilbury Lane answering the phone and talking to taxi-drivers over the radio. So I've got ten to fifteen blokes who can vouch for me last night. They all know when I'm on duty. We have some good laughs over the short wave, I can tell you.'

'And Chief Inspector Wigfull is investigating damaged cars now? Are you sure of this, Ada?'

'Sure? Of course I'm bloody sure. I wasn't brought in here for my health. I'm his number one suspect, or I was until I put him straight.'

This was difficult to believe. No officer of Wigfull's rank looked into minor acts of vandalism unless there was an overriding reason. 'Do you happen to know whose car it was? Not a police vehicle, I hope?'

She told him. 'One of them people up the Crescent. Alley something, is it?'

'Allardyce, I expect.' Diamond was intrigued.

'That was it and that's why Wigwam fingered me. He reckons I got a grudge against them because of my friend Hilde dying up there. It's not true, Mr Diamond. I don't blame them for what happened to Hilde. I never even met them.'

Diamond turned to Julie. 'Would you see Ada safely to the door?'

Julie gave him a mutinous look.

He explained, 'I want to get things straight with JW. This is a development I hadn't expected.'

Ada said, 'Throw the book at him. He's out of order, victimising innocent women.'

'Come on, love,' said Julie. 'Don't waste our valuable time.'

'And you're no better,' Ada shouted at Diamond as she was led away. 'What about poor Rose, then? If you lot had the sense to listen to me, you'd solve your bleeding cases and have time to spare,' was Ada's parting shot.

He spent twenty minutes with Wigfull, going over the implications of the slashing of Allardyce's tyre. Now that Ada had been eliminated as the suspect, Wigfull fell back on his original theory that it had been a random act by a teenager.

Diamond was like a dog with a bone. 'Did you ask Allardyce if he could think of anyone holding a grudge against him?'

'I did.'

'And what did he answer?'

'Negative.'

'Was he being totally honest?'

'What do you mean?'

'Was he hiding anything? Bad feelings with someone else?'

'Why should he?' Wigfull said, reasonably enough. 'If he'd wanted to keep it quiet he wouldn't have come to me in the first place. A slashed tyre is no big deal. He could have put on the spare and got on with his life.'

'You see, if it *was* deliberate, the circle of suspects is fairly small. Not many people knew where he'd left his car last night. Not many would know his car anyway. You said it was new.'

'He's not the sort who makes enemies of his neighbours,' said Wigfull. 'There's nothing to dislike in him. The only person I could think of who might have taken against him was Ada. She's still upset about Hildegarde Henkel's death at the party they had, and she's an unstable personality anyway, but she's got this alibi for last night. I really think we're wasting our time talking about it.'

Diamond carried on as if nothing had been said. 'Is the car still up there at the Circus?'

'I've no idea.'

'Did you go to see it?'

'What would have been the point?'

He picked up Wigfull's phone. 'Get me William Allardyce, will you? . . . The Crescent, yes.'

Wigfull tapped his fingers on the desk and looked out of the window at the early evening traffic jam, trying to appear nonchalant while listening keenly to Diamond's end of the conversation.

'Who is this? . . . Mrs Allardyce. Peter Diamond here, from Bath Police. . . . He isn't? Well, I have the pleasure of speaking to you instead. I was perturbed to hear about the damage to your husband's car this morning . . . After you'd left for work? You must start early. Of course, you do. I forget the television runs right through the day. Personally I prefer the radio in the morning . . . Do you have a car of your own? . . . I agree. The train is much the best way to travel if you can . . . Yes, it only just reached my attention. We're having a meeting about it right now. Tell me, has he had the tyre fixed yet? . . . He has? No use me trotting up to the Circus to look at the damage, then . . . I dare say the filming has finished in the Crescent, so he'll be able to park in his usual spot tonight . . . These things happen, sadly, but I think it's unlikely. Just in case, I'll ask our night patrol to keep a lookout . . . No trouble at all. Just tell him we're working on it, would you? Thank you, ma'am.'

'Perturbed, are you?' said Wigfull.

'Yes, John, I am. Let me know if you get any further with it, won't you?'

He returned to the incident room, now transformed into a bustling workplace. Halliwell had a message from Jim Marsh: would Mr Diamond call if convenient?

'*If convenient*?' He snatched up the phone and got through. 'Well, John?'

'It's a match, Mr Diamond. The hair from the clothing comes from the same individual as the two hairs found at the scene of the murder.'

'So Rose was definitely in the farmhouse?'

'That's for you to say. I was looking at hairs.'

'And now you're splitting them.'

'I'm simply reporting our findings.'

Diamond turned and gave a triumphant thumbs-up to the entire incident room. 'Cheers, mate,' he said into the phone. 'You can bill me for that beer next time we meet.'

'Double Scotch.'

'What?'

'It was a double Scotch you offered before.'

'Was it? Mad, impetuous fool. You're on, then.'

The news buoyed everyone up. Few had been willing to back Diamond when he picked on Rose as the main suspect. Now they had to admit he was justified. It wasn't quite the surge of exhilaration that comes when a case is buttoned up. They didn't shake him by the hand or pat him on the back, but they clustered around him, united in support. Then in the passion of the moment the computer operator who had called him a great oaf gave him a hug and retired immediately to the ladies.

He took the whole thing equably (even the hug, which no one would forget), reminding everyone that the time to celebrate would be when they picked up Rose and she admitted everything.

So there was no popping of corks. Just a quiet coffee in Bloomsburys. Alone.

This should have been a defining moment in the inquiry. It was . . . and yet. He found himself thinking increasingly not of Rose, but the people in the house in the Royal Crescent – the Allardyces and the Treadwells. The trivial incident of the ripped tyre would not bed down with the rest of the day's events. It niggled. It had brought the two couples back into the frame, *his* frame, anyway. Speaking on the phone to Sally Allardyce, the slim, softly spoken black woman working in television, he was reminded of the tensions he had noticed. Superficially, they were good neighbours and firm friends. Their ill-starred weekend had started with an evening in the pub. Together they had coped with a party much larger than they anticipated. In the aftermath they shared the inconvenience of policemen taking over their apartments. They had got up a card game to pass the time when their Sunday was so disrupted. But under questioning, the men, in particular, had taken different stances over the party, Turnbull agitated and resentful, while Allardyce was more tolerant.

If anyone had deliberately slashed Allardyce's tyre, the betting was strong that it was somebody from that house. Who else would have known where it was parked on that one night? Another neighbour, maybe. Less likely, though.

Why was it done then, then?

Out of malice, sheer frustration, or for a practical reason?

In his mind he could cast Guy Treadwell as a tyre-slasher with no difficulty. The young man bristled with resentment. Exactly why it should be directed at his neighbour was another question, except that people like Treadwell rarely got on with their neighbours.

Emma Treadwell? A woman could rip a tyre with a sharp blade as easily as a man. If anything, she was a more forceful personality than Guy. '*Infirm of purpose! Give me the daggers.*'

And what of Sally Allardyce? She had left early for work that morning. Her walk to the station would have taken her through the Circus, very likely when it was still dark. If she had wanted, for some reason, to limit her husband's movements that day, she could have done the deed.

The motive? In each case he could only guess, and he didn't do that.

He would find out.

Twenty-nine

He crossed the street from Bloomsburys and returned to the police station the quick way, by the public entrance. Before going home, he meant to have a few pointed words with Halliwell about manning the incident room at all times. But he got no further than the enquiry counter. The sergeant on duty had spotted him.

'Mr Diamond.'

'At your service.'

'You're wanted upstairs, sir. A taxi-driver came in ten minutes ago, reckons he knows where your missing lady is.'

Caught in freeze-frame, as it were, Diamond let the magic words sink in. In his experience taxi-drivers didn't volunteer information unless it was reliable. This had to be taken more seriously than the so-called sightings up to now.

Two old men and a dog were waiting by the enquiry window. As one, they turned to see who it was who needed to find a missing lady. And he was so elated by the news that he performed a slow pirouette for them – with surprising grace for a big man.

'The incident room?'

'Your office.'

'I'm on my way.'

Upstairs, Halliwell, caught off guard again, sprang up from Diamond's chair and introduced Mr John Beevers, from Astra Taxis.

John Beevers did not spring up. He was in the one comfortable armchair in the room, basking in limelight and cigar smoke. He took a cellophane-wrapped corona from an inside pocket and held it out to Diamond in a way that was faintly vulgar.

'Non-smoker. What have you got to tell us?'

Now the driver produced the *Bath Chronicle* from his car-coat. 'This woman in the paper. You want to find her, m'dear?'

Diamond had worked in the West Country long enough to be used to being a stranger's 'dear' or 'love', but it grated when coming from someone he disliked on sight. 'That's the general idea.'

'Well, I got news for you. I had her in my cab. Her and another woman.'

A vulgar quip would have been all too easy. 'When was this?'

'Two and a half weeks back, I reckon. It was her, no question.'

Diamond's hopes plummeted. 'As long ago as that?'

'If 'tis no use, m'dear, I'll save my breath.'

'It could still be useful. Go on.'

The driver exhaled copiously in Diamond's normally smoke-free office. 'I can't tell you the date. 'Twere the afternoon and it had been raining. The first woman – not her you're looking for – hailed me in Laura Place, by the fountain. She wanted Harmer House, the women's hostel in Bathwick Street.'

So it was that far back in Rose's history. Diamond's elation was ebbing away.

'I gave her a close look to see if she were a paying customer. You hear the word "hostel" and you got to be careful, if you understand me. She were quite respectable actually. Mind, I weren't over-pleased with the job. It were no fare at all from Laura Place. No more than six hundred yards, I reckon. I told her, polite like, she'd do better to walk it and save herself the fare, but she said she were picking someone up, with luggage. She wanted me to bide awhile outside, and then we'd go up St James's Square.'

'Tucked away behind the Royal Crescent?'

'Right. That sounded more like a job of work to me. I warned her it would all be on the clock, and she weren't bothered. So that's what we did.'

'What was she like?'

'The one who hired me? Now you're asking. This were some days back, you know.'

'Try.'

'Dark-haired, I b'lieve. Thirty, maybe. Bit of a madam. She weren't having no lip from a common cabbie.'

'The hair. Can you tell me anything about it?'

'What do you mean, m'dear? I said it were dark. I can't tell one style from another.'

'Curly?'

'No, not curly. Straight, and combed back, fixed behind her head. What do they call that?'

Diamond knew, but he wasn't going to put words into the witness's mouth.

Beever was getting there by stages. ''Orse-tail. Is that it?'

Halliwell looked ready to supply the word, so Diamond cut in, 'We've got to hear it from you to be of any use, Mr Beever.'

''Orse-tail, I said. No, that b'ain't right. Pony-tail. She had a pony-tail. If you ask me, pony-tails look nice on little girls and really scrawny women. Her'd had too many good dinners to get away with it.'

'And the face. Can you picture the face?'

'You want a lot for nothing. 'Twere the other woman I came in about. Well, I don't know if this be any help, but she made me think of them women in boots.'

'Boots?' said Diamond.

'The tarty ones on the make-up counters. Heavy on the war-paint.'

'Ah, Boot's the chemist.'

'I was telling thee what happened. She made a great to-do about could she rely on me to wait. I told her if she were paying, I didn't mind how long it took. So that's what happened. We drove to Bathwick Street. I bided my time outside Harmer House, reading my paper for a good half-hour, maybe longer. Then she came out with this other woman, the one you're trying to find. She'd said sommat about luggage, but it were only a couple of carrier bags, so I didn't open the boot. I drove them up to St James's Square—'

'Was anything said?'

'Could have been. I don't recall. When we got up to the Square – off Julian Road, behind the Royal Crescent—'

'We established that.'

'Be that as it may, m'dear, nine out of ten people couldn't

take you to it without a map. When we got up there, she pointed out the house. I can't tell you the number. It were on the south side, with a red door. That's all I got to say, really. She settled the fare – something over twenty-five by that time – and I give her a receipt and out they got. They went in with their bags and I haven't seen hide nor hair of them since.'

'Did she let them in with a key, or did someone come to the door?'

'Couldn't tell you. I didn't look.'

'Is your taxi in our car park?'

'I bloody hope so. That's where I left 'er.'

'Right. You can drive me to the house. One of our patrol cars will meet us there.'

St James's Square is one of Bath's tucked-away Georgian jewels, located on the slope above the Royal Crescent and below Lansdown Crescent. You come to it from the scrappy end of Julian Road, where pasta-coloured housing from the 1960s cuts it adrift from the dignified end of the city. But the spirit soars again when you come upon John Palmer's charming square dating from the 1790s, noble buildings with Venetian windows and Corinthian pilasters facing across a large lawned garden with mature trees.

John Beever said as he double-parked outside the house with the red door, 'It be too much to hope that I can charge this to the police, I reckon.'

'I reckon, too,' said Diamond, and added, 'Nice try, m'dear.'

'Do I have to stay?'

A patrol car was entering the square on the far side, so he was content to let John Beever drive away in search of a paying passenger.

There were lights at the windows of the two upper floors. The bell-push gave names for all four flats. He pressed the top one first. Angus Little.

Meanwhile the patrol car had pulled up. Two uniformed constables got out and joined him.

'You know what this is about?'

They did not.

He explained succinctly. There was ample time before

anyone came to the door. This house was not equipped with an answerphone.

Angus Little from the top flat was silver-haired, sixtyish and deeply shaken to have the police calling.

Diamond showed his ID and the picture of Rose.

Little took off his glasses and examined the picture. Then shook his head. 'Can I ask you something?'

'Go ahead.'

'Would you mind terribly turning off the flashing light on your car? It's a bit of a poppyshow, if you know what I mean.'

'Can't do that, sir,' said the driver. 'We're blocking the street.'

Diamond asked, 'Do you live alone, Mr Little?'

He did.

'Tell me about these other tenants.'

As if he had never previously noticed the names listed against the four bells, Mr Little bent close to inspect them. His own was a printed visiting-card, David Waller's had been produced on a printer, made to look like italic writing; Adele Paul's was a peel-off address-label; and Leo and Fiona (no surnames) had typed theirs on pink card.

'What do you want to know?'

'Who are they? Young people, married couples with kids, pensioners?'

'There's only Mr Waller underneath me now. He's single, like me, and quite a bit younger. The other flats have been empty for months.'

'So Adele Paul and – who is it? – Leo and Fiona aren't living here although their names are showing?'

'That's my understanding. Nobody has bothered to remove the cards, that's all. It may be deliberate, for security, you see. You don't want people knowing that some of the flats are unoccupied. I expect the agent is having trouble finding anyone prepared to pay the rent. It's pretty exorbitant. I had the impression Miss Paul was a student at the university. Well-heeled parents, I expect. She must have left last June.'

'Have you noticed anyone using either of the empty flats recently?'

'I can't say I have, but then I'm out so much. I'm in the

antique business. Buying and selling clocks and watches. You might do better asking Mr Waller. He spends more time here. He's a computer expert, I believe, and he tells me he can do most of it from home, lucky man.'

Mr Waller could be saved for later, Diamond decided. He wanted to see inside the two allegedly empty flats. The door to the ground floor one was just ahead. He knocked, got no reply, and asked the more solid of the constables to force it.

Mr Little protested at that. 'Shouldn't you contact the landlord first?'

'Who is the landlord?'

'I'm not entirely sure. But we pay our rent to an agency called Better Let. Do you know it? They have an office in Gay Street.'

'So we don't know the landlord, and the agency is closed by now. What are you waiting for, constable?'

The door sprang inwards at the first contact of the constable's boot.

The flat had the smell of many months of disuse. They didn't spend much time looking at the even spread of dust on the furniture. 'We'll try the basement.'

Mr Little was returning upstairs, probably to confer with Mr Waller. No one had mentioned a search warrant yet, but the computer buff might.

No answer came to Diamond's rapping on the basement door.

'Get on with it, lad.'

This one was harder to crack. The door-frame withstood a couple of kicks and it took a kung fu special to splinter the wood.

Diamond felt for the light-switch. The result was encouraging. The mustiness upstairs was not present here, even though the apartment was shuttered and below ground. He stepped through the living-room to the kitchen, confident that the fridge would yield the clue, as it had in Rose's London flat. But it was switched off, empty, the door left ajar as recommended by the makers.

He looked into the cupboards. There was a tin containing tea-bags, and a jar of instant coffee. The label had a 'best before' date of December 1996 – evidently bought some time ago.

The bedroom, then: a small, cold room with a window placed too high to see out of. Twin divans, a wardrobe, dressing-table and two chests of drawers, empty. No sign of recent occupation.

Quite an anticlimax.

As he returned to the living-room, he heard people coming down the stairs. A youngish, cropped-blond man in a blue guernsey and jeans appeared in the doorway. He had a silver earring. 'Do you mind telling me what this is about?'

'You are . . . ?'

'David Waller from upstairs.'

'The one who works from home? As you see, Mr Waller, we're police officers. Do you happen to know if anyone has used this flat in the last three weeks?'

Waller answered, 'The tenants left ages ago.'

'That isn't what I'm asking. This doesn't have the look of a flat that's been empty for months. Where's the dust?'

The young man gave a shrug. 'It's no concern of mine, is it?'

'You seem to think it is, coming downstairs to check what we're doing. I'm not blaming you. It's the responsible thing to do. I just wonder if you've caught anyone else letting themselves in here.'

'Squatters, you mean?'

'This is potentially more serious than squatting,' Diamond told him. 'Two women were seen entering this building some two weeks ago. We're anxious to question them both. Did you see them?'

'No.'

'So they weren't visiting you?'

Waller rolled his eyes as if to say it was obvious that he didn't entertain women.

'Nor me,' said Mr Little, stepping from behind the door, where he must have been waiting unseen, but more out of discretion than deceit. 'Do you think you might have come to the wrong house?'

Diamond concentrated on Waller. 'You're in here working most days, I gather. Are you sure you didn't hear anyone downstairs?'

'Have you ever lived in a well-built eighteenth-century

building? I'm two floors up, aren't I? It's solidly constructed. I don't hear much at all, except when Mr Little uses a hammer or some such. You could have a rave-up in here, and I don't think the sound would travel up to me.' He paused, fingering his earring. 'But there was something that struck me as strange a couple of weeks ago. We put out our rubbish on Mondays. Black plastic sacks by the front door. Mine was out the night before, and on Monday after breakfast I found I had some other items to throw out, so I went downstairs intending to chuck it in the sack. I unfastened the sack, and much to my surprise it was practically full. I was certain I hadn't filled it up. There were food cans and a cereal packet and some magazines that I knew hadn't belonged to me. Very odd – because it was the only sack there. Mr Little hadn't brought his downstairs at that stage.'

'What magazines were they?'

'That was what puzzled me,' he said. 'They were women's magazines: *Cosmopolitan* and *She* and *Harper's & Queen.* The current issues, too. Someone had gone to all the trouble of unfastening the wire tag on my sack, adding their rubbish to it and fastening it up again. I didn't seriously think anyone else had moved in downstairs. I'm not sure what I thought, except it didn't seem too important. But now that you mention this, I wonder.'

'So do I,' said Diamond. 'But you don't remember seeing anyone in the building?'

'No. They'd have needed keys, wouldn't they? One for the front door and one for the flat – unless they were experts at picking locks.'

'Tell me about the people who were here before. Leo and, em . . .'

'Fiona. They didn't stay long. Leo was an ex-prisoner, I heard. He did eighteen months in Shepton Mallet for stealing underwear off washing-lines. Fiona worked for the Theatre Royal, didn't she?' he asked Little.

'She was in the box office,' the older man confirmed. 'I hinted that I wouldn't say no to some complimentary tickets, but it didn't work.'

'Would their keys have been returned to the agent when they gave up the flat?'

'That's the drill,' said Waller.

'Better Let, in Gay Street?'

'Yes.'

'You said they weren't here long. Who were the previous tenants?'

'An old couple: the Palmers. Mr Palmer died last year and his wife went into a retirement home. After that the place was redecorated and let to Leo and Fiona.'

'What was their surname?'

'Leo and Fiona? I didn't enquire.'

'Nor I,' said Little.

'Were they married?'

'I never enquired. Did you?' David Waller asked his neighbour.

'They were only ever Leo and Fiona to me. Whether they were married is their business.'

Such is the innate respect of the British for their neighbours, Diamond mused. They give you their prison record straight off, but they won't be drawn on their marital status.

'Thanks,' he said, and turned his back on them. He wanted another look at the bedroom. Waller started to follow until Diamond looked over his shoulder and said, 'Do you mind? This is police business.'

The flat had been used by Rose and Doreen, he felt sure, but why, and for how long? The magazines in the rubbish-bag were about the only clue. If they suggested anything, it was that the women had spent time here and needed something to fend off boredom.

He went into the bedroom and began looking behind cupboards for objects that might have been accidentally left behind. The longer the women had remained, the better chance there was of finding some trace of their stay. They had gone to some trouble to leave the place as they had found it, but things occasionally fall out of sight.

Whilst he worked, pulling out pieces of furniture and feeling along the spaces behind, he pondered the reason why the woman who called herself Doreen Jenkins had gone to such trouble to annexe Rose and bring her here. The cover story had been that they were going back for at least one night to Bathford, where Doreen was staying with her partner Jerry. Patently this had been untrue. Doreen was not a visitor to Bath, here on a weekend break, as she had claimed. It was clear that she had planned all along to bring Rose to this address. Very likely she had brought in food and bedding in advance. To have set it all up, she must have obtained a set of keys, but who from? Mrs Palmer, the old widow, now in a retirement home? Leo, the ex-con? Fiona, former box-office person at the Theatre Royal? Or the agency, Better Let, in Gay Street?

His fingers came in contact with something small, hard and lozenge-shaped behind the wardrobe. 'Help me, will you?' he said.

The more burly of the constables tugged the massive piece of furniture away from the wall. Diamond retrieved his find, and held it in his palm. The lozenge-shaped object was a cough lozenge.

He let the two constables go back on patrol, saying he would walk back.

Alone, he searched for almost another hour before giving up. By then he had been through all the rooms and the finds amounted to the cough-sweet, two hairpins that could have belonged to anyone, a piece of screwed-up silver paper and threepence in coppers. Who said police work is rewarding?

David Waller had lingered in the hallway and was waiting for Diamond when he came up the basement stairs. He asked what was going to happen about the doors that had been forced.

Diamond said it would be up to Better Let. He would notify them.

Outside the house, he looked over the railings to see if there was a separate basement entrance. He hadn't noticed one from inside. If there had ever been one, it was bricked over. The only means of entry was inside. The windows had an iron grille over them.

It was quiet on the streets in this upper part of the city. He supposed it would be around nine-thirty, maybe later. All the night life – and there wasn't much in Bath – took place in the centre. Facing a twenty-minute walk to the nick, he stepped out briskly. One of Bath's advantages was that you had the choice of different and interesting routes wherever you were heading. This time he decided to take in Gay Street.

This once-grand street built on a knee-straining slope has a strong literary tradition, home at some point to Jane Austen, Tobias Smollett and Mrs Piozzi, the friend of Dr Johnson. Diamond was on the trail of a less exalted connection. He had a recollection of some information that he scarcely dared hope to confirm: not literary, but commercial. First he had to find the premises of Better Let, the renting agency. It was on the right, almost opposite the George Street turn. A recently cleaned building. Some attempt had been made to display photos of flat interiors at the windows, but it was still essentially residential in appearance. All these houses were protected from the modernisers and developers.

The only other clue to its business use was a plaque on the wall by the door – something about rented accommodation. Peter Diamond didn't bother to read it. His attention was wholly taken by the distinctly superior brass plaque above the Better Let notice:

Guy Treadwell ARIBA
Chartered Architect
Emma Treadwell FRICS
Chartered Surveyor

His memory was accurate, then. They did have an office in Gay Street, and as far as he was concerned, it couldn't have been at a more interesting address.

Part Four

Upon a Dark Night

Thirty

Peter Diamond was not built for jogging, nor fast walking, but he covered the distance to Manvers Street in a sensational time by his standards. His brain was getting through some work, too, putting together the case that buried Emma Treadwell up to her neck in guilt. The descriptions of 'Doreen Jenkins' from Ada, Imogen Starr and the taxi driver all matched Emma's solid appearance and svelte grooming; and now he had the damning fact that the Treadwells' office was in the same building as Better Let. How easy to help herself to the keys to vacant furnished flats.

He called Julie at home.

'Can you get here fast? I'm about to nick the Treadwells. I want you on board.'

She didn't take it in fully.

'They're the link to Rose.' He went on to explain why in a few crisp sentences.

The dependable Julie said she would come directly.

What a wimp of a young man, Diamond thought. It was almost eleven when Guy Treadwell, in silk dressing-gown and slippers, opened the door and saw the outsize detective with Julie and two uniformed officers beside him. Treadwell's hand went to his goatee beard and gripped it like an insecure child reaching for its mother.

'What is this?'

'Shall we discuss it inside?'

'If it's about the damage to the car, I think you want our neighbours, the Allardyces.'

'No, Mr Treadwell, this concerns your wife. Is she at home?'

He stared. 'You'd better come in.'

Diamond gestured to the two officers to wait in the hall. He and Julie followed Treadwell into the living-room.

'Your wife,' Diamond prompted him.

'She isn't here. I'm expecting her soon. She went out. Some meeting or other.'

Diamond turned immediately to Julie. 'Tell the lads to move the cars away, or she'll take fright and do a runner.'

Treadwell looked in danger of bursting blood vessels. 'What on earth is going on?'

'I have some questions for your wife, sir. And for you, too.'

'About what?'

'You might like to get some clothes on. I intend to do this at the police station. You'll come voluntarily, won't you?'

Horrified, Treadwell mouthed the words 'police station'. 'Are you seriously proposing to arrest us?'

'Didn't you hear? This will be voluntary on your part.'

'We've done nothing unlawful.'

'No problem, then. Shall we go upstairs? If you don't mind, I'll stay with you while you put your clothes on.'

Speechless, shaking his head, Treadwell led Diamond to the bathroom on the first floor where his day clothes were hanging behind the door. Diamond waited discreetly on the other side holding it open with his foot.

'I don't see the necessity of this,' the voice in the bathroom started to protest more strongly. 'Coming at night without warning. It's like living in a fascist state.'

Diamond chose not to tangle with him over that. In a few minutes the young man came out fully attired. Some of his bluster had returned now that his bow-tie was back in place. 'I can't imagine what this pantomime is about, but I tell you, officer, you're making a mistake you may regret. I need my glasses.' With Diamond dogging him, he crossed the passage to the bedroom opposite, where a single bed and a single wardrobe made their own statement about the marriage. The half-glasses were on a chest of drawers. He looped the cord over his head and looked ready to play the professor in a college production of *Pygmalion*.

On the way downstairs Diamond asked him if his wife made a habit of coming in late.

He said defiantly, 'There's no law against it.'
'That wasn't what I asked.'
'We're grown-ups. I don't insist that she's home by ten.'
'Was she out last night and the night before?'
'There's plenty to do in Bath. Emma belongs to things, she has friends, she doesn't want to sit at home each evening watching television.'
'So the answer is "Yes"?'
'Haven't I made that clear?' A direct answer seemed impossible to achieve.
They joined Julie in the living-room. While they waited for Emma, Diamond interested himself in the glass-fronted antique bookcase. Two shelves were filled with bound volumes of the *Bath Archaeological Society Journal*.
'You're seriously into all this, Mr Treadwell?'
'The books? I got those for next to nothing at a sale. I don't have the time to be serious.'
'I remember someone telling me you're a whizz at digging up relics.'
'They were exaggerating.'
'I'm sure. We were talking about this good luck you seem to be favoured with. If the truth were told, you have to know a bit about the site before you know where to dig. Isn't that so?'
'It helps.'
'It's like the cards. They call you lucky, but you have to know how to play the hand as well.'
'That is certainly true.'
He was clearly reassured by Diamond's change of tone. Then they heard the front door being opened. Treadwell grasped the arms of his chair, but Diamond put out a restraining hand. Instead, he gestured to Julie, who stepped into the hall to explain to Emma Treadwell why there would be no need to take her coat off.
Emma reacted more coolly than her husband had. 'It's a little late in the evening for all this, isn't it?'

She was still composed in the interview room at the police station. She had spent the evening, she claimed, with a woman friend. No, she could not possibly divulge the friend's name. The poor woman was going through a personal crisis. To pass on her name to the police would be like a betrayal, certain to undo any good she had been able to achieve.

Not bad, young Emma, Diamond thought, not bad at all.

And Julie was thinking that this was the most casual Emma had looked. The baggy sweater and jeans, and the fine, dark hair looking as if it could do with a brushing, supported the story. You don't get dolled up to visit a distressed friend.

Diamond asked, 'Is your friend in trouble with the police?'

'I didn't say that.'

'We only want her to vouch for you.'

She raked some wayward hair from her face, smiled, and said, 'What am I supposed to have done? Pinched the Crown Jewels?'

'We just want it confirmed where you were.'

'At this moment, her situation matters more to me than my own.'

'You've spent a lot of time with her lately, haven't you?'

Emma had no way of knowing how much her husband had already divulged. Guy Treadwell was seated in another room with a copy of the *Bath Chronicle*, some lukewarm coffee in a paper cup and only a bored constable for company. 'It's confidential,' she insisted.

'This woman: is she local?'

'Look, I don't want to be obstructive, but haven't I already made clear why I can't tell you anything about her?'

Reasonable as she appeared to be, she was rapidly sacrificing any rapport with Diamond. What Ada called the lah-de-dah voice grated on him. No doubt she could keep stonewalling *ad infinitum*. He changed tack. 'You have an office in Gay Street?'

'Yes.'

'Above the agency that lets flats. Better Let, isn't it?'

She nodded.

'Obviously, you're on good terms with the people in Better Let. Is there a business tie-in?'

'Do you mean are we connected with them? No.'

'You understand why I'm asking this?'

She said without even blinking, 'No, I don't.'

'One of their flats, a furnished basement in St James's Square, was used by two women a couple of weeks ago. An unofficial arrangement. The place is supposed to be vacant. The women must have acquired a set of keys. There was no break-in.'

The pause that followed didn't appear to unnerve Emma Treadwell.

'One of the women fitted your description,' Diamond resumed. 'The other is called Christine Gladstone, known to some people as Rose, or Rosamund Black. She was in the care of Avon Social Services until recently, suffering from some form of amnesia. Do you have any comment?'

She said as though the subject bored her, 'I did see something in the local paper about a woman who lost her memory.'

'She was seen in the company of this woman who's a dead ringer for you. We have three independent witnesses. We can hold an identity parade in the morning if you insist on denying that it's you.'

'All right,' she said, still without betraying the least concern in her still, brown eyes. 'Let's do that. May I go home now?'

As neat a hand-off as he'd met, and he was an ex-rugby forward. 'You don't seem to realise how serious this is.' He found himself falling back on intimidation. 'It isn't just a matter of illegally occupying a flat. Christine Gladstone is under suspicion of murder – the killing of an old man – her own father – at Tormarton a few weeks ago. If you've been harbouring her, this makes you an accessory.' He watched for her reaction and it was negligible.

'So?'

'If there's another explanation, now is not a bad time to give it.'

Her response was to look up at the ceiling.

He said, 'I can arrest you and detain you here until we get that identification.'

'That sounds like a threat.'

He paused, and then tossed in casually, 'Did you get the fuses you were looking for in Rossiter's?'

She blinked twice. For a fleeting moment her guard seemed to be down. Then she recovered. 'What did you say?'

'The fuses. You were seen in Rossiter's yesterday afternoon asking for electric fuses. They don't sell them.'

She managed to smile. 'I know that.'

'You don't deny you were there?'

She gave Julie a glance as if to invite contempt for this man's stupid questions. 'It must have been someone else, mustn't it?'

But he was certain he'd hit the mark. 'You were seen there by Ada Shaftsbury, who was in the same hostel as Christine Gladstone. She recognised you as the woman who presented herself at Harmer House and claimed she was the sister. I really think you ought to consider your position. I can bring Ada in tomorrow morning.'

That look of indifference remained, so he heaped on everything he had.

'I can bring in Miss Starr, Christine's social worker. I can bring in the taxi-driver you hired – the one who waited for you and then drove you both to St James's Square, to the vacant flat that Better Let had the keys for. St James's Square – that's just behind the Royal Crescent, isn't it? Five minutes from where you live?'

Unperturbed, she rose from the chair. 'Let me know what time you want me tomorrow, then.'

'You can't leave.'

'Why not?'

'We haven't finished.'

Still in control, she said, 'The hell with that. I'm not sitting here any longer, being put through the hoop about things that don't concern me. I know my rights, Mr Diamond. I'd like to go home now.'

She managed to seem convincing, whatever she had done.

He said – and it sounded like a delaying tactic even to him: 'We haven't talked to your husband yet.'

'That's your business.'

'You wouldn't want to leave without him.'

'And that's mine.'

The flip response revealed more than she intended.

'Working together, as you do, you must see a lot of each other.'

'So?'

'Puts a strain on your relationship, I reckon.'

She gave him a glare. 'You're getting personal, aren't you?'

'From what he was saying, you don't share many evenings out.'

Nettled now, she said, 'Oh, for pity's sake. I've heard enough of this garbage.' She moved to the door, but the constable on duty barred her way. 'What is this? Tell this woman to let me pass.'

Diamond said in his most reasonable manner, 'Emma, you may think this is over, but it's hardly begun. I'm going to have more questions for you presently, after we've spoken to your husband.'

'You can't keep me here against my will.'

'We can if we arrest you.'

'That would be ridiculous.'

He gave her one of his looks. 'And that's exactly what I'm about to do. Emma Treadwell, you are under arrest on suspicion of being an accessory after the fact of murder.' He turned to Julie and asked her to speak the new-fangled version of the caution he'd never had the inclination to learn. She had it off pat, even if she spoke it through gritted teeth. He supposed she felt put upon.

But outside the interview room, Julie had more than that to take up with him. 'You won't like this, but I'm going to say it. I don't think we can justify holding her.'

'Have a care,' he warned. 'This has been a long day.'

'It's a house of cards, isn't it? The case against Rose isn't proved yet, and now you're pulling this woman in as an accessory.'

'She's obstructing us, Julie.'

'All you've got is the fact that she works above the agency.'

'She matches the descriptions of Jenkins: mid to late twenties, sturdy build, with dark, long hair, posh voice.'

She sighed and said, 'I could find you five hundred women like that in Bath.'

'Carry on in this vein, Julie, and I may take you up on that.

We may need an identity parade. She'll go on ducking and weaving until someone fingers her.'

'Who would do that? Ada?'

'The husband is worth trying first. He's brittle.'

'But how much does he know?'

'Let's see.'

In the second interview room, Guy Treadwell had discarded the newspaper and shredded the coffee cup into strips. He told Diamond as he entered, 'You've got a damned nerve keeping me here like this.'

'Yes.'

'You haven't even told me what it's about. I have some rights, I believe.'

'Let's talk about your business as an architect,' Diamond said.

'My practice,' he amended it.

'You're in Gay Street, above Better Let.'

'Yes.'

'They're a renting agency, am I right?'

Treadwell's eyes widened. He said with a note of relief, 'Are they the problem?'

'Is there independent access to your office, or do you go through their premises to get to yours?'

'We share a staircase, that's all.'

'I expect you know the people reasonably well?'

'We're on friendly terms.'

'Friendly enough to go into their office for a chat sometimes, coffee and biscuits, catch up on the gossip or whatever?'

'Very occasionally, if something of mutual interest crops up, I may go down and speak to the manager.'

So pompous. He was half Diamond's age, yet he made the big man feel like a kid out of school. 'Good. You can help me, then. You know the layout. What do they do with their keys – the keys to the flats they have to let?'

'They hang them up in a glass-fronted case attached to the end wall.'

'Does it have a lock?'

'I haven't the faintest idea.'

'I suppose they wouldn't need to keep it locked while the

office is occupied,' Diamond mused. 'And your wife – is she on good terms with the Better Let people?'

'Reasonably good.'

'Nips down for a chat with the girls in the office?'

'No.'

'No?'

'Emma is a Chartered Surveyor. She doesn't fritter away her time with office girls.'

Diamond was forced to accept it, put like that. Trapped in his middle-aged perspective of the young, he'd lumped Mrs Treadwell with the legion of women from eighteen to thirty, forgetting that they had a hierarchy of their own. 'Tell me something else,' he started up again. 'I came past your office building tonight. I noticed you have a security alarm.'

'Of course.'

'Sensible. I imagine that's a shared facility.'

'Yes.'

'So how does it work? A control panel somewhere inside with a code number you enter if you want to override the system?'

Treadwell nodded.

'Where's the control panel housed? Not in the hall, I imagine?'

'Inside the Better Let premises. I have a key to their office for access purposes.'

'Exactly what I was about to ask. You keep the key where?'

'On a ring, in my pocket.' He took it out and showed Diamond.

'And does your wife have a key to Better Let for the same reason?'

'Yes, in case one of us is away. Those alarms have a habit of going off at the most inconvenient times.'

'I know, sir,' said Diamond, with a glance at Julie, cock-a-hoop that one of his theories had worked out. 'There you are, you or Emma, working late, and the darned thing goes off for no reason, disturbing the pigeons and all the old ladies within earshot. But happily you're safe in the knowledge that either one of you can deal with it. You can get into the Better Let office at times when they aren't there.'

Guy Treadwell looked at him blankly.

Diamond explained about the basement flat in St James's Square and the suspicion that Emma had taken the missing woman Christine Gladstone there. 'She can let herself into Better Let whenever she wants. She could have picked up the keys to this empty flat and used it, you see.'

Treadwell shook his head. 'Emma isn't stupid, you know. She wouldn't risk her career. She doesn't even know this woman. You're way off beam here.'

The force of the denial tested even Diamond's confidence. Surely Treadwell was implicated if Emma was. What else had he thought she was doing on her evenings out? Highland dancing?

'I'm keeping her here overnight for an identity parade tomorrow.'

'Do you mean she's under arrest?'

Diamond gave a nod. 'She'll be comfortable.'

'This is absurd!'

'We're not talking parking offences, Guy. Christine Gladstone is wanted on suspicion of murder. We think your wife knows where she is.'

Treadwell looked away and said bleakly, 'Are you going to lock me up as well?'

'You're free to go. We all need some sleep.' Diamond leaned back in the chair and stretched his arms. 'Talking of sleep, I noticed you don't share a bed with your wife.'

He flushed crimson. 'Bloody hell, what is this?'

'Don't share a bedroom, even.'

'Our sleeping arrangements are nothing to do with the police.'

'They are if they provide your wife with an alibi. She's out most evenings. Gets home late. If she isn't with Christine Gladstone, who is she with?'

Treadwell stared back, his face drained of colour.

'I'm still trying to understand her behaviour,' Diamond continued in his reasonable tone. 'Back at your house you told me she's got this social life that takes her out in the evenings. Forgive me, but you don't seem to be part of it. Who are these friends?'

Treadwell leaned forward over the table, covered his face, and said in a broken voice, 'Sod you. Sod you.'

Diamond lifted an eyebrow at Julie, whose eyes were registering amazement. Then he dealt quite sensitively with Treadwell, before the self-pity turned more ugly. 'It has to be faced, Guy. Not all marriages work. I'm no agony aunt, but maybe you both entered into it thinking you were an ideal team, the architect and the surveyor. Working out of the same office can be a joy when you're man and wife, but it can also be a strain.'

Without moving his hands from his face, Treadwell said in a low, measured voice, as if he were speaking into a tape-recorder, 'I knew Emma rejected me physically, but I never thought she was seeing a woman until you told me. I thought she was with men. And now I discover it's this Gladstone woman and it's tied in with murder. I'm gutted.' He looked up, his eyes red-lidded. He hooked a finger behind the bow-tie and tugged the knot apart. 'I don't know what else you want from me.'

'There is one thing: did you stick the knife into your neighbour's car-tyre?'

His startled gaze flickered between Diamond and Julie. 'God, no. What makes you think . . .' he started to say, then answered his own question. 'You thought I suspected William and Emma were at it. Well I did, to be honest. There were times when I noticed the pair of them looking at each other as if they knew things I didn't. He's more outgoing than I am, smiles a lot, so I couldn't be sure. Emma laughs at his remarks as if he's the wittiest man she ever met. And that irritates me. I *was* jealous, let's face it. I once saw them by chance coming out of the Hat and Feather in London Street. And quite often she'd come in at the end of an evening and a few minutes later I'd hear the front door open quietly again and he'd creep upstairs to his flat. You can torture yourself imagining things. But I wouldn't do anything so sneaky as to take it out on his car.'

'Who did, then?' said Diamond, more to himself than Treadwell.

'Sally?' suggested Julie.

Thirty-one

Treadwell had been silent during the short ride. Diamond left him locked in his own misery until the patrol car swung onto the cobbles in front of the Crescent, jerking them all out of semi-slumber.

'In the morning we'll put your wife on an identity parade. These things take hours to set up, so it can't be much before noon. I advise you to get your solicitor there.'

Troubled questions welled up again. 'What's Emma really supposed to have done? You don't think she was involved in the deaths of these people?'

'Will you sleep any better if I give you an answer?'

'I don't know,' he said, unable to decipher such a Delphic utterance.

'How's your cooking?'

'What?'

'Cooking. Pretty basic, is it? Boiled eggs and baked potatoes?'

'I don't follow you.'

'Go out in the morning and buy a decent cookbook. She's not coming home for a long time.'

The wretched man trudged towards the front door like the closing shot of a sombre East European film.

Inside the car, Diamond yawned. 'My place next.'

Only it was not to be. Julie, seated in the back, with a better view of the house, had spotted something she did not understand.

'Hold it.'

'What's up?'

'The door's already open. Someone is there.' She wound down the window for a better view. 'I'm sure of it.' Without another word, she got out and crossed the pavement. Guy Treadwell heard her, turned and stopped.

She ran straight past him. The figure she had glimpsed for a moment in the doorway had retreated inside. Shouting, 'Stop. Police!' she dashed in and across the hall.

Diamond, still in the car, roused from his torpor, swung open his door and followed.

Treadwell had halted uncertainly outside his house.

Diamond asked him, 'Who was that?'

'I didn't see.'

'Which way?'

'Upstairs.'

Inside, the sounds of a struggle carried down from an upper floor. The place was in darkness. He fanned his hands across the wall for a light-switch and couldn't find one. Groped his way to the banister rail and took the stairs in twos. The gasps from above sounded female in origin.

Blundered up two flights of stairs.

Moonlight from a window on the second-floor landing revealed two figures wrestling. There was no need to pile in. Julie had her adversary in an armlock. A young woman.

'You want help?' Diamond asked. 'Cuffs?'

'You don't have any cuffs,' Julie reminded him. She eased her grip slightly, allowing the woman to turn her head.

Sally Allardyce's eyes gleamed in the faint white light, the more dramatically against her black skin. She was wearing a blue dressing-gown over a white nightdress. Her feet were bare.

'Let her go, Julie.'

Released, Sally sat up and rubbed her left arm, moaning.

'I called out,' said Julie. 'And you took off.'

'I was scared,' Sally said. 'I saw the police car.'

Diamond loyally did his best to justify Julie's conduct. 'What were you doing, peeking round the front door?'

'I thought it was my husband coming in.'

He hesitated, playing her answer over in his head. 'He's still out? Where?'

'God knows.' Her voice faltered. She swallowed hard, pulling the dressing-gown across her chest, getting command of herself. 'I heard a car draw up outside. I wanted to catch them sneaking in together.'

'Catch who?'

'William and Emma.' Speaking the names caused a torrent of resentment to pour from her. 'I'm sick of all the deceit. I've known about it for months, the way they look at each other, the secret meetings, the evenings out together, the restaurants on his credit card statements, pretending it's business when I know bloody well what it is. I want to catch them creeping in. Tonight I was sure. I waited up. I knew they were together.'

So it was cards on the table with a vengeance.

'But he isn't with Emma,' Julie told her.

'Don't give me that. I know bloody well he is.'

'You're wrong, Sally. Emma came back a good two hours ago and we picked her up. She's in a cell at the police station.'

Sally stared at her. 'What for? But I heard her go out at seven, seven-fifteen, or something, and he was looking out of the window, waiting. He didn't know I was watching. It was like a signal to him, like she was some bitch on heat. He was off down those stairs without even telling me he was going out.' She paused, letting Julie's statement sink in. 'If he isn't with her, where is he, then? If she's locked up, where the hell is William? What's he doing at this hour of the night?'

The same question was troubling Peter Diamond. He thought of a possible answer that would be no comfort to anyone. Instead he asked, 'Someone slashed a tyre of your husband's car yesterday night. Was that you?'

'Me?' She looked bewildered. 'Why should I do that?'

'You've just told us. You're an angry young woman with a two-timing husband, that's why. You walk to the station early on your way to work, when it's still dark. You go through the Circus, where you know it's parked. You could easily—'

'I didn't,' she said in a tight, controlled voice. 'I wouldn't demean myself.'

Back in the car, he told the driver, 'Change of plan. Switch on the beacon and back to the nick. Fast.'

Above the surge in acceleration, Julie said, 'If this is to do with me—'

'It isn't.'

'I know I was out of order to scrap with her.'

'Will you listen, for Christ's sake? Another killing may have taken place tonight.'

'William Allardyce?' Her voice rose high. 'You think he's been murdered?'

'No chance. I think he's the murderer.'

After a pause, to be sure that he was serious, she spoke her mind. 'This is an about-turn, isn't it? You've been telling all and sundry that Rose is the killer.'

'Of the farmer, yes.'

'Is she, then?'

The lack of contact between them had never been so apparent. 'No, Rose is innocent.'

'After all that you've been saying?'

Unwisely, he was still trying to claim some credit. 'The way I prefer to put it, Julie, is that I confirmed my earlier theory. Allardyce was our main suspect from the day we met him. Remember the missing shoe? You can't have forgotten us watching his car for hours.'

She said, 'We were investigating something else.'

'Right. I hadn't connected Hildegarde's death with the farmer's. This new information that Emma has been hiding Rose stands the whole thing on its head. William is our man.'

'Both murders?' she said in disbelief. 'William Allardyce?'

'Don't tell me you like the man.'

'That's neither here nor there.'

'But . . . ?'

'He was easier to deal with than the rest of them. He went out of his way to be pleasant.'

'His job,' Diamond cynically dismissed it. 'PR.' He swayed against her as they swung left into George Street. 'God, don't you hate being driven fast?'

The car's speed didn't bother Julie. Being crushed against the arm-rest didn't either, but being crushed by force of personality was something else. She said nothing. She was waiting for him to make his case against Allardyce.

Instead, he asked, 'Did you believe what Sally just told us?'

'About what – her husband with Emma?'

'The tyre, Julie. The slashed tyre.'

'Yes, I believed her.'

He sighed. 'So did I.'

'What is it about the damned tyre?' she asked. 'You won't let go.'

'I won't let go because it's crucial to the whole shooting match.' Competing with the engine, he explained, 'We have two angry spouses, Guy Treadwell and Sally Allardyce: reason enough to sabotage the car. I put it to them both and they denied it, and we believe them, right?'

Julie nodded.

'And there's no earthly reason, is there, why Allardyce would have done the slashing himself and then reported it?'

'I can't think of one.'

'So who else knew where the car was parked last night?'

She pondered the options. 'Only Emma. But she's supposed to be his lover. She had no reason either.'

'Oh, but she had,' he said. 'She had a reason, Julie, a far better reason than anyone else.'

Emma was not sleeping. She was lying in the cell wrapped in the blanket, but that was to keep warm. When the door was unbolted, she sat up and swung her legs over the edge of the bed.

'Straight answers, now,' Diamond demanded. 'Where did you take Rose?'

Her mouth tightened.

He told her, 'William Allardyce isn't home yet. We just came from there. His wife says he followed you when you went out this evening soon after seven.'

She drew in a sharp breath and still said nothing.

'Emma, you don't want another killing on your conscience. You've been protecting Rose. That's why you disabled his car last night. Isn't that so?'

She stared away at the blank wall, absorbing what he had said.

'You put his car out of action to stop him following you. But he's out there now and he came after you tonight. How long is it since you left Rose?'

Now, giving way to emotion at last, her face creased in anguish.

'You loved the man,' Diamond went on, still taking the tolerant line with her. 'You had an affair and it went horribly wrong. He's a killer twice over, your lover. He shot the old farmer, didn't he? And he threw the woman off the roof of your house. You know he won't stop at two. If Rose isn't dead already, she will be shortly. Where is she, Emma? Where are you keeping Rose?' He grasped her arms and practically shook her.

She turned her terrified eyes on him. 'Prior Park Buildings.'

'Where's that? You're coming with us.'

In the short drive across the Avon and out along Claverton Street, Diamond got some more things straight with Emma.

'He was using you – you realise that? Putting you out front, getting the plans of Marton Farm through your official duties as a surveyor. No doubt you were excited by his stories of a fabulous hoard waiting to be dug up. But did you know he was willing to kill for it?'

She was ready to talk now that she understood the danger Rose was in. 'William was jealous of Guy. He was so reasonable in every other way,' she said in a voice drained of all emotion. 'Totally charming and civilised, much more in control than my husband.'

'You say "in every other way".'

'He had this obsession – there's no other word for it – with beating Guy at his own game. Guy seems to lead a charmed life. You've heard us talk about his good luck, and it's true. Well, his hobby is archaeology.'

'William wanted to beat him at that?'

She nodded. 'By making a sensational find. He read about an Anglo-Saxon sword dug up during the war.'

'The Tormarton Seax.'

Diamond's status improved several notches. She said after a surprised interval, 'That's right.'

'Go on.'

'Well, you seem to know about it. The family have never allowed anyone onto the land. Because of the war and the dog-in-the-manger attitude of the family, nothing actually happened after the sword was found. William researched the site. He sent me to the County Planning Office – which, of course, I'm familiar with – to copy maps of local burial sites. He read everything he could about the Anglo-Saxons and decided there was a real chance that other objects were waiting to be dug up. He believed it was worth buying the farm to make a search.'

'Buying it? He was as confident as that?'

'Massively confident.'

'And you encouraged him?'

'He didn't need encouraging.' She sighed and coloured a little. 'It was the sure way of pleasing him.'

'So what happened? He offered to buy the land?'

'At a fair price. But old Mr Gladstone wouldn't sell.'

'One stubborn old farmer stood in his way. Wouldn't even let you run a metal-detector over it.'

'That wasn't suggested. William was careful never to mention why he was interested in the farm. He said to me – and I think he was right – that any talk of possible finds would wreck the deal for ever.'

'So when he couldn't acquire the land by lawful means, he shot the old man.'

She was quick to close him down. 'It wasn't so crude as that. William visited the farm and made a good offer that Mr Gladstone turned down. He refused to leave the cottage. He'd been born there and he would die there, he said.'

'And he did.'

She ignored that observation. 'Then William went back with a better idea. He would buy the land and the cottage on the understanding that Mr Gladstone would remain in the cottage as tenant – and for no rent. And William would pay for renovations as well. But it just seemed to inflame the old man.'

'When was this?'

'The Friday evening before . . .'

'Before the body was found? And you were there?'

To confirm this could easily make her an accessory to murder, but she answered without hesitation, 'Yes. The old man became angry. He ordered us out. He grabbed his shotgun off the wall and started waving it about really dangerously. I was terrified. William wrestled the gun away, holding it by the barrel. Mr Gladstone came at him and

William swung the gun at him. The heavy part you hold – what do you call it?'

'The stock.'

'Yes. The stock crashed against his head and he fell. I was appalled. It all happened so suddenly, and there he was lying on the floor. William was calm. He knelt beside him and tried to feel for a pulse to see if he was still alive. I was in a terrible state by then and he sent me out to the car. I waited there a long time, praying and praying that he wasn't dead. Then to my absolute horror, I heard a shot. Terrible. I ran back and looked through the window. It was the worst moment of my life. The sight of that old man, what was left of him, propped in the chair.'

'Did you go in?'

'I couldn't possibly.'

'What did William tell you?'

'That he'd made it look like a suicide. The only thing to do, he said, because the old man was dead from the blow to his head. He sat the body in the armchair and propped the gun under the chin and fired. It caused a massive injury to the head, so much that you wouldn't have known he'd been hit previously.'

'He was right about that.'

Better Let would have described the street as a superior terrace dating from the 1820s in a secluded location south-east of the city, set back from Prior Park Road by steeply banked gardens and the novel feature of a shallow canal. They left the car in Prior Park Road and approached the house by the path skirting the canal.

Emma, handcuffed, remained in the car, guarded by the driver. She had pointed out the house, and there was no reason to think she was bluffing. She wanted Rose to survive. Say what you like about Emma, in all her actions over the past days, Rose's safety had been paramount.

Two response cars had been ordered to the scene, bringing six uniformed officers – not bad, Diamond reckoned, for the small hours of the morning. Bath was not geared up to night emergencies.

Three men went to the garden at the rear of the house to cover a possible escape through the alley.

No lights were on in the house Emma had named. But they were turned on next door, and the curtains twitched.

'The Neighbourhood Watch strikes again,' muttered Diamond, rolling his eyes.

The curtains had not been drawn in the ground floor flat where Rose was supposedly in hiding. He shone a torch through the window. Nothing moved inside.

Over the personal radio, the officers at the back reported that no one was visible in either of the two rooms at the rear.

'We'll go in, then.'

They forced the front door and made a search. Signs of recent occupation encouraged them, a half-eaten chicken sandwich in the kitchen that was still soft and moist to the touch and a faintly warm teapot. But no one was there. No signs of a scuffle, even.

'Where's he taken her?' said Julie.

'Anywhere from Pulteney Weir to Clifton Suspension Bridge. Fake suicides are his m.o.' He returned to the car and contacted headquarters. They already had a call out on Allardyce's BMW. No one had sighted it.

He got into the back seat beside Emma. 'You know where he must have taken her, don't you?'

She shook her head.

'I think you do. We need your help, Emma, if we're going to save Rose's life.'

She cried out in anguish, 'I'd tell you if I knew. I'm on her side. God, I've spent the last two weeks hiding her from him.'

'What state is she in mentally? Is her memory back?'

'Hardly at all. I've told her some things I thought she should know. She knows what happened to her father, but I don't think she remembers finding him.'

'She *found him dead*?'

'A couple of days later, yes.'

'So she knows her father was murdered?'

'No. I simply said he was found dead with a shotgun beside him. I was trying to be truthful without saying everything.'

'She still thinks you're her stepsister?'

'Yes.'

'And William. She has no suspicion that he killed her father?'

'She doesn't know who William is. I told her a little about the farm being a possible Anglo-Saxon site. I said the man who tried to force her into the car the other day must be a treasure-hunter who thinks she knows about precious objects her father may have unearthed.'

'And that was Allardyce, of course?'

'Yes.'

'Who was driving?' Julie asked.

'I was.'

'You?' said Diamond.

'Wearing a baseball hat.'

'Nobody got a look at the driver,' said Julie.

'There's something wrong here,' Diamond said. 'That car wasn't the BMW Allardyce uses. It was a red Toyota according to Ada.'

'A Toyota Previa. It took a dent in the side from Ada. He had to get it off the road until it was repaired, so he rented the BMW, until yesterday, when he got his regular car back,' Emma said.

He hesitated. 'You're telling me the BMW isn't his damned car? Julie, we're looking for the wrong motor. What's the Toyota's number?'

Emma told him and he radioed central communications.

He turned back to her. 'You say she doesn't know who William is, but she knows a man is pursuing her. She knows he's dangerous.'

'He terrifies her.'

He leaned back in the seat and closed his eyes. The tension was getting to him. He was striving to second-guess the outcome of this meeting between the terrified young woman and the double murderer. 'If she isn't killed straight off – and I don't think she has been, because he'll want to dress it up as a suicide – her only chance is to bluff him. Does she have the self-control to do it?'

He'd been speaking his thoughts and he didn't expect an answer, but Emma said, 'To do what?'

'You say he's obsessed with the idea of finding a hoard. You mean really obsessed?'

'It's taken over his life.'

'Does Rose know he's so fanatical?'

'She's in no doubt about that. I had to get her to understand why I was trying to protect her.'

Diamond leaned forward and grasped the driver's shoulder. 'Tormarton. We're going up to the farm.' He lowered the window and shouted to Julie to get in. In seconds, all three cars were moving at speed in convoy, with beacons flashing, up Pulteney Road, heading north.

'She's bright enough to have thought of it, but is she cool enough?' he said to no one in particular.

Julie turned to look at him.

He said, 'The surefire way to buy time from a killer like this is to offer him the thing he craves – an Anglo-Saxon hoard. She tells him what? What would I tell him? What would either of you tell him in desperation? She bluffs. She says it's a family secret that the stuff was dug up years ago and stored away in the house. Yes, inside the house. She's willing to show him. It's all his if he'll spare her life.'

Julie digested this. 'It's asking a lot – for her to think up a story as good that.'

'If she hasn't come up with something, we might as well get some sleep and drag the river in the morning.'

Thirty-two

With Emma, the softly-softly approach seemed to be the right one. Diamond spoke with more steadiness than he felt whilst being driven through the cluttered streets of Bath at a speed appropriate to a three-lane motorway.

'This help you're giving us won't be forgotten.'

She didn't respond.

It was crucial to discover the likely behaviour of the killer they hoped to find at Tormarton.

'Emma, we're trying to save Rose's life. We need to know more about his dealings with her. When did he first meet her?'

'When she turned up at the farm on the Sunday afternoon.'

He paused, trying to follow the sequence of events. 'Let me get this straight. You told me old Mr Gladstone was killed on the Friday evening. Now you're talking about Sunday afternoon?'

She nodded. 'A couple of days after.'

'You say William went back to the farm?'

'He went back on the Saturday and the Sunday.'

'What for?'

'To go over the ground. Use the metal detector. Dig for gold or silver or whatever is buried there.'

He breathed out audibly, vibrating his lips. 'With the old man lying dead in the house? He was taking one hell of a risk.'

Emma, beside him, spread her hands. 'That's how fixated he is. I told you it's an obsession. There's no other word for it.'

'The chance to get rich quick? Does he have money problems?'

'They live beyond their means, but it's more personal than that. He's desperate to prove something.'
'To you?'
'To himself. Oh, he started out wanting to impress me, to show me that he's a winner, much smarter than Guy.'
'By stealing you from your husband?'
She was silent a moment. 'I haven't thought of it like that. I was carried along by the passion he put into it. Stupidly, I thought he was doing it all for me. A treasure hunt, with just the two of us sharing a secret. Flattered, yes. Any woman would be, to have a man care so much about her. I let him make love to me. But it's been brought home to me that I'm of secondary importance. He'll carry on regardless of anything I say.'
'An old-fashioned lust for gold?'
She shook her head. 'It goes much deeper with William. It's about his self-esteem. He has this terrific opinion of himself and very little to show for it. His public relations business is going nowhere. If he could discover a new planet, or an unknown element, and have his name on it, he would. He's sure he's on the brink of a brilliant discovery. You have to know someone as single-minded as that. He thinks about nothing else but the finds he is going to make at that site. With the old man dead, he could get onto the land at last and use his metal detector. That's how blinkered he is.'
Diamond understood. It was the kind of all-or-nothing motive that made a man into a hero, or a crook. Certain individuals had this supreme belief in themselves that in the right conditions produced great art, huge discoveries and inspiring leadership. But the same self-importance spawned dictators and murderers.
'So he spent the weekend at the farm, searching,' he said. 'Worth the risk, I suppose. It could have been weeks before anyone else turned up there. Old Gladstone didn't welcome visitors.'
'Believe me,' Emma stressed, 'if it had been Queen Square in the centre of Bath, he would still have been there with his metal detector.'
'So? Any joy? We saw the places where he dug.'
'Only bits of scrap.'
'What a let-down.'

'He won't accept that nothing is there. He still believes in this hoard.'

'That's the hope we're hanging onto,' said Diamond. 'You were starting to tell me about that afternoon when Rose turned up at the farm.'

'I've only heard William's side of it. Rose doesn't remember.'

'Let's have it.'

'He told me time was getting on and he'd just about decided to stop for the day, when he heard a car come up the lane. It was a taxi, and it stopped in the yard, right beside William's parked car. William took cover behind the chicken house. He heard someone get out, and the taxi driving off.'

'This was Rose?'

'Yes. William saw this woman arrive and he didn't know who she was, or what to do. He stayed hidden while she walked up to the cottage and went in.'

'It was open?'

Julie, in the front passenger seat, turned and reminded him, 'It doesn't lock automatically when you close it. There's a key that works from both sides.'

'I get you,' he said. 'If it had been locked on the outside, then the suicide theory would have looked very dodgy indeed. So she went in.'

Julie put in, 'Which is why two of her hairs were found at the scene.'

He didn't like being reminded of his earlier theory. Ignoring that, he asked Emma, 'What did Allardyce do?'

'His first impulse was to run back to his car and drive off. But he had his metal detector lying on the ground where he'd left it and he went to pick it up and everything happened too quickly. She came rushing out in a state of hysteria. She saw William and ran towards him, for help, I suppose. She was gibbering, unable to speak. She must have had the most horrendous shock you can imagine, finding her own father like that. He'd been dead for two days. Enough—'

'To blow her mind?'

Emma returned Diamond's gaze. 'That's what happened, isn't it?'

'Something shut down in her brain, for sure.'

'William didn't know what to do with this frantic woman. But she calmed down quite quickly, and he tried talking to her, yet still couldn't get any sense out of her. Couldn't even get eye contact. He asked who she was, and where she came from, and she just stared ahead, like a zombie, he said. Obviously she was in deep shock at finding the body. That suited William. His best plan was to get her away from the farm while she was still confused. So he put her in the car and drove off.'

'And shoved her out a couple of miles down the road.'

'Well, yes.'

'Letting her take her chance with the traffic on the A46. Charming. What happened next? You read in the paper that she survived and was the mystery woman who lost her memory, right?'

'Yes. William saw her picture. He was really alarmed. The report said she'd recovered her power of speech. He didn't know if she remembered enough to give the police a description of him, or lead them to the farm. People might lose their memory for a short time, but they usually get it back.'

'So he made the botched attempt to snatch her outside Harmer House – with you at the wheel?'

'Yes.'

'Using his red Toyota. If Ada hadn't dented it, we would have made the connection sooner, wouldn't we, Julie?'

Julie didn't look round, or speak.

He turned back to Emma. 'You drove the car knowing what you'd got yourself into.'

'No.' She was adamant. 'In my worst nightmare I didn't think Rose would come to any harm. I thought he wanted to talk to her, give her some story that would reassure her and keep her quiet. I was so upset about what had happened already that I didn't think it through. It was only after he was so violent trying to get her in the car that I knew what danger she was in.'

'You feared for her life.'

'And I still do. I fear for it now.'

As if he were tuned in on the radio, the driver in the police car ahead switched on his siren. With blue lights flashing, the convoy of three slipped past the line of traffic at the junction of the London Road with the A46, jumped the traffic lights and started the long climb up Nimlet Hill.

Diamond had to wait for the siren to stop before he picked up the thread. 'You meant to stop him from harming her. You say you were too upset to think straight, but you must have got your thoughts in order.'

'I had to.'

'Your plan was more subtle than his, and it worked. You went to Avon Social Services and told them you were Rose's stepsister. They were taken in because you had those photos. Where did the pictures come from? Rose's handbag, I suppose.'

Emma nodded. 'The bag was in the car the evening he drove her away from the farm. That's how we found out who she is. Her name, Christine Gladstone, was on a chequebook and the credit cards. William asked me to get rid of it for him. He kept involving me at each stage. Going through the bag, I found the pictures and kept them. Old photos are precious. Everything else is at the bottom of the river.'

'You won over the social worker with those pictures. She was the crucial person.'

'Yes. The others were uneasy, I could see, but they weren't taking the decision.'

'So you had to hide her away. You nicked a set of keys from Better Let and took her to the basement flat in St James's Square. But you moved her soon after. Why?'

'William spotted her in the street.'

He said in surprise, 'You let her out?'

'I wasn't capable of keeping her hidden all the time. She thought I was family and she co-operated. It was just bad luck that William saw her. I suppose it was good luck that he didn't see me with her. Anyway, he followed her to St James's Square. He appeared at the window. Of course Rose recognised him as the man who'd tried to snatch her outside Harmer House. She heard someone let him into the house and she panicked. Climbed out of the kitchen window at the back. Those houses are built on a steep gradient and it was a long drop, longer than she expected in the dark. When I found her next morning, she'd spent the night lying in pain in the yard. I had to get her to hospital.'

'Hospital?' His voice piped high. 'Are you saying she's injured?'

'A broken ankle.'

'That's all we need.'

Julie said, 'In plaster?'

'Yes.'

All that softly-softly stuff went out of the window. Diamond clenched a fist and brought it down hard on his thigh. 'Jesus Christ, you're telling us she's immobile?'

'She has crutches.'

'Terrific.'

He was temporarily lost for words, so it was Julie who asked, 'Didn't the nurses find out who she is?'

'They're terribly overstretched. In the Triage Room all they wanted was her name and date of birth. I gave it.'

'Yes, but in Casualty Reception . . . ?' Julie knew the procedures at the RUH.

'I told them we were sisters visiting Bath and made up an address and the name of a GP in Hounslow and they were satisfied.'

'Rose didn't speak up?' said Julie.

'She didn't know any different.'

'They must have asked how the accident happened.'

'I told the truth, or most of it. A fall from a window. I said she was trying to hide from someone and underestimated the drop. Accidents often sound stupid when they have to be explained.'

'And Rose went along with this?'

'She was feeling pretty bad at the time, and was happy for me to do the talking.'

'She trusted you?'

'I hadn't been unpleasant to her. What she couldn't understand was why we didn't go back directly to West London, where I said we lived. I'd made up a story about being on holiday with my partner and wanting to spend a few more days in Bath for his sake.'

Diamond chipped in again, needing to press on urgently. Already they had reached the approach to Dyrham. 'So after she had the foot plastered, you moved her to Prior Park

Buildings, to another furnished flat. What about Allardyce? At which point did he start to suspect you were double-crossing him?'

'I don't know,' Emma told him. 'He heard from somewhere that her family had collected her and she didn't remember anything and at first he was relieved. I think it must have been the evening of the party when he got suspicious.'

'Suspicious! He killed the German girl.'

She swallowed hard. 'Yes.'

'That party. Was it really got up that night as you told me, with no planning?'

'It was just as we told you. Thanks to Guy's lucky streak we won a small prize on the lottery and our house was taken over. I was glad of the distraction, to tell you the truth. The tensions had been pretty bad in the house.' She sighed. 'I can't tell you much about the poor girl who was killed except that she was behaving strangely, very inquisitive, looking into store cupboards and trying to get into the basement at one point.'

'And the attic,' Diamond enlightened her. He had long since worked out what Hildegarde had been up to that night. 'She was looking for Rose. She didn't speak much English, but she got about, and she was sharp-eyed. She was a witness to the kidnap attempt outside Harmer House. She tried to report it to us.'

Emma's eyes registered surprise.

'We got a translation and filed the statement,' he said. 'Put it down as a scuffle in the street, unfortunately. We had the same story from Ada. They both lived in the hostel.'

'Oh.'

'Later, Hildegarde thought she recognised you when you came to the hostel to collect Rose. Her suspicions were fuelled, but she didn't have enough English to discuss it with Ada, who was the obvious person to talk to. Instead, she made the fatal mistake of doing some investigating of her own. She followed you that Saturday night when you met in the Grapes. She was a regular there, and she saw you and the others come in. She was positive she knew you this time, because Allardyce was with you. She was right about so much, but wrong in one crucial matter. She suspected you were keeping Rose at the Royal Crescent, and the chance of getting into your house was too good to miss.'

With an insight that impressed even Julie, he was drawing together strands of the case she had not thought about until now.

'At the party, she checked everywhere in the house she could imagine as a possible place where Rose was kept and finally she was left with the attic room. Allardyce had noticed her prowling around. He was worried about this woman's strange behaviour. He noticed her looking at him suspiciously. He may have seen her previously, tracking his movements out on the streets of Bath. So when she went through the bedroom and up the stairs to the attic, he followed. Hildegarde heard him and opened the window and climbed out onto the roof. Fatal. He saw his chance to be rid of her. Pushed her off. There must have been a struggle, because one of her shoes came off – something Allardyce didn't know until the body was found by the paper-boy. The shoe was still up on the roof. Too late to place it beside the body, he disposed of it. Only he knows where. I don't suppose we'll find it.'

Julie explained, 'He had to get rid of it after handling it. Forensic traces.'

Diamond asked Emma, 'Did he tell you any of this?'

She shook her head, visibly shaken at hearing her lover's callous conduct set out in full.

Pitying her, he said, 'Don't be in any doubt. Your efforts to hide Rose saved her life.'

But she shook her head. 'He'll have killed her by now.'

They had reached the Tormarton interchange. The convoy crossed above the motorway and took the right turn that would bring them north of the village and out another mile to the Gladstone farm.

He spoke over the radio to the other cars. This was a covert operation, he informed them. They were to switch off the beacon lights immediately. They would park on the main road opposite the farm and cut their lights, and not under any circumstances drive up the track. All personnel would assemble at the near end of the track leading to the farmhouse and await instructions.

'And now pray to God our hunch is right,' he told Julie.

The first car drew up as instructed. Diamond ordered his own driver to stop in a position that sealed the lane. He had Emma moved to one of the other vehicles at the roadside. An officer had to be spared to guard her. That left seven, including Julie and himself.

In a subdued voice, he issued orders. They would know at once, he said, if the suspect was present in the farmhouse because his car, a red Toyota Previa, must be in the yard. If so, it was to be disabled as a precaution, and one of the officers was deputed to do this. The others would surround the house. The suspect, Diamond went on, was not known to possess a firearm, but extreme care was to be taken. This was a potential hostage situation, complicated because the hostage was a woman whose leg was in plaster.

They started along the mud track. Diamond had not gone more than a few steps when he spread his arms to signal a halt. His heart pumped harder. The Toyota was standing, as he had predicted, in the yard in front of the farmhouse.

What he had failed to predict was that the engine roared, the lights came on full beam and the car raced towards them.

Thirty-three

Ever since she fell from the kitchen window in the St James's Square basement and broke her ankle, Rose had been shackled, physically and mentally. The plaster was an obvious constraint; so, also, was her flawed relationship with Doreen. She was not deceived. Yes, her memory had stalled, but not her logic. She knew for certain that the whole truth about her life was being denied to her. There were times when Doreen refused point-blank to answer questions. Her actions – the daily shopping, the care for her comfort and safety – were decent, sisterly, genuine – but whenever Rose asked for more freedom, more space, Doreen was rigid and unforthcoming. She was not malicious; Rose would have detected that. But the trust was absent.

Until this evening.

Doreen's entire manner had been different when she had arrived in the flat in Prior Park Buildings. Usually so well-defended, she seemed uneasy, as if her strength were undermined. When Rose had asked for the umpteenth time about her family, Doreen had spilled it out, confiding astonishing things to her. The truth was deeply distressing, so painful that she could appreciate why Doreen had delayed discussing it with her. Her father, an elderly farmer living alone, had recently been found dead with half his head blown away by a shotgun. Rose had visited the farm expecting to find him alive. The dreadful scene had affected her brain. In effect, she was denying her own existence to shut out the horror.

She heard all this with a sense that it must be true, but still without remembering any of it. She had no recollection of being at the farm, or walking in on the bloodbath within, or what happened after. She was left emotionally drained.

After a while, Doreen had told her other things. She had talked of the family's unusual claim to fame, her grandfather's discovery of the Tormarton Seax during the war. Two generations of Gladstones had resisted all requests to excavate the ground. They wanted only to be left alone to earn their living from farming. But now her father was dead, there was renewed interest in the site, even rumours that other objects had been recovered by the family. The smiling man who had tried to abduct her was almost certainly acting on the rumours.

Rose was white-knuckled thinking about that evil predator. Thank God Doreen had moved her to another flat. This place seemed even more tucked away than St James's Square. Unless you knew it was here, masked by trees and up the steps from Prior Park Road, you would probably go straight past.

Doreen had stayed with her until late. She left about ten-thirty. Afterwards, horrid images churned in Rose's brain and she knew she would not sleep. For distraction, she switched on the TV. An old black and white film was on, with James Mason looking incredibly boyish as an Irish gunman on the run from the police. She watched it intermittently while clearing the table. Everything she did was slowed by the crutches, but she liked to be occupied, and she had insisted Doreen left the things for her to carry out.

On about the fourth journey between kitchen and sitting-room she happened to notice two slips of paper lying on the armchair. They must have fallen out of Doreen's pocket when she took out a tissue. At a glance they were only shop receipts. She left them there; when you depend on crutches, there is a limit to the number of things you stoop to pick up.

She finished washing up and went back to the armchair. The film was reaching a climax. The girlfriend had found James Mason in the snow surrounded by armed police. She would surely draw their gunfire on to both of them.

Involved in the drama, Rose gripped the underside of her thigh and her hand came into contact with one of those scraps of paper. When the film ended, Doreen's receipts were lying in small pieces in her lap. While watching the last tragic scene she must have been shredding them. Stupid.

They didn't belong to her. They might have been needed for some reason.

To make sure they *were* only receipts, she spread the pieces on the table and put them together, jigsaw fashion. *Astra Taxis,* the first said, *From: Bath Stn. To: St Jas Squ. + waiting, with thanks £30.* She had seen the transaction herself, watched the receipt being handed across after the drive from Harmer House to St James's Square. Her short-term memory couldn't be faulted.

The other was a credit-card slip for the lunch at Jolly's. Doreen had settled that one at the till.

She stared at the name.

But it ought to read Doreen Jenkins.

The date was the correct one. *Two lunches,* it said. The name of the card-holder was *Mrs Emma Treadwell.*

Emma?

Frowning, she stared at the name for some time. There was only one conclusion. Her so-called stepsister was caught out. Here was proof that she had been lying about her real identity.

She was crushed by the betrayal. If Doreen concealed her own name, could anything she said be trusted? The story about her father and his horrible death could be pure fabrication, as could the stuff about the Tormarton Seax.

Soon after, the doorbell rang.

Her first thought was that Doreen must have come back. No one else knew who was staying here. That would be it: she had just discovered she'd mislaid the receipts and she was back in a panic.

She called out, 'Coming,' and hastily scooped up the bits of paper and put them in her own pocket, hoisted herself up and on to the crutches and picked her way across the floor to the hall.

There was no second ring. She knows I'm slow, she thought. She unfastened the door and opened it the few inches the safety chain allowed.

A mistake.

A metal-cutter closed on the safety-chain and severed it. The door swung open, practically knocking her down, and Smiling Face walked into the flat and slammed the door closed.

She gripped the crutches, terrified.

'Move,' he ordered, pointing to the armchair.

She hobbled across the room. She was turning to make the awkward manoeuvre of lowering herself when he grabbed one of the crutches away and pushed her in the chest, slamming her into the chair. He kicked the other crutch out of her reach.

As if she were no longer there, he walked through and checked the kitchen and the bedroom. Satisfied, he sat opposite her, resting a brown paper carrier on his knees. He was in a suede jacket, white sweater and black jeans.

In a shaky voice she asked him what he wanted.

'You don't know?' It was an educated voice, no more comforting for that. His mouth curved in that crocodile smile. 'Come now, Miss Gladstone, you're not stupid. You know you've got to be dealt with, and it needn't hurt. You swallow the sleeping tablets I give you, helped down with excellent cognac, which I also happen to have in my bag, and you don't wake up. It's the civilised way to go, and it works.'

'You want to *kill* me?'

'Not at all.' The smile widened. 'I want you to commit suicide.' From the carrier he produced some cheap plastic gloves, the sort garages provide free at the pumps, and put them on. 'Oh, and so that no one is in any doubt, I'll fix a new safety-chain before I leave, reassuring anyone with a suspicious mind that you must have been alone here.'

Rose had not listened to any of it.

He took out and placed on the low table between them a silver flask and a brown bottle full of prescription capsules. 'Fifteen should do it. Twenty will make certain.'

Terrified as she was, her brain went into overdrive. This man would snuff out her life unless she found some way of outwitting him.

'Why?'

'Why what?'

'What have I done, that you want to kill me?'

He unscrewed the bottle and tipped some capsules on to the table. 'Take a few.'

If anything Doreen had said could be believed, the man

was a treasure-hunter. She knew nothing else about him, so she would have to gamble on its being true.

She said, 'It's revenge, isn't it?'

'For what?'

She held his glance and began to unfold a story worthy of Scheherazade. 'Because you didn't find the necklace and the other things that belong to my family.'

He gazed at her blankly, unconvinced. 'Just what are you wittering on about?'

'Certain objects my father dug up years ago.'

His brown eyes were giving away more than he intended. 'You're bluffing. There's no record of anything being found there after 1943.'

He *was* a circling vulture.

'There wouldn't be,' Rose said, trying to sound calm, 'because Dad didn't report it. He didn't want some coroner declaring them as treasure-trove and belonging to the nation. My grandfather made that mistake with his find.'

'Nice try,' he said, getting up. 'I don't buy it. I'll fetch you a glass from the kitchen.'

Elaborating wildly, she called out, 'I've tried on the necklace. Dad re-strung the gold beads and the garnets himself. The original string rotted in the soil.'

Smiling Face was silent for some time.

When he returned from the kitchen he was holding a tumbler. 'It isn't the right shape for a decent cognac, but it will have to do. I don't believe a word you're saying. You don't remember a damned thing about your father, let alone any gold objects, so swallow these and give us both a break.' He took the cap off the flask and poured some brandy.

Her brain grappled with the complexities. In this poker game her life was the stake and the cards had been dealt to her by Doreen, an impostor. In spite of the denials, the man had appeared at first to be interested. She had no choice but to play on as if she held a winning hand.

'Don't you want to know why I came down here to visit my father?' Without giving him time to respond she answered her own question. 'Dad invited me to collect the hoard, as he called it. He wrote to say it would be safer with me. People had visited him, wanting to excavate. If he agreed, he said, they'd find nothing and there was a danger they would turn nasty. He felt vulnerable, being elderly. He was afraid they would break into the house.' While she was speaking, her eyes read every muscle movement across his face. She was encouraged to add, 'He said the coins would bring me a steady income sold in small amounts and to different collectors.'

The mention of coins drew a better result than the necklace had. His grin lost a little of its upward curve. 'What coins?'

'The ones he dug up.'

'You mean old coins?'

'I don't know how old they are. Silver and gold mostly. They must have been in a pot originally, because they were mingled with tiny fragments of clay.'

His façade was crumbling, even if he tried to sound sceptical. 'And where are these fabulous coins kept now? In a bank vault?'

'No. He wouldn't trust a bank. They're in the farmhouse.'

'Oh, yes? Where precisely?'

If she named a hiding-place, he wouldn't be able to resist checking. He might disbelieve her, but he was too committed to let any chance slip by, however remote. The challenge was to keep him interested without telling him enough to let him believe he could go alone. 'He didn't tell me exactly where.'

He was contemptuous. 'Convenient.'

'But there can't be more than four or five places they could be. I knew the farmhouse as a child.'

'Now you're lying through your teeth,' he said. 'It's common knowledge that your memory is gone. You know sweet FA about what happened when you were a kid.'

Rose harangued him with the force of Joan of Arc in front of her accusers. 'Wrong. It came back a couple of nights ago. I woke up in the small hours and remembered who I am and everything about me.' A huge claim that she would find impossible to justify if put to the test, but how much did Smiling Face know of her life? She started talking at the rhythm of a sewing machine, stitching together a patchwork of what Doreen had told her and what sprang to mind. 'I'm twenty-eight, and I live in Hounslow and I work in a bookshop. My parents separated when I was very young and I've seen very little of my father since. I came down from London the other day at his request and when I got to the farmhouse I found him dead, shot through the head. The rest you know.'

He reached for the brandy and drank some, caught in indecision.

'If you like,' she offered in a more measured tone, squeezing her hands between her knees to stop them trembling, 'we could go to the farmhouse and find the hoard. You can have the coins and all the other things except the necklace.' Trying to do a deal over the non-existent necklace was an inspiration. 'Dad always promised me the necklace.'

He said tersely, getting in deeper, 'You're in no position to bargain. If I believed you for one moment, I could go there and turn the place over. I don't need your help.'

'Believe me, you do. Cottage hiding-places are really cunning. People centuries ago needed to keep all their valuables secure. The places they used were incredibly clever. You have to live there to know where to look.'

He passed a gloved hand uncertainly through his black hair.

At the limit of her invention, she added, 'We can go there now. I'll show you where to look.' She pointed at the plastered ankle. 'I'm not going to run away.'

In the Toyota, he said with his habitual grin, 'If your memory is back, I'm surprised you want to get into a car with me.'

She didn't know what he meant, and didn't care to think about it. She said with disdain, 'It's better than the alternative.'

'I wouldn't count on it.'

They had been on the road about twenty minutes, going further and further from the lights of Bath, past places with strange, discomforting names like Swainswick, Cold Ashton, Nimlet and Pennsylvania. How this would end, Rose did not dare think. With her injury, she had no chance of running away. Her plan, such as it was, amounted to no more than delaying action – but for what? The Cavalry wouldn't come riding to her rescue.

The car swung right and up a bumpy track. A stone building, pale in the headlamp beam, appeared ahead. It was essential to pretend this was familiar ground. She felt her mouth go dry. The bluffing was over. He would expect her to deliver now.

'Out.'

'I can't move without my crutches.'

He got out and took them off the back seat and handed them to her. He produced a heavy-duty rubber torch and lit the way across the yard to the house.

Strips of yellow and black police tape were plastered across the front door. Smiling Face kicked it open and clawed the tape away.

He told her, 'There's no electricity. We'll have to do this by torchlight. Where first?'

She'd spent the last twenty minutes asking herself the same question. Without any memory of this house, it required swift decisions. She had to put up a show of familiarity. 'Could I hold the torch a moment?'

He handed it to her. She cast the beam rapidly around the kitchen. 'There used to be a loose brick against the wall there,' she improvised, training the torch on one section, 'but it seems to have been cemented in.' She hobbled out of the kitchen, hoping the floors might be of wood – for loose floorboards – but they were flagstoned.

This was the living-room. She shone the torch over a wooden armchair and a small table, a chest of drawers and a bed against the wall. One other hope was dashed: the place had no phone. On the walls and ceiling were a number of stains encircled with chalk. Her own father's blood? She made a huge effort to put death out of her mind. Then she spotted the faint outline of a pair of footprints in chalk, and a shudder passed through her. 'There used to be a special flagstone with a cavity under it. I'm trying to remember which one.'

Smiling Face kicked the mat, uncovering most of it. He wasn't saying anything, but his impatience was obvious.

'It definitely wasn't one of these,' she said. 'Perhaps if you rolled the mat right back . . .'

'And you cracked me over the head with the torch? No thanks,' he said. 'Your time has run out.' Even so, he moved the mat with his foot and exposed more flagstones. It was obvious from the dirt impacted in the cracks that none of them had been disturbed for years.

'I wonder if the stone I'm thinking of was in the back room,' she speculated, switching the torch-beam to the door at the end.

'Full of junk,' he told her acidly. 'No one has been in there for years.'

Undaunted, she crossed the room and shone the torch over a forest of furniture and household objects. 'Well, I'm beginning to wonder if it's at the back, by the wardrobe.'

To reach the wardrobe, he would have to remove a rocking-chair, a table, a dog-basket and a hat-stand, all coated with an even layer of dust.

'Let's face it,' he said. 'This has been a total waste of time. You haven't any more knowledge than I have about this place. Give me that.' He grabbed back the torch.

She started to say, 'I didn't promise to—'

He swung the torch viciously and cracked it against her head. She felt her skull implode. Briefly, she saw fireworks, brilliant, multicoloured points of light. Then they went fuzzy and faded away.

The darkness was absolute, but some of her sensations returned. Shallow breathing. She was cold, freezing cold, there was a roaring in her ears and she was being buffeted.

This uniform blackness was scary. Her eyes were open. She could feel them blink, and she could see nothing, not the faintest grey shading at the edge of her vision.

Blind?

I will not panic, she thought. Try to work out a rational explanation.

She seemed to be lying on her right side in a hunched position. Her foot – the one not in plaster – was in contact with something solid that made it impossible for her to stretch.

And there was a smell that made her nose itch and her eyes water.

Petrol fumes. I am in a car. It's an engine that I'm hearing. I'm being driven at high speed.

By degrees, she remembered the incident immediately prior to blacking out. This, she deduced, must be the red Toyota. Smiling Face is at the wheel, driving at a terrifying speed, and only he knows where.

I'm locked in the boot. He knocked me senseless with the torch and carried me to the boot and now he's going to dispose of me somewhere. He wants me to die. He made that clear. He may even think I'm dead already.

The strange thing about it is that I'm beginning not to care. I'm freezing and uncomfortable and I want to be sick.

Some instinct for survival insisted that she do something about it. Car boots had linings. If she could wrap some of the lining around herself she would get some insulation. She reached out in the dark, probing with her fingertips for the edge of the felt she was lying on. Some of her fingernails broke. The effort was almost too much. But a strip of the material came away from the bodywork. More followed. She drew it to herself like a blanket, or a shroud.

Thirty-four

Diamond's physique had thickened and, it has to be said, slackened since he gave up rugby, but his reactions were still quick. He grabbed Julie and dived out of the path of the advancing car. It whooshed by so close that he felt the rush of air on the back of his neck.

Scratched and winded, but basically unhurt because his colleague's soft flesh had cushioned his fall, he hauled himself off her and out of a hedge that was mainly bramble.

'You okay?'

She thought she was. He helped her up.

'See if Rose is in the farmhouse.'

Leaving Julie, he started running up the lane after the Toyota, confident that a patrol car was blocking the exit to the road.

From up ahead a screech of brakes pierced the air. But the expected impact didn't happen. There was the high note of the engine in reverse, then a change of gear.

He was in time to see the Toyota mount the verge to avoid the police car, rip through the hedge, advance into the field, rev again, switchback over the uneven turf and bear down like a tank on a wooden gate at the edge nearest to the road. Like a tank it smashed through.

'Get after him then!'

One of the cars was already turning to give chase, its blue light pulsing. Diamond hurled himself through the open door of another and they were moving before he slammed it.

The rear lights of the Toyota were not in sight.

'He'll make for the motorway,' Diamond told the driver. 'Can you radio ahead?'

On an undulating stretch north of Tormarton, the skyline

momentarily glowed in the high beam of headlights. At a rough estimate, Allardyce was a quarter of a mile ahead. There was no chance of catching him before the M4 interchange.

A message came through from headquarters. Diamond could just make out through the static that Julie had radioed in from the farmhouse to say no one was in there, but she had found Rose's crutches.

'I don't like the sound of that. I didn't see her in the car, did you?' he asked his driver.

'No passenger, sir. I had a clear look.'

'What's your name?'

'PC Roberts, sir.'

There was a hairy moment when they rattled the wing mirror in passing a stationary car. They were doing eighty along country lanes.

'Been driving long, Roberts?'

'Since my seventeeth birthday, sir.'

'How old are you now?'

'Eighteen, sir.'

The problem at the approach to the motorway was how to divine which direction Allardyce had taken. At the roundabout, Diamond watched the patrol car ahead speed up the first slipway eastwards. 'Then we go west,' he told PC Roberts. They swung with screaming tyres around the long turn and presently joined the Bristol-bound carriageway. At this time of night the traffic would be sparse.

Diamond was trying to hold down the nausea he always felt at high speed. It was compounded by concern over Rose. If she was not at the farmhouse and her crutches were there, what had Allardyce done with her?

'No sign of him, sir,' Roberts said. 'I reckon he took the other route.'

'Is this thing as fast as the Toyota?'

'Should be. He should be in sight by now.'

'Keep going.'

This stretch of motorway had no lighting whatsoever. They had the main beam probing the three lanes. In the next minute Diamond thought he could discern a dark shape ahead.

'Isn't that something?'

'You're right, sir. He's switched off his lights, bloody idiot. He's all over the road.'

As they got nearer, they could make out the outline of a car without lights veering erratically between the lanes.

Roberts said, 'I think his electrics are buggered. He braked just then and the brake lights didn't come on.'

'Flash him. Let him know we're here.'

'He knows that, sir. My God, he's going!'

They watched the car sheer towards the crash-barrier in the centre, hit it in a shower of sparks and skew left across three lanes and the hard shoulder. It thudded into the embankment, reared up like a whale, rolled over and slid upside down with a sickening metallic sound, spinning back across two lanes of the motorway.

In trying to avoid it they got into a skid themselves. Their vehicle did a three-quarter turn before coming to a halt.

Diamond hurled open the door, got out and sprinted towards the up-ended Toyota on legs that didn't feel like his own, only to discover that the impact had pancaked the superstructure to the level of the seats. The driver and anyone inside must have been mangled.

PC Roberts joined him and warned, 'You can't do anything. It could easily catch fire, sir. I've radioed for help.'

It was good advice which he ignored, for he had noticed something Roberts had not. The force of the crash had ripped open the Toyota's luggage compartment. The lid was hanging open under the upturned wreck and a dark form wrapped in a roll of fabric was lying in the angle. Projecting from it was a white tubular object shaped like an angled section of drainpipe, but it was patently not a drainpipe because just visible at the end were five toes.

'It's her,' he said. 'She's wrapped in something.'

Steam was rising from the wreck, but it had not yet caught fire. On his knees, Diamond reached into the darkness and got his arm around the body. Roberts was beside him.

'I've got her legs, sir.'

Diamond tried talking to Rose and got no response. The hope was that the limited size of the compartment had restricted her movement as the car somersaulted. She was wrapped in the felt lining.

They prised her out and carried her to a place of relative safety on the grass embankment.

Diamond gently removed part of the felt that was covering her face. She had a bloody nose, but she was breathing. Her eyes opened.

'You'll make it, love,' he told her.

'Allardyce? The fire service got him out eventually, sir, what there was of him,' he told the Assistant Chief Constable next morning.

'Looking at it from a cost-effectiveness standpoint,' said the ACC, who usually did look at things that way, 'I suppose it saves the community the expense of a long trial and keeping him in prison for a life term. And the woman?'

'Do you mean Emma Treadwell? We're still holding her. We'll send a report to the CPS, but I can't see them proceeding on any of the more serious charges.'

'I meant the woman you rescued.'

'Christine Gladstone? They kept her overnight in the RUH. She escaped with some ugly bruises. Being in the luggage compartment, where Allardyce put her, she was in the one reasonably secure part of the car.'

'Secure? I'd say she was damned lucky.'

'Some people are, sir. You're right. Considering she caused the crash, she was bloody lucky.'

'She caused it, you say?'

'Being in the boot, she grabbed the wiring and ripped it out. His lights went, and the next thing he hit the barrier.'

The ACC cleared his throat in an embarrassed way. 'Good thing you were close behind. I think it's in order to congratulate you on your prompt action, Peter.'

'No need, sir. It was a team effort.'

'Yes, that's a fact. You and John Wigfull between you.'

'Oh, yes?' Diamond half-smiled, suspecting that this was humour.

But it was not. The ACC was serious. 'I think of you two as the Castor and Pollux of Bath CID.'

'The what?'

'Castor and Pollux. It's a compliment, Peter. They were the twin sons of Jupiter, a formidable duo.'

'I see,' said Diamond. 'And which is which?'

The ACC frowned. 'I don't think it matters.'

'If it's all the same to you, sir, I'll take Castor, and Pollox to John Wigfull.'

At home the next evening, he was less buoyant. He ate one of his favourite meals of salmon *en croute* almost in silence. Stephanie didn't need telling that he was badly shaken.

She suggested an evening walk.

'If you like.'

They had not gone far when he said, 'Julie's leaving. She asked for a transfer and they've found her a job at Bristol. No warning. It's fixed.'

'I know,' Stephanie admitted.

'You do.' He stopped.

'She came to see me, Pete.'

'To see you? When?'

'A couple of days ago. She was pretty unhappy. She has a lot of respect for you, but she feels too much of her time is spent smoothing the way.'

'For me, you mean?'

'Don't sound so surprised. You know you're hell to work with. She's young for an inspector, ambitious. She's entitled to move on.'

'We were a bloody good team.'

'Too good for your own good.'

'What does that mean?'

'You told me yourself that you're underworked most of the time, and it's bad for your health. Julie in her quiet way has been batting for you all the time, making your life easier. I didn't tell her about the hypertension, of course, though it wouldn't surprise me if she's aware of it. But we agreed that a trouble-free life isn't necessarily what you want.'

'It's what I expect from my deputy.'

'She's too good at it. Let her go, Pete.'

He sniffed. 'When she meets that lot at Bristol, she'll realise I'm not such an ogre.'

'She didn't say you were. She said some very complimentary things.'

They walked on for some distance before he spoke again.

'It's going to be tough without Julie. I'll keep an eye on what happens at Bristol.'

Stephanie said, 'No. When the path is slippery it is safer to go two paces forward than one pace back.'

'Who says that?'

'The book you keep by the bed.'

'Kai Lung? I don't subscribe to everything he says.'

Thirty-five

At the other end of winter, when millions of daffodils were brightening all the approaches to Bath, a visitor came to Harmer House and called on Ada Shaftsbury.

'Bless your little cotton socks,' said Ada, with a bear-hug. 'If it isn't my mate Rose!'

'Christine, actually.'

'I know, petal. I saw it in the papers. You're looking well, Rose. Did you get your memory back?'

'In time for Christmas.' She laughed, so much more relaxed now. 'I was in Oxford Street looking at the lights, and suddenly I knew I'd been there years ago with my mother. It was amazing, just like the clouds parting. And now I know why I came to Bath. It was to see my father. After Mother's death I had a difficult time, but I felt closer to my dad than I ever had. I really wanted to see him. Then finding him dead like that, with the shotgun at his side, I blamed myself for neglecting him so long. I just blanked everything out. Anyway, I've picked up my life as it was, living in my flat in Fulham and working again.'

'What are you doing here, then?'

'Two things. I've just been to see that policeman who pulled me out of the crash. I wanted to thank him.'

'Old gutso? What did he suggest as a thank-you – a jumbo burger and chips?'

'Oh, Ada.'

'Say it, blossom. Next to me, he's a sparrow. What's the other thing you came for?'

'To sort out the farmhouse. It's officially my property now.'

'Are you selling the farm?'

'Definitely. I'm having the house demolished first. The solicitor advised it after what happened there.'

'And all the furniture?'

'I've arranged for one of those house clearance firms to take it all away. I'm meeting them there this afternoon.' Christine nervously touched her hair, twisting a length of it between her finger and thumb. Her new, confident look softened into something like the diffidence Ada remembered. 'I'm a bit uncomfortable about going there alone. Would you have the time to come with me?'

Invited to choose a present from the farmhouse, Ada picked an old milking stool, which she said she would rest her feet on while thinking of all the years of honest work it represented.

'It isn't much. Don't you want anything else?'

'You know me, love. I only ever take what I can carry away. I'd have the kitchen range if I could. I was born in a cottage. Spent the first ten years of my life in a place like this.'

'You're welcome to take the range if you want. The clearance people won't have any use for it.'

'Can you see Imogen's face if I had it sent up to Harmer House?'

They decided to light a last fire while waiting for the van. Soon the flames were giving an orange glow to the dark room.

'Have I got it right?' Ada asked. 'Allardyce brought you here to look for some old treasure your dad was supposed to have salted away?'

'That was only delaying tactics on my part. I made it up, telling him there were hiding places in old cottages.'

'There wasn't anything?'

'Only the Seax, and that was dug up half a century ago.'

'Two innocent people died for bugger all?'

'I'm afraid that's true.'

They watched the flames for a while. Finally Ada said, 'All this was an open hearth once. In the old days they used to roast on a spit, over an open fire. You can see where they bricked in the space they didn't need any more.' She picked up her milking stool by one leg and tapped it firmly against the wall to the right of the range. 'Hear it? Hollow.

I'll tell you for nothing, blossom, it's a perfect place to hide anything. If I had some hot stuff I wanted to salt away – not that I ever do, mind – I'd chip out a couple of bricks and put it in there.'

They both looked at the wall. Each of them spotted the loose bricks at floor level on the left of the range.

'Well, if you're not going to look, I am.'

Ada planted her stool by the bricks and lowered herself onto it. She withdrew the bricks with ease and put her hand into the space behind. 'Wouldn't it take the cake if there really was . . .' Her voice trailed off and she stared at Rose with saucer eyes. She took out her hand and showed something that glinted gold in the fire's glow.